PRAISE FOR

The Anatomist's Wife

"A riveting debut. Huber deftly weaves together an original premise, an enigmatic heroine, and a compelling Highland setting for a book you won't want to put down."

—Deanna Raybourn, *New York Times* bestselling author of the Lady Julia Grey novels

"Lady Darby is an engaging new sleuth to follow . . . [A] history mystery in fine Victorian style! Anna Lee Huber's spirited debut mixes classic country house mystery with a liberal dash of historical romance. Fans of Tasha Alexander and Agatha Christie, rejoice!"

—Julia Spencer-Fleming, *New York Times* bestselling author of *One Was a Soldier*

"Anna Lee Huber has delivered a fast-paced, atmospheric, and chilling debut featuring a clever heroine with a shocking past and a talent for detection. I'm already anticipating Lady Darby's next adventure."

—Carol K. Carr, national bestselling author of *India Black and the Shadows of Anarchy*

"Lady Darby is an unusual and romantic heroine, haunted by a deadly past and trying to be herself in a society that wants to silence her—and worse."

—Judith Rock, author of *A Plague of Lies*

"Huber's protagonist is complex and likable and the well-plotted mystery is filled with fascinating secondary characters . . . You'll be engaged right to the end."

—*RT Book Reviews*

"Huber's debut . . . reads like a cross between a gothic novel and a mystery with a decidedly unusual heroine."

—*Kirkus Reviews*

Berkley Prime Crime titles by Anna Lee Huber

THE ANATOMIST'S WIFE
MORTAL ARTS

MORTAL ARTS

ANNA LEE HUBER

BERKLEY PRIME CRIME, NEW YORK

THE BERKLEY PUBLISHING GROUP
Published by the Penguin Group
Penguin Group (USA)
375 Hudson Street, New York, New York 10014, USA

USA I Canada I UK I Ireland I Australia I New Zealand I India I South Africa I China

Penguin Books Ltd., Registered Offices: 80 Strand, London WC2R 0RL, England
For more information about the Penguin Group, visit penguin.com.

This book is an original publication of The Berkley Publishing Group.

Berkley Prime Crime Books are published by The Berkley Publishing Group.
BERKLEY® PRIME CRIME and the PRIME CRIME logo are a registered trademark of
Penguin Group (USA).

Library of Congress Cataloging-in-Publication Data

Huber, Anna Lee.
Mortal arts / Anna Lee Huber.—Berkley Prime Crime trade paperback edition.
pages cm.—(A Lady Darby mystery ; 1)
ISBN 978-0-425-25378-6 (pbk.)
1. Detective and mystery stories.   I. Title.
PS3608. U238M67 2013
813' .6—dc23
2013018566

PUBLISHING HISTORY
Berkley Prime Crime trade paperback edition / September 2013

PRINTED IN THE UNITED STATES OF AMERICA

10 9 8 7 6 5 4

Cover illustration by Larry Rostant.
Cover design by Lesley Worrell.
Interior design by Tiffany Estreicher.

For the veterans of all wars,
in all times and in all places,
who suffered from what we now call
PTSD (post-traumatic stress disorder).
Your cries may have gone unanswered and,
in ignorance, your courage may have been questioned.
But we hear you now.
And we honor your bravery and sacrifice.

ACKNOWLEDGMENTS

Writing a book is much like the old adage about raising a child—it takes a village. And I would like to offer my heartfelt thanks to the following people for all of their help in creating *Mortal Arts*.

To my editor, Michelle Vega, for your enthusiasm and your unswerving devotion to making this book better. To all the staff at The Berkley Publishing Group, including Lesley Worrell, Larry Rostant, Tiffany Estreicher, Aurora Slothus, and Kayleigh Clark for your skills and expertise.

To my agent, Kevan Lyon, for being my staunch and dedicated advocate. I take great comfort in knowing you always have my back.

To my writing group partners, Jackie Musser and Stacie Roth Miller, for your confidence in me and all of your invaluable feedback.

To all of the authors and other publishing industry professionals who welcomed me so warmly into their ranks, and showed such kindness and encouragement to me.

To my parents, my siblings, and all of my friends and family for showering me with so much love and support. I'm so incredibly blessed to know each and every one of you.

To my Pita, for being the adorable, fun-loving kitty you are.

To my husband, Shanon, words will never be able to

express my gratitude for all you have done, and all you continue to do for me. I truly am the luckiest woman in the world. Thank you for loving me through thick and thin, for sharing this incredible journey, and for being my most steadfast supporter.

To God, for the amazing and wonderful gift of life, and for the drive, the abilities, and the grace to see this dream come true. Every perfect gift comes from above.

CHAPTER ONE

Art is not what you see, but what you make others see.

—EDGAR DEGAS

OCTOBER 1830

It was the groan of death.

Or so one would think. But after five interminable days of listening to my sister moan and carry on as we trundled across Scotland toward Edinburgh, her grumbles and whimpers had lost their ability to alarm me. I had seen death, even if I hadn't exactly heard its guttural conclusion, and despite the dark circles around Alana's eyes and her wan complexion, I could tell my sister was far from its door.

Although, with each excruciating hour I was trapped inside the carriage with her the closer she became.

Alana was merely expecting, and the child inside her had decided to protest this journey persistently and forcibly. I had already decided that this troublesome niece or nephew would be my favorite. A child who could so unsettle my sister while still confined to the womb certainly merited my affection.

"Kiera," my sister whined, rolling her head to the side so that she could see me, "do you have any more of that bread?"

My lips tightened. "Yes."

Her hand lifted from her stomach and reached toward me. "Give me some."

"Why? You'll only vomit again and delay our arrival by another hour."

A frown pleated Alana's brow. "Why are you being so cruel?"

"I'm not. I'm simply stating facts. *And* hoping to salvage my last traveling dress," I couldn't help adding.

"You know I didn't do it on purpose . . ."

"*Twice.*" I leaned forward to point out. "You got sick on me *twice.*"

"But that was yesterday . . ."

"And you splattered my boots just this morning."

Alana pouted and turned to stare up at the ceiling of the carriage. "Well, if you had held the slop bucket for me, I wouldn't have dropped it."

"That was how you vomited on me the second time. The next time you begin to retch I'm going to leap out the carriage door. And, as I don't wish to break my neck by falling from a moving vehicle, I'm going to make certain there *isn't* a next time." I inhaled deeply and turned to stare at the crimson curtain covering the window. When next I spoke, I had managed to banish most of the anger from my tone. "At the last stop, Philip said we would halt for luncheon in a few hours' time. You can eat then." Though whether she would keep it down for more than a quarter of an hour after we rolled away from the roadside inn was doubtful.

Alana huffed. "What does he know?" Clearly she was still irritated with her husband after their argument earlier in the day. I was also none too happy with my brother-in-law for abandoning me to my sister's irritability and illness while he rode alongside the carriages, though I couldn't blame him for doing so. Had I brought a suitable mount, I might have done the same.

"It could be another hour before we reach our stop," she complained. "I cannot last that long. I need to eat now."

I crossed my arms, unmoved by her plea.

Her eyes widened in entreaty. "Please, Kiera. I think it will settle my stomach."

I shook my head.

She scowled. "Kiera. Give it to me."

"If you want it so bad, get it yourself."

"Fine," she snapped, pushing herself upright. Almost immediately her already pale face bleached of all color. She groaned and sank back against the cushions.

Despite my annoyance, I was not without compassion or concern for her. I sat forward to take hold of her hand, offering her what comfort I could while she struggled to hold down the small amount of water she had managed to sip since the last time she'd lost the battle with her stomach.

When the worst passed and a faint tinge of pink returned to her complexion, she opened her eyes to look up at me. "I'm fine," she murmured, squeezing my palm weakly.

"Do you want a sip of water?"

She shook her head and swallowed. "Not just yet."

I reached up to brush a stray curl of chestnut hair away from her brow, fighting to keep the worry I felt from showing on my face. Either I didn't do a very good job or my sister simply knew me too well.

"I'll be fine once we reach Edinburgh."

"I know," I replied with a tight smile. I pulled the curtain over the window aside. Dense forest met my view. "I just wish we would get there already." I glanced back at my sister, whose cheekbones had noticeably thinned in the past two months of her confinement. "We made this move in hopes of improving your health, not diminishing it."

Her hand squeezed mine again, stronger this time. "Edinburgh is home to the best medical minds in the world, is it not?"

I nodded.

"Then I wish you and Philip would stop questioning your decision to take me there. You believe our physician at Gairloch is a quack, and there is not another medical man or midwife for miles around. If I'm going to deliver this child safely, you had no choice but to take me to Edinburgh."

A lump formed in my throat at hearing her state the matter so bluntly. After the complications she had faced during her third child's birth less than a year and a half earlier, she had been warned of the difficulty she might face in delivering any more children. Alana and Philip had taken the physician's counsel seriously, but, despite their precautions, Alana once again found herself heavy with child. I couldn't say that I was surprised. My sister and her husband had a very loving and affectionate marriage, and the natural result of such a relationship was children, whether planned for or not.

Upon learning of Alana's delicate state, Philip and I considered the available options for her care. We agreed that Gairloch Castle, located in the wilds of the western Highlands, was not the ideal place for such a potentially difficult confinement, especially as winter set in, closing off the roads to the outside. By our calculations, the child was not due until mid-April, but winter was long and hard in the Highlands, and it was not uncommon for the roads to remain impassible long into spring. Neither of us wanted to take any chances with Alana or the child's health, so it became apparent we needed to travel somewhere with better access to medical care. Edinburgh was the natural choice.

The fact that someone I very much wanted to see might also be in Edinburgh had not factored into the decision, though it had not been far from my thoughts.

So, before the chill of winter could settle over the land, Philip, Alana, their children, and I set out for Edinburgh. As the Earl of Cromarty, Philip already owned a town house on Charlotte Square in the Georgian New Town. Much of his household had been transferred to the city ahead of us, along with a large portion of our luggage. Only the personal servants and the nanny lagged behind, the latter of whom was to ride with the children in the carriage that followed ours. Malcolm and Philipa had begun the trip in our carriage, but Alana's illness had swiftly necessitated their removal to the second coach, where they had joined their baby sister Greer, already in the nanny's care.

I released Alana's hand and sank back against the squabs with a weary sigh. "If we ever arrive." I felt my sister's eyes on me as I reached up to peer outside the curtains once again at the autumn forest. I braced myself to refuse yet another one of her pleas for bread, but the careful tone of her voice alerted me there was something far more perilous on her mind.

"You know, there will be a great deal of society in Edinburgh."

"Yes," I replied neutrally, hoping she wasn't about to suggest that I accept every reluctant invitation I received. I might have been less nervous about reentering civilization than I had been two months prior, but that did not mean I was ready to jump in with both feet just yet. Society had not yet forgotten my forced involvement in the dissections my late husband, the great anatomist Sir Anthony Darby, had carried out, or the subsequent charges of unnatural tendencies. And even though my assistance in helping the authorities capture a grisly killer two months ago had done much to calm their fear of me, I knew that just one such incidence of heroics was unlikely to repair my reputation. As such, I had decided to approach my reentry into society with great care. Any minor faux pas could destroy all the good my turn as an investigator had done, and since I had never been very interested in following the rules to begin with, I was already at a distinct disadvantage. Fortunately my sister and brother-in-law would be there to guide me. As long as Alana's health improved once we reached Edinburgh.

"And, if I remember correctly, didn't Mr. Gage venture to Edinburgh upon leaving Gairloch?"

I could tell my sister's casual observation was far from innocent, just as I knew her memory was far from faulty in regard to this matter. "I believe so," I replied obscurely.

"Perhaps he's still there. Wouldn't it be lovely to see him again?"

My heart tripped at the possibility. Not that I hadn't already thought of it, had *been* thinking of it ever since Philip and I realized we would need to take Alana to Edinburgh. In fact, Mr. Sebastian Gage had not been far from my thoughts since the night I trailed him down to the makeshift crypt below Gairloch's chapel to assist him with the murder investigation I helped to solve. I had been uneasy with my fascination with him back then, and still was, especially considering my ignorance of his feelings toward me. The idea that we might meet again in Edinburgh both thrilled and terrified me. But I wasn't about to admit any of that to my sister.

I could tell that, upon his departure two months ago, Alana had suspected some sort of involvement between Gage and me, but we had never discussed it. I preferred it that way, not able to name my feelings for the exasperating inquiry agent even to myself, let alone someone else. I still didn't want to have that conversation, least of all when trapped in a carriage with my nosy sibling. So I proceeded with caution.

"Of course," I replied, satisfied that neither my voice nor my face gave away just how anxious I felt about seeing Gage again.

Alana narrowed her eyes up at me from her reclined position. "Of course? That's all you have to say? The man saved your life, for heaven's sake."

I stiffened. As if I could forget. "What do you want me to say? Yes, it would be lovely to see him."

Her mouth pursed in frustration. "I thought you'd grown fond of him. Philip thought you two were getting along rather well near the end."

I ran my hands over the skirt of my russet brown traveling dress, trying to hide the tension vibrating through my frame. I wondered just how much my brother-in-law had told my sister. Had he witnessed the kiss I thought Gage and I had shared in the loch just before I fell unconscious? Did he tell her about our final confrontation on the morning Gage departed? I had not believed Philip to be a tattler, but perhaps relaying such information to one's spouse was not considered tattling.

"I did. We were." I sighed in exasperation. "I don't know what you expect me to say. The man helped me unmask a murderer and then went on his merry way. I doubt he expects to see you or me again, just as I never expected to see him.

So, *yes*, it would be lovely to see him, but it's not a blessed event." I sank back against the squabs and scowled at the curtains blocking the light from hurting Alana's eyes but also obstructing my view.

"Are you angry about that?"

"What?"

"Are you angry that he 'went on his merry way' with no intention of seeing you again?" my all-too-perceptive sister clarified softly.

"What? No," I lied. "The only thing I'm angry about is that you keep trying to make more of this than there is." I glared at her and she lifted her hands in a staying gesture.

"All right, all right. I'm sorry I pressed you."

I crossed my arms over my chest. "Besides, chances are he's not even in Edinburgh." I ignored the sick feeling in the pit of my stomach at the thought. "He probably returned to London weeks ago. So this entire discussion is for naught."

"Probably," Alana agreed.

I watched her prone form suspiciously, but her eyes were closed and her face, for the moment, relaxed and free of the pallid cast it had taken on so frequently over the past few days. I decided to hold my tongue, in hopes that she might actually be resting.

Unfortunately, that left me all too alone with my thoughts of Gage, my worries about Alana's health, and my anxiety over society's reaction to my arrival in Edinburgh. I realized I preferred to argue with my sister.

CHAPTER TWO

True to Philip's word, a few hours later we stopped at an inn on the outskirts of Linlithgow and piled out of the carriages and into the private parlor he had procured for us. Typical of a roadside tavern, the furniture was shabby and worn, but its cleanliness and sturdy construction were a testament to the innkeeper's pride in his establishment. The ruddy man grinned cheerily as he ushered us into the room before bending over the enormous rough stone fireplace to add more wood to the flames.

By the time the meal was delivered and the children settled, Alana's illness had subsided enough to allow her to eat. Philip spread butter across a slice of fresh-baked bread while I piled small amounts of string beans and apple compote on her plate. By unspoken agreement, we all knew the slices of mutton in rich gravy would be too much for Alana's tremulous stomach.

Trying to ignore my sister's strained expression as she nibbled at her bread, I sliced into my meat and turned to Philip. "Did you speak with that rider who passed us a few miles back?" An approaching horse's canter had slowed to a trot as it came upon our carriage and when I peered through the window, it was to see Philip's steed dropping back.

He made a grunt of remembrance and set aside his knife

to reach into the pocket inside his navy blue frock coat. Swallowing the bite of food in his mouth, he unfolded the letter. "It was a messenger sent by my aunt Jane. You remember Lady Hollingsworth?"

I nodded. She had attended Alana's house party at Gairloch Castle a few months back, along with two of her children. I had grown quite fond of Philip's cousins, but chosen largely to avoid his aunt, a rather formidable matron who felt no qualms about making known her disapproval of me. To the Dowager Marchioness of Hollingsworth, society and decorum were everything, and I was considered far too disreputable.

My sister was also not particularly fond of her husband's aunt, though, for the sake of familial harmony, she tried to keep her disparaging thoughts to herself. Unfortunately the aversion was mutual, and Lady Hollingsworth was not so circumspect. Alana and I shared a look of wariness.

Philip continued on, either oblivious to or choosing to ignore our unspoken exchange. "It appears my cousin Caroline is engaged."

Alana looked up at her husband in surprise, a welcome flush of color entering her cheeks. "Oh, but that's wonderful. Do we know the groom?"

"We do." Philip smiled. "It's none other than our Mr. Dalmay."

I leaned forward. "*Michael* Dalmay?"

"One and the same."

"I didn't know Caroline and Michael were acquainted."

"Apparently so."

Alana forked a bite of her beans. "Now I understand why he expressed so much regret about not being able to attend our house party in August. He must have been courting Caroline even then." She paused, her head tilted in thought. "I wonder why your aunt never mentioned the possibility of such a match."

I was thinking much the same thing. I would have

thought Lady Hollingsworth would have considered a possible alliance with the wealthy and well-connected Dalmays something to crow over.

Alana's eyes dropped to the note in her husband's hands. "So she went to the great trouble of sending a messenger to find us on the road to Edinburgh just so that she could share such news?"

His smile faded and he glanced back at the missive. "I'm afraid not. It appears there is some kind of unforeseen problem with Caroline's betrothal."

Alana and I shared another speaking glance.

"What kind of problem?" I queried.

His brow furrowed. "She doesn't say. But she pleads with me to join her at Dalmay House immediately."

"She doesn't say anything more?" Alana leaned forward to see the letter Philip held.

He tilted it so that she could read it. "I'm afraid not." He sighed. "Aunt Jane is never one to elaborate when she thinks demands and histrionics will get her way."

"But surely she would give you some clue as to the source of the trouble," I pressed. Lady Hollingsworth was a woman used to having her every request met with the bare minimum of effort on her part, but I would have expected her to treat her nephew with more consideration.

Philip's face tightened, likely entertaining a similar thought. "Not even a hint."

Alana glanced up from her perusal of the letter. "Do you think it has something to do with Michael?" she asked, doubt stretching her voice.

He seemed almost appalled by the suggestion. "Surely not. I may not have seen much of him in the past two years, but I doubt the man has changed so much in that time." He contemplated the matter for a moment and then shook his head. "No. I can't believe there is anything objectionable to be discovered about Michael Dalmay."

I had to agree with him. Michael had been one of Philip's closest friends since attending Cambridge, but Alana and I had known him even longer. We had grown up with Michael and his siblings, running through the forests and meadows of the Borders region, and rowing our boats back and forth across the River Tweed. The meandering river was all that divided our families' properties, much as it divided Scotland from England. Blakelaw House, my childhood home, was located just outside of Elwick, England, while Swinton Lodge stood across the river in Scotland.

The Dalmay family's residence at Swinton Lodge was only supposed to be temporary, while the new manor Michael's father had commissioned to be built on the Dalmay estate to replace their old, drafty castle could be completed. However, numerous delays had dragged the project out longer than expected, and it wasn't until late 1817 that the majority of the family had decamped to Dalmay House along the Firth of Forth, north of Edinburgh.

It had been many years since I had seen Michael Dalmay, but, knowing the young man he had been, I had a difficult time believing Lady Hollingsworth could find any great fault with him.

"What could it be?" Alana asked, biting her lip. "Surely it can't be anything with the marriage contracts. There wouldn't have been time to draw them up. And, in any case, such matters would be conducted between Michael and the head of the family, her eldest son, the current Lord Hollingsworth, not Aunt Jane herself."

Philip shook his head. "No. It can't be that."

We ate in silence, each of us lost in our own thoughts.

"Do you think it has to do with the title?" Alana suggested.

He glanced up at her from his contemplation of his mutton. Her eyebrows arched, urging him to consider the matter. "Possibly," he hedged, and then sighed. "Likely."

"What do you mean?" My gaze darted back and forth between them. "What title?"

"The barony of Dalmay," Philip replied.

"What about it?" I asked.

Philip and Alana both stared at me as if I was the one who wasn't making any sense. "Aunt Jane is probably pushing Michael to petition the Court of Chancery to have his brother declared dead so that the title can be legally passed on to him," he explained.

I was stunned. "He hasn't already done so? But William . . ." I felt an odd pang in my heart at speaking his name after so much time. "He's been missing for, well . . . it must be nearly a decade now."

"Aye. And Michael's been urged to do so since his older brother's disappearance passed the seven-year mark. But Michael refuses. Or, at least, he still was very much against it the last time I spoke to him." He stabbed his fork into his pile of string beans and twirled it around. "He insists that William is alive, and he won't rob him of his inheritance."

I stared morosely down at my own plate, wondering if I would do the same should my brother or sister go missing. How did one accept a loved one's death without proof of it, or at the very least, word of where, when, and how it had happened?

"He's acting in his brother's stead."

Philip nodded. "Yes, but that's not the same as his holding the title outright."

"And Lady Hollingsworth would certainly see the difference," Alana pointed out with a wry twist to her lips. "I can't imagine her being happy with such a circumstance when her daughter could be made a baroness instead."

Neither of us argued with such an assertion, for we both knew it to be true. Lady Hollingsworth was nothing if not calculating. She had likely agreed to the betrothal thinking she could convince her future son-in-law to petition for the title, and now that he was proving difficult she wanted assistance from Philip in doing so. The dowager did not know her nephew very well if she thought he would simply bend to her demands. Philip would speak to Michael about it, but he would never threaten or force his friend to do such a thing.

Philip frowned and sat back in his chair, crossing his

arms over his chest. "Aunt Jane is placing me in a difficult position. I do not want to show up at Dalmay House uninvited, no matter my aunt's assurances of our welcome, but I also cannot justify ignoring her summons. Not when her oldest son, James, has only recently seen the birth of his son and heir. I would hate to see him called away from his wife and child at such a time, and I know Aunt Jane will send for him if I do not rush to her aid."

"What do you wish to do?" Alana asked.

He sighed and rubbed the back of his neck, staring down the table at his chattering children. "I hate to make such a detour with your stomach giving you so much trouble. Your health . . ." his gaze dropped to her still nearly flat abdomen ". . . and that of the babe, is more important than whatever catastrophe my aunt has imagined."

She rested a hand on his arm. "Yes, but Dalmay House is on the road to Edinburgh, is it not?"

"Yes," he admitted somewhat reluctantly.

"Then a stop there will not take us much out of the way." She smiled in reassurance. "My health can handle a slight detour. In fact, it might do me some good to stand on solid ground for longer than a twelve-hour span. Once this matter is resolved, we'll continue the two or three hours to Edinburgh."

Philip's gaze softened at his wife's valiant display of unconcern. My brother-in-law and I both knew this stopover was no small matter. Being ill in one's own home was one thing, but being forced to endure a queasy stomach in unfamiliar surroundings was quite different. We were both eager to see Alana settled in Edinburgh and replace the weight she had lost on the journey.

He reached out to take hold of the hand she had placed on his arm and lifted it to his lips. "Thank you, my dear. I promise we shall not stay longer than necessary."

I dropped my gaze to my plate, trying to squash the uncomfortable surge of jealousy I felt flooding me—a sensation that had been happening more and more often of late.

In the past their displays of affection had always warmed me, but now they left me feeling itchy, anxious. I knew they were not the ones to blame. I was the one who had changed. Somehow in the short space of a few months my life had begun to chafe. Where once I had felt comfortable and content in my exile, I now felt frustrated and alone.

I welcomed the move to Edinburgh if for nothing else but the change of scenery and the opportunity for new company. I loved my sister and her family, but their constant companionship had recently begun to pall. That the annoyance had been sufficient enough to motivate *me* to seek other associations should be indicative of the severity of the situation. I, who hated society and its insipid conversations, who despised petty gossip, was willing to venture out among the lions simply to indulge in a bit of idle talk with someone other than a family member.

So to hear that we would be stopping at Dalmay House where I might speak with old friends, who were far less likely to judge me or flay me with their barbed tongues, should have made me quite pleased. After all, Michael Dalmay and his sister, and even Philip's cousins, were sure to be excellent company, regardless of the problem with Michael and Caroline's betrothal. However, I felt a surprising amount of distress at the postponement of our arrival in Edinburgh.

It wasn't difficult to understand why. Despite my mixed emotions concerning the man, and my fervent denials— even to myself—that I did not care for him, I evidently had been looking forward to seeing Gage. I reminded myself that it was ridiculous to think he would leave the city in just the two or three days we would spend at Dalmay House, if, in fact, he was even still residing in the Scottish capital, but my taut nerves would not be persuaded.

I sighed, resigned to our detour. I wasn't about to argue with Philip and my sister about the necessity of stopping at Dalmay House, not when they were certain to see through my excuses to the truth of the matter. Besides, it seemed a bit heartless to ignore Caroline's plight, though I could have cared less for her mother's distress. And I did want to see Michael Dalmay again.

So I did not give voice to my disappointment when, upon suddenly recalling my presence, Alana turned to ask me, "Is that all right, Kiera?"

"Of course," I replied with forced indifference, not that my opinion mattered anyway. "I'm in no rush. And, in any case, it will be lovely to see the Dalmays again."

Alana smiled. "Yes, it will."

CHAPTER THREE

"Oh, my," I gasped as I leaned forward to peer out the window as the carriage emerged from the shelter of trees onto a circular drive. "It's rather . . ." Words failed me.

"Sprawling? Ostentatious?" Philip supplied wryly, joining me at the window. Following luncheon, he had elected to join us in the carriage, allowing his horse to be led along behind the coach. He laid his hand against his wife's head, careful not to jostle it where it lay on his lap. "Yes. The old Lord Dalmay never did anything by halves."

I felt that might be the understatement of the century.

Perched on the crest of a small rise, Dalmay House dominated the landscape. The rambling Gothic manor, with its ornamental Coade stone chimneys and highly decorated crenellations, was so sharp and delineated as to be almost aggressive, like a warrior attired in a full suit of armor and ready for battle. No plants or flowering bushes softened the harsh lines of the south front or lightened the color of the stalwart gray stone. Even the chimneys, beautiful as they were, seemed to stab forcefully toward the heavens like daggers and pikes.

As we rounded the drive, the manor's numerous wide, mullioned windows glistened in the late afternoon sunlight, blinding me. I turned to the east to see that the lawn, which was a brilliant green next to the drab stone, stretched down toward the dark water of the Firth of Forth, whose choppy waves eventually spilled out into the North Sea. Ancient forests stood sentinel on either side in golden autumn finery, as if guarding the processional route from the house to the sea.

"It's quite something, isn't it?" Philip said on an exhale. I nodded.

The carriage pulled to a halt and within moments the dark double doors were thrown open to reveal a coterie of blue-and-gold-clad footmen. While Philip helped Alana to sit up and straighten her appearance, I allowed one of the waiting footmen to assist me out of the coach onto the gravel drive. I couldn't stop my gaze from traveling upward. From this angle, the glittering façade was even more imposing.

"Oh, my," my sister exclaimed in an unconscious imitation of my earlier reaction as she stepped out of the carriage beside me. I turned to see that her chestnut hair and Prussian blue traveling costume were restored to order. But for a few wrinkles in her skirts and the paleness of her complexion, one would never have known she had fallen ill again after luncheon. My appearance was all the more shabby for the stark comparison, in an old russet brown dress with tendrils of hair escaping their pins to trail down my back, per usual. Even had Alana not soiled my two best traveling ensembles, I still would have appeared a bedraggled mess next to her. It was not that I was unkempt; I simply could not be bothered to notice or care that my hair was mussed or my gown wrinkled, until it was too late to alter the opinions of the people scowling at me. As was the case now.

An expression of disdain flickered briefly in the Dalmay butler's eyes as he stared down his rather hawkish nose at me before he ushered us into the entryway. Ignoring the servant's condescension, I handed him my cloak, bonnet, and gloves and moved toward the stone archway leading into the entry hall.

My eyes widened in appreciation. The soaring two-story chamber was topped with a decorative hammer-beam ceiling, and its walls were covered in portraits of the Dalmay family's many noble ancestors. Such artwork was a feast for my eyes, and I planned to spend many an hour over the next few days devouring their canvases, dissecting the pieces to discover just how the various artists had achieved their effects. It had been quite some time since I had been given the opportunity to study another's artwork—I had long ago exhausted the paintings at Gairloch Castle of their educational value—and I felt a thrill at the chance to do so now.

Philip and Alana joined me in my examination of the beautiful chamber. Black-and-white tiles covered the floor, leading to the creamy marble of the staircase and the red runner trailing up the center of each riser. The stair rail was molded in black rod iron and topped with warm oak. The furniture positioned in the room had appropriately been kept to a minimum. Two red wingback chairs and a round table topped with a floral arrangement of fragrant asters and bellflowers were all that occupied the space.

As we stood absorbing our surroundings, a man rushed in to greet us through a door on the left, his footfalls echoing off the walls of the cavernous chamber. A wide, boyish grin flashed across his face, summoning an answering smile to my own.

"Cromarty, I'm so glad you could join us," Michael Dalmay exclaimed.

"Glad you could accommodate us," Philip responded, clasping his proffered hand.

A subtle undercurrent of tension tightened Michael's shoulders, as if in the excitement of seeing us he had forgotten our real reason for being there. "But of course. You're always welcome," he demurred. His eyes still warm and bright, he turned to bow over my sister's hand. "Lady Cromarty, how lovely it is to see you."

"Thank you," she replied with obvious pleasure. "But when did we become so formal? Alana, if you please. After all, were you not the young man who took a pair of scissors to one of my braids?"

I laughed, having forgotten about that particular incident.

Michael's gaze flicked toward me, his soft gray eyes dancing with mirth. "Aye. And I discovered I wasn't too old for my father to take a switch to me. I couldn't sit for nearly a week."

"Well, it was no more than you deserved," Alana proclaimed with mock indignation. "My other braid had to be lopped off at the shoulder to even it out. I was mistaken for a boy for almost half a year."

"Oh, Alana, you could never have been mistaken for a boy. Even at the age of nine."

She blushed becomingly, giving her wan cheeks a welcome wash of color.

"And it taught you an important lesson." He leaned toward her. "Young ladies should never spy from haylofts upon adolescent boys. Not if they don't want an eyeful."

"And an earful," Alana added with a teasing arch to her brow.

This time it was Michael's turn to blush. Nearly all of the tension that had tightened his frame moments earlier was gone, and I was grateful to Alana for putting him at ease, whether it had been her intention or not.

He turned to take my hand, flashing me the same dimpled grin I remembered from childhood. Even at eight years my senior, Michael had never acted too old or important to pay attention to a quiet little girl. Nor too mature to tweak my nose when I was ignoring him in favor of my sketchbook. "Lady Darby. Kiera," he corrected, likely hoping I wouldn't also dredge up some embarrassing story about our shared past. "You are looking very well. The Highlands must agree with you."

"They do. Though I cannot say I will miss their cold and darkness this winter."

His grin widened in agreement. "Still painting, I hear."

"I am," I answered in some surprise.

"Caroline has spoken of little else in the past few hours," he replied by way of explanation, though it only served to perplex me further. But before I could ask for clarification a loud commotion called our attention to the entryway. "Ah, the children," our host exclaimed.

The next few moments were occupied in assisting the rather frazzled-looking nanny in wrangling the children. They were all introduced to Michael and then herded up the stairs toward the nursery. "Laura's babe is also there. I imagine the little scrapper will enjoy the company," Michael told us.

"Oh, yes. I had forgotten your sister welcomed her first child but a year ago," Alana said. "What is the lad's name again?"

"Nicolas. And what a charmer he is. You'll see." His eyes shone with genuine affection for his little nephew. "Now, I imagine you would like to rest and refresh yourselves after your journey. We normally dine at six o'clock," he declared, opening his pocket watch and then snapping it shut again. "I would be happy to ask Mrs. MacDougall to postpone it another half hour if you would like to join us. Or I can have trays brought to your rooms." The last was directed at Alana with some measure of sympathy. The man had not missed the signs of her recent illness.

"Oh, we don't wish to be an imposition," Alana began.

"No imposition," he declared, interrupting her. He reached out to take her hand between his own again. "I'm simply glad you are all here." He smiled warmly in turn at each of us, but I thought I detected some measure of sorrow in his eyes. The somber emotion confused me. The tautness that had returned to his frame I could understand, as he undoubtedly knew why his future mother-in-law had sent for us, but sadness seemed oddly out of place. Unless he worried Philip would advise his aunt to end Michael and Caroline's engagement, or be unable to convince her not to. But what could Michael have done to warrant such a drastic measure?

In the next moment, he blinked and the sheen of grief was washed away, making me wonder whether I had seen it there at all. "What shall it be?" he asked Alana.

My sister glanced at her husband, who gazed down at her, waiting for her to make the decision. "We will dine with you," she said with a smile.

"Excellent. Then, if you'll follow me." Michael offered me his arm and guided us toward the stairs, allowing Philip and Alana to fall into step behind us.

Catching my gaze on the portraits hanging above, he patted my hand where it rested on his arm. "Still painting mostly portraits?"

"Yes." I waved my arm at the array of artwork decorating the chamber. "This is quite a collection."

He nodded. "Aye. The whole host of Dalmay ancestors since the barony was granted over three hundred years ago. There's more hanging in the dining room, the drawing room, and the library." My eagerness must have shown in my eyes, for he chuckled. "You are welcome to wander at your leisure."

"Thank you."

He waved it away. "Someone should appreciate it."

I glanced up at the wry tone of his voice.

He smiled tightly. "I'm afraid I find the gaze of all my forefathers bearing down on me rather heavy."

I did not reply—not knowing what to say—but I was more certain than ever that the conflicting emotions I had seen in Michael's face had been real, and I was intensely curious as to why. Was the possibility of losing his fiancée all that distressed him, or was there something more?

Before I could ask, however, our host's attention was diverted by a man at the top of the stairs. Michael's arm stiffened beneath my hand, and I glanced between the two men, trying to read the silent communication passing between them, for it obviously distressed Michael in some way. Even though the man was not attired in the Dalmay livery, from the hunched posture of his shoulders and the worn appearance of his clothing I could see that he was a servant. A gardener, perhaps, or the stable master? But what one of those employees would be doing on the upper floors of the manor, I could not fathom.

Out of the corner of my eye, I caught Michael's subtle nod, and then, as quickly as the man appeared, he was gone.

"I must apologize." Michael turned back toward me to announce, "There is a matter I must see to." His soft gray eyes were strained. "I'm afraid it cannot wait."

"Of course," Philip replied. "Think nothing of it." The tone of his voice told me he believed the matter had something to do with the usual running of an estate, but I was not so certain.

And if the gaze Michael continued to level at me was any indication, he was aware of my interest. He did not seem worried by it, merely attentive, and this in and of itself heightened my curiosity even more. I wished we were alone, so that I might ask him. Only Alana's and Philip's presence behind us kept me from voicing the questions forming on my lips.

Michael's gaze broke away from mine. "Mrs. MacDougall will see you to your rooms," he informed us as we approached the landing where his housekeeper stood waiting for us. "I look forward to seeing you at dinner."

Then, with a quick bow, he hurried around a corner and out of sight, in the same direction the mysterious servant must have gone. I glanced over my shoulder to see if my sister and her husband had noticed the strange altercation, but they seemed consumed by their own worries for Alana's health and the reasons behind Lady Hollingsworth's summons.

I turned back to the housekeeper, listening absentmindedly to her greeting while most of my attention remained with Michael and the grizzled servant. I couldn't help wondering if there had been something Michael wanted to say to me. Would he approach me later, or would time and distance persuade him to hold his tongue? I was anxious to join the others in the drawing room before dinner, if for no other reason than to catch a few moments alone with our host.

CHAPTER FOUR

Having washed the dust of the road from my face and hands, I dressed quickly in a marine blue gown with ivory lace trim, the least rumpled of my evening gown choices, for it lay at the top of my trunk. Its sloped shoulders and slightly puffed sleeves were the latest fashion, or so Alana had told me when she'd ordered it for me six months before. After affixing the matching marine blue belt around my waist, I allowed Lucy, my maid, to fuss over my deflated hair; however, I refused to let her curl the fashionable ringlets that graced the sides of most ladies' heads. I was impatient to see Michael, and ringlets would take far too long to perfect. A simple knot would have to do.

Ignoring my maid's petulant expression, I slipped out of my chamber to retrace my steps to the entry hall, when the sound of a shrill voice brought me up short. The sound was emanating from the suite my sister shared with her husband across the hall, and, though I had never heard the ever-proper marchioness speak in such a strident manner, the voice was undoubtedly Lady Hollingsworth's.

I hesitated, wondering whether I should join the members of Philip's family gathered in his suite. The shrieks and outrages Lady Hollingsworth uttered penetrated the wood door, as well as the calmer rumble of Philip's voice, but the words were indistinct. I could not have eavesdropped on their conversation even had I wanted to.

Curious as I was to understand why Lady Hollingsworth had insisted her nephew attend her to sort out whatever problem there was with Michael and Caroline's engagement, I was none too eager to encounter Philip's stodgy aunt again, particularly while she was in the midst of a tirade. Shaking my head at her display of theatrics, I turned away from the door to my sister's suite and marched down the hall. Alana would inform me later of everything I needed to know, and I could avoid falling under the marchioness's critical gaze for a little while longer.

Trailing my fingers over the smooth oak of the banister, I descended the stairs toward the entry hall. Unbidden, my eyes lifted once again to the vast number of portraits plastering the walls from floor to ceiling. I felt like a honeybee buzzing among the flowers of the garden of Versailles, overwhelmed by the beauty and abundance and uncertain where to alight. My gaze drifted toward the wall on my left as I approached the first landing, falling on the portrait of a Georgian lady. A delicious shiver of excitement ran through me as I leaned closer, certain Gainsborough must have painted this. The knowing look in the young lady's eyes, the almost poetic positioning of her amid the deep shadows of an arbor—classical techniques of the famous artist—were aspects I had tried to emulate in my own paintings.

So caught up was I in tracing Gainsborough's brushstrokes with my eyes that I failed to notice the footsteps descending the staircase behind me. In fact, it was not until an all-too-familiar voice spoke just over my shoulder that I realized I was not alone.

"If I did not know you better, I would suspect you were ogling the young lady in that portrait, Lady Darby."

I stiffened in surprise.

"As it is, I imagine you're making her quite uncomfortable with so close an examination of her . . . attributes."

His voice was husky with amusement, and I did not need to turn to look at him to know his pale blue eyes were twinkling wickedly. My gaze lifted anyway, to ensure that the devil behind me was truly there and not conjured by my active imagination. Handsome as ever, Sebastian Gage stood before me, making my heart trip over itself inside my chest.

He looked past me at the portrait and tilted his head in thought. "Although, for all we know, she might be quite the saucy minx and thoroughly enjoy your intimate inspection."

I scowled as the impish smile curling the corners of his lips stretched even wider. "I was not ogling her breasts," I protested, feeling my cheeks heat even as I spoke the words.

"I'm sure you weren't," he murmured in agreement, though the light in his eyes seemed to belie his words. "Of artistic interest, was it, my lady?"

"It's a Gainsborough," I declared. The artist's name should be explanation enough.

His eyes lifted to the portrait once again before returning to me. "I see." And clearly he did, for he did not taunt me or request that I elaborate.

We stared at each other, and for the first time the significance of his appearance struck me.

Vivid recollections flooded my mind and tangled my emotions into knots. Memories of Gage verbally sparring with me over the facts of the murder we had solved at my sister's house party. Of him cradling me in his arms as we floated in the loch after I had been shot, and the kiss he may or may not have pressed on my icy lips. Of the last time I had seen him, when he had tried to sneak away in the predawn light without even saying good-bye.

No one had ever created such conflicting emotions inside me—irritation, fondness, longing, and anger. He challenged and confused me, and the moment I thought I knew who he was and what he wanted he would do something to alter my opinion. One moment he had turned his back on me callously, and the next he was gazing at me with such tenderness that it took everything inside me not to throw myself into his arms. I couldn't understand him, or my reactions to him, and that made me agitated and wary. And more than a little resentful.

"You look well," Gage said just as I snapped, "What are you doing here?"

The flush in my cheeks turned fiery at the petulant tone of my voice, but I refused to retract the question. Especially since my annoyance only seemed to amuse him further.

"I was invited," he replied much too calmly. "Michael Dalmay and I are old friends from our university days."

I could not dispute his assertion. As my brother-in-law had been friends with both Gage and Michael at Cambridge, it only made sense that the two men were also acquainted. However, I was suspicious of his so-called invitation, particularly when, to my knowledge, all of the other guests were in one way or another related to the betrothed couple.

"I thought you were working an investigation in Edinburgh."

He arched an eyebrow. "I was. I finished what needed to be done there about a fortnight ago before accepting Dalmay's *gracious* invitation."

I narrowed my eyes, uncertain if he was mocking me.

"I suspect *your* invite was at the hands of Lady Hollingsworth. Or should I say, Cromarty's was."

I frowned at his subtle dig and lifted my chin. "You suppose right. Although I can, perhaps, claim a longer friendship with the Dalmays than either of you."

Gage's gaze turned curious.

"We grew up together, on neighboring estates."

"But Dalmay must be almost eight years older than you."

"Aye," I replied with a small smile. "As are you."

He scowled.

"I assure you, such an age difference did not stop him from pulling our braids or indulging in rowing races on the River Tweed." I smiled wider at the memory. "Nor did the seven-year age gap between Michael and his older brother prevent Will from joining in our antics, as well. When he was home," I added as a saddened afterthought. It had been many years since I had allowed myself to think so much about the older Dalmay boy, and the memory of him tugged at something inside me.

My mention of Will seemed to have a similar effect on Gage, for his gaze turned watchful. "You knew William Dalmay, then?"

I nodded. "He was a good man." I glanced over my shoulder at the Gainsborough portrait. "And a gifted artist in his own right." I sighed. "Who knows what he would have become had it not been for the war."

I turned back to find Gage watching me closely. I furrowed my brow in question, wondering why his gaze was now so concerned. He opened his mouth to speak, and then, as if thinking better of it, shook his head.

"Shall we join the others in the drawing room?" he asked, unclasping his hands from behind his back and offering his arm to me.

I stared up at him, wondering if I could force the information out of him that he had decided not to share. I suspected not. Not when his brow had been wiped so clear of any trace that his thoughts had ever turned dark. I knew from experience that this man would not be driven to answer any questions he did not already want to. And so today's enigmas would be added to the already long list of unresolved business between us.

I pressed my lips together and reluctantly accepted his escort.

At the bottom of the stairs, Gage drew me across the hall toward a set of double doors fashioned from slats of mahogany. One door stood wide open, allowing the tones of a far warmer conversation than the one being conducted upstairs to drift out into the hall.

Our host was the first to see us, crossing the room to take my hand in greeting. And try as I might to focus solely on Michael's words, I found my gaze wandering over his shoulder to one of five intricately woven tapestries displayed on the creamy walls. They had obviously been designed and crafted with much skill. My fingers itched to trace the threads.

Fortunately, from Michael's delighted grin, I could tell he did not feel slighted by my interest. "I'm glad our artwork has met with such satisfaction. Our mother must have done an adequate job of selecting accomplished pieces."

"Indeed. Who is the designer?" I could not stop myself from asking as my gaze was drawn once again to the tapestries.

"Some fellow named Goya, my sister tells me. Procured from one of the Spanish royal palaces."

I gasped. "Francisco de Goya?"

"But of course," Laura Dalmay, now Lady Keswick, replied, joining in her brother's amusement.

I blushed, realizing how rude I was being to take more interest in the tapestries than in my old friends. "Forgive me. I fear I've been away from the city and all of its art exhibits for far too long," I offered by way of explanation.

Laura brushed my apology aside. "It is no matter. I am only glad to see you looking so well." She took my hand in hers with a warm smile.

"Likewise," I replied, taking in the sight of the sprightly young girl I remembered all grown up.

She was now a statuesque woman, though with the same light brown hair and charming sprinkling of freckles across her nose she had sported since the age of three. Being a few years older, I could remember when Laura's mother had begun to despair at the freckles' unfashionable appearance, but I found them to be charming. Laura was quite beautiful, but in a warm, approachable way that drew you closer rather than pushing you away to admire from afar. No, indeed, her prettiness was best appreciated up close, while basking in her bright smile. She was very much like her brother Michael in that regard.

She nodded to the man standing beside me. "I see you have already met Mr. Gage."

I glanced up at Gage, who was observing our conversation attentively. "Lady Darby and I are already acquainted."

Laura's gaze turned wary. "Really?"

"Yes," he replied, still looking down at me. "We met at Lord and Lady Cromarty's house party several months ago."

"Oh," she gasped in relief. "Thank goodness! I thought maybe . . ." Her words trailed away awkwardly, and I suddenly realized why she had appeared so concerned. She worried our acquaintance had been made in London, during the inquiry into the charges my husband's colleagues had leveled against me after his death. I had been acquitted and released, but that had not put a stop to the scandal surrounding my name or the rumors that still haunted me.

Laura blushed, and I felt an answering heat rush to my cheeks. "I forgot about Lady Cromarty's party," she rushed on to say. "I know Michael was sorry to miss it, as were we. Especially knowing as we do now that his lovely fiancée was also in attendance." She glanced over her shoulder, as if looking for Caroline, but Philip's cousin had not yet entered the room.

Her gaze alighted on her husband, and she beckoned him forward. "Oh, but allow me to introduce you to my husband." She laced her arm through his. "This is my Lord Keswick." She pronounced it in the same way as the name of the town in the Lake District of Cumberland—*KEZ-ik*.

"Lady Darby, my pleasure," he murmured, bowing over my hand from his very great height like a sapling bending in the breeze. Keswick was quite possibly the tallest man I had ever met—taller even than Mr. Gage—and whippet-thin. At perhaps five and twenty, his wheat-blond hair had already begun to recede from his head, and I suspected by forty he would be bald.

"Dalmay tells me you grew up on the Northumberland side of the Tweed," Keswick said. "Have you ever had occasion to visit Cumberland?"

"No," I replied. "Though I hear the hills and lakes there are beautiful. That is where you are from, am I correct?"

His smile deepened. "It is. I believe it the loveliest place in all of England."

"And deathly dull."

Lord Keswick stepped back to reveal the deliverer of this pronouncement. A young lady in rose-colored satin sat flipping the pages of a periodical so rapidly it was doubtful she was reading. Her gaze lifted once from the paper to glance at me through the sweep of her lashes before dropping back to the pages before her, but not before I saw the twinkle in her eye.

"Perhaps compared to London or Edinburgh," Keswick replied in obvious irritation. "But the Lake District is hardly dull."

Her laughing gaze met mine again and she rolled her eyes as if I were in on some private joke. "Only to you," she protested. She set aside her periodical and rose to her feet.

"Lady Darby," Laura rushed to say before her husband could voice the displeasure tightening his lips. "Allow me to introduce my sister-in-law, Miss Elise Remmington."

I could see the resemblance now—the pale blonde hair, the slim physique, the caramel-brown eyes.

She offered me her hand. "My pleasure."

"Likewise."

"Miss Remmington recently had her first season in London," Michael supplied, possibly explaining her earlier expressed opinions.

"I take it you enjoyed it," I said.

"Oh, yes," she replied. "Although . . ." Her expression was all innocence, but I did not miss the spark of devilry in her eyes. "From what I've been told, it seems it would have been much more exciting had you joined us in town."

I stiffened. "Indeed."

Michael cleared his throat uncomfortably and stepped forward to slip his arm through mine. "Kiera, allow me to show you the tapestries you were so admiring."

I allowed him to escort me away from Miss Remmington, whose face creased momentarily into a cheeky grin, flashing a pair of dimples, telling me she'd meant no real malice. Her brother did not witness this exchange, however, and I doubted it would have done much to ameliorate his temper in any case, for his face was red with fury at her impertinence. I suspected theirs was a very interesting sibling dynamic, and wondered whether I should pity Laura for getting caught in the middle of it.

Gage, for his part, seemed quite amused by the girl's cheek, if the laugh lines crinkling at the sides of his eyes were any indication. I arched my brow at his merriment before turning back to Michael.

"I must apologize for Miss Remmington," he was saying. "I'm sure she meant no insult."

"No worries," I assured him, laying my hand over his where it pressed against my arm. "I have met Miss Remmington's like before."

He sighed. "She is such a lively, pretty girl, but she can be a bit . . ." He struggled to find the right word.

"She is a hoyden."

Michael smiled tightly in acknowledgment. "I fear Keswick despairs of reining her in. And this gathering is proving a bit trying for him. The stiffer the personage, the more shocking Miss Remmington seems determined to be."

"And Lady Hollingsworth is certainly not . . . flexible."

"Nor her son."

"Lord Damien?" I asked in some surprise. I had never thought of Lady Hollingsworth's younger son as being particularly stuffy, but perhaps Miss Remmington's extreme impishness had proved too much for him.

"She particularly delights in tweaking his nose."

We paused before one of the tapestries. The rich palette of browns, gold, forest green, and burgundy wove together to form a depiction of children at play. I allowed my eyes to slide over the pleasing lines and hues, but kept my mind firmly fixed on our conversation.

Speaking of Damien and his mother had made me all too aware of their continued absence, as well as that of Michael's fiancée and Philip and Alana. Michael would have to be a fool not to notice the significance. That I was the only one here in Philip's family's stead made me more than a little uncomfortable, and uncertain whether I should tread lightly.

"You are well?" I asked, pretending to study the tapestry.

He turned to face the tapestry as well, with his back to the room. "As well as can be expected, under the circumstances," he surprised me by admitting.

We fell silent, listening to the rumble of the others' voices across the room as I contemplated my next question and whether to pry at all.

His gaze flicked toward me. "How much do you know?"

"Almost nothing," I admitted, allowing him to take the reins of the conversation.

It took him so long to respond I began to worry he would not tell me. I could press him with questions, but it would be so much easier if he willingly confided in me. The tension I had witnessed earlier was still in him; I could feel the muscles in his forearm tighten beneath my hand.

"Do you remember Will?" he finally asked, his voice heavy with repressed emotions.

I glanced up at him. "Of course."

His gaze met mine, seeming to scour my face for information, as if my expression could tell him something he wanted to know. "There was such a large age gap between you, and then he was off fighting on the continent. I wasn't sure."

"Fifteen years," I confirmed. "But he stayed at Swinton Lodge even after the rest of your family decamped for Dalmay House and London." I looked away, suddenly unwilling to let him read my face as I relived my memories. "I daresay I saw more of him during that last year than anyone. He acted as my drawing master while Father struggled to find a replacement when Signor Riotta resigned."

Michael appeared genuinely surprised. "Really?"

I nodded. "For almost six months." I stared unseeing at the Goya tapestry, my mind conjuring the soft gray eyes of William Dalmay shadowed with the pain that had seemed ever present in his gaze. Even when he laughed it had been there in the tight lines at the corners of his eyes. "Your brother might have been the best drawing master I ever had," I added in a soft voice.

"I never knew that," he murmured. "Father said he'd been painting again that last summer. But I never thought . . . I guess I just always assumed he was alone."

I felt his curious gaze on me, and I knew why. In my mind's eye, I could see one of Will's last paintings, the grotesque images, the distorted bodies. Even within context, they were bizarre and disturbing. As a fifteen-year-old girl they had given me nightmares, though I never mentioned them to Will. I couldn't add to his already heavy burdens.

"Did you . . ." Michael struggled to voice the worry tightening his features. "Did he ever show you his artwork?"

I turned to him, able to answer honestly. "No." He had never *shown* me. I had seen them by accident.

He exhaled in relief and turned back toward the tapestry. I studied his profile, wondering why, if at all, Will's paintings mattered to Michael's current troubles. Had he kept them? Was that what troubled Lady Hollingsworth? Had she or Caroline seen them, and worried what they meant— what ghastly secrets the Dalmay family hid?

"Michael, what is going on?" I asked, tired of dancing around the issues at hand. "Why did Lady Hollingsworth send for Philip? And why did that servant's presence at the top of the stairs earlier trouble you so?"

"Ah, you saw that, did you?" He spoke lightly, but I could tell he felt anything but amused.

"Yes. And if Philip had not been so concerned for my sister's health, I suspect they would have seen the oddity in it as well. *What* is going on?"

He sighed and closed his eyes, as if gathering the strength to speak, when the soft tread of feet pulled our attention toward the door.

I believe he would have answered—that the truth would have come out right then and there—had my brother-in-law and sister and Lady Hollingsworth and her two children not chosen that moment to enter the drawing room. I had been flustered by their continued absence, and now I was irritated by their sudden appearance. Had I been a four-year-old I would have stamped my feet. Only the looks on Philip's and Alana's faces kept my frustration in check. Something was definitely wrong. My sister's gaze sought me out, and the grooves between her eyes seemed only to deepen.

Crossing the room toward her, I glanced around at the others to see what their reactions were to the newcomers' presence. The strained smiles and cordial greetings were all to be expected, as was Lady Hollingsworth's pinched expression. However, the manner in which Gage's eyes remained steadily trained on me, as if he was interested in my response to Michael's troubles, stretched my already taut nerves.

I wrapped my fingers around Alana's arm. "How are you feeling?"

Her bright blue gaze flickered, searching mine. "Better," she replied before offering me a weak smile that did not reach all the way to her eyes. "I think it helps that the room is not swaying."

"Yes." I wanted to pull her aside, to demand she tell me what she knew, what had upset her so. But I knew I could not. Not with an entire roomful of people watching, waiting on us to go into dinner.

The conversation around us was stilted, the mood uncertain, as if no one knew exactly how to proceed. And so good manners, the fallback of the genteel, took over. If all else fails, proceed with unbending civility.

Laura smiled tightly. "Let's go into dinner, shall we?"

The others eagerly complied, naturally falling into pairs according to precedence. I could see the strain on Michael's face as he was forced to offer his arm to Lady Hollingsworth, but I knew his worry over her acceptance was needless. The marchioness would rather suffer the touch of a leper than break protocol.

"Lady Darby." Laura laid a hand against my arm. Distress

tightened her features. "I'm afraid I must apologize. Our numbers are uneven this evening. We had hoped our party would balance out, but . . ." she offered me a sad smile ". . . things do not always go as planned."

"A blessing, under the circumstances," Lady Hollingsworth sniped as Michael led her through the door.

I frowned at the marchioness's back before turning to place a hand over Laura's where it rested on my arm. "There is no need to apologize," I assured her. As the lowest-ranked lady in precedence, I had expected to walk in alone. "After all, you were not anticipating three more guests to join you. How could you be expected to make up the numbers on such short notice?"

Her expression was unreadable. "Yes. Well. Thank you for being so understanding."

My brow furrowed in puzzlement. Once again I felt I did not understand something that should have been clear. But before I could decide whether to press her about it, Gage deftly linked my arm through his left one.

"No worries," he declared, flashing Laura and me one of his most charming smiles. "I'm quite happy to claim a lady on each arm."

"An excellent solution," Laura proclaimed in relief before I could protest. "Thank you, Mr. Gage."

"No need for thanks," Gage said. "Not when I'm clearly the one who benefits from such a predicament." He grinned first at Miss Remmington on his right and then at me.

My face felt tight from the effort it took for me not to frown at his good humor.

"Well, since that's settled." Laura touched my arm again before turning away toward her own escort.

Seeing the reassurance Gage's offer had given my hostess, I bit my tongue against the urge to argue. It would be ungracious to reject his escort now, even if his close proximity did less than comfortable things to my insides.

"Shall we?" He leaned closer to ask as the last couple before us exited the drawing room.

"Of course," I replied, relieved to hear that my voice did not betray the emotions tumbling about inside me.

Gage's lips curled up at the corners, as if he was imparting a forbidden secret, and then he straightened to escort us from the room.

Instantly I began to wonder why Gage seemed to be exerting his charm upon me. He had rarely done so before, and then only when he wanted something from me. I scolded myself for being taken in, even if only for a second, by his charisma. I, more than anyone, knew I had to keep my wits about me when I was dealing with Gage. My attraction to him aside, he was a very clever and enigmatic man. And I was not about to become another member of his slavering horde of female followers. If Gage was suddenly determined to befuddle me, I was resolved to find out why.

CHAPTER FIVE

Dinner was an awkward affair of stilted attempts at conversation and Lady Hollingsworth's determined efforts to steer all discussions back to topics concerning her family. Matters were not improved by the fact that I was seated between Lord Keswick and his sister, whose sole purpose seemed to be to further antagonize her sibling, as well as Lord Damien.

I had taken an immediate liking to Lady Hollingsworth's second son upon meeting him at Gairloch two months prior. Quick to laugh and chivalrous to a fault, Damien had been more than one lady's champion at different occasions during the house party, including mine. However, listening to him scold and rebuke Miss Remmington, I doubted the cheeky girl would ever be able to count him among her defenders.

I couldn't fault the meal or the setting, even if the attitude of some of our dinner companions left something to be desired. The room absolutely sparkled with candlelight; the china, crystal, and silverware glistened on a tablecloth of pristine white under the glow of a chandelier and candelabras, which spanned the length of the buffet, the sideboard, and the fireplace mantel. A fire crackled merrily in the hearth, holding back the chill of the autumn evening and lending the spice of cedarwood to the heady scent of the wine and the rich aroma of the food.

I was relieved to see Alana hungrily consume dainty spoonfuls of her split pea soup. However, observing my sister as I was, I also couldn't help but notice Gage, who was seated to her left, and the way he seemed to be noting my every movement. It was not overtly done. Gage would never have been so gauche as to stare openly at a person across the dinner table. All the same, I knew where his focus lay, and it was disconcerting.

The fact that Michael periodically sent anxious looks in my direction only made matters worse. Did he regret our not being able to finish our conversation in the drawing room? And just what exactly had he been about to confide?

I could not stop my mind from going over the clues that had been dropped in my hearing. As far as I could tell, everything still pointed to Philip's supposition that his aunt's displeasure with Michael and Caroline's engagement had to do with Michael's refusal to petition the Court of Chancery for the title. But, then, why the sadness in Michael's eyes? William had been missing for almost a decade. Was Michael only now beginning to accept that his brother would never return, that he was, in fact, dead?

And why was Lady Hollingsworth so intent on antagonizing the Dalmays? Surely such a display of disdain was not the way to win them over to her way of thinking.

After three courses, I was no closer to uncovering what was going on than I was before, and infinitely more aggravated.

"Lady Darby does not seem to be enjoying herself. Perhaps we should pursue a different topic of conversation," I was jolted from my introspection to hear Lord Damien say.

"Why ever shouldn't she be?" Miss Remmington insisted. "We're merely discussing the merits of city life compared to country life. I daresay she's experienced both."

"Yes, but the last few weeks she spent in London were not the happiest."

I stiffened at his oblique reference to Sir Anthony's death and the subsequent charges brought against me for unnatural behavior.

Miss Remmington forked a bite of delicate, flaky cod and swirled it in its mustard cream sauce. "Well, I'm not the one who brought up such an insensitive subject. You are."

"Yes, but *you* are the one who caused it by mentioning London at all." Damien's brow was lowered in a ferocious frown. "She was bound to think of it."

"Please," I interrupted before their argument could become even louder and more embarrassing, for me, if no one else. "Lord Damien, it's quite all right." I shifted my gaze to Miss Remmington, who was watching me curiously. "I do miss London sometimes," I admitted. "Especially the museums," I added with a tiny smile. "But, by and large, I find I prefer the country. The air and light are so much better, you see." I did not add the fact that there was also less society, and people's sharp tongues and penetrating stares, to contend with, though from the sharpening of Miss Remmington's eyes I was certain she was aware of this.

However, she did not question me on it. "I had forgotten that Laura said you were an artist."

"And quite a good one," Damien declared, determined not to be left out of the conversation. "Mother says her portraits will soon be all the rage. Everyone will want to be painted by the notorious Lady Darby." Damien's eyes widened and a blush reddened his cheeks as he belatedly realized what he had said. "Well, that is . . ."

"Really? The *notorious* Lady Darby?" Miss Remmington pressed, a smirk stretching her face.

I felt a tightness in my chest at his words, but held no rancor toward the young man, for I knew he was only repeating something his mother had said. And in an attempt to show up the vexing Miss Remmington he had uttered the epithet without thinking.

Miss Remmington, on the other hand, was taking advantage of the opportunity to cause trouble by plaguing Damien for his faux pas. I knew her type, unfortunately. She thrived on conflict. The bigger the reaction she got out of you, the more it pleased her. And the more likely she was to continue goading you. The swiftest way to beat her at her own game was to refuse to engage, be it with anger or discomfiture.

"I'm sure he meant no harm," Laura murmured, trying to smooth over the awkwardness that had once again descended.

"Of course not," I replied, not wanting everyone to make more of it than it was. I refused to become a target for Miss Remmington. "And, in any case, there's no harm in speaking the truth. After all, I suppose I *am* rather notorious," I added, forcing the jest past my lips. Almost everyone seated at the table smiled.

"I'm truly sorry," Damien began earnestly, leaning forward to see past Miss Remmington, but I cut him off before he could continue.

"Damien, it's quite all right," I assured him with a tight smile, feeling my own cheeks begin to heat in embarrassment. If the boy didn't cease protesting, he would expose the anxiety beneath my veneer of careful indifference.

"Yes, if I were Lady Darby, I would actually begin to capitalize on that sobriquet," Gage said. He flashed me an encouraging smile before nodding to the table. "I have had more than one acquaintance inquire as to whether she would be accepting portrait commissions again. They seemed quite eager to hear that she would."

I couldn't withhold my surprise, at both the fact that people had actually been asking after me and the fact that they had asked Gage, of all people.

"I, too, received more than one inquiry," Lady Hollingsworth reluctantly admitted.

"Well, then, that is excellent news." Philip smiled warmly at me over his wineglass. "For I'm sure she won't mind me telling you that she plans to take on new commissions once we settle in Edinburgh."

I fought against the urge to squirm as the others expressed their delight at the news. I was excited to begin painting the likenesses of real persons again, instead of the imagined subjects I had been portraying since I had tired of depicting my sister and her family months ago, but I was not accustomed to so much praise or attention. The works I had created since the scandal and my self-imposed banishment from London had been sold anonymously, and though they fetched higher-than-expected profits, I rarely encountered the buyers, and then usually with my secret identity still intact.

"Oh, then you must take me on as your first commission," Lady Caroline declared. Her face flushed a fetching shade of pink as everyone turned to look at her. "That is, I remember that you painted Lady Cromarty's wedding portrait. Your sister was kind enough to show it to me while we were at Gairloch Castle."

I nodded. The portrait hung in the master bedchamber.

"Well, it was ever so lovely. And . . ." Her cheeks reddened deeper, nearly matching her skin tone to the cherry-red ribbon laced through the neckline of her gown, as she glanced down the table toward her fiancé. "I wondered if . . . you might be willing to paint mine."

Complete silence fell over the table as Caroline innocently broached the topic of which everyone was thinking, but no one dared speak. Eyes darted around the table, as if uncertain how the others would react and whether anyone would actually pursue the matter. As much as I wanted to demand that they explain what exactly had everyone so on edge, I knew that now was not the time. A confrontation at the dinner table could only end in heartache, at Michael's and Caroline's expense. I simply couldn't open them up to public ridicule like that.

So, instead, I adopted a bright smile and addressed Caroline. "I would be honored."

Her gaze flew back to mine from where it had been pinned on her mother. "Truly?"

"Of course."

Her joy and excitement were so evident in her shining eyes and dazzling smile that I couldn't help but respond in kind.

"If there is a wedding," Lady Hollingsworth muttered crisply.

The happiness faded from Caroline's face like the sun disappearing behind a cloud, and it was clear to me, if nothing else was, how very much Philip's cousin wanted to marry Michael.

I wanted to reach down the table and pinch the marchioness. Two months ago, Lady Hollingsworth had tried to match her daughter with a horse-mad brute who had ended up compromising one of the other young ladies at my sister's house party. I had been as unconvinced then that the marchioness had her daughter's best interests at heart as I was now.

After Lady Hollingsworth's rude comment, the conversation could easily have dissolved into bickering and infighting. I was almost more shocked when no one snapped back at the marchioness than that she had behaved so impolitely in the first place, priggish as she was. She was plainly beyond overset if she was willing to break the very rules she clung so tightly to.

Everyone seemed inordinately determined to remain civil, and though I supposed this could have stemmed solely from the same desire I felt to spare Michael's and Caroline's feelings, I sensed there was something else holding everyone back, even Miss Remmington. What it could be, I didn't know, but it cast a different light on the glances that Gage and Michael, and even my sister, continued to send my way. I couldn't tell whether they were merely uneasy about my continued state of ignorance or if they were afraid of my reaction once the truth was known. But why should my response matter?

I frowned down at my plate and pushed my food around with my fork, having lost all appetite. I could only hope someone would take it upon themselves to remedy the situation following dinner and tell me just what exactly was going on.

After Lady Hollingsworth's rude outburst, no one seemed eager to talk, except for the lady herself, who, whether out of nerves or anger, proceeded to yammer on about her family and her connections, boring us with her stories. By the time the dessert course was served, I had ceased to really listen, let alone take part in the discussion. Everyone appeared resigned to silence except Michael and Laura, who as hosts seemed to feel responsible for the steady decline of the evening.

"Lady Darby," Michael proclaimed, pulling me from my solemn reverie. I glanced up to find him smiling at me determinedly while Lady Hollingsworth scowled at the interruption. "I understand your husband, Sir Anthony, served as a surgeon for the army during the war with France," he said in what I thought was a particularly adept attempt to redirect the conversation from what I believed had last been a rather mind-numbing description from Lady Hollingsworth of her sister's encounter with an incompetent medical man who was supposed to treat her goiter.

"Why, yes. Early in the war," I replied, unwilling to expound, even to prevent Lady Hollingsworth from speaking. Sir Anthony's disparagement of His Majesty's troops was not worthy of being repeated, no matter the urgency of our current predicament. Especially to a family who, for all intents and purposes, had lost their eldest brother to the war. In any case, my late husband would not have wished to discuss any part of his medical career prior to the surgery he performed to remove a cyst from the then prince regent's scalp, for which he had received his baronetcy. And I had no wish to discuss it at all.

Prior to receiving his baronetcy, Sir Anthony had not been a lofty enough personage even to walk through the front door of a nobleman's residence, as everyone knew surgeons entered through the back door like a servant. Only physicians, who were often gentlemen themselves, were allotted that privilege. As a surgeon, even an anatomist, Sir Anthony had not ranked high enough to merit that respect, let alone to marry the granddaughter of a baron, even if he had been friends with Father. His baronetcy had changed all that, and my life, forever. I was not inclined to feel grateful to King George IV for the honor he paid to my late husband.

I could feel Gage's sharp gaze on me, as if he could read my thoughts. For the first time, I found myself wishing I hadn't shared so much of my past with him during our investigative partnership two months prior. At the time it had been a necessary evil and brought me surprising comfort when he did not reject me after I allowed him to know so much about me. No one outside my family had been privy to such details. But now it made me feel vulnerable, as if he could probe inside my mind for the truth. Particularly since he would not return the compliment, and instead insisted on remaining as tight-lipped as ever about his past.

I refused to meet his gaze, even though I could feel him silently urging me to.

Michael shifted in his seat at the head of the table. "Will mentioned he'd met Sir Anthony once." He smiled tightly, but with good humor. "Said he was a bit of a tyrant, but skilled at his profession. Patched up his friend, but not without a great deal of grousing."

From the looks of the others' startled reactions, I wasn't the only one surprised to hear him mention his brother in such a casual manner.

"He told you he met Sir Anthony?" I asked in confusion.

Michael nodded.

A tingling sensation began at the base of my neck and I felt Gage's eyes intent on my face, but I would not look away from Michael. Somehow knowing that what he said next would change everything. "When he returned from the war?" I pressed for clarification.

He hesitated, and I held my breath waiting for him to speak, as did everyone at the table. He sensed the mood shift, and I could see him consider not saying anything further. My muscles tightened in protest, wanting to force the answer from his lips. Then his gaze met mine warily.

"No. A few weeks ago."

The blood drained from my face. "You spoke to . . . William . . ." I swallowed ". . . a few *weeks* ago?"

"Yes," Michael replied calmly as everyone else observed

our exchange with avid interest. "In fact, I spoke with him just today."

I wavered in my chair and slammed my hands down flat on either side of my plate to steady myself. It was so difficult to breathe, I wondered if my corset was too tight. Lord Keswick reached out to cradle my elbow, helping me remain upright.

"Perhaps this conversation should wait until later," Gage argued, half rising from his chair, at the same time that Philip demanded, "Your brother is *here?*"

Michael's gaze passed from Caroline, who was clutching her napkin to her chest, to Philip, and then to me. "Yes. He's upstairs."

Pandemonium broke loose.

Lady Hollingsworth shrieked and threw down her serviette. "You've allowed that madman into this *house*! While we're *visiting*!" She shrieked again before almost toppling from her chair, which necessitated Lord Keswick to release my elbow so that he might attend to the marchioness.

Lord Damien turned to argue with Miss Remmington, insisting somehow she was to blame, while Laura tried to calm him. Caroline was weeping into her napkin, while Philip rounded the table to stand behind his wife. He clutched her shoulders and demanded an explanation from Michael, who had also risen from his chair, along with Gage, who urged the men to remain calm. Alana sat with a hand pressed to her mouth, as if she didn't know what to say.

My eyes lifted to the ceiling, as if I could see past the layers of wood and plaster to the floors above to verify the truth of Michael's statement. Will was here? And . . . alive? I could scarcely comprehend it. Could it really be true?

Ignoring the shouts and accusations swirling around me, I sought out Michael's face. "Will is alive?"

Michael halted midsentence in whatever he was telling Philip and turned to stare at me.

"Will is alive," I repeated, stronger this time. Some of the others looked up at me. "But I thought . . . that is . . ."

I shook my head, as if I could clear away the confusion. "I thought . . ." I swallowed again, feeling sudden anger well up inside me. "This isn't some kind of terrible jest?"

His eyes widened. "No! Of course not." Then his gaze turned gentle, seeming to realize that, whatever the others had been told about the matter when William disappeared, my fifteen-year-old self had not been given the truth. And neither had anyone seen fit to inform me since my arrival at Dalmay House. "Kiera, I understand you must have been led to believe otherwise, but . . . Will is very much alive. And he has been for the last decade." As I watched, his face seemed to age before my eyes, draining of all light and happiness. "Our father had him put away. Locked in a lunatic asylum."

CHAPTER SIX

Ten years after the fact, I could not remember exactly what, if anything, I'd been told had happened to William Dalmay, or if I'd just been allowed to believe what I wished, for he'd simply been there one day and then gone the next. But in that moment I knew that whatever lie I'd been told, or told myself, would have been a far kinder fate than his reality.

I felt sick, in stomach and at heart. It was true that the man I remembered had been damaged somehow, scarred by his experiences, but he certainly had not been beyond reason, or in any way violent or dangerous to those around him. He had simply been trapped in his own private hell, and some days, as I had witnessed, had been harder than others for him to break free of it. To discover now that he had returned home to the bosom of his family only to be locked away in another kind of hell—one where there was even less hope of escaping—chilled me to the core.

I knew what lunatic asylums were like. Black holes of filth and degradation where the unfortunates were, at the very best, drugged and left to rot, but more likely tortured until they turned into the very beasts they were alleged to be. Sir Anthony had taken me to tour one about a year into our marriage, dangling the threat of incarceration when my cooperation in sketching his dissections had wavered. And upon his death, his colleagues had threatened to have me thrown into one when they learned the truth about who had completed the drawings for Sir Anthony's anatomy textbook, and accused me of unnatural tendencies and desecrating bodies. Even after my husband's death and the dismissal of the charges against me, the threat had never actually vanished, and neither had my nightmares that I might one day find myself caged inside such a place. Locked inside a cell where people could pay a penny to stare at me and laugh.

I had heard of asylums that instituted "moral treatments" of their patients, but those were few and far between, and often derided for their methodology. I was quite certain the old Lord Dalmay, Will's father, who was a heartless despot, had not sent his son to one of those.

I pressed my hands into the hard wood of the table, hoping its stability would calm the swirling in my head and in my stomach. Questions flooded my mind, overwhelming me with the need for answers, and yet I was unable to speak them. Lord Keswick leaned over to ask if I was well, and somehow I managed to nod.

"Surely this is not an appropriate conversation for the dinner table, let alone a young lady's ears," Lady Hollingsworth proclaimed in disgust, apparently having regained control of herself after all of her shrieking.

It was obvious now what had upset her enough to send an urgent missive to Philip and threaten to call off the engagement. She was undoubtedly concerned with how Will's mental state would affect her family. After all, marrying your daughter into a lineage with known madness was no small matter. I fully grasped what a blight even a hint of mental illness could be to a family. It called into question the stability of every member and made one fear for the sanity of future children.

However, I was quite certain Lady Hollingsworth was more concerned with the ramifications to her family's reputation than whether Will's alleged insanity could be catching.

I turned to glare at her, wanting to snap at her for her ridiculous comment. *The tragic past of a beloved family friend is not appropriate dinner conversation, and yet the treatment of your sister's goiter is?*

Whether or not he had seen the venomous look I sent his aunt's way, Philip took control of the situation. "Perhaps the gentlemen should skip their port tonight, and we should *all* adjourn to the drawing room."

The others murmured their assent and began rising from their chairs. Still dazed and disoriented, it took me longer to follow. I simply could not convince my limbs to obey. I sat there, staring at the remnants of my mostly uneaten cheese and fruit, chasing the same thoughts round and round my head.

It wasn't until Gage bent over me and asked if I was finished that I was jolted out of my trance. The warmth of his hands at my back as he pulled out my chair and supported me by the elbow was somehow bracing and yet comforting at the same time. It was exactly what I needed. Though by no means was I returned to myself when he pulled my arm through his and escorted me from the room.

The others were already gathered in the drawing room when we entered, seeming to have drawn up flanks. Lady Hollingsworth had settled on a pale blue and white damask settee between her two children. Damien appeared as fierce as his mother, but Caroline was plainly miserable, torn between her mother and brother and the man she loved seated across the room. Michael sat in a rather ornate golden chair between his sister and Lord Keswick on one side and Miss Remmington on the other. Obviously having chosen to play the mediator, Philip took up a position off to the side, behind where Alana rested on an indigo-patterned settee, glancing worriedly between the two opposing factions.

Gage guided me over to them. I sat next to Alana, who promptly took hold of my hand. While the others continued to square off in silent accusation, I seemed to be the only one who noticed when Gage crossed the room to take up what I knew to be his customary position before the fireplace mantel. One arm rested negligently against the shelf of wood, somehow avoiding the delicate porcelain figurines littering its surface, as he crossed one ankle over the other and slouched against the wall. He seemed to be settling in to watch a show, which I resented. Shouldn't he be offering his friend Michael his support, or at least helping to arbitrate matters, rather than distancing himself from the gathering as if he were a spectator?

"Now, then," Philip said. "Dalmay, I think we deserve an explanation."

Michael's gaze shifted from the occupants of the settee across from him to look first at Philip and then at Alana and me. He sighed and reached up to rub his temples with one hand. "Yes. Yes, you're right. But first I must apologize to Lady Darby. I did not know that you believed Will was dead. Or that no one had given you at least some idea of the matters that called your brother-in-law here." His eyes darted toward Lady Hollingsworth and back. "Otherwise I would never have broken the news in such a thoughtless manner. Please accept my sincere regret."

I nodded.

"What about the rest of us?" Lady Hollingsworth demanded. "Do we not deserve an apology? First you court my daughter under false pretenses. And then you invite us under the same roof as a madman!" She nearly shrieked the last. "I have never been so ill-treated in all my life."

"I apologize for not informing you of his presence immediately, but surely you can understand the matter is delicate. No one knows where William has been." Michael made a sweeping gesture to include all of us. "No one besides those of you who are here. And I want it to remain that way." He glared at Lady Hollingsworth. "When my brother is ready to reenter society, we will develop a fiction about his whereabouts for the last ten years."

The feathers in Lady Hollingsworth's hair quivered in indignation. "Reenter society? Are you as daft as your brother? He's a madman! No one will be safe if he's let loose."

"My brother is *not* a madman! And he's *certainly* no danger to others. He just needs more time to . . . readjust before he enters the world again."

"Surely if Lord Dalmay had him locked up, he deserved to be there," Lord Damien said, trying to sound reasonable.

"Father didn't know what he was doing," Laura replied heatedly, bright color staining her cheeks. "Will didn't *do* anything wrong." Her gaze dropped to her lap, where she plucked at the embroidery on her goldenrod skirts. "It's not a crime to be sad. Or to have nightmares."

I wondered how much Laura remembered of her oldest brother. She had been twelve when he . . . disappeared. Had she been told the truth of William's whereabouts? The thought horrified me. At that age Laura would never have been able to understand.

Lady Hollingsworth sniffed. "I saw a lunatic once. And he was *raving*. Flailing his arms and shouting, spittle flying from his lips. He fought the men who tried to take him away. Broke one of their noses."

"Will wasn't like that," Michael declared, shaking his head. He flung his arm out toward me. "Ask Lady Darby. He acted as her drawing master during the months before his . . . detainment."

I gazed morosely back at the others as they turned to stare at me. I found it odd that of all the statements just made, this one should be met with the most surprise. Even Gage seemed unsettled by it, straightening from his slouch.

"I had forgotten that," Alana murmured beside me, concern pleating her brow.

Philip lifted one of his hands from my sister's shoulder to forestall further comment. "Now, hold on. Before we start collecting everyone's testimony, there are a few things I don't understand." Alarm tightened his voice. "How long have you known William was locked in an asylum?"

"Almost three years," Michael admitted. "And as soon as

our black-hearted father admitted what he had done, I worked every single day to obtain his release." His jaw was rigid with anger.

"Why did your father finally tell you?"

His eyebrows arched contemptuously. "Because he'd recently been ill. And seven years had passed. He wanted us to petition the Court of Chancery to have William declared dead and assert my claim to the title."

I pressed my hand to my mouth in shock.

"I insisted he tell me how he knew that William was dead, and when he finally told me the truth . . ." Michael shook his head. The muscles in his jaw jumped.

At this display of emotion, Caroline shifted in her seat on the settee across from him, but her mother draped her arm over her daughter's lap, preventing her from going to her betrothed. Laura reached out to touch her brother's sleeve, and his Adam's apple bobbed as he swallowed, gathering his composure.

"I begged him to tell me the location of the asylum where William was being held, but he refused. He simply would not listen to reason. I pleaded with his secretary and estate manager, and our solicitors, but none of them would admit that they knew anything. Either they truly were ignorant or they were too afraid of my father to confess."

"And so you refused to make the petition," Philip said.

Michael nodded. "And threatened to tell everyone the truth if he tried to push it through without me."

"I don't understand," Miss Remmington said. "Couldn't your father have just had your brother declared insane? Wouldn't that have disinherited him and made you his rightful heir?"

Philip shook his head. "A man cannot disinherit his heir. And entailments cannot be broken by cause of insanity, only a conviction of treason or murder. So the most Lord Dalmay could hope for by having his heir proved legally insane was that the guardianship of William and the Dalmay interests would be given to Michael. But even then Michael could not inherit the title or its entailed property outright until William died."

"But dragging William into the courts in search of a verdict of insanity would only tarnish the Dalmays," Lord Keswick pointed out. "And the last thing Lord Dalmay wanted was to taint his own illustrious name."

"Is that how you were finally able to obtain his release?" Philip asked. "Lord Dalmay never attained such a verdict against his son?"

Michael lifted his eyes from the swirled pattern of the rug. "When my father died I was able to search through his papers to uncover where he had sent my brother. Even then, I almost found nothing, just a scrap of paper tucked away in his file at our solicitor's office, as if the foul deed had never occurred." He pounded his fist on the arm of his chair. "And then it took me two more months to extract him from that villain Sloane's custody. Father had signed some document giving him total authority over William's care. I had to threaten the man with kidnapping and causing bodily harm to a peer of the realm and actually had to go so far as to petition the local magistrate before Sloane would release him to me. That was over nine months ago."

"And he'd been locked away all that time?" I could barely mouth the question.

Michael's voice was graveled with anguish. "Nine years. He spent *nine years* in that cesspit, while we were all blissfully unaware."

The room fell silent while everyone contemplated his words. I felt sick, unable to fathom being trapped in such a place for nearly a decade. Good heavens, what he must have been through. A knot formed at the back of my throat and I had to swallow hard to force it down.

Feeling a pair of eyes on me, I looked up to find Gage watching me. His face was inscrutable, but that in and of itself was telling. Why, in this moment, was he so intent on shielding his emotions from me? Surely he could only feel empathy for the Dalmays' plight.

"Who is Sloane?" Philip queried, moving around to perch on the arm of the settee beside his wife.

Michael's face twisted. "The doctor who convinced my father that my brother was mad in the first place. He owns the Larkspur Retreat where William was detained."

Retreat, indeed. I had heard of asylums that misleadingly adopted such innocuous-sounding names in order to lure the public into believing that their patients were well cared for and simply having a rest.

"Where is this . . . *retreat* . . . located?" Philip asked, not missing the irony in the title.

"On Inchkeith Island."

My brother-in-law's eyes widened. "Rather a harsh, isolated environment for such an institution."

And one that was far too close to Dalmay House for my comfort. Perhaps twenty miles away, Inchkeith Island perched in the middle of the Firth of Forth just at the point where the waterway began to open into the North Sea. It was practically on the Dalmays' back doorstep. How had William's father managed to not be eaten alive by guilt when he knew his son was so close?

"That was precisely my thought," Michael said, responding to Philip's observation. "But apparently the matter did not concern my father." His hands fisted in his lap. "He was more worried about the taint to our family's good name than what was best for Will. I don't know how the two met, or why he was asked to examine my brother in the first place, but somehow Sloane . . ." he almost snarled the name ". . . convinced my father that William could be dangerous and the best thing for him was to be put away where he could never hurt anyone."

"But he wasn't mad," I protested, unable to keep silent a moment longer. "And he certainly wasn't *dangerous*." Philip and Gage exchanged a glance that spoke volumes. "I mean, I realize he fought in the Peninsula campaign with Wellington, and at Waterloo, and later he was part of the occupation force. And I know he came back from the war changed. Or so everyone told me. But he wasn't violent or frightening. At least, not to me. He just got lost in his memories sometimes." Michael looked startled by this revelation. "That's how he explained it to me." I dropped my gaze, embarrassed to have revealed so much of what Will had told me. It felt like betraying his confidence. But how else was I to make them understand?

"Will talked to you? About his . . . troubles, I mean."

I looked up at Michael, hearing more than confusion in his voice. There was hurt there as well.

"Yes," I replied cautiously, knowing he must be wondering why his beloved sibling would have confided in a fifteen-year-old girl rather than his grown brother. "During my drawing lessons. Sometimes . . ." I pleated the ivory lace trim of my gown between my fingers ". . . it's . . . easier to talk . . . when your hands are distracted," I tried to explain.

Everyone was sitting very still in their chairs, as if afraid to voice whatever thought was in their head. It was Michael who finally gathered the courage to ask. "Did William ever . . . That is to say . . . were you romantically involved?"

I frowned. "Of course not." The forcefulness of my response seemed to relieve him. "Will was nearly fifteen years my senior, and I was not of age. He would never have acted in such an inappropriate manner." Not that my fifteen-year-old self had not contemplated it. At the age of thirty, William Dalmay had been very handsome, in a dark, brooding sort of way. And there had been something in his eyes, something in the premature lines etched at their corners that called to a rather lonely and melancholy girl in a way that charming urbanities never could have. I could admit to myself now that I had been rather infatuated with Will. But I couldn't imagine what impressionable young girl wouldn't have been.

"When did he become your drawing master?" Laura asked in curiosity.

I tried to think back. "Let's see. It would have been about April of 1820. Father had been having a difficult time finding someone to replace Signor Riotta after he quit, and Will stepped into the gap." I didn't need to mention that the position of drawing master to a young lady in the far reaches of Northumberland was not exactly a sought-after position. And the fact that I was talented only seemed to make matters worse. I had learned at a very young age that men did not want to be outshined by women, especially girls who had yet to reach their majority.

"You won't remember it," I told Laura, "because you had already moved here to Dalmay House with your father upon its completion. And Michael was away in London." I nodded to him before turning to indicate my sister. "Our brother Trevor was at Cambridge and Alana was in our aunt's care for her first season in London. So it was only Father and I rambling around Blakelaw House." I glanced at Philip. "You were in London, as well, I believe. Resisting Alana's charms."

A light blush heated his cheeks, which amused me.

"It was another year until you finally took notice of her, though it took her near engagement to Lord Felding to do it." I suppressed a smile when Philip frowned in irritation. It was a common jest between him and my sister, who had been in love with him from the tender age of twelve. That it had taken her ignoring him to finally gain his favor had provided no small amount of banter in their household.

"I was shocked to discover you had turned into such a respectable gentleman," Gage said, joining in the good-natured teasing. "That always seemed to be more of Michael's purview. But you surprised us by being the first to fall into the parson's mousetrap."

"Well, you could hardly expect us all to have remained the same when you returned from Greece," Philip pointed out.

Greece? Gage had gone to Greece?

My gaze turned to the man in question, who did not miss my sudden interest.

"True," he answered guardedly.

I opened my mouth to question him further, when Lady Hollingsworth, who had been sitting quietly through Philip's questioning, spoke up. "What does any of this have to do with the matter at hand?" She pinned Michael with a look. "No matter your protestations, the truth is your brother is . . . damaged." That she had searched for and used such a diplomatic word told me just how much our conversation had engaged her sympathy. "If not before he was locked away, then certainly after. You cannot expect us to stay under the same roof with such a man."

"He is not dangerous to any of you," Michael insisted. "And he has made a great deal of progress in the nine months since his release. In fact, he was supposed to join us for dinner tonight, except . . . he had a small relapse."

Lady Hollingsworth gasped.

"It is nothing to be alarmed about. And in any case, every precaution has been made for our safety should for some reason he turn violent. He's being housed on the floor above our bedchambers far from anyone else."

"What of the children?" the marchioness demanded, gesturing to Alana, who stiffened. "Your own nephew? Are they not in the nursery on the same floor?"

I squeezed my sister's hand and scowled at Lady Hollingsworth. While perhaps a legitimate concern, she needn't have voiced it in such a way. Alarming my already overtaxed sister did not help matters.

"The children are as far away from William as we are, with many doors locked between them."

Lord Damien narrowed his eyes. "Then you do admit you fear for their safety. If you've taken such precautions, you cannot be as certain of your brother's inability to do harm as you protest."

Gage shifted in his stance, drawing my attention. There was a tightening in the muscles of his face, a sharpening of his eyes that I knew signaled intense interest.

"I . . . I do not believe William would hurt anyone," Michael stammered. "At least, not on purpose. But if he were confused . . . I simply thought it best to ensure our guests' comfort and his."

"And is he often confused?" Gage asked.

I wanted to glare at him for assisting Will's detractors, but I knew it was a reasonable question.

"No . . ." He sounded uncertain. Raking a hand through his hair, he leaned forward over his knees and sighed. "Sometimes. Though less and less often." He glanced sideways at Laura. "He's never hurt my sister or Keswick."

"But that doesn't mean he won't," Gage pointed out doggedly.

I did glare at him this time.

Michael stared down at his hands, considering Gage's words. "No," he asserted, shaking his head. "No. I don't believe it. Will would not hurt anyone."

Gage looked as if he would like to argue, but held his tongue.

Lady Hollingsworth was not so circumspect. "And what of this missing girl?"

I sat up straighter, glancing at Michael in confusion. I noticed that Miss Remmington and Laura, seated on either side of him, had done much the same.

He frowned. "What do you mean? Will has nothing to do with her."

"How can you be so sure?" she demanded.

His eyes narrowed in warning.

"Wait." Philip held up his hands to interrupt, evincing the same perplexity I was feeling. None of the others seemed similarly lost. "What missing girl?"

"A man stopped by a few days ago to tell us a girl went missing from the neighboring village of Cramond," our host replied impatiently, still glaring at Lady Hollingsworth.

A tingle of unease crept down my spine.

"He wanted to know if we had seen her or noticed anything suspicious." Michael leaned forward. "And we *haven't*," he bit out.

Lady Hollingsworth lifted her chin, staring down her nose at him. "Yes, but how can you be so certain your brother was not involved?"

"Because he never leaves the house without an escort." He

sneered. His sister glanced at him in concern, and he took a deep breath to calm himself before adding, "And, far as I know, he isn't acquainted with anyone from Cramond."

I inhaled my own calming breath. Given those facts, it did seem rather unlikely that Will had anything to do with her disappearance. And even if Will did know the girl, and had been given the opportunity to meet with her alone, it seemed rather precipitous to accuse him of a crime just because of his recent enforced stay in an asylum. He had never been dangerous before, and it seemed unworthy to suppose he would be now. But, nevertheless, I couldn't seem to shake the disquieting feeling that had crept over me.

I glanced at Gage, curious how he had taken this news. His emotionless mask was back in place, his pensive gaze contemplating the floor at his feet. For once he didn't seem to be eager to question Michael on the matter. I could only assume he didn't know what to think of it either.

Lady Hollingsworth huffed. "Well, regardless, I do not want my daughter within ten miles of your brother."

Caroline shifted anxiously. "Mother . . ."

"And I am furious that you would risk her safety in such a manner," she continued, heedless of her daughter. "You have misrepresented yourself since the moment you presented yourself to her, and I will not stand for it."

Michael's temper exploded again. "I never misrepresented myself. *You* were the one who assumed I would petition the Court of Chancery for my brother's title." He stabbed his finger at the marchioness. "I never mentioned doing any such thing, and I always flatly refused whenever I was questioned about it."

"Well, you should have known it would be expected. What self-respecting mother wouldn't wish for her daughter to have a title? And your failure to mention the mental illness that runs in your family was inexcusable." She rose stiffly from the settee. "This engagement is at an end. We will be leaving first thing in the morning."

"But Mother!" Caroline gasped, tears already streaming down her cheeks.

"Hush! I'll hear no word from you. To bed."

Michael rose to try to stop them, but Keswick put a hand out to prevent him. "Not now," he said with a shake of his head.

Michael watched in misery as Lady Hollingsworth ushered her children out the door. Caroline glanced over her shoulder one last time before her mother forcibly pulled her from the room.

CHAPTER SEVEN

Michael dropped back into his chair and stared forlornly at the door. Seeing him like this, I wanted to do nothing more than run after Lady Hollingsworth and shake some sense into her. Couldn't she see what a good man Michael Dalmay was? What tough decisions he'd been forced to make? Couldn't she see how much he cared for her daughter?

But for all the displeasure I felt at the marchioness, I knew she was right to question Michael's behavior. He *hadn't* been completely honest. And, regardless of his reasons for doing so, and whether his intentions had been good, she wouldn't have been looking after her daughter if she did not at least call him to task for it. Her ending of their engagement had been a bit precipitous, but perhaps she could be made to see reason in the morning.

The others seemed to be of the same mind-set.

"Take heart, old boy," Keswick told his brother-in-law, clapping him on the shoulder as he slumped forward. "I predict cooler heads will prevail tomorrow."

Michael nodded absently, his elbows braced on his knees.

"Keswick's right," Philip said. "We may yet be able to resolve this matter to everyone's satisfaction or at least give you some more time to prove your brother is stable. But not tonight."

Michael lifted his head. "I'm sorry, Cromarty. I didn't

think. I should have realized you'd be alarmed to hear your children were sharing the same floor with my brother."

I glanced at my sister, whose complexion was paler than normal. I couldn't tell whether that was due to her recent illness or worry over her children. Either way, it was impossible not to think of the manner in which she had reacted to the news of the murders two months past, locking herself in Gairloch's nursery with her three children.

"But, I promise you, they are safe," he vowed to Alana, clearly realizing she was the one he needed to convince of his sincerity. "I would never allow them to come to harm. But if you would like to have them moved, to the room next to yours or somewhere here on the ground floor, I will do whatever you feel is necessary."

Alana looked up at her husband, who was waiting for her to decide what should be done. She smoothed her hands over the creamy satin of her skirts. "I know you would never place our children in danger." Her gaze flitted toward Laura and Keswick. "And if little Nicolas is safe in the nursery, I'm sure our children are as well."

"You're certain?" Michael pressed, anxiety stretching his voice. "I do not want you to worry."

She took a deep breath and exhaled before offering him a reassuring smile. "I'm certain."

Michael nodded.

"We're going up to say good night to Nicolas," Laura said. "Would you like to join us?"

Alana perked up. "Yes. Yes, I would."

"Go on," Philip told her when she turned to him. His eyes warmed with affection. "I'll be up shortly."

"Come along, Elise," Keswick told his sister as they passed by her chair.

Miss Remmington, who had been listening to us quietly, with a far more earnest expression on her face than I had yet to witness, glanced up at her brother. "Oh, I'm wide awake," she replied, doing a marvelous job of masking whatever concern she felt. "I believe I'll stay up a bit longer."

"Then you can read in your room."

Miss Remmington blinked up at him through her eyelashes and her lips formed into a pretty pout—an expression that was certain to have any number of men eating out of her hand. Unfortunately for her, it had no effect on her brother.

"Now, Elise!"

"You're so stodgy." She flounced out of the room after her brother.

Philip shook his head. "Thank goodness I never had any sisters."

"Thank goodness mine was well behaved," Michael muttered in commiseration.

Philip shifted off the arm of the settee to sit beside me. "Are ye well?" he asked, lifting his eyebrows in query.

"Yes."

His eyes remained locked with mine for a moment longer, as if assuring I spoke the truth, and then he nodded in satisfaction. "So, Dalmay. Now that the others are gone, give us the truth. How is he really?" He frowned. "And what about this missing girl? Are ye acquainted?" I could hear his brogue slipping now that most of the house had retired and the fatigue of the day was setting in. Philip could speak as well as any English-bred gentleman when he chose to, but the truth of his Highland roots was never far away, especially when he let his guard down.

Michael passed a hand over his face. "I was honest before. Will has his good days and his bad. And, at this stage, they *are* more often good." He sighed and settled back in his chair. "As for the girl, her name is Mary Wallace. I'm acquainted with her father—a respectable, generally good-natured fellow. He owns a small estate south of Cramond. I met his daughter once . . . Oh, for heaven's sake," he snapped, turning to glare at his friend still lounging against the fireplace mantel. "Sit down, Gage. I will not keep craning my neck to include you in the conversation."

Amusement twinkled in Gage's eyes as he crossed the room toward the settee Keswick and his wife had vacated.

"I don't know why you feel you have to be so damned . . ." Michael's gaze darted to mine ". . . *dashed* mysterious all the time. Apologies," he told me.

I waved it away. He wasn't the first gentleman to curse in my presence, and I was certain he wouldn't be the last.

His scowling visage returned to Gage. "What was all that about?"

Gage shrugged. "I wanted a vantage point where I could see everyone's faces."

Michael huffed. "This isn't one of your investigations."

Michael might not think so, but I wasn't so sure. My eyes narrowed on Gage, remembering the way he had interrogated Michael about his certainty of William's harmlessness.

A slight tensing of Gage's shoulders let me know he was aware of my interest. "Well, old habits die hard," he replied vaguely.

Michael's expression said clearly that he thought that was cock-and-bull.

"Ye said tonight William had a small relapse?" Philip prompted, trying to steer the conversation back to more important matters.

He nodded. "For weeks he's been making steady progress. Conversing with others. Taking interest in what's going on around him. Behaving more and more like the brother I remember. But this evening, just after you arrived . . ." He sighed. "He . . . went away again."

Philip's brow furrowed in confusion. "What do ye mean he 'went away' again?"

"I don't know how else to describe it. It's as if one minute he's there with me, and the next he's not. His mind, it . . ." Michael lifted his hand in defeat ". . . goes somewhere else."

"Was that why the servant at the top of the stairs called you away when we arrived?" I asked.

"That was Mac. He's an old family retainer, and one of Will's caretakers."

I nodded, remembering Mac from a decade earlier when he'd acted as Will's manservant at Swinton Lodge. Mac's hair had thinned and grayed considerably in the years since I'd last seen him, but now that I knew it was him, I could see his resemblance in the stoop-shouldered servant who had stood at the top of the stairs.

Michael's face dragged with worry. "I knew when he appeared that something was wrong."

Gage tilted his head to the side in thought. "What does he do when his mind . . . goes away? Anything?"

"Well . . ." Michael looked at me ". . . he draws."

"He draws?" Gage repeated in puzzlement.

"Yes."

I don't know why I was shocked to hear this, but I was. "He's returning to what he feels most comfortable with." Philip and Gage turned to stare at me and I endeavored to explain. "It's what I do. When I feel troubled." I shrugged one shoulder. "It's what he did before."

Michael's gaze turned apprehensive. "I thought you said you had never seen any of his paintings."

I licked my lips. "No. You asked if William had ever shown me any." He narrowed his eyes at my splitting hairs. "And he didn't. But . . . I did see some of them."

His hands flexed on the arms of his chair, and I knew he was seeing the same images I was. The memories Will had brought back from Spain and Portugal and France.

"What paintings?" Gage demanded.

Michael shifted uncomfortably, making the legs of his chair creak beneath him. "I don't quite know how to describe them."

"I think they're scenes from the war," I replied when he hesitated to elaborate. I hoped that would be explanation enough, and we wouldn't have to describe the war-ravaged countrysides on his canvases and in his sketches. The abject suffering. The horrors perpetuated by both friend and foe alike.

I was both relieved and alarmed to see understanding in Gage's pain-shadowed eyes. The starkness of his features seemed too pronounced for a man with only abstract knowledge of what I spoke.

"Then they were disturbing?" he murmured.

I opened my mouth, to deny it, to try to explain it, I don't know, but I couldn't make such convoluted excuses. Not when the truth was so straightforward. "Yes."

They *had* been disturbing. Particularly to my sheltered, untested fifteen-year-old self. I had known nothing of war, or the pain and devastation it caused. The only casualty of my acquaintance had been a younger son from a neighboring estate, a gentleman I barely knew. The newspapers did not report the worst for our sensitive ears, and as I was barely ten when the battle of Waterloo was fought, I paid little attention.

But Will's paintings and sketches brought the truth home to me as nothing else could. Will was an artist, like me. He captured images on canvas, noting details with one blink of an eye that others would never see had they stared at the same scene for hours. To have such terror imprinted in your head, reappearing over and over in your mind's eye, was a living nightmare. I knew from experience.

The cadavers Sir Anthony had forced me to watch him dissect had plagued my thoughts and troubled my sleep so badly that I had dropped a stone in weight. Until I learned to accept them, to see the beauty in the bodies and not the gruesomeness of the undertaking, I found no rest. Even so, those first few corpses sometimes still haunted my dreams, particularly Frederick Oliver, the young man whose body had been the subject of my first dissection. How much more disturbed had Will been by the memories he carried home with him from war?

"Who else saw them?" Gage asked.

Deep furrows pleated Michael's brow. "I don't know. Father showed them to me when he told me the truth about my brother's whereabouts. I think he believed they would convince me of the rightness of his actions."

Gage sat taller. "He kept them?"

"Yes. I admit it seems a bit odd now that I think about it. Wouldn't he want to destroy all evidence of his son's malady?" He sighed and shook his head. "I can only suggest my initial assumption was correct. That he believed they proved his blamelessness, and he kept them in his defense, should someone question his decision. As far as I know, they're still in the attic."

A shiver ran down my spine at the thought of them.

It was apparent to me now that those paintings and sketches had been the primary source of Will's trouble. That they had been the evidence Dr. Sloane used to convince Lord Dalmay that his son was insane and that he should be confined to this Larkspur Retreat, without following proper protocol. It wasn't the aimless wandering or the sometimes frantic pacing. It wasn't the lapses into silence or the startled reactions to seemingly innocuous noises or the haunted look in his eyes. It was the art he continued to create, the visual depictions of what he was seeing in his mind, those frightening images.

"What your father never understood," I told Michael, "was that, as disturbing as they were, those drawings were merely memories. Remembrances of a time he wanted to, but could not, forget. They weren't representations of what he wished to do. They were images of the past."

"But how can you be sure?" Gage's skeptical tone of voice made me believe even more strongly in what I was saying.

"Because I am. None of you were there during the days and weeks leading up to his disappearance. I saw him almost every day. And I could have sworn he was improving. I know I was only fifteen, but I was not unobservant." Especially when it came to Will. I lifted my gaze to a portrait of William and Michael Dalmay's mother, whose image flickered in the firelight, and thought back on those last few weeks spent with Will. "He seemed . . . lighter somehow. Less restless. And he'd gained at least a stone of much-needed weight."

I felt the weight of Gage's gaze as he studied my face, but I ignored him in favor of Michael, whose eyes were lowered toward the floor. I could tell he was wrestling with some emotion. I waited, knowing he would speak when he was ready.

"Do you . . ." He cleared his throat and looked up at me. His gray eyes were bright. "Do you think he could do it again? Fight his way back from . . . whatever is troubling him. If he started to draw again?"

"I don't know," I admitted honestly. "Maybe. You said he already sketches?"

"Yes." Michael seemed to hesitate, and I wondered if the drawings contained more disturbing images.

"There aren't any art supplies in his rooms, not that I saw," Gage pointed out, and I realized that he had been to see Will.

For some reason that set me on edge. I didn't want Gage visiting him without me being present.

"Where does he draw?" he persisted.

I felt indignant. As if Michael would lie.

Michael glanced from me to Gage to Philip. Then he sighed, as if he'd just made some kind of troubling decision, and pushed to his feet. "It might be easiest if I just show you."

I blinked in surprise, rising to follow.

Gage's eyes darted to me as he stood. "Is that really wise? After all, you just told us he's been unwell this evening, that he had a relapse."

"Yes, but when he's like this he's very docile." He turned his face to the side, showing us his profile. "As long as you don't try to stop him from doing what he wants to do."

A quiver of alarm stirred in my gut, but I refused to heed it. Will had been my champion and confidant. He had believed in me when everyone around me was disparaging my talent. My mother dead, and all but forgotten by my sister and brother, who were off in London and Cambridge, I was left floundering after enduring months of belittlement at the hands of my drawing master, Signor Riotta. When he abruptly quit and Father complained about the time and expense it would take to lure another art instructor to the relative wilderness of Northumberland, I had almost told him not to bother. Then Will had taken me under his wing.

He had taken one look at my sketchbook and cursed Signor Riotta roundly for a fool.

Without Will's confidence and guidance I might never have found peace with my talent. I remembered well the turmoil of my early adolescence—the frustration and inadequacy, the raging emotions. Will had helped me to channel it into my artwork, to embrace my gifts instead of deny them. I owed him much.

And because of that, I couldn't allow a little fear to persuade me to turn my back on him now. Not when the very least I could do was visit him in his chamber.

Unfortunately Gage seemed hell-bent on preventing it. "Then it's not safe. What if we startle him? Who knows what the man is capable of when he's out of his head?"

"He's never truly harmed anyone," Michael argued.

"That doesn't mean he won't." The fact that Gage sounded genuinely distressed did nothing to cool my anger at his interference. "Cromarty, I have seen unwell men wring the life out of another human being while in the throes of a mania."

Philip frowned, and I knew he was considering Gage's words. There was enough truth to them to give anyone pause. But I could not let Gage keep me from Will, whatever his motivations were for doing so.

"Will would *never* hurt me," I insisted, scowling at him. *"Never."* I turned to Michael for his corroboration but his eyes said that he was not as certain of such a thing as I. A knot of fear lodged in my throat.

"He may not be able to comprehend who you are," Gage answered, his gaze far too compassionate for my liking.

"Well, what is he at his worst?" I knew I surprised the men by asking, particularly Michael, whose face visibly paled. "Does he attack anyone when he's lost in his head? Has he ever been in the grips of a . . . mania?" I had difficulty repeating the word. "Has he become violent?"

"Not in many months," he admitted. "And even then, he would only fight you if he thought you were going to confine him or dose him with medicine he didn't want, and then just until he made his escape. He's far more likely to be so engrossed in his thoughts he won't even know we're there."

"Then I don't see what we have to fear," I stated defiantly. And then, before Gage could voice the objection forming on his lips, I rushed on to say, "Besides, with the three of you gentlemen there with me, should something go wrong, I'm certain you could protect me." It was a challenge, and perhaps one made in poor taste, but I was not about to let Gage's fears, well-founded or not, stop me from seeing Will.

Gage's eyes narrowed and, knowing he could no longer appeal to my good sense, he turned back to Philip. "Cromarty, this is a bad idea. There is far more at stake here than physical danger from a man in the grip of a mania."

I glared at Philip while he thought over Gage's words, daring him to deny me this. He seemed torn between Gage's appeal for my safety and the emotions he must have sensed in me. I wanted to curse Gage, knowing that his display of protectiveness had probably brought back memories of my being shot and nearly drowned in the loch next to Gairloch Castle not so many months ago.

I didn't understand Gage. Was his conscience troubling him that his stubborn refusal to listen to my doubts regarding the initial findings of our investigation had almost cost me my life, and he wasn't about to see me in harm's way again? Or was there something else, something specific about Will?

He was an enigma. One sent to torment me. For all that seemed to lie between us was unanswered questions, unspoken words. That silence was filled with so much noise it was deafening.

Philip leaned toward Michael. "You believe Kiera will be safe?"

"I would not have thought to take her to him had I not."

Philip rubbed the stubble just beginning to show along his jaw and nodded.

I hurried to take Michael's arm, lest Philip change his mind. As it was, I was worried Gage would make another protest, but he surprised me by remaining silent.

Michael led us into the entry hall and up the central staircase. At the top, he turned right, away from our assigned bedchambers. A door opened a few feet down the hall to reveal another set of stairs. Though less grand than the approach to the first floor, the flight to the second was still far from ordinary. Rich wooden panels covered the walls from ceiling to floor and the same red carpet as the central staircase ran up the middle of the stairs. A large window covered the wall on the landing, allowing plenty of moonlight to spill into the shadowed space. It looked out onto the front drive, providing a fine view of the trees straddling the lane that led away from the estate.

At the top, he guided us through a heavy door on the left, which he opened with an ornate key. "The nursery is back in the other direction. Facing the firth."

I nodded but could not manage a reply. Tension had mounted tighter and tighter inside me with every step we took that brought us closer to Will. As we turned right down another passageway, I realized my fingers were gripping Michael's arm like talons through his coat. This part of the manor house seemed deserted, but the walls and floor were well maintained.

Michael came to a halt outside a door near the end of the hall. He lifted his arm to knock, and then hesitated with his hand hovering there next to the wood. I could feel his doubt quivering inside his muscles, his uncertainty that bringing me here was the right thing to do.

I inhaled deeply to calm my racing heart and pressed my hand to his biceps, hoping he could sense my good intentions, my desire to help. The floorboard creaked as either Gage or Philip shifted behind us. I closed my eyes to pray they wouldn't voice an objection now.

The sound of knuckles wrapping lightly on wood

brought my eyes open with a snap. A few seconds later, the same stoop-shouldered man I had seen at the top of the stairs opened the door. Mac's head was covered in grizzled gray hair and his face was lined with age, but he still appeared hale and hearty—more than capable of handling a man half his age. I knew that his slouch was more a matter of poor posture than a crooked spine.

He eyed each of us belligerently, studying me a moment longer than the others, before stepping back from the door to let us into what looked to be a parlor.

"They're here to see William," Michael told him while I took in the sturdy but elegant furnishings. "How is he?"

Mac grunted and lifted his hand toward a door on the far side of the room. "See for yoursel'."

I followed Michael across the room. He rapped once on the gleaming wood and then turned the doorknob.

The room was dim, lit only by the fire crackling in the hearth. It cast flickering shadows over the walls and furnishings, revealing an unmade bed and a toppled chair. I swallowed the acrid taste of fear coating my mouth and stepped over the threshold. Beyond the signs of recent distress, I could tell the room was clean and well kept. No must or smoke fouled the air.

Inching forward, my toe brushed against something. I looked down to discover a simple sheet of paper, but as my eyes traveled along the gleaming wooden floor, I realized it was merely the first in a tangled trail of parchment and charcoal sticks littering the room. I bent closer to examine the foolscap and saw that it was covered in drawings.

Most were merely childish scribbles, as if the artist had been too overwhelmed to do anything more than thrust his elbow back and forth in the most elemental of movements. But others were inscribed with terrible images. Of pain and anguish. Of despair. Of men and women shuffling around a courtyard, some barely clothed, hopelessness dragging down their faces. On one page two men grappled while others cheered them on; in another a man scratched at the wall with his fingernails. And in still another a man huddled over his knees, surrounded by scribbles of darkness.

Blinking away the burning wetness from my eyes, I focused on the room before me, searching for the artist. And I found him, hunched in the far corner, scrabbling at the wall with his charcoal, as if, having run out of paper, he was forced to inscribe his memories onto the blank canvas of the wall. I sucked in a sharp breath at the sight of him. His hair standing on end, his shirt hanging open over one pale shoulder—the flesh covering it so thin that I could see clearly the sinew and bone.

Biting my lip to withhold a sob, I moved farther into the room, pulling Michael along with me. I heard the crinkle of paper as either Philip or Gage picked up some of the pages on the floor I had stepped over, but I had no concentration to spare for them. It was all focused on Will. He seemed not to notice our presence, so consumed was he by the task before him.

"Will." Michael spoke so gently, as if a word too harsh would send his brother spiraling to his death. Or flying across the room in a wild rage. Either possibility tested my resolve to stand there and witness it, no matter the obligations I felt toward Will.

"Will," he repeated. "We have guests. You remember Kiera St. Mawr, don't you?" he said a little louder, giving him my maiden name. "She married Sir Anthony Darby. You . . . you remember, you told me you had met him once."

Through this entire exchange, Will made no movement to show that he even heard the words, let alone that he understood them. His focus remained resolutely on the wall before him, scratching softly with his charcoal against its surface. He was lost. Lost in one of his memories.

"I'm sorry . . ." Michael began to say as I pulled my arm from his grasp and moved deeper into the room.

"Kiera," Philip warned as I came to a stop to stare up at the wall Will was sketching on.

Mini murals in black and white covered its surface from the floorboards to as high above his head as he could reach. The flickering light of the fireplace seemed to hide and reveal them in haunting patterns, illuminating first the image of a woman chained to a bed, and then a man with rivulets of what appeared to be water running down his arms, though from the trails' starting points at the undersides of the figure's elbows, I realized, with a chill, that it also could have been blood. A third sketch depicted a man, his head drawn over-large to show the dilated pupils of a person who stared at a ceiling where insects and other winged things seemed to hover. A fourth illustrated a man with his head being held underwater by two men standing over him.

My steps slid toward Will, trying to see what he was drawing now.

"Kiera," Philip cautioned again, shuffling closer. I held up my hand to hold him off.

The sour stench of body odor assailed my nostrils and I wrinkled my nose. I feared it was coming from Will, but as I moved closer it dispersed, as if it had never been.

I leaned forward to see that this drawing was no different from the others—a frantic scrawling of lines depicting exaggerated proportions and faces—but the emotion was somehow altered. The others were frightening and definitely tormented in their portrayal. But this one was worse, even though the subject matter was by far the least disturbing.

Will had utilized the corner of the wall to draw himself trapped into it. The imagined room surrounding him was stark and bare like the others, and empty of all save his huddled and broken body quivering against the cold stone. His arms raised to cover his face, it was impossible to see his expression, but the posture, the abject misery and despair etched into each line, told everything.

Before I could change my mind, before I could doubt my actions, I stepped closer and rested a hand on Will's shoulder. One of the men behind me sucked in a harsh, worried breath, but Will did not even flinch. He simply continued to sketch in the lines of his feet. I pressed into his thin flesh more deeply and then kneeled to pick up a discarded nub of charcoal, settling onto the floor beside him. Silently I reached up to continue shading the wall of his all-too-real prison.

Several moments passed when all that could be heard was the scratching of our charcoal across the plaster. No one else moved, or breathed, the chamber was so still.

And then Will's movements began to slow and then falter. I could feel his awareness shifting, like a tangible presence. He blinked his eyes at the wall in front of him. Not wanting to alarm him, I lowered my hand and waited to see if he would acknowledge me. Slowly his head turned, and his stormy gray eyes, the pupils almost swallowing their depths, stared back at me.

I willed my breath to remain calm, my gaze unchallenging and unclouded by emotion. A minute ticked by, and then two, and then a glimmer of something sparked in his vacant eyes. His brow crinkled and his mouth worked. And on a sliver of sound, he spoke.

"Kiera?"

CHAPTER EIGHT

Never in my life had I felt so much sadness and so much joy in the same breath. The two opposing waves crashed inside me, enveloping me and threatening to pull me under. Emotion clogged my throat until I thought I might choke on it. Swallowing desperately to dislodge it, I nodded my head, worried I would lose him again if I did not answer. "Yes," I murmured. "Yes, Will. It's me."

Will's eyes traveled over my face, as if hungry for the sight of me, of anything outside the nightmarish memories in his mind. I forced a smile to my lips, even as I felt the first hot tear slip free from my eye and slide down my cheek. Will focused on it for a moment before returning his gaze to my eyes.

I reached out carefully to take his hand, removing the charcoal from between his fingertips. He stared down at it in confusion and then allowed his eyes to slide up the wall beside him at the drawing there as I held fast to his chilled fingers, grimy with charcoal residue. His gaze trailed over me to the men standing behind me. I did not turn to see their faces, absorbed as I was in watching the play of light and thought across Will's. He seemed all too willing to accept the fact that so many virtual strangers had observed his odd behavior. I wondered if he was simply resigned to it or if embarrassment was now beyond his ability to feel.

"Will," Michael said, his voice husky, "you didn't eat your dinner. Shall I have Mac bring you another plate?"

Will's shoulders suddenly seemed to slump under the pressure of holding his head up. He shook it listlessly. "No. Too tired." The tone was gravelly and broken, either from fatigue or disuse.

I heard feet moving across the floor and then Michael stood over us, leaning down to help Will up. "You have to eat something, Will. Please."

Will looked at his brother and then me. He nodded.

We guided him toward a wingback chair positioned near the hearth, and while Michael settled him comfortably, I turned to call out to Mac.

"He's gone for his dinner," Philip told me from the doorway. At some point, he and Gage had retreated to the parlor.

I nodded and turned back to help Michael. We righted the overturned chairs and began gathering up the papers scattered across the floor. And all the while, Will's gaze seemed to float about the room as if unable to focus on anything. Suddenly feeling like an intruder, I touched Michael gently on the back and told him I would wait for him in the parlor.

Will's head perked up at the sound of my voice and his gaze sought out mine. "You'll return?"

Stunned by the request, I could only stare at Will's earnest face flickering in and out of the amber light cast by the fire. His face was so gaunt, his eyes shadowed.

Michael paused in his tidying to stare first at his brother and then at me.

"Please," Will added as the silence stretched.

"Of course," I replied, feeling ashamed that my astonishment had forced him to utter such a word, so close to begging. "Yes. I'll return. Soon," I promised him, hoping he could sense my sincerity.

His gaze held mine another moment before sliding away. I took that as my cue to leave, exiting through the doorway just as the surly manservant returned with Will's dinner.

He glared at me as we passed, shutting the door to the bed-chamber behind him.

I stared at the wooden barrier for a moment longer, unable yet to face Gage or Philip. My insides felt scoured and raw, and dark emotions bubbled too close to the surface.

"Do not take it personally," Philip said to my back, forcing me to turn. He leaned awkwardly against the back of a Hepplewhite chair, his body still taut from the scene in the bedroom. "Ole Mac is always like that."

I wondered if the man even remembered me. After all, if I hadn't recognized him immediately, how much more must I have changed in the last ten years from age fifteen to twenty-five. "Is he really the best person to be looking after Will?" I questioned, unaccustomed to servants displaying such blatant aversion for those they served.

"Oh, aye. You won't find a more loyal man to the Dal-mays than Mac, particularly when it comes to William. He was his personal servant during the war," Philip explained.

I knew that much, but loyalty wasn't the only thing to be considered.

"And he's not the only one Michael hired to assist his brother." Gage's voice was stiff, and I couldn't tell whether it was because he was angry or merely uncomfortable with what we had just seen. "There's another man, named Dono-van. I met him the other day. He seems to have some kind of medical experience."

I nodded. Perhaps a former surgeon's assistant or an apothecary's apprentice.

I worried my fingers and glanced back at the door to the bedchamber. I couldn't help but wonder how many times similar events had played out in the last nine months since Will's release. Michael had told us that he was improving, that these . . . lapses . . . were happening less and less often. But how many times had they occurred to begin with?

The memory of Will crouched in the corner scrabbling away at the wall with a stub of charcoal kept flashing before my eyes and made my chest ache. I wrapped my arms around myself against a sudden chill.

The bedchamber door opened and Michael reappeared. He was exhausted. Dark circles had formed under his eyes and his face was pale and drawn. How many nights had he lain awake, worrying about his brother? How many times had he been called from his bed to deal with a problem concerning Will?

He sighed and closed the door, but not before I saw Mac bending over Will, helping him manage the spoonful of soup he was ladling into his mouth. Will's hand shook from the effort.

Michael crossed the room to lean over a sideboard that rested against the wall near the hall door. The emotional strain of the last few minutes seemed to tighten the muscles across his back, stretching the fine fabric of his evening coat. I tensed, uncertain if he was angry with me for approaching Will in the manner I had.

I knew he had every right to be upset with me. I had disregarded his warnings and walked straight into the lion's den, so to speak. If Will had turned on me and harmed me, I knew neither Michael nor Will would have been able to forgive themselves. And it would have been my fault.

Michael inhaled deeply, pressing his hands into the smooth slab of oak so hard that it jostled the glasses and decanters lined up along its surface, making them tinkle and clatter. I braced for whatever reprimand was coming.

"I have *never* . . . seen Will react that way." His voice was soft with bafflement. He shook his head. "Not with anyone." Pushing away from the sideboard, he turned to look at me. "How did you know he wouldn't hurt you?"

"I . . . I didn't," I admitted. "But . . ." I swallowed around the dryness in my throat. "It seemed logical that as long as I didn't alarm him or try to force him to stop drawing, he wouldn't be upset. I'm much the same way, you see." I offered him a weak smile. "When I'm immersed in a painting, I don't note the servants coming or going with trays of food—left untouched because I don't recognize my own hunger or thirst." I laughed nervously. "Sometimes I don't think I would notice if my studio caught fire. Only the passing of daylight captures my attention, because once it's too dark to see I have to light lamps in order to continue."

"Are all artists like that?"

"No," I admitted, hating to squash his hopes. "I'm a bit . . . eccentric." That was the word my grandmother had taught me to use many years ago.

"But is it possible . . ."

I shook my head, cutting him off. "Will was never like that before."

He nodded and turned his face toward the wall.

"How does he usually come out of these trances?" Philip asked.

"Sometimes he just all of a sudden stops and blinks his eyes, like he's waking up from a deep slumber. Other times he tires himself out and falls asleep. But he's never come out of it with the help of someone else before."

I looked up from my examination of the rug below my feet to find Michael studying me in silent contemplation. I didn't have to glance at my brother-in-law or Gage to know they were scrutinizing me in much the same way.

"It's not really so surprising," I said defensively, wrapping my arms tighter around me. "He wasn't likely to feel threatened by a female. And I didn't demand anything of him." I ran the toe of my slipper over a burr in the rug. "I was just letting him know I was there."

"We know, Kiera." Philip rested a hand on my shoulder in a gesture meant to reassure me. "Ye did well."

But I could tell that something I had said had bothered Michael. Had I not been looking him in the eyes as I spoke I might have missed it, but I had seen the flicker of emotion, the flinch that had tightened his shoulders before being masked. His gaze had slid away from mine and fixed on the point where the rug met the floorboards. I frowned, confused by his reaction.

"It's late," Philip declared, seemingly unaware of the change in his friend's demeanor. "If there's nothin' else pressing, perhaps we should continue this conversation in the morn."

Michael cleared his throat. "Of course."

Philip rubbed a hand over the stubble on his jaw wearily. "I'll speak to my aunt and Caroline then, and we'll try to sort everything out. But I canna promise ye anything. Ye did lie to them, Dalmay. And it might be best for all involved if there was some distance between ye for the time bein'. The engagement need not be so hastily broken, but a little space and reflection are not unwarranted."

Michael nodded, having not raised his gaze through this entire speech. "I understand. My thanks, Cromarty."

Philip joined me in my study of our friend's down-turned head, but did not comment further. "Come along, Kiera." He pressed a firm hand to the small of my back, guiding me toward the door.

I glanced over my shoulder at Michael, and then Gage, just before Philip steered me through the door and out of sight. The taut expression Gage aimed at my back did little to reassure me.

I was surprised to find my lady's maid waiting for me in my bedchamber. I eyed her suspiciously as she rose from her perch on the edge of the vanity seat, hands folded before her, wondering what had brought on this sudden change in routine. Normally I was forced to ring for the girl, sometimes several times, in order to get her to attend to me. Which suited me just fine. Nothing annoyed me more than to have someone flitting about me, forever fussing with my appearance.

But, then again, Lucy had been acting strangely ever since we'd left Gairloch Castle. I suspected she missed her rather large family and found the uncertainty of each new location more of a trial than she wished to admit. So I decided to overlook the oddity of her prompt presence and crossed the room to allow her to begin unfastening my dress.

However, after enduring several minutes of her sharp movements, jerking and jostling me as she unhooked my garments, it became apparent I was not going to be able to ignore her unusual behavior or the evidence from her over-wrought sighs that she had something to say. "Out with it," I ordered her, reaching out to steady myself on the bed pole. "What's got you in such a dither?"

"I dinna like it here, m'lady." Her thick brogue was heavy with condemnation. "Ye said we'd be stayin' in Edinburgh t'night."

"We were supposed to." My voice wavered with each of Lucy's tugs. "But unforeseen circumstances have impelled us to stop here, and we shall likely remain for a few more days."

Lucy fell silent, but I could tell from the continued roughness of her movements that she was far from mollified. "Why don't you like it here?" I persisted.

"It's no' for me to say," she replied crisply.

I stifled a sigh. "I can't do anything to make it better if you don't tell me what the problem is," I reminded her, feeling as if I were talking to my five-year-old niece.

"There's naught ye can do, m'lady." She pulled the dress up over my head without warning, smothering me in fabric.

I sputtered and turned to glare at her, but she had turned away to lay the costly gown over a chair. "Lucy, if you don't tell me what has made you so determined to maim me . . ." I threatened.

She flushed and dropped her gaze to the floor. "Sorry, m'lady. It's just . . ." She began to worry her hands, darting a look at me. "I ken I shouldn' be listenin' to the gossip. 'Tis likely just the maids flappin' their tongues. But . . ." She glanced about her as if worried someone might be listening and then leaned toward me to murmur in an exaggerated whisper, "They say a *madman* lives here." Her eyes were wide with fright. "And I dinna think my mum would like it if'n he murdered me in my sleep."

I frowned. I shouldn't have been surprised that Lucy had heard about Will from the Dalmay servants, but I was. Especially when he was spoken of in such terrifying terms. I wondered if Michael knew what rumors his staff were spreading. If he hoped to keep the truth about Will's whereabouts during the last ten years a secret, he had best look to getting his servants in line first.

"There are no madmen living here," I answered in a calm voice, unwilling to classify Will as such no matter what had been said. "And you are *not* going to be murdered in your sleep." Of all the nonsense . . .

Lucy's brow puckered doubtfully.

"William Dalmay is just . . . ill. He's quite incapable of hurting you."

She considered my words, as if trying to decide if I was telling her the truth. "So . . . they was just feedin' me gammon? The other servants?"

I hesitated, not certain precisely what had been said belowstairs. "It's likely."

Lucy scowled, evidently not liking the idea of being manipulated for someone else's amusement. At Gairloch Castle she had been related to half of the staff and had grown up with the rest. A bit of teasing there was all in good fun. Among strangers it was not so kind.

She helped me out of my corset and petticoats and then set about straightening the garments while I sat down to remove my stockings and slippers.

"That Mr. Gage is here, isna he?" she surprised me by asking when she returned to begin removing the pins from my hair. "His valet was at dinner." From her fierce expression in the reflection of the mirror, I could tell she didn't like the man.

"Was he the one who told you Mr. Dalmay was mad?"

"Nay. But he dinna correct them."

"Then what is so distasteful about him?" I pressed.

Her mouth screwed up. "He's a might too high in the instep."

I smiled. "I'm afraid that's how most valets are."

"Barnes isna," she said, referring to Philip's manservant. "And neither are the men who serve the Dalmays." She uncoiled my rope of hair and began dividing it into three sections to braid it.

"So you've met Mac," I asked, curious to get her opinion on the ill-tempered man.

"Nay. They be Clark and Donovan."

I perked up at the mention of Will's other manservant. "What did you think of Donovan?"

A coy smile brightened her face. "Oh, he's a bit o' all right."

"Lucy," I scolded, blushing at the admiring tone of her voice.

"What? A big, strappin' lad like that. I couldna help but notice."

"And do the other maids notice him as well?" I asked, interested despite myself.

"Oh, aye."

I watched her in the mirror as she tied a ribbon around the end of my braid, not having failed to miss the telltale flush of attraction cresting her cheeks. "Well, just be careful there," I felt compelled to warn her. At Gairloch Castle she was relatively safe from men with dishonorable intentions, surrounded as she was by three brothers and a handful of female relatives to look after her. At Dalmay House, she had only me.

"I will, m'lady. But no worries. He's no' likely to fancy me."

I wasn't so certain about that. With her creamy skin and buxom figure, Lucy was attractive enough to draw most men's attention. I wondered if her sheltered existence had made her blind to that.

"Did Donovan mention anything about his former employment?" I asked, thinking back to what Gage had told me about him having some kind of medical experience.

Lucy helped me pull my nightdress over my head. "Nay, m'lady. Did ye want me to ask?"

She seemed far too eager to have any excuse to talk to the man. "Only if it seems natural to do so," I told her, not wanting the girl to seem too keen.

"Aye, m'lady." Her eyes twinkled. "He willna ken why I'm askin'," she promised, misunderstanding my reason for concern.

I didn't correct her, figuring the maid would take more care if she thought concealing my interest was the reason I requested her discretion. She helped me into my warm, midnight-blue wrapper, and then I dismissed her to seek her own bed.

I wandered the room restlessly, my mind too busy yet for sleep. The chamber assigned to me was swathed in shades of pale pink and warm chocolate brown in the most sumptuous of fabrics—velvet and silk and satin. The walls were hung with ivory silk speckled with pink flowers, which matched nearly perfectly the pearlescent pink marble of the fireplace. I did not know whether Michael and Laura had elected to place me in a premier chamber, or if all the bedrooms were decorated so lavishly.

A handsome landscape held pride of place over the hearth, depicting the sweep of a bay and the softly lapping waves of the sea. The tumbled rocks of the cliffs were shaded with sweeps of palest pink, tying the piece to the room's color palette. I studied the painting, wishing momentarily that I was as skilled at bringing to life earth and sea and sky as I was at capturing it in the human face and form. Then I brushed the thought away, reminding myself to be grateful for the gifts I had been given instead of wasting my time longing for the things I couldn't change.

Will tried to teach me that—the summer he spent as my drawing master.

I crossed my arms over my chest and moved to the window, lifting aside the heavy velvet drapes to peer out at the moonlit countryside beyond. A wide swath of lawn stretched before me, ending in the thick shadows of forest that extended inland toward Dalmay village, and then farther on to Queensferry. Will would have liked such a setting.

During that summer, which seemed so long ago now, Will had enjoyed teaching my lessons outdoors whenever he could. On warm, dry days, whether the sky was clear and blue or piled with towering clouds, he had escorted me out to one of the neighboring hillsides. Sometimes we carried easels and canvases, and sometimes merely sketchbooks, but without fail, on fair weather days we trudged across the countryside to capture one scene or another with brushes or charcoal.

At first I had hated those excursions, wanting to remain inside engrossed in my latest effort at portraiture. Painting people was safe, comfortable, and I felt relatively competent in the task. Landscapes were a different matter. They left me feeling frustrated, overwhelmed, and wholly inadequate. After a day spent sketching the River Tweed as it rambled past St. Cuthbert's Church or painting the towering oaks of Dunstan Wood, I was left certain I had as little talent as my past tutor, Signor Riotta, claimed.

Then one afternoon in late June, after yet another failure to capture any sense of light or movement or life in the landscape before me, I threw my paintbrush down with a cry of exasperation. I was tempted to tear the canvas from the easel, throw it to the ground, and stomp on it, but for the fact that it took time and effort to prepare new canvases, and I had no desire to waste the ones already stretched and coated with noxious gesso.

"Why do you make me do this?" I demanded, pacing back and forth in a tight circle before our easels. "You *know* I'm incompetent at landscapes."

Will continued to focus on his own efforts, leaning toward his canvas as he applied the paint on his brush to some detail. "Because you have skills yet to learn."

"But I don't want to paint landscapes," I insisted, growing angrier in the face of his calm. "I don't care if I know how."

He sat back to study his efforts. "Perhaps. But there are still elements that can be learned from painting a landscape that apply to a portrait or a still life."

I planted my hands on my hips. "Such as?"

He glanced up at me for the first time since my outburst and I felt my cheeks heat under his regard. "Light and shadow. The tone and depth of your hues. Texture."

I frowned. "I can learn those just as easily on a portrait."

He shook his head. "How will you learn the way sunlight affects your subjects? The way it saturates color or distorts texture?" I opened my mouth to protest, but he continued on before I could speak, lifting his eyebrows in silent chastisement. "And don't tell me that all of your portraits will be composed inside. What if one day you are asked to paint a subject on a terrace or beside a window?" I snapped my mouth shut, angry that I had to concede this point. He turned back toward his canvas. "All of the skills you will study while painting landscapes will translate to your portraits."

I watched him for a moment, frustration simmering inside me like the water heating in a teakettle. "But I'm not any good at it," I blurted out.

Will looked up at me again, as calm and unruffled as before. "Do you have to be?"

I watched the way the wind ruffled his too-long hair across his forehead and considered his words. "But it's not any fun to do something I'm not good at."

The corners of his handsome mouth quirked upward into a smile. He set aside his paintbrush and rose from his stool. "And, ignoring your previous drawing master's idiotic comments, you have been good at everything else you've tried to paint, haven't you? Even as a small child, I bet you could draw far better than most adults."

I hesitated, knowing it was impolite to brag.

His grin widened. "It's all right. You can speak the truth."

"Yes," I admitted.

Humor danced in his eyes. "Well, I'm sorry to tell you,

but it was inevitable that you should come up against something that gave you trouble. Even geniuses and prodigies have their weak points. The trick is not to let those bothersome bits stop you. Persevere and you'll be better all around for the effort."

I looked up into Will's soft gray eyes and wondered at what he'd had to persevere. Little as I knew about it, Will had shown me that war was a terrifying, difficult thing. And I knew he had struggled, still struggled every day to leave it behind.

The amusement faded from his eyes and his smile turned sad, as if he understood exactly where my thoughts had taken me. "Now, see here," he said, pointing to the leaves of my trees. "Your sense of shade and definition have improved significantly in just the past few weeks. I noticed it in the portrait of Mrs. Caldwell you've been working on."

I blinked at the blurs of foliage on my canvas. "Really?"

"Most definitely."

I gestured to the painting. "But the forest still looks dead. Like a flattened, lifeless slug."

He chuckled. "Oh, it's not quite so bad as that. Even your worst efforts are far better than most can ever aspire to. But in any case, you don't want to paint landscapes. You said so yourself." He tilted his head and smiled, chiding me gently. "So stop worrying so. Approach them as the exercises they are, and concentrate on your brushstrokes, the play of light." He gestured to the admittedly lovely panorama around us. "And enjoy the sunshine. You spend far too much time cooped up in your smelly studio."

I sighed, willing to concede that point. "It *is* easier to breathe out here."

He laughed outright and I felt a flush of pleasure at the sound. It was deep and husky, and far too rare.

"I imagine so," he murmured, bending over to pick up my brush. Blades of grass stuck to the paint-smeared tip. "Now," he said, handing it to me, "study the way the sunlight glistens off that stream and try to re-create it."

I glanced at the flat blue-gray strip of water depicted on my canvas and nodded.

Will truly had been an excellent teacher. Patient, understanding, and far better at motivating me to do the things I didn't want to do than anyone had been since I had outgrown the care of my nursemaid.

And now . . . look at what had become of him.

Tears burned the backs of my eyes, their salty bitterness curdling my tongue. I pressed my forehead against the cool glass of the window, knowing it would leave a smudge, but not caring. I needed to feel the shock of cold against my skin. Gritting my teeth, I fought against the sob building inside me. It pressed hard on my chest. If I wept it would do no one any good, least of all Will. But in spite of my struggles, a single tear escaped to etch a trail down my cheek.

I swiped the wetness away angrily, and then turned to slam the flat of my palm against the window casing. It smarted, but I welcomed the pain.

Damn the old Lord Dalmay! How could he do this to his son? What kind of unfeeling bastard locks away his own flesh and blood in such a cesspit and then proceeds to erase him from his life?

And Lady Hollingsworth along with all the other loose tongues here at Dalmay House should be ashamed of themselves. After everything Will had been through—his service during the war, his unjust confinement—he should be given a hero's welcome, not spoken of in disgust and shunned like some criminal.

My breath sawed in and out of my chest, rasping like a wounded animal, and I was forced to grip the drapes on either side of me and press my face to the cool glass again, trying to slow my racing heart. My breathing calmed, but the tightness in my chest remained, squeezing my breast every time I closed my eyes and saw Will's haunted face.

If only I could turn back the clock, return to the summer Will acted as my drawing master. Return to the months before he was locked away. Maybe I could convince Lord

Dalmay not to fear his son. Or persuade Will to go to his brother in London. Surely there was some way we could have stopped it all from happening. If only I could fix this. If only I could make it right.

I lifted my face from the windowpane, staring out at the shadowy landscape before me dusted with silvery moonlight.

There had to be something I could do. Some way that I could help him get back what he'd lost, to return him to himself, to the man he was before he'd been confined to that asylum. Before all of those years of torment had been inflicted on his still-fragile mind.

Knowing that I still had not beaten my own demons, it seemed somewhat naïve to think I could help Will to defeat his, but it felt even more wrong not at least to try, to offer whatever support or guidance I could. Too many people had turned away from Will—during the years prior to his confinement, when he struggled to escape the exhaustion and melancholia that had followed him home from war, and in the months since his release from Larkspur Retreat. I couldn't be one of them. Not when I had experienced a similar shunning I was just beginning to fight my way back from.

For all the things Will had done for me that summer as my drawing master and more, he deserved my friendship and my loyalty. To turn my back on him now would be a betrayal. I wasn't sure I could live with myself if I behaved so callously.

Of course, I didn't know exactly *what* I could do for him. Despite the years of enforced tutelage by my late husband studying the intimate workings of the human body, I was not medically trained. I had no idea how to treat a man suffering from the manias and melancholia Will endured. But Michael must have consulted a physician—someone with experience with this sort of thing, someone who knew how to care for patients like Will. I could follow their direction.

I worried my lower lip between my teeth. Unless the physician had told Michael to return his brother to the asylum.

That seemed to be the answer for anything that baffled a medical man, and the more arrogant the man, the more adamant his protestations that nothing could be done. At least, that had been my experience. And as Sir Anthony's wife, I'd had plenty of opportunities to witness prideful displays from him and his colleagues.

In any case, Michael had told us his brother had improved significantly in the nine months since his release, so continuing on the present course must be better than sending him back. Perhaps all Will needed was more time and everyone's patience, and his mind would heal itself. If he was sketching those frightening images on spare sheets of paper and his walls to purge his mind of them, then maybe he was already making great strides to mend himself. Maybe if I encouraged his efforts, let him know I understood, he could rid himself of those haunting memories once and for all.

I rubbed my fingers against my right temple, knowing full and well it wasn't quite so simple. Was I not still plagued by the images from my past? Pacing the floors of my room on some nights, unable to sleep?

My fingers tightened their grip around the drapes, wrinkling the costly velvet.

But surely it was better to at least try. Maybe Will would never be completely rid of his nightmares—maybe no one ever was—but he could at least fight them. What other option did he have? Giving up, giving in was intolerable.

Struggling as I was with such dark thoughts, I nearly missed the soft click of the door opening and closing behind me. It was latched with care not to disturb those in the other rooms nearby.

I knew better than to suppose Lucy had forgotten something and come back to fetch it. Or that my sister was ready for a chat, when fatigue from her recent illness had marked her steps as she exited the drawing room after dinner. No one else should have been so presumptuous as to visit my room in the middle of the night, or to enter it without even knocking, but I knew who it was without turning. And somehow I felt I should have been expecting it.

The anger I had only recently dampened flared back to life, sweeping swift and hot through my veins. I almost felt grateful for the chance to vent my spleen, especially on the man who was my intruder.

Dropping the drapes, I whirled around to glare at him. "This is becoming rather a bad habit, isn't it?"

CHAPTER NINE

Gage was not the least intimidated by my angry stare. In fact, despite his casual pose, leaning back against the doorjamb with his ankles and arms crossed, I could feel the full force of his displeasure across the twenty-foot room that separated us. It only served to enrage me further.

"What are you doing here?" I demanded.

He lifted one shoulder in the semblance of a careless shrug, but his posture was too stiff. "I thought we needed to talk."

"At midnight in my bedchamber?" I could hear my voice rising with my temper and made an effort to check it.

"It was the only time and place where I knew we would have some privacy."

I narrowed my eyes, uncertain whether there was a hidden barb in there somewhere. "You are aware that just because I gave you leave to enter my chamber twice during your visit to Gairloch does *not* give you permission to do so now."

"Three times."

I had sucked in breath to offer him a set-down when his words caught me off guard. "What?" I snapped, shaking my head in agitation.

"I entered your chamber three times," he clarified. He

pushed away from the door, stalking across the room toward me as he ticked off the encounters on his fingers. I stumbled back a step, but then planted my feet, refusing to give him the satisfaction of watching me retreat. "Once after Lord Westlock coshed you over the head, once when I brought champagne to celebrate Lady Stratford's detainment, and once while Sir Graham Fraser questioned you after the ordeal in the boat."

The ordeal in the boat? That certainly wasn't how I thought of it. And I was surprised Gage could refer to it in such mundane terms. "You mean when I almost *died?*"

He stiffened, his steps faltering to a stop a few feet from me. "Yes. I well remember the more serious implications of that struggle," he replied in a measured voice. He turned his face to the side and I could see the muscles in his throat working before he added in a huskier undertone, "I will never be able to forget them."

My cheeks flushed with heat and my eyes dropped to his cravat and the sapphire stickpin glistening among its snowy white folds. Of course he remembered. He had saved my life, at no small risk to his own. And how did I repay his discretion, his avoidance in bringing up such a sensitive subject, but by chastising him like a resentful harpy? What was it about this man that so riled me that I could forget all prudence and decency?

"I . . . I'm sorry," I murmured, stumbling over an apology. "Of course you remember."

He shifted uncomfortably and cleared his throat. "Yes, well . . ."

I regained the courage to look him in the eye, noticing the faint lines at the corners of them. His finely sculpted cheekbones seemed tanner, as if he had been spending a great deal of time outdoors since last I saw him. If possible, I thought it made his already devilish good looks even more arresting, even at this late hour, with nary a stray beam of sunshine to highlight his golden hair. I had decided a portrait of Gage was best painted in the daylight, but now I wasn't so sure. Here in the flickering shadows, his features might actually be more interesting.

"You look well," he said meaningfully, and I realized that even as I had been standing there studying him, he had been doing the same to me.

I wrapped my arms around myself, suddenly self-conscious. Especially when I realized I was wearing naught but a thin night rail and my wrapper. When Gage had visited my chamber in the past I had always been properly attired in an evening gown or a morning dress, not bedclothes. "Thank you," I murmured, praying he would not mention my state of dishabille.

"Cromarty told me you've suffered no lasting effects from your injuries."

"Ah . . . no," I told him. "Just a tiny scar."

"Good."

I pivoted to the side, fiddling with the long rope of my braid where it lay over my shoulder. "And you?" I asked, glancing at him out of the corner of my eye. "Are you well?"

"Yes. Yes, I am. Thank you for asking."

I nodded, wondering if we could possibly have become more staid or polite. Either we seemed to argue with one another or we turned to stilted small talk. And I wasn't certain I didn't prefer the arguing. At least it didn't leave me standing here feeling foolish and uncertain, wondering what Gage was thinking.

"You said you wanted to talk," I prodded, unable to stand the awkward silence a moment longer.

"Uh . . . yes." But he hesitated to say more, his gaze turning cautious, as if he wasn't certain how to voice his next words. Or he was wary of how I would react to them.

I tilted my head, considering him. Beyond his ruffled hair, which I knew he was prone to comb his fingers through when he was frustrated or impatient, he was still impeccably turned out in his evening kit. Even his cravat had not become rumpled through the evening's events. I suspected he had been planning to make this midnight visit before we even parted company, and he had been pacing his room, biding his time, until he knew he could steal into my chamber without being seen. I had but one guess as to why he was so eager to speak with me, and it made sense he would be cautious in bringing it up.

"This is about William Dalmay, isn't it?"

Gage did not try to insult my intelligence by denying it or couching it in gentler terms.

I sighed in frustration, knowing what he was going to say. "I have no intention of discussing him with you."

"Be reasonable," he said, an edge returning to his voice. "I'm concerned for your well-being. The man is simply not safe."

I glared over my shoulder at him. "Says who? You?"

His mouth tightened into a thin line.

"You have no right to speak to me on this matter. I think I know William just a little bit better than you do."

"Perhaps you *did*," he replied, emphasizing the past tense of the word. "But he's not the same man he was before he went into the asylum. You can see that."

"And what do you know of the matter? You were in London or Greece . . ." I gestured with my hand ". . . or wherever you were when he was locked away. And you've been here at Dalmay House all of—what? A week? How does that make you an authority on William Dalmay?"

"It doesn't. But I would wager I know far more than you about the inmates of lunatic asylums and just what they're capable of."

"Will isn't just some nameless *inmate*," I snapped, hating that detestable word. "He's my friend. And I am not going to let you scare me or turn me against him. He needs our help, not our condemnation." I turned to walk away from him, but Gage's hand shot out to grip my upper arm.

"I'm only asking you to be sensible," he growled, his face tight with frustration. "The man is, at the very least, unpredictable. And I don't like erratic, potentially volatile men."

"Will is not volatile." I stared up into Gage's angry gaze, trying to make him understand. "I *know* him. He would never hurt me."

Gage's eyes searched mine and in my gaze I pleaded with him to listen to me, to stop this ridiculous campaign to keep us apart. His hand pulled me closer to him, tightening almost painfully around my arm, and then loosened, though he still did not release me. "Who is William Dalmay to you?" he surprised me by asking.

I blinked up at him in confusion.

"Was there really nothing between you?"

Heat blossomed in my cheeks as I realized what he meant. "No. I already told everyone we were just friends. He would never have behaved so dishonorably."

Gage's gaze sharpened beneath his furrowed brow. I wanted to turn away, to hide from his all-too-knowing eyes. "But you wished he would?"

My heart squeezed sharply, whether from the remembered heartache of my adolescent self or my current mortification, I wasn't certain. Either way, I could not maintain eye contact with the man in front of me. "I was fifteen," I offered by way of explanation. "And he was a handsome war hero."

He considered my words while I contemplated the lapels of his frock coat. "And a tortured one."

His insightful response drew my gaze back to his. "Yes," I admitted.

Gage nodded.

"Didn't you ever become infatuated at fifteen? Whether it was wise or not?"

His mouth quirked wryly and a glimmer of humor returned to his eyes. "The young women of Devon were never more safe than when I left for Cambridge."

I arched my eyebrows.

Seeing the look in my eyes, he coughed. "But let's not discuss my adolescence, shall we?"

I allowed the matter to drop, not certain I wanted to hear about Gage's youthful conquests.

He studied me closely, and at such a close range I felt a little like an insect beneath a magnifying glass. I tugged against his hold and he released me, allowing me to move to a safe distance. His gaze dropped to my upper arm where I was rubbing the spot where he had gripped me, not so much because it hurt, but because it still tingled from his touch, even through the thick fabric of my wrapper.

"Did I hurt you?" His voice was concerned.

"No."

He searched my face as if trying to decide whether I was lying. He must have decided I wasn't, for he turned away, raking a hand back through his hair. After a moment's contemplation, he spoke carefully. "You realize it's probable William Dalmay will never fully recover from this."

My eyes dropped to his feet. I wanted to deny it, but the pain twisting in my chest told me that I already knew this, even if I didn't want to admit it even to myself.

I felt Gage's worried gaze on me. "He will never return to the man he was. Too much has happened. Too much has changed."

"Are any of us the same people we were ten years ago?" I asked.

It was meant as a rhetorical question, a feeble defense against the truth of his words, but from the ringing silence, I knew Gage had taken the query seriously.

I lifted my eyes to find him watching me, his pale blue gaze torn with indecision. He inhaled swiftly and parted his lips to speak, but then, as if he'd thought better of it, he stopped. The words died on his tongue and his mouth drifted shut in resignation.

I could almost feel the gravity in the air between us of whatever confession he had been about to make. Another secret unspoken. Another thought left unsaid.

Frustrated by his continued refusal to share, his determination to keep me off balance, I tried asking him myself. "What happened in Greece?"

His gaze turned stony. "I'm not going to talk about Greece."

"Why? Did something happen there?"

"No."

Irritated, I racked my brain trying to remember what might have been going on during that time period. "Were you caught up in the Greeks' war for independence?" I asked, trying to recall when that conflict had actually begun. I knew very little about the Greek revolution, and those things I did know, I had read in the newspapers. I must admit I had not been very interested in following the events of a war so far from home, but now I wished I had paid more attention.

I knew I had hit on something of the truth when the muscle in his clamped jaw jumped. "I did not come here to discuss the Greeks' struggle for independence from the Ottoman Empire." He stabbed a finger at the middle of my chest. "You are attempting to distract me."

I turned away with an aggravated huff. Why did the man insist on being so secretive? It seemed ludicrous that I could be so drawn to him when I really knew almost nothing about him except the few facts I had been able to glean from others. Certainly I felt I knew his character after all we had been through at Gairloch. I could even understand his desire for privacy—I myself prized it highly—but his stubborn refusal to share anything about his past upset me. I had shared so much of myself with him already—parts of my life that I discussed with no one—that it smacked of betrayal when he did not reciprocate.

Upon his departure from Gairloch, I had accepted his decision to remain quiet about his reasons for ignoring my doubts about the initial findings of the investigation we had conducted. If he had believed, as I did, that we might never see each other again, I could understand his unwillingness to share private information with someone who would return to being a stranger. I hadn't liked it, but I could understand it. However, now that we had been thrown together again, for who knew how long, I could not comprehend his continued silence.

"I understand that you care for Dalmay," Gage said in a calmer voice. "And I can understand that you wish to help him, but just stop and consider the matter for a moment." He leaned closer and I looked up, reluctantly meeting his troubled gaze. "He is damaged. Even Dalmay himself would admit that."

I scowled.

"He is not always himself, as we witnessed this evening."

I opened my mouth to argue, but he cut me off.

"*Yes*, he did not harm anyone tonight. But that doesn't mean he is incapable of it," he added carefully.

I lifted my eyebrows, letting him know I was tired of hearing this same refrain.

He quickly came to the point. "How do you think Dalmay would feel if he emerged from one of his stupors to discover he had hurt you?"

My stomach clenched. Damn him, he was right. If Will were to accidentally injure me while in the grips of one of his melancholies, he would never forgive himself. I had admitted as much to myself earlier this evening when I thought Michael was angry with me for approaching his brother.

Frustrated that he had backed me into a corner I could not reason myself out of without disregarding Will's best interests, I glared daggers at Gage. "I can't just walk away and ignore that he needs my help," I challenged him. "What kind of person would I be to abandon a friend in such a manner?" I heard distress creep into my voice and shook my head in aggravation. "I can't do it, Gage. I owe him too much."

His brow furrowed in consternation. "Because he was your drawing master for a few months?"

I closed my eyes, trying to find the words to make him understand. "Because he believed in me when no one else did. Because he was my friend when everyone else had abandoned me." I sighed. "Because without Will's encouragement I would likely have given up my portraits, and then where would I be?"

I opened my eyes to find Gage watching me with a

strange glimmer in his eyes. I knew he understood how much my artwork meant to me, how lost I felt without it. How desperate I had been when Sir Anthony had threatened to take it away from me if I dared defy him in his quest to complete his anatomy textbook—the textbook for which he needed my sketches. I had only ever admitted to Philip and my brother Trevor how far Sir Anthony was willing to go to carry through on his threats, but I suspected Gage had inferred more than I had let on. Even if he hadn't guessed that my late husband had threatened to break my fingers, I knew he presumed something similar.

I could tell from the concern in his eyes that his thoughts had traveled along the same path as mine, and I dropped my gaze. Even eighteen months after Sir Anthony's death, the hurt was still too raw.

Gage surprised me by cupping my jaw with his warm hand and gently forcing my gaze back to his. The callus on his thumb rasped against my skin as he brushed it back and forth across my cheek.

For one breathless moment, I thought he was going to kiss me. His face was so close that I could smell the smoky scent of whiskey on his breath, telling me he must have indulged in a tot or two before venturing forth to confront me. His gaze dropped to my lips, making them tingle, but he never brought his mouth closer to mine.

"I can understand why you want to help William Dalmay," he said. His voice sounded huskier than before. "But you need to consider what would really be best for him."

I backed away from his touch, and his hand fell away. Turning my back to him, I took several steps toward the fireplace, needing to put some distance between us. I was shaken by how disappointed I felt that he hadn't kissed me, and thrown off guard by his persistent efforts to keep me away from Will.

Struggling to maintain my composure, I pressed a hand to my forehead. "Why are you so concerned about this?" I finally managed to ask him. When he didn't approach or offer an explanation, I turned to look at him. He stood with his hands at his sides, watching me with a faint look of consternation on his face. "If it's because you feel some sort of responsibility for my safety because of what happened two months ago, I assure you, there's no need. You saved my life. Had you not jumped into the loch after me . . ." I smiled sadly. "Well, let's just say we wouldn't be having this conversation. Any obligation you felt toward me in not taking my concerns seriously has been fulfilled."

His voice was soft. "Kiera, I will never stop feeling responsible for your safety."

I wrinkled my brow in puzzlement.

"But I'm not warning you because of what happened two months ago," he added briskly, closing the distance between us again.

"Then why?"

"Because someone needs to. Cromarty and Michael Dalmay clearly aren't thinking."

I arched an eyebrow. "Isn't that rather high-handed of you?"

A smile quirked his lips. "Perhaps. But you have a stubborn streak. Someone needs to rein you in."

"I resent that," I gasped, planting my hands on my hips. "You were prepared to name me as your chief suspect for the murder at Gairloch if I did not help you find the real culprit. And I only insisted on continuing the investigation after you were done because I knew *you* . . ." I pointed a finger at him ". . . had apprehended the wrong suspect."

"Yes, well, nothing I have seen of you since your arrival here at Dalmay House has convinced me you are not as willful as you were at Gairloch."

I frowned. "Then I'm sorry to disappoint you further. Because you're not about to see anything from me now that will change your mind."

He scowled. "Kiera . . ."

I lifted my hand to halt the flow of his words. "No, Gage. I have heard your objections, and I appreciate your concern, but nothing you say is going to keep me from visiting with William Dalmay. I will, of course, take appropriate precautions, for my own sake as well as Will's, but I'm not going to avoid him like he's got some deadly disease."

Gage clenched his hands into fists. "You don't understand what you're doing. William Dalmay spent *nine years* in that asylum. Who knows what he's endured or how it's changed him? I don't know that you can comprehend what vile things he may have been forced to do in order to survive." His voice lowered. "A man does not last long in such a place without having to do things that would make grown men tremble."

I wrapped my arms around my waist and turned to stare at the fire crackling in the hearth, unwilling to let myself contemplate what he meant. What could Gage really know of the matter? He was just trying to scare me. He was accustomed to persuading people around to his way of thinking, and if his weapons of choice, wit and charm, wouldn't work, apparently he wasn't above using fear and intimidation.

He acted as if he knew what he was talking about, but how could he? Even if Michael had related more of the details of Will's confinement to him than the rest of us, surely Gage couldn't know enough to speculate on what Will did or didn't do while locked away.

Unless there was more to the matter than he was letting on.

"Why are you here?" I demanded, glancing up at him out of the corner of my eye. "At Dalmay House." He opened his mouth to speak, but I interrupted him. "And let's try the truth this time."

His eyebrows snapped together. "I never lied. Michael Dalmay invited me to visit, and I accepted. End of story."

"I see," I murmured, feigning interest in the lamp painted with delicate flowers positioned on one of the side tables. "When did Michael extend this courtesy?"

"About a fortnight ago, when I was wrapping up my investigation in Edinburgh. As I *told* you earlier."

"What fortuitous timing. You might have left Edinburgh without him ever knowing you were there."

Gage's hesitation was slight, but telling. "I wrote to him, of course, when I arrived in Edinburgh, on the off chance that he might venture into town."

I locked eyes with him, trying to understand why he was lying to me. Or, if not lying, why he wasn't telling me the complete truth. I faced him head-on. "Did he confide in you about his brother?"

"Upon my arrival? Yes. Michael is very worried about him."

"Did he ask for your help?"

Gage tilted his head quizzically. "Why would he ask for my help?"

I studied his face, wishing I knew the right questions to ask. Something was definitely suspicious about Gage's presence here. His explanation was certainly feasible, and under ordinary circumstances I wouldn't have questioned it. But Gage had shown an inordinate amount of interest in the comments made about William Dalmay since the moment I'd first mentioned him during our encounter on the stairs. I suppose, given the situation, that would seem understandable, but I knew better. Gage did not get that gleam in his eyes unless he was contemplating something serious.

I just wished I knew what it was. If Michael hadn't asked him to look into the matter, then why was he giving such sharp attention to it?

"Kiera, I wish you would listen to me," he began again, taking advantage of my silence to hark back to his familiar refrain.

I shook my head fiercely and crossed the room toward the door.

"You're being foolishly obstinate. What about this missing girl?" he asked, crossing the room in just a few angry strides.

"What about her?" I snapped, surprised by the question.

"Aren't you the least concerned that Will is involved somehow?"

"No."

"No? How can you be so certain?"

"Because I know Will. He would never have harmed that woman," I replied, sick unto death of repeating myself. "Besides, Michael told us it would have been impossible for him to be involved. Why would he lie?"

"Why, indeed?" Gage muttered under his breath.

I felt a moment's alarm at his exasperated words. Had he noticed Michael's odd behavior in his brother's parlor as well? I had wondered for a moment if Michael had been lying to us, but then dismissed his strained expression as concern for his brother. But if Gage had questioned it, too . . .

I shook my head, irritated with myself for allowing him to plant seeds of doubt in my head. "I believe it's time for you to go," I declared, placing my hand on the doorknob.

His angry gaze returned to mine. "Don't think this is over. I will speak to Cromarty and Dalmay about what we've discussed."

"Don't you dare," I hissed, worried about being overheard by someone in the corridor. "Philip has enough to worry about with Alana's health. I don't need *you* adding to his concerns."

"It would be *you*, with your foolish disregard for your own safety, who is adding to his concerns, not me."

I glared up at him, infuriated with his interference. So be it. I would just have to make sure I spoke with Philip first and warned him of Gage's buffle-headed nonsense.

I wrenched open the door and nodded with my head, telling him to leave. Now.

He dipped his own head sharply once and strode out the door.

I would have liked to slam it, but, mindful of my sister and her husband sleeping in the chamber across the hall, I eased it shut and turned the key in the lock with a pointed click.

CHAPTER TEN

I spent a sleepless night tossing and turning and trying fruitlessly to pull my mind away from thoughts of Will and Gage. But the harder I tried, the more stubborn their faces became fixed in my mind and the more incessant their voices became.

So, frustrated and weary, I welcomed the first light of dawn as it seeped across the sky in shades of yellow and then pink. It seemed doubtful by that point that sleep would ever find me, so I bathed my face in the chill water left on my washstand and dressed in a simple morning gown and pelisse. Then, eager to escape the house, I slipped out of my room, in hopes the brisk morning air would clear my head.

Philip stepped out of the room across the hall just as I was closing the door to mine. Taking in my warm Venetian blue walking ensemble, he smiled. "It seems we've had the same idea." He spoke in a soft voice, presumably so as not to wake Alana.

I smiled sympathetically in return. Judging from the dark smudges under Philip's eyes, I wasn't the only one who'd passed a restless night.

"Would you care if I joined you?" he asked, running his fingers around the brim of the hat in his hands.

"I'd like that," I replied, realizing it would give me the perfect opportunity to speak with him in private before

Gage could. "But . . ." I glanced down the hall ". . . weren't you going to speak with Lady Hollingsworth this morning before she leaves?"

"No worries." His eyes twinkled. "Aunt Jane was never one to rise before midmorning, even when facing the most harrowing of crises." He came forward to take my arm and lead me down the hall. "Caroline told Alana that when her eldest brother's wife went into labor in the middle of the night, her mother called it the height of rudeness."

I stifled a gasp of horrified laughter.

"Luckily for Aunt Jane's new grandson, he didn't decide to make his actual entry into the world until almost noon the next day; otherwise I'm certain he would never hear the end of it. In any case, in the event that she should take it upon herself to rise earlier than expected, I still estimate that will be a good two to three hours from now. And I've left a note requesting an interview and more or less ordering her to stay put until we've had a chance to talk."

I smiled, imagining how Lady Hollingsworth would take such a dictate from her nephew, even though I was certain Philip had couched it in the gentlest of terms.

We exited through a door on the north side of the manor and turned east toward the firth. Philip guided us down a well-worn path that led away from the house and underneath the towering trees of the wood. The air was crisp and ripe with the damp of early morning dew and the musk of decaying leaves. I inhaled deeply, welcoming the cold air into my lungs.

The path widened as we exited the canopy of trees and approached the water. A solid block of craggy stone rose before us to pierce the crystalline blue sky.

"Banbogle Castle," Philip explained when I turned to him curiously. "The Dalmays' old stronghold."

"Now I understand why Michael and William's father felt the need to build Dalmay House," I admitted, staring up at the decaying tower. Banbogle Castle must have been falling down around their heads.

Moss and lichen clung to the cracks in the pale stone and grime coated the windows that were not broken and exposing the interior to the elements. Though the gaping hole in the western wall would undoubtedly have been more troublesome to its inhabitants. Elsewhere, the stonework had steadily begun to crumble away to reveal the interior layers of masonry, giving the outside a jagged, uneven appearance. Some spots looked so worn that they were, undoubtedly, a mere layer or two away from creating additional gaps in the exterior.

"And not a moment too soon," Philip said. "Barely a month after Lord Dalmay moved his family to Swinton Lodge, while work began on the new manor house . . ." he nodded to the yawning gap ". . . that wall caved in on the nursery."

I gasped, unable to find words adequate enough to describe the horror of such an occurrence had any of the Dalmay children or their nursemaids been inside at the time.

"Precisely," Philip concurred. "William and Michael's grandfather had largely ignored the family's estate, leaving his wife and heir at the castle while he took up residence in Edinburgh and London. And by the time their father, the old Lord Dalmay, came into his inheritance, it was too late to undo the damage the years of neglect had wrought."

I gazed out across the steel-blue water of the firth, close enough now to smell its brine. "I always remembered Lord Dalmay as a rather stern man. Constantly lecturing us on our duty." A sad smile tugged at the corners of my mouth. "He wasn't keen on the idea of his children wasting their time trampling about the countryside or racing boats down the Tweed. Alana, Trevor, and I knew to avoid Swinton Lodge whenever he was in residence. Which was, fortunately, not so often." My grin widened. "When she was still alive, Lady Dalmay would hang a pennant out one of the south-facing windows when her husband had gone, signaling my mother the 'all clear.'"

Philip chuckled.

But my face fell as I remembered. "Even in the few months between my mother's death and hers, she continued to fly her pennant for us when Lord Dalmay was away. Though, instead of bright red, it was black." I conjured the image of Lady Dalmay, having trouble seeing any of her with clarity except her kind, gray eyes, so like her sons'. "Lady Dalmay was a caring lady. I suppose you could have called her a sort of surrogate parent to us."

"Yes," Philip murmured. "Alana admitted as much to me once."

I glanced at him, knowing I shouldn't have been surprised to hear so. But Alana rarely spoke of that time. Our mother's death had been difficult for her, more difficult than it had been for Trevor and me, perhaps because of her age—twelve, the very cusp of womanhood—or because she was so like our beautiful, spirited mother. She did not get along well with our more serious-minded father, which couldn't have helped matters. Without our mother there to buffer for her, Alana and Father had butted heads like two rams in a pasture. Alana had exasperated and troubled our father. Trevor had tried his patience, while still managing to make him proud. And I had merely baffled him.

That Alana had talked about this with Philip should have been expected. They had been married for eight years, and her husband was her closest confidant and friend. Closer even than me. I ignored the twinge of jealousy I felt at that thought. I certainly didn't begrudge my sister that intimacy with her husband, but it made me all the more aware of what I lacked.

Philip patted my hand where it lay on his arm and guided me forward down the path. It skirted the hulk of Banbogle Castle and then joined a wide, trampled dirt lane that stretched north and south down the shoreline. I commented on the well-worn trail.

"It's an old road," he explained. "From a time long before the foundations of Banbogle Castle were laid. The Dalmays have always allowed the people in the neighboring villages and estates to make use of it. It's sort of a tradition. The vantage is simply too pretty to keep to themselves."

And indeed it was. The view out over the water of the Firth of Forth was magnificent. The morning sun reflected off the waves, sparkling like gems in the clear light. The northern coast across the estuary was rockier, but the same brilliant autumn colors swathed its forests. High above, soft wisps of clouds had streamed out across the pale blue sky, while crying kittiwakes and razorbills wheeled about below them. In the distance, I could see a small island resting in the middle of the water, not far from the southern shoreline. It was too close to be Inchkeith. The isolated island where Dr. Sloane's asylum was located stood too far out in the firth to be seen easily from this shore. And thank goodness for that. I wasn't sure I could have stomached the sight.

The waves lapped playfully against the shore, inviting us to remove our shoes and run through them, but I knew the waters coming in off the North Sea were never warm, and with the stiff breeze whipping across the inlet, stinging my cheeks, they would be downright icy. I shivered at the thought and Philip glanced at me in query. Not wanting him to cut our walk short, I smiled in reassurance and hugged my arms tighter to my body to conserve warmth.

He nodded and we returned to our contemplation of the bay. I knew I had a limited amount of time in which to discuss William with him before we returned to the house and Gage sought him out, but it was difficult to gather my thoughts. And in the end, it was Philip who broke our companionable silence.

"I'm taking Alana and the children to Edinburgh this afternoon."

I swung my gaze from the water to his troubled visage.

"I would like you to join us," he added, turning his head to look down at me.

For a moment, I was speechless. I had not expected him to say anything of the like, and I couldn't quite form a response.

"I realize that you care for the Dalmays, we all do, but this . . ." He shook his head. "This is too much. Alana's health is already worrying without the added anxiety of sleeping under the Dalmays' roof."

I understood then. "Neither of you slept much last night."

Philip sighed wearily and stopped walking and turned toward the sea. "No. I knew we should have brought the children into our room after everything that Dalmay revealed, but I let Alana convince us it would be all right. I don't think she rested for more than a quarter of an hour at a time. She couldn't stop thinking of the murders at Gairloch and fretting for the children's safety."

"But this isn't like what happened at Gairloch."

"I know. But you know your sister isn't always reasonable when it comes to the children. She locked herself in the nursery with them, remember, swearing she wouldn't emerge until the murderer was caught. I can't risk her attempting something similar here." His face firmed with resolve. "It would be best simply to remove them to Edinburgh. She can settle herself at the town house, and the physician who was recommended to us can examine her."

I knew he was right. Alana's health had suffered on our journey, and I knew the last thing she needed was to worry over her children. I couldn't even blame her for feeling that way. As much as I believed Will to be harmless, I still felt a sliver of doubt. A sliver that had been there even before Gage had expressed his concerns in the middle of the night, though I had tried to deny it. I could not ask my sister to put up with that uncertainty, especially when it wasn't necessary for her even to be here.

I hunched my shoulders against the chill wind and watched a small boat bob across the water toward the tiny island. "What will you tell your aunt?"

"I don't know. Michael *did* withhold information from Caroline and her family." I opened my mouth to argue and Philip held up his hand to ward off my protest. "Perhaps it wasn't their right to know about William while they were courting, but he certainly should have informed Caroline and her oldest brother, James, about him when he asked for her hand."

I frowned at the frothy whitecaps racing toward the beach like pale horses. Philip was right. Michael had misled Caroline and her family, and no matter his intentions in doing so, it had been wrong. Sir Anthony had done the same thing to me and my father, though his reasons for doing so had been infinitely less honorable, and his purpose far more nefarious. Had we known that my future husband was marrying me so that he could force me to illustrate the anatomy textbook he was writing, saving the money it would cost to hire an artist and keeping the credit for himself, my father and I would never have agreed to the match. In truth, my father would likely have blackened Sir Anthony's name.

But his deception had not come to light prior to the ceremony, and I had said my vows, and entered my new husband's household, ignorant of what he had planned for me. That I hadn't revealed the truth to anyone while Sir Anthony lived had been my choice. Fear and shame and despair had ensured my silence as much as my husband's threats.

However, Michael's deception had been quite different from Sir Anthony's. While still poorly handled, at least Michael's dishonesty had been well-intentioned. Sir Anthony's had been purely self-serving. And at least Michael had had the decency to reveal the truth about his brother long before the wedding vows were spoken.

"In any case," Philip continued, unaware of my unsettled thoughts, "I'm not going to try to convince her to stay here, even if I thought that were possible. It just doesn't seem right for me to insist that Aunt Jane and Caroline remain here when I'm removing my own family."

"Does that mean you think Caroline shouldn't marry Michael?" I asked in distress.

He frowned, looking down at the crumbled leaves at his feet. "No. It's obvious they care for each other. And I don't know that you could find two finer people. But this problem with William . . ." He inhaled deeply and shook his head once. "It's not going to be smoothed over with just a heart-felt apology."

"Because Caroline won't be made a baroness after all," I guessed, knowing that Michael's dishonesty was not the insurmountable issue. "Unless, of course, William eventually dies without issue."

"Yes, that, and William's mental state."

Surprised by his answer, I turned to face him. "But surely it's obvious that his problems do not stem from a feeble family line. None of his ancestors were mad. And his current mental weakness can clearly be traced to the strains of war and his time spent in that asylum."

"It's probable that you are correct, but Aunt Jane won't see it that way. And I'm not certain I can either."

I stared at him, unable to believe what I was hearing. When I was finally able to speak, it was in a hard voice. "You think Will is unsafe."

"Kiera," he murmured in a placating voice. He reached out to cup my elbow, but I shifted out of his reach. He scowled. "I honestly don't know what to think about him. But I know that I don't feel comfortable with you spending time alone with him."

I narrowed my eyes at him. "Has Mr. Gage spoken with you?"

Philip's eyes crinkled at the corners. "About your safety?"

I stifled a curse, wondering how he'd gotten to Philip before me. Had he knocked on his door in the middle of the night? "I told him to stay out of this," I snapped.

"Yes, I heard you quite clearly in the Dalmays' drawing room," my brother-in-law told me almost in scolding.

I blinked up at him in confusion, trying to understand why he was talking about the confrontation in the drawing room.

His gaze sharpened as I realized Gage had not discussed me with him yet. "Unless you spoke with him another time."

"Of course not," I replied quickly. I wasn't about to admit

the man had visited me in my room later that night. Who knew how Philip would react? In his current state of mind, he might just do something foolish. Like call his friend out. Or, perhaps worse, insist Gage do the honorable thing and marry me—an outcome I couldn't even fathom.

"His behavior yesterday evening just proves that he has taken the same overprotective stance that you seem to have adopted," I rushed on to say before he could question me further. "Do I need to keep repeating myself? Will would never hurt me."

Philip stiffened, straightening to his greatest height, and I saw the muscle in his jaw twitch just like it did when he was refraining from saying something to my sister he knew he would regret later. I had never seen him do it while facing me before, but then, Philip and I seldom argued. "I don't care if you believe I'm being overprotective." He spoke carefully, enunciating his words. "But the fact is that while you are a part of my household, I am responsible for you. I am not going to just turn my head in the other direction and allow you to do whatever you please, particularly if your actions are so foolish as to threaten your safety in any way."

Something in my chest pinched at his words. I had always felt that Philip and I understood each other, and to hear him speak to me as if I was just another silly, irrational female hurt more than I would have admitted. "If you felt me to be so lacking in sense, I wish you would have told me before," I replied in a clipped voice. "I assumed you valued my intelligence. After all, you were the one who asked me to assist Gage with the murder investigation at Gairloch." An undertaking that had certainly threatened my safety. I had a scar on my side from a grazing bullet to prove it.

Philip's brow furrowed in distress and I instantly felt contrite for even bringing up the matter of my near death. I turned to stare out at the water, hugging my arms tighter to my chest. What was wrong with me? First I threw the shooting in Gage's face and then my brother-in-law's. I had never been one to go about deliberately hurting others before.

"Kiera," Philip murmured, stepping closer. He waited until I looked up at him to continue speaking. "I do value your intelligence. You know that."

My gaze dropped to the collar of his black greatcoat. I nodded.

"And you know I regret that you were harmed during Lady Godwin's murder investigation. Sometimes I feel like I should regret ever having asked you to take part in it." I opened my mouth to object, but he raised his hand to halt my words. "But I don't," he admitted.

I searched his gaze, trying to understand what he was telling me.

"I know that had you not taken part in that investigation, we may never have caught the real culprit, and several more people might have lost their lives."

I felt a surge of pride at his admission. After the removal of everyone from Gairloch Castle, we had avoided any discussion of the events of those dark days. I had no wish to relive those memories—well, most of them—more because of the pain and anger they caused me than any prolonged trauma or regret. But I had never stopped to consider why my sister and brother-in-law refrained from mentioning them. Was it possible that Philip, like Gage, had been feeling real guilt for what had happened to me?

"Perhaps that makes me a horrible man . . ."

"No," I said, reaching out to take hold of Philip's hand. I shook my head. "You are not going to take responsibility for the injuries done to me," I told him firmly. "And if you are going to insist on trying to, then you are also going to have to take responsibility for all the good that came of it."

His face was blank, clearly not understanding what I meant.

I turned away, knowing it would be easier to find the words if I wasn't looking at him. "I . . . was hiding, Philip," I began hesitantly. "We all know it. And the investigation forced me to move beyond that. To exert myself in ways I hadn't been. Not for many months. Not since . . ." I let my words trail away, knowing he understood. I took a deep breath to continue. "In a way, that investigation gave me a second chance to fight for myself again." I shook my head. "I never got to do that in London, after Sir Anthony's death, after those charges were brought against me. I was too beaten and scared to even try."

I risked a glance at Philip and saw the memory of the fragile, broken creature I had been when I first came to live with his family eighteen months ago reflected in his eyes.

I smiled sadly. "Lady Godwin's murder investigation gave me the chance to finally step forward and defend myself against the accusations made against me. To defy society's small-mindedness. And most importantly it proved to me that I *was* strong enough to survive this. That maybe I didn't have to spend the rest of my life hidden in the shadows." I squeezed his hand. "And none of that would have happened if you hadn't believed me capable enough to assist Mr. Gage. Despite his protestations to the contrary," I added at the last.

We shared a look of wry amusement.

"He was rather irritated with me for that at first," he admitted.

I scoffed. "Not nearly as irritated as he was with me. I had to work alongside the man, after all, and I was initially his chief suspect."

"But that didn't last long," Philip pointed out.

"No. He came around. Reluctantly."

Philip smiled. "Gage doesn't do anything that matters without reluctance. I think it's because of his mother."

"What do you mean?"

"She was quite ill for a long time, most of his boyhood, and died during his second year at Cambridge. He never talks about her, but I know they were close. Especially since his father was away at sea much of the time."

My heart clenched. The loss of a parent was always difficult, but something about the way Philip said he never talked about her told me Gage had taken his mother's death harder than most.

I followed the flight of a squawking kittiwake as it wheeled about the azure sky overhead before soaring toward the crumbling battlements of Banbogle Castle behind me.

"You know, you haven't answered me yet," Philip pointed out. His tone was well modulated, but I could see the tension in the turn of his neck as he looked out over the firth.

I didn't pretend to be ignorant about what he referred to. "I think you're right about Alana and the children. They are certain to be more comfortable in Edinburgh." I hesitated, not wanting to argue with him further, but prepared to do battle nonetheless.

"But?"

"But I would not. Not knowing I didn't at least try to help Will." I turned to meet his gaze, letting him know I was serious. "I'm through with being a coward, Philip."

He searched my eyes, as if looking for some sign of weakness. When he found none, he sighed. "And what am I supposed to tell Alana? You know she's going to worry about you."

"She'll understand," I assured him, hoping it was true. I knew I couldn't stop my sister from fretting, but I thought I could at least put my decision into perspective for her.

He frowned at the trees standing between Dalmay House and us. The colors of the leaves were brilliant in the early morning light, a feast for my artistic palate. The earthy scent of them only whetted my appetite more. It had been a long time since I'd painted someone against an autumnal backdrop, and I suddenly itched for my oils and a canvas. Perhaps I could convince Miss Remmington to pose for me here. As little as I cared for her troublemaking, her pale features would benefit greatly from such a colorful backdrop.

Philip turned to me, his features tight with frustration. For a moment I thought he knew how far my attention had wandered from the matter at hand, but then I realized that was unlikely. I waited for him to speak.

"All right," he said. "I will allow you to stay here."

I bristled at his choice of words, but knew better than to say anything if I was getting what I wanted.

"On one condition."

I lifted my eyebrows, wondering what it could be.

"You must promise me that you will not visit William Dalmay without Mr. Gage accompanying you."

I scowled at him fiercely. "No!"

"Then you will be journeying to Edinburgh with us if I have to drag you bodily into the carriage myself," he declared as calmly as if he were discussing the weather.

"Why can't it be Michael or one of Will's caretakers?"

"Because I don't trust them to have *your* best interests at heart."

"You don't trust Michael?"

"No," he stated decisively, surprising me with his forcefulness. "He has already shown he is willing to lie for his brother's benefit, heedless of the effect those lies have on the welfare of others. Think of how Caroline must feel. She clearly cares for Michael, and was ecstatic to be marrying him, and yet now she faces a broken engagement as well as the knowledge that her fiancé lied to her when his first consideration should have been for her above everyone else."

His argument silenced me, but only for a moment. "Then what about Lord Keswick?"

"Gage is the only one I trust to see to your safety, Kiera."

I clenched my fists at my sides. "But he does not want me to even speak with Will. He will keep me away from him, and then how am I supposed to help him or prove him harmless?"

"I will tell Gage that he must allow you to meet with Dalmay. However, you will have to yield to Gage's judgment as to whether he is in a calm state of mind." Seeing my livid expression, he shook his head against the other arguments forming in my mind. "I will not budge on this. If you wish to remain at Dalmay House, you will have to accept Gage's escort."

I ground my teeth in frustration and paced away from him to consider the matter. I was furious that Philip was playing me so easily into Gage's hand. How was I supposed to do Will any good with that infuriating man hanging over my shoulder? For all I knew, Gage would interfere with any attempts I made to meaningfully engage with Will.

No, that wasn't fair. Gage was not unreasonable. His presence would make my interactions with Will awkward, but not impossible. Gage might even have something useful to contribute; if he could set aside his ridiculous notions that Will was out to hurt me.

I huffed and returned my gaze to Philip, who waited for me to speak. I knew my brother-in-law was just looking out for me in the best way he thought he could. He couldn't know the history between Gage and me, how the man tied me in knots. Although he must realize that things had not ended happily between us at Gairloch. After all, he was there the morning I confronted Gage before he departed with the dawn mist. Being in such close proximity to Gage was going to be uncomfortable at best, particularly as he seemed determined to prove that Will was dangerous.

But then again, I suspected there was more to Gage's presence here than a simple visit to a friend, and I had a sinking feeling it had something to do with Will. How was I to uncover what that was if I avoided his company?

"Agreed," I bit out.

Philip looked as if he might want to press me on the issue but held back. I had never given him reason to doubt my word. Forcing the point would be insulting, and he clearly realized this. He gave me a single, decisive nod, and the matter was finished.

CHAPTER ELEVEN

Philip and I returned to the house via a path that wove through the woods south of Dalmay House to meet up with the drive several hundred feet from the manor. We passed through the main door we had entered upon our arrival the day before and into the grand entrance hall with its portraits and sweeping staircase. But before we could begin our ascent toward our assigned bedchambers, the butler intercepted us.

"My lord, my lady," he pronounced in solemn tones, "Mr. Dalmay wished to see you upon your return from your constitutional. May I have your things sent up to your rooms?"

Philip and I glanced at each other. Clearly the majordomo took his job seriously. He wasn't going to allow us to escape without following his master's wishes. I stifled a grin and permitted the man to help me out of my pelisse, and then handed him my gloves and bonnet.

"Very good. This way, please."

He led us through a set of doors and down a hallway carpeted in the same plush crimson as the stairs. Marble-topped tables stood between each doorway, each holding a vase of fresh flowers or the bust of some ancient Greek or Roman. On the walls above the flowers hung mirrors, reflecting the light spilling through the tall window at the end of the hall, while various uninspired landscapes graced the spaces behind the busts. At the second-to-last door on the right, the butler rapped twice before pushing it open.

We stepped into what appeared to be Michael's study, a rather masculine affair swathed in seal brown, coffee, and tan. Three of the walls were covered in dark oak paneling with recessed bookcases. A small fire crackled in the fireplace fashioned from the same wood on my left, but the majority of the light came spilling through the windows spanning the length of the wall across from me. The creamy tan brocade curtains had been thrown open to show the view across the sloping lawn all the way down to the firth. I wondered if the room's occupants had been able to see Philip and me traversing the path that skirted its shoreline just a short while ago, but from the looks of their expressions, I doubted they would have even taken notice.

Michael appeared to have been halted in the midst of pacing and stood awkwardly at the corner of his cluttered desk. Whatever he had been saying to Gage, who was seated in one of the Queen Anne–style chairs with cabriole legs clustered around the hearth, had not been agreeable. Gage's brow was pleated, his mouth tight with displeasure.

"Cromarty, Kiera, there you are." Michael strode toward us, a strange mixture of anxiety and relief stretching his features. "I trust you enjoyed your walk."

"Ah, yes, we did. Your grounds are lovely." I spoke up when Philip made no effort to reply. Out of the corner of my eye I could see him studying his friend. There was a suspicious gleam in his eye. One that Michael did not fail to notice.

"Excellent." The tone of his voice belied the wariness I saw creep over his features. "That will be all, Tomson."

The door clicked shut, and then Michael extended a hand toward the fireplace. "Won't you have a seat?"

I passed between the two men, hoping to break the tension that seemed to tether them like a taut cord. My ploy did not work, for the air remained heavy with their strained silence, but at least I heard their muffled footsteps follow me across the rug. Reaching up to finger the amethyst pendant I almost always wore, I selected the chair across the low table from Gage and farthest from the hearth. I found the atmosphere in the room cloying enough without the heat of the fire on my skin.

I glanced up to find Gage watching me, a wry smile twisting his lips. He looked at Philip and then back to me, and I understood what he was saying. I lifted my chin, determined not to feel defensive about speaking to my brother-in-law before he did this morning, for all the good it had done me. I was just glad Gage did not yet know he had gotten his way without even trying, for if he did, I knew his smirk would be insufferable.

Michael cleared his throat and shifted in his seat. "There's something I need to tell you." His gaze darted back and forth between Philip and me before finally settling on the floor between our feet. "I . . . haven't been entirely honest with you."

His eyes lifted briefly to see how we had taken this revelation and I had to struggle to keep my sense of foreboding from showing on my face. A quick survey of the others told me they had not taken the news any easier. Philip's countenance was dark, and Gage's brow was puckered again, but I couldn't say that either man appeared shocked.

"I told you that my brother never leaves the house without an escort. Well, that's not strictly true." The knuckles of his hands turned white where he gripped the arms of his chair. "He's escaped before. Twice."

"I thought you said he was secure," Philip said in a hard voice.

"I did," Michael admitted and then hastened to explain. "And he should be. That lock on the door at the end of the corridor is a recent addition, and he's yet to escape through it."

I swallowed the sour, acidic taste at the back of my mouth, hating to hear William spoken of in such terms. The man wasn't a criminal or a raving lunatic. At least, I didn't

124 · *Anna Lee Huber*

believe so. I glanced up at Michael through the screen of my eyelashes. But if he had lied about this, what else had he failed to disclose?

I suddenly wished I were seated closer to the fire.

"Where did he go?" Philip asked.

"I don't know. But both times he was found a short while later down by the firth, staring out at the water as if he'd simply gone for a stroll." Michael shrugged as if this baffled him.

"Was his appearance altered in any way?"

I did not fail to note that it was Gage who asked this question, but I did not react, wanting to know the answer myself.

Michael narrowed his eyes at him. "There were no signs of a struggle, if that's what you're hinting at. No, he actually looked peaceful, happy, if you can believe it." He tilted his head in thought. "I attributed it to his love of the water. You know, we thought he would join the Royal Navy. But in the end he surprised us all by following the family tradition of soldiering with the cavalry." A small but proud smile curled his lips. "The first ancestor of ours to do so was a Sir Roger Dalmay, a knight who went off to fight in the Crusades. Legend says his faithful dog kicked up such a fuss when Sir Roger tried to leave him behind, howling and crying, that he was forced to take the hound with him to the Holy Land. However one night, months after they'd gone, the residents at the old castle swore they heard the dog howling again, so loudly as to wake the dead. Not long after, they discovered Sir Roger had been slain about the same time. Tradition says the dog's howling is a portent of death to the lairds of Banbogle."

I shivered at the thought of a ghostly dog presaging my death, but Michael seemed to relish the tale.

Philip was not so easily distracted. "Then what of this missing girl? Is it true that William is not acquainted with anyone from Cramond, or was that also a lie?"

Michael frowned and looked as if he would like to protest

his friend's harsh words, but he must have accepted that the question was justified. "As far as I know, he is unacquainted with the people of Cramond, and I have no reason to suspect otherwise. William did not move here with the rest of us when Dalmay House was completed in 1817, choosing instead to remain at Swinton Lodge. And he seemed to have no memory of the building when I brought him here from Larkspur Retreat nine months ago."

"He could have met the girl during one of these escapes," Philip pointed out, somewhat needlessly, I felt.

"Yes. Yes, he could have," Michael admitted. Worry crinkled his brow.

"Now, just wait a minute," I interjected, surprised by their willingness to jump to conclusions. I glared at all three of them in turn. "There is no evidence to suggest that William has done anything wrong. So he escaped. I would think all of us would chafe under the confines placed around him, no matter how necessary or well-intentioned they are." Michael shifted guiltily in his seat. "You are making wild suppositions to suggest he sought out this girl and did some kind of harm to her before . . ." I waved my hands, trying to find the right words ". . . disposing of her body. Or do you think he's keeping her locked away somewhere, since no one can even say for certain that she is dead?" I added scornfully.

Gage arched his eyebrows at my tone, telling me just how little he was impressed by my scolding, and Philip seemed absorbed in his own thoughts. Only Michael appeared the least bit contrite, staring forlornly down at his feet.

I scowled at the gleaming wooden surface of the tea table, furious with each of the men before me. Why had Michael decided to lie? I could understand his desire to protect his brother, but all of this deception . . . it only compounded the problem. How could any of us know now whether he could be trusted? I had been counting on his support, his dependability, as I tried to help his brother, but how was I to trust that another of his half-truths wouldn't turn around and bite me?

And then there was Philip and his protective measures. Could he not see how unjustified his stance was? A year and a half earlier, had he and my brother made half the assumptions about me that they were making about Will, based on hearsay and conjecture, they would have gone along with Sir Anthony's friends and the rest of London's fickle mob and seen me hanged. If Philip was going to condemn Will, he should do it with fact, not fear and speculation.

As far as Gage was concerned, I simply wished he would stop interfering. He had walked away two months before without looking back, but now he wanted a say in how I conducted myself? He had sacrificed that right, if indeed he'd ever had it, when he climbed into his carriage and drove away from Gairloch. There had been no promises made between us, no intentions made clear, only the camaraderie of our investigation and the brief flare of attraction. He refused to share himself with me, and yet he continued to force his protection on me. Did he not realize how frustrating that was, how inappropriate? How it continued to tie me to him in a way I could not understand?

"There's something else, isn't there?" Gage said, breaking the silent standoff.

I followed his penetrating gaze to Michael, who sat hunched forward in his chair. He was eyeing Gage warily out of the corner of his eye. "What do you mean?"

"There's another reason you felt you should bring this to our attention. Lady Darby's right." He nodded to me. "You would not have doubted your brother's innocence with evidence as flimsy as this."

Philip sat forward, plainly believing Gage had a point.

I studied Michael's haggard face. It was obvious he had gotten as little sleep as Philip and I that night, maybe less, and I began to suspect he'd had many such nights. His complexion was wan, his features drawn, and dark circles ringed his eyes. He'd appeared healthy enough the previous evening, but another night of disturbed slumber had reclaimed its toll on his appearance. If I felt the weight of my own sleeplessness dragging at me, how much more so did it pull at Michael?

He shifted in his chair again, his leg twitching in time to his thoughts. "I'm simply worried for my brother. Lady Hollingsworth's words last night rattled me."

"As did Lady Darby's interaction with William?"

Michael's gaze, wide with panic and uncertainty, darted to Gage.

"It was clear to all of us how much it affected you," Gage elaborated. His voice was calm and unhurried, as one would speak to a sobbing child or a riled animal. "But was there something more to it?"

I watched him, wondering what he was hinting at. For whatever it was seemed to be disturbing Michael greatly. He jumped up from his chair and moved toward the fireplace, leaning over the flames with his hand pressed against the mantel.

I watched as Gage and Philip shared a look of grim anticipation. It stretched my already taut nerves past my endurance. "Whatever it is, I'm sure it can't be so awful," I told our host. "What could William possibly have done that has you so rattled?"

Gage's eyes were solemn, and I frowned at him in confusion.

"I'm not certain he did anything," Michael said to the fire. He heaved a sigh and pushed away from the hearth. "In fact . . ." he scraped a hand back through his hair ". . . I don't know why I'm giving Dr. Sloane's words any credence at all."

"The man who controls the lunatic asylum?" I asked in surprise.

He nodded. "He told me something when I returned with my petition signed by the local magistrate to collect William. Something I never believed, something I *still* don't believe. But . . ." His words trailed away.

"This girl's disappearance is making you doubt him," Gage guessed.

Michael nodded wretchedly, sinking back into his chair.

"What did Dr. Sloane say?" Philip prompted.

"He said . . ." He swallowed and tried again. "He said that William had . . ." he choked on the words ". . . raped and murdered a girl, a fellow inmate in the asylum."

I felt as if all the air had been sucked from my body. All I could do was stare at Michael in shock.

"When?" Gage seemed to be the only one with the presence of mind to ask questions. "How?"

Michael shook his head. "I don't know. I told him he was lying. I never wanted to hear any of the details."

"And he only told you this after you returned with the petition forcing him to allow you to remove your brother?" Gage's tone of voice held a tinge of skepticism in it—one most would not have heard, but I did—and I blessed him for it.

"He kept telling me I was making a terrible mistake by removing William from his care, but I refused to listen. The man was an oily, underhanded bastard." He pounded the arm of his chair with his fist. "I was not going to leave my brother in his institution." His breath rasped in and out of him as if he was imagining doing bodily harm to this Dr. Sloane. But then his face crumpled, and I could see the fear and doubt return. "But what if I was wrong?"

"You're not," I declared. "It doesn't matter what kind of gammon this doctor tried to feed to you. He obviously can't be trusted. Just look at William." I gestured toward the ceiling. "He *clearly* did not prosper under his care. I would rather see your brother consigned to perdition than returned to that man's tender mercies."

Michael began to look more hopeful, and then Gage spoke up. "Now, let's not be too hasty. I agree that this Dr. Sloane is not the right man to handle Lord Dalmay's care. And he certainly seems capable of lying to get his own way. But we must ask ourselves why he would do so. Why would he be so anxious to keep Lord Dalmay in his care that he would fabricate a heinous crime?"

"My father was paying him a significant amount of money every year for my brother's upkeep," Michael said.

I gestured to our host. "Well, there you go."

"But I told him I would no longer pay the fee," he added in dismay. "I said I refused to lend support to such a dishonest establishment."

"But if you hadn't gotten your brother released, would you really have done that?" Philip asked, looking at his friend kindly for the first time that morning. "Would you really have been able to withhold the funds without worrying that this Dr. Sloane would have punished William for it?"

Michael sank his head into his hand. "I don't know."

"And Sloane would have seen that weakness. So it still could be about the money."

"Were you allowed to visit William in his room?" I asked Michael. "Were you allowed inside the asylum at all?"

"No. Not past Dr. Sloane's office, at any rate. He has burly guards stationed at each of the doors, and I wasn't allowed even a peek past them into the confines of the asylum."

"Not even when you returned that last time to collect your brother?" Gage asked in some surprise.

He shook his head. "No. William was brought out to me." His face darkened. "They had him in chains."

Anger sparked inside me, and I stoked it, wanting it to burn away the other uncomfortable emotions churning in my gut. "Then William's release could mean the loss of another valuable commodity for Dr. Sloane."

The three men turned to look at me.

"Secrecy."

I could tell I had grabbed their attention, particularly Gage, who seemed to be mulling something over in his mind that he didn't like.

"Has William talked about what happened to him there?" Philip asked.

Michael frowned. "Not much. He's mentioned a few

things to me, but most of what I know has come from studying his drawings."

I leaned forward. "Like the ones we saw last night?"

He nodded.

"Would he talk to his manservants?" This would seem a sensible question to Philip, who was far more familiar with his valet than most gentlemen.

Michael narrowed his eyes, considering the matter. "Maybe Mac. But I really don't know."

Philip blew out a long breath and sank deeper in his chair. "So we don't actually know what William witnessed in the asylum, or whether it would cause Dr. Sloane alarm if it got out."

"I think just the fact that he was willing to bypass the proper channels to take Will in as a patient says a lot about Dr. Sloane and his 'retreat.' " I sneered.

"Why on earth didn't your father get a second opinion?" Philip asked in bewilderment.

We lapsed into silence. There was no answer to that. None of us knew what the old Lord Dalmay could possibly have been thinking, least of all Michael, who looked utterly overwhelmed and dejected.

"It's been troubling you greatly, hasn't it?" Gage told Michael. "What Dr. Sloane told you?" His friend slowly lifted his head to look at him. "You don't want to believe it, and yet you have no way of disproving it without asking your brother. But you don't want to ask him, because you're afraid of what he will say. Will he admit to it? Will he deny it? Will he even remember it at all?"

The stricken look on Michael's face was all that was needed for us to know that Gage spoke the truth. "He was so fragile. You should have seen him when I first brought him here. He could barely recall my name." He shook his head. "I couldn't ask him about it. I didn't want to ask him about it. I didn't want to make him think I doubted him."

I wrapped my arms around myself and turned to stare out at the bright light pouring through the windows. I wished I were standing next to the firth again with the sun beating down on me, no matter how stiff the wind.

"What if William genuinely doesn't remember? How will we ever discover the truth?" I demanded of myself as much as them, desperately wanting an answer.

Philip's voice was kind. "With so little to go on, we may never know."

Gage frowned. "But if he killed a woman . . . ?"

"*If. If* he killed a woman, that's what's key here. And all that connects William Dalmay to a dead woman is Dr. Sloane's word."

Gage rubbed his finger over his lips, considering what Philip had said. "But what about this missing girl?"

"What about her?" I asked.

"Well, clearly Dalmay is worried that his brother may have had something to do with her disappearance; otherwise he would never have brought any of this up for discussion."

I turned to Michael, disheartened to see that Gage was right.

"I don't think he did." He tried to sound assertive. "I don't think he knew her at all. But . . . how am I to be absolutely certain?" He seemed tormented by the possibility, and I couldn't bear to see him doubting his brother that way. I couldn't bear feeling that I doubted him myself.

"Then we'll just have to go about proving he's not involved," I declared.

Michael looked confused. "How do we do that?"

"We'll simply have to find this missing girl."

"But we know nothing of her disappearance," Gage said dampeningly, but I could see the spark of interest in his eyes.

"Well, that's easily remedied. Michael, can you arrange a meeting with the girl's father as soon as possible?"

"Of course."

"Then we should pay a visit to whatever authorities are handling the investigation into her disappearance and learn what they've uncovered so far."

"They won't appreciate our interference," Gage told me, though I noticed he had inferred his assistance in the matter by using the word *our* instead of *your*.

My heart began to beat faster at the realization that Gage and I would be working together again.

"Maybe not." I arched my eyebrows. "But has that ever stopped you before?"

A slow smile spread across his face. "No."

An answering smile curled my lips. "I thought not."

CHAPTER TWELVE

"Philip tells me you've decided to stay." Alana's voice was carefully modulated, but I could hear her concern and see it in the reflection of her bright blue eyes in the mirror. I was relieved at least to hear that my brother-in-law hadn't decided to resume his campaign to convince me to retreat to Edinburgh with them. After the revelations in the study, I had been prepared for further objections or, even worse, for Philip to make good on his threat to remove me forcefully from Dalmay House.

I watched as her maid secured the last few pins in her hair. "Yes."

She reached out to fiddle with the hairbrushes on the vanity before her. "Do you think that's wise?"

The maid moved to the corner of the bureau, bottles clinking as she repacked my sister's valise. It was clear that she was listening even if she was trying to be as unobtrusive as possible.

"I'm not sure that wisdom is the predominating consideration in this matter, but, yes, I believe I'm using good judgment."

My sister's gaze locked with mine. "Jenny," she told her maid. "Give us a moment."

The maid glided silently across the carpet and closed the door behind her with a soft click.

Alana inhaled deeply. "Are you sure you won't reconsider?"

I crossed the room to rest my hands on her shoulders and smiled sadly at her reflection. "Yes."

She sighed and dropped her head. The scent of her French perfume wafted up, so similar to the fragrance our mother had worn, and made my heart clench. I knew she had chosen that particular cologne on purpose, but I wasn't sure she realized I was aware of its sentimentality.

Alana nodded in resignation. "I knew it was silly to ask, but I guess I felt I had to try." She grinned sheepishly and reached back to clasp my hand where it rested on her shoulder. "Of course I realized you couldn't remain with me forever, but I never thought I would be saying good-bye so soon."

I squeezed her shoulder in reassurance. "It won't be for long. Just until William is better able to cope. You understand why I must try to help him?" I asked, suddenly anxious for her to know I wasn't abandoning her.

Her penetrating gaze told me she understood far better than I could have hoped. "I do."

I leaned forward to wrap my arms around her, pressing my cheek to hers. "Promise me you will take care of yourself. And this troublesome little one," I added, making my sister sniffle and giggle. "Listen to what your physician tells you. Unless he tells you nonsense, like you should be eating less. You're eating for two, and once you get to Edinburgh and your stomach stops protesting, you need to put some weight back on." I stood up to shake my finger at her. "I expect you to have gained at least a stone the next time I see you."

"All right . . ."

"Don't let Philip and this physician naysay me on this. You and I know better what you need than two silly men."

Alana turned to grab hold of my wagging finger. "Kiera . . ."

"And I expect you to send for me if you need me. No

hesitating. I'll be the one to decide whether you're being daft once I see you."

"Kiera," Alana said in a sharper voice, pulling me closer.

"Promise me," I ordered, feeling terrified that something might go wrong with Alana or the baby while I was away. I had never seriously considered such a thing happening, but now I was worried I was doing the wrong thing by staying at Dalmay House.

Alana clasped both of my hands between her own and stared reassuringly into my eyes. "I promise."

I nodded and dropped my gaze to her too-flat belly. Swallowing against the lump that had formed at the back of my throat, I reached out to press my hand to the deep claret fabric of her traveling costume. "And you behave in there, you hear me? Or you'll have your aunt Kiera to answer to." I had intended to be stern, but my voice emerged much more like a caress.

I straightened to find my sister watching me with a strange smile curling the corners of her lips.

"What?" I demanded.

She shook her head. "I've just always been the mothering one. It's a bit strange to find our roles reversed."

I crossed my arms over my chest and turned my head to stare out the window to my right.

"And . . . kind of nice," she admitted.

I glanced back to find a welcome glow cresting her wan cheeks.

I reached out to run a thumb over the dark purple circle under one of her eyes. "Did you get any sleep last night?"

Alana tilted her head. "Are you saying I don't look my best?"

I arched an eyebrow in scolding.

"Don't worry, dearest," she told me, rising to her feet. "The drive to our town house is less than ten miles. I'll be able to rest tonight."

I knew she was right, but I wouldn't stop worrying about her until I knew she had received a full night's sleep and passed a few days without losing the contents of her stomach. "Send me a note to let me know you've arrived safely," I requested, sinking into the chair she had vacated.

"Of course."

Alana pulled the evening gown she had worn the previous night out of the wardrobe and laid it over the golden coverlet on the bed, and then turned back to pull out two more dresses. I knew my sister had no intention of actually doing the packing—that was her maid's job—but she needed something to do with her hands while she worked around to asking me about whatever was on her mind. I suspected it had something to do with William Dalmay, but I should have guessed my sister was contemplating something far more treacherous.

"Philip told me about the promise he extracted from you."

"Yes?" I replied cautiously, knowing that careless tone. Wiser people than I had failed to heed it and walked straight into whatever trap Alana had set for them.

Realizing I wasn't fooled, she turned to look at me. "Why are you pretending to be so adverse to his company?"

"Whose company?" I asked, feigning ignorance.

"Give over, Kiera. You know exactly who I'm speaking of." She crossed her arms over her chest and leaned into the bed with her hip. "You can't just ignore him. You're going to have to speak with Mr. Gage."

I glared at the pale silk wallpaper between the bedchamber's two windows and wished my sister would mind her own business. If I had wanted her advice on Gage, I would have asked for it.

"Are you worried there's something between him and Miss Remmington?"

I scoffed. "No."

"Because if you are, that's just silly . . ."

"I'm not," I told her firmly.

"Good," Alana replied, seeming to be at a loss for words. Unfortunately that lasted only for a moment. "Then why are we back to the same antagonizing behavior that began your acquaintance?" I opened my mouth to deny it, but she spoke over me. "Don't think I missed the looks you sent his way last night. And Philip told me about your argument after I left the drawing room. You do realize the man is showing every sign that he cares."

I scowled and mumbled under my breath, "Except being honest with me."

She frowned. "Did you ask him why he left Gairloch the way he did?"

I glanced up at her, suspecting for the first time that she really did know more about what went on between Gage and me than she let on. "I tried, but the man is as tight-lipped as a corpse. You realize, I know next to nothing about him. And what I do know I've had to glean from others' comments."

Alana smiled in commiseration. "I'm sure you know far more about him than you think. At least, as it pertains to what matters. You're just missing some of the details."

"*All* the details," I groused.

Alana crossed the room to rub her hand over my back. "Give him time," she told me gently. "Men are secretive creatures—Mr. Gage more than most. When he's ready, he'll tell you. And when he does, you'll know just how much he esteems you."

M y maid was harder to convince of the necessity of my staying at Dalmay House. Upon returning to my chamber to change out of my walking ensemble into a morning dress, I found Lucy preparing to pack my bags. And when I told her to do the reverse, and unpack the rest of the gowns that had remained in my trunk, she didn't hold back from conveying her displeasure. She pouted and fussed and, as she'd done the previous night, tugged and jostled me as she helped me to dress. I was so out of sorts with her by the time we finished that I nearly ordered her to return to Gairloch on the next mail coach. The Dalmays would have a maid I could borrow for the duration of my stay, and I could find a new lady's maid when I reached Edinburgh. All that kept me from doing so was a last-minute confession in which Lucy once again admitted her anxieties about William's much-gossiped-about "malady." But, in light of Lucy's generally poor attitude and performance over the past week, my sympathy extended only so far, and I left my bedchamber before I said something I would later regret.

Charging down the corridor, I turned the corner to find Gage and Philip standing near the top of the grand staircase in heated conversation. My brother-in-law's back was to me, but I could hear him speaking in sharp, clipped tones, even if I could not make out the words, while Gage glared at him.

My steps slowed. I did not particularly want to encounter either of them at that moment, but given my intended destination and my promise to Philip, I knew I couldn't avoid Gage for long. I considered postponing my plans and retreating to my room, where more of Lucy's theatrics awaited, or to Alana's room, where her maid would simply ignore my presence, but at that moment Gage's gaze shifted, bringing me into view over Philip's shoulder. I could see the icy displeasure he had aimed at Philip in the depths of his eyes. Philip glanced my way to see what Gage was looking at, his face still tight with anger, before turning back to finish whatever he had been saying.

I narrowed my eyes, having a strong suspicion they were discussing me. I stiffened my spine and marched toward them as both men turned to observe my approach.

"When will you be departing?" I asked Philip.

"Within the hour."

I nodded coolly. "I shall be there to see you off. In the meantime . . ." I turned to face Gage, deciding now was as good a time as any to test his compliance with Philip's and my wishes. "I would like to pay a visit to William. Will you escort me?" The words tasted like dirt coming from my lips, but I managed to choke them out with what I thought was an admirable display of indifference.

I was sure Gage was aware of my displeasure anyway, but either because of Philip's mitigating presence or his own decision to exercise restraint, he chose not to make an issue of it. His eyes flicked to my brother-in-law before returning to me. "Certainly."

He offered his arm and I grudgingly accepted it, allowing him to steer me toward the staircase leading to the next floor. We were silent as we climbed the steps, both wrestling with our own thoughts. I knew that Gage didn't want to consent to my seeing Will as much as I didn't want him to accompany me. Neither of us was happy with this arrangement. At least we were in agreement on that.

I turned to him in question as he reached into his inside coat pocket and extracted a key.

"Dalmay gave me a copy of the key when Cromarty informed him of his . . . stipulation for your staying here," he explained.

I frowned, wondering what exactly Philip had told Michael and Gage, but was glad I hadn't been present for the conversation. I wasn't certain I would have been able to hold on to my temper.

He hesitated at the door, and I looked up to find him studying me. He seemed to be weighing his words. "Kiera," he began, "I never meant to . . ."

"Please," I interrupted, holding up my hand. "Let's not do this. Not now." I was so tired of arguing. I didn't want to have yet another quarrel with Gage. Especially not when my thoughts should have been focused on Will so I could prepare myself for whatever I was about to encounter.

I pressed my free hand to my temple and risked a glance at Gage's face. A pucker across his brow told me he was not happy that I'd cut him off, but he turned back to the door without a word to insert the key into the lock. His shoulders were rigid with tension.

I could tell I had hurt his feelings in some way. Perhaps he had been about to make a peace offering, and I had silenced him before he could speak. But I couldn't be certain, and in my present state of mind, I simply couldn't risk the possibility of another disagreement.

The lock released with a twist of the key, and Gage pushed open the door on its well-oiled hinges.

"Did Michael even really need to give you a key?"

He looked down at me with a frown.

I nodded toward the keyhole. "You probably could have picked that lock with unsettling ease." I tilted my head. "Unless the skills you bragged to me about at Gairloch were exaggerated."

Gage arched a brow. "I never bragged. But, yes, I could undoubtedly pick this lock." He ran his fingers over the metal.

I watched as he locked the door behind us, using the key. "I taught myself to pick the lock to my art studio door," I told him, wondering why I felt the need to share this bit of information.

"Did you?" he replied with indifference.

I fought a frown. "It was more difficult than I expected, but I think I've mastered it now." I was rather proud of the accomplishment, even though I wasn't certain that said much for my character.

"You mean you've mastered the ability to pick that one type of lock," he informed me. "There are many more."

This time I did scowl at his insufferably pompous tone. "I know that. But it's a beginning."

At this proclamation, he finally looked down at me. He sighed in resignation. "I have no one to blame but myself, do I?"

I tilted my head in question.

"I should never have told you I could pick locks or shown you how easily it could be done."

I only smirked.

We drew to a stop outside Will's rooms and my anxiety returned. I wasn't certain in what state we would find him. Michael had said that the episodes similar to what we witnessed the night before rarely happened now, but how did his brother behave in the meantime? Because Michael thought it necessary to keep him behind locked doors, I found it hard to believe he behaved like his normal self, and I was more than a little afraid I wouldn't be able to handle whatever I saw without losing my composure. Fatigue always blunted my self-control, making it far too easy for me to lose my temper or, worse, the reins on my softer emotions, and the last thing I wanted to do was to break down in tears in front of Will. But I'd promised him I would visit him again, and I couldn't be certain when I would have another chance. I didn't want him to think I had lied, not for a second.

I pressed a hand to my hollow stomach. I had barely eaten anything at breakfast, too uneasy after our discussion in Michael's study to eat more than a piece of dry toast and sip a cup of tea. I wondered if I would soon regret that.

Gage turned to look down at me, much as Michael had done the evening before. I summoned my courage and nodded with as much assurance as I could muster. He hesitated a moment longer before lifting his fist to knock.

A strange man opened the door to our summons, and I realized that this must be Donovan, Will's other manservant, the one with medical training.

He certainly was brawny, as Lucy had alluded to, with short-cropped brown hair. His plain lawn shirt stretched tautly across his shoulders and chest, and I could see the outline of his biceps through the material. Even his forearms, clearly visible at the edges of his rolled sleeves, were well-defined. He eyed us neutrally, though I knew he must have been at least a little curious as to why we were there.

"We're here to see Lord Dalmay," Gage told him.

Donovan took Gage's failure to elaborate in good stride and stepped back to allow us entry. I hoped Michael had warned him we might be stopping by and that he wasn't always so unconcerned about the visitors William received.

"He's through there," he said with a nod toward the

bedchamber door, which stood ajar. He paused to examine us one moment longer before striding across the room. "M'lord, ye have visitors," he called through the doorway.

I tried to ignore the pounding of my heart as I allowed Gage to guide me across the parlor and into the bedchamber. All that had been toppled and tousled the night before had been put to rights. The drapes covering the room's tall windows had been thrown open to allow in the morning light, illuminating all the dark corners and crevices that had been cast in shadow a dozen hours before. In fact, only the crude sketches covering two of the walls, which I tried to ignore, and the haggard appearance of the room's occupant hinted that anything unsettling had ever happened at all.

Will sat in a sturdy chair positioned before the window. The sunlight shining through the glass haloed his honey-brown hair and allowed me to see that it was now liberally dusted with silver. Unfortunately the bright light did nothing to soften the harsh lines of his gaunt face or to hide the dark circles around his eyes that gave them a sunken, bruised quality. He was dressed like any country gentleman, minus the frock coat, in a pale waistcoat and buff trousers; however, the clothing hung awkwardly on his too-thin body. They were not ill fitting—I could tell they had been tailored for him—he simply did not have the flesh and muscle to fill them out. A half-full glass of beige liquid stood on the table at his elbow next to a book left unheeded.

When we entered the room, he seemed as if he had been lost in thought, his face turned toward the window and his chin propped on his fist, and it took him a moment to return to the present. A subtle wash of pleasure spread across his features at the sight of us. It was a small display of emotion, but in so sharp a contrast to the blankness of his features and the dimness in his eyes the night before that it made something tight inside my chest loosen.

"Kiera. Mr. Gage." His voice had the same husky quality as before, but it was much less strained. He shifted forward as if to rise, but I waved him back down.

"I may be an invalid," he scolded, ignoring my motion, "but I can still rise when a lady enters the room." The soft light in his eyes removed any of the sting from his words, but I flushed regardless.

He reached out to me slowly. All of his movements seemed sluggish and blurred, as if each action took great thought and effort. His hands trembled in my grasp as he pulled me closer, trailing his gaze over my face with keen intensity, as if he was starved for the sight of me, of anyone familiar. "It's wonderful to see you," he murmured.

I blushed brighter. "You, too."

And it was. Last night had been a shock. Today, with the bright sun chasing away the shadows, and some of the light returned to Will's eyes, it felt more like I was welcoming home a long-lost friend. I could embrace the joy, the sweetness of it, and feel some pleasure in his presence, even with my lingering worries over his health and the state of his mind, not to mention the concerns Michael had shared with us earlier in his study.

Releasing me, he stretched out a hand toward Gage. If his greeting was not particularly warm, it also held no rancor. Gage responded in kind, though I could also read the watchfulness in his gaze. He was suspicious, and more than a little curious about our interaction. And, if I was interpreting him correctly, even a bit displeased by it. I didn't know whether I felt annoyed or flattered. Perhaps a little of both.

Will's arms shook slightly as he lowered himself back into his chair, and I could tell he was not fully recovered from his incident the previous evening. I hoped his energy was sufficient enough to endure our visit without him suffering for it later. I had no wish to impose on him the overwhelming fatigue that had made it impossible for him even to carry a spoonful of soup from the bowl to his mouth the night before. In any case, our visit would need to be brief if I was to see my sister and her family off.

I settled into the chair closest to Will's, glancing over my shoulder out the window where he had been staring when we entered. "Oh, my," I gasped. "What a view." His rooms looked out over the trees northeast of the manor house toward the ruins of Banbogle Castle in the distance. On such a fine autumn day, the forest blazed with fiery color and the gray stones of the castle glistened in the sun. The sounds of twittering birds and rustling leaves came in through the window, which was open a crack. In the distance, I thought I could even detect the bass rumble of the firth's water rolling against the shoreline. How peaceful it must be for Will.

"Yes," he told me, staring at the vista beyond my shoulder. "My brother made certain I had the best view in the manor."

And, I couldn't help but think, it must be far nicer than the outlook from his cell at the Larkspur Retreat. If, in fact, he'd had any view at all.

Inchkeith Island was a treeless lump of granite in the middle of the windswept Firth of Forth, with nothing to recommend it save for its isolation. At least once in known history it had been used to quarantine people with disease, and a bizarre scientific experiment commissioned by King James IV had taken place there in the late fifteenth century to discover the original language of mankind. The only reason I knew anything about it was because of my late husband's fondness for medical absurdity, as well as his appreciation of the novelist Sir Walter Scott, who had derided the test, and its clearly feigned results, for its utter foolishness.

"Will there be anythin' else, m'lord?" Donovan asked Will as he bent over the table next to him and gathered up his employer's breakfast dishes. I noticed that much of the food had gone uneaten.

Will looked to me. "Tea?"

"Uh, no, thank you."

Gage shook his head.

Donovan nodded in confirmation. The china clinked together as he hefted the tray. I frowned as he disappeared through the door, leaving it standing open behind him. I wondered why the servant had not tried to get Will to eat more of his breakfast. Or was my old friend just much more willful than I remembered?

I turned back to find both men watching me. Gage's stare was knowing, as if he had followed the bent of my thoughts and shared my curiosity, while Will's was more thoughtful. He seemed content to sit in comfortable silence and enjoy our company. Perhaps his time in the asylum had taught him the value of such companionable stillness.

I, however, felt no such ease. I shifted in my seat while I racked my brain trying to find a safe topic of conversation that was neither inane nor prying.

"It's all right, you know," Will surprised me by saying. "We can talk about it. I promise I won't fly up into the boughs." He smiled sadly. "Contrary to what you saw last night, I am usually in my right mind."

I flushed. Was my discomfort so easy to read?

"Oh, I know," I hastened to assure him. "Michael told us how much you've improved since your . . . release. He explained how last night's . . . ah . . ." I fumbled, trying to come up with the right word ". . . episode has become a rarity."

"And yet that must be hard to believe, since you've seen me no other way," he replied, not unkindly, before glancing significantly toward Gage.

I burned with shame, cursing Philip for forcing me to bring him along as a guardian. Will was not fooled. He knew why Gage had accompanied me.

"It's all right," he assured me, yet again. "I understand why Mr. Gage is here." His gaze shifted to him. "And though I would like to be insulted, I can't. Not knowing I would insist upon the same thing were our situations reversed."

Gage, who had at least had the grace to look uncomfortable when Will was speaking, now shared a more level look with the man.

Still smarting with embarrassment, I blurted out, "Well, I didn't want him to come." Gage's eyes snapped to mine. "His presence seemed entirely unnecessary."

"I can well believe that." Will's eyes crinkled with

amusement. "You always were quite stubborn and independent."

I scowled, wanting to scold him for calling me stubborn, especially after Gage had done so unjustly only the previous night, but I couldn't. Not when the humor that had flickered so briefly in his gray eyes faded.

"But . . . perhaps . . . it is necessary."

I searched his face, not wanting to believe he truly meant those words. But from the pain and uncertainty that tightened his features, it was all too apparent he did. A chill ran down my spine like an icy raindrop.

"You can't believe that," I protested. "I know you would never hurt me."

His words were bleak. "I hope not."

I wanted to stop up my ears, to deny what I was hearing. Did he not understand how that sounded? I could feel Gage's eyes watching him, watching me, weighing the truth of his words. What was Will thinking? What did he know?

"Why would you say such a thing?" I demanded, my voice cracking in distress.

"Kiera." Will leaned toward me. His voice was gentle, as it had been ten years before when he was soothing a distraught fifteen-year-old who had been told her paintings were no good. "I *want* to believe that I would never harm you. That I would never harm *any* woman. And, in my right mind, I know I never would. But . . ." He sank back into his chair with a dejected sigh. "I'm not always myself," he admitted guardedly.

There was such despair in his gaze that it wrenched something inside of me.

"I don't know what happens to me. And I can't seem to control it." He shook his head in obvious frustration. "I thought I was getting better, that I had finally put those moments behind me." His voice dropped to almost a whisper. "I guess I was wrong."

I glanced at Gage, who was studying Will with a mixture of wariness and compassion.

"Do you have any recollection of what happens to you during those times?" I ventured to ask him. "Michael suggested it's like you go someplace else. Somewhere he can't reach you."

His brow furrowed. "All I know is that one moment I'm fine and the next I'm not. I'm . . . there."

My stomach clenched. "The asylum?"

He nodded. His eyes were unfocused, staring off into the distance.

"Do you ever . . . return . . . to the war?" I asked, remembering all he had told me a decade before about his time on the continent during the war with France.

His gaze lifted to meet mine before drifting away again. "Sometimes. But usually it's that *hellhole*." He spat out the word angrily.

I couldn't fault the man for his rage, and, in fact, I welcomed it. It was comforting somehow to see him express his fury at what had happened to him. I found it far more disturbing when he faced me with such resigned acceptance.

"And the drawings?"

He looked up at me as I worked out how to ask my question.

"Is that . . ." I tried again. "Are they representations of what happened there?"

Will had never hid the darkness inside of him from me before, even if he had hidden his paintings, and he didn't do so now either. "Yes. Exaggerated. But . . ." He heaved a sigh. "Yes."

I glanced at Gage, who was watching me, his brow furrowed in concern. I turned away to look up at the wall on my left, covered in Will's crude sketches, for the first time since our arrival. The light of day had softened the charcoal's harsh lines, but the drawings' contents were still disturbing, particularly if they depicted fact and not just the fevered imaginings of a troubled man. My gaze snagged on the image of the man having his head held underwater by two burly figures standing behind him.

I swallowed the lump that had formed in my throat before asking cautiously, "Did these things happen to you?"

Will seemed hesitant to respond, and that, in and of itself, was answer enough. "Some of them," he reluctantly admitted as I rose to my feet.

I wrapped my arms around myself and paced before the wall of drawings, no longer able to sit still. My stomach churned and my nerves prickled. My legs were ready to take flight, to carry me far from here so that I wouldn't have to face what had happened to Will. So that I wouldn't have to accept that human beings could be so cruel.

But, of course, I already knew they could. I had paced my bedchamber in Sir Anthony's town house in much the same manner on the night he had told me I would be assisting with his dissection the next day or be forced to live without my art forever. And on the evening not long after his death when his colleagues had accused me of unnatural tendencies and promised to send the Bow Street Runners for me. My mind had rebelled just as assiduously then as it did now, wanting to block out the truth of Will's words, the painful reality etched in his eyes.

"Perhaps I shouldn't have been so frank," Will said. "But . . . Michael told me a little bit about what happened to you. About what your husband made you do."

I stopped pacing to look at him.

"And I thought, maybe, you, of all people, would understand, even just a little bit." His gray eyes flickered with a hope that I could tell he was afraid, and possibly ashamed, to feel. "You always saw more than most people did."

I had no words for him. The knot inside my chest was too tight. So I simply nodded.

His head dropped back onto his chair cushion with relief and he closed his eyes. I could see the tight lines around his mouth and the ashy cast to his complexion, and I worried we had exhausted him.

"We should let you rest now," I told him.

Will didn't even try to object, or rise from his chair,

which told me just how tired he truly was. "But you will come again?"

"Of course," I assured him.

He nodded listlessly. "Then you can tell me how you ended up married to that cantankerous sod in the first place."

His irreverent comment surprised a smile out of me.

Gage waited for me near the doorway, and I glanced over my shoulder one last time to find Will already nodding off to sleep. I turned back to see Donovan seated to the side of the door in a straight ladder-back chair. His placement had enabled him to listen to every word of our conversation. Although there was nothing outwardly wrong with his presence or the chair's positioning, it bothered me nonetheless, perhaps merely because I had been unaware of it.

Donovan rose to his feet as we passed and I could feel his eyes tracking me across the room, but when I peeked in his direction they were carefully directed elsewhere.

CHAPTER THIRTEEN

"Thank you," I told Gage begrudgingly as we turned onto the corridor that would lead us back to the staircase and the main part of the house.

He glanced down at me in question.

"For not directing Will's and my conversation where you wanted it to go." Which is what I'd fully expected him to do.

He turned his face forward again, hiding his eyes from me. "I thought it best to allow it to wander where it would."

I crossed my arms over my chest. "His admission didn't mean anything, you know. Just because he accepted your accompanying me on my visits as necessary doesn't mean he's truly dangerous to me, or anyone else."

"I know," he said.

I glanced up at him, expecting to receive another lecture on Will's potential for violence and my not taking chances, but he surprised me.

"In fact, I'm actually heartened by the fact that he's so wary of himself, contrary as that may seem." He stopped before the locked door and turned to look down at me, catching my frown. "A man who was more certain of himself, even as he lapses into these trances, would be far more dangerous. Simply the fact that he has contemplated what he might be capable of when he's not in his right mind says a great deal in his favor."

I pondered his words.

"Now, that does not mean I believe it's safe for you to visit him alone," he hastened to add before the argument could even enter my head. "But . . ." He pursed his lips, not seeming eager to continue. "I'm less uneasy."

I nodded, knowing that I shouldn't push but accept his admission as the peace offering it was. I stared down at the toes of my slippers peeking out from the hem of my dress. "He seemed genuinely distressed by the possibility he might be capable of harming someone."

Gage was quiet for so long that I looked up to see if he was listening. His eyes were trained on me with a strange intensity. "Yes, he does," he finally admitted.

I tilted my head, trying to read his inscrutable gaze. "But I don't think he has. I believe if he thought he had, or found some kind of evidence to suggest he had, he would admit it. To someone."

He sighed and fingered the key in his hand. "You may be right. But what if he doesn't know?" I opened my mouth to protest, but he pressed on, determined to make his point. "What if someone covered for him?"

I frowned, understanding what he was hinting at, and not liking that I had to consider it.

"You can't tell me that Michael wouldn't do just about anything to protect his brother."

"But he's the one who mentioned his worries over the missing girl and Sloane's claims that he murdered someone at the asylum. Why admit what he did if he wants to protect his brother?"

"Maybe he feels guilty. Maybe he doesn't know for sure his brother did anything wrong. Perhaps he covered up more than just the fact that his brother escaped the manor a few times unescorted. Michael wants to know the truth, but he's not ready to condemn his brother yet."

I scowled at him. "That's an awful lot of supposition."

"You're right," he admitted easily enough. "But the point I'm trying to make is that, while I believe William Dalmay is being honest, at least as much as his mental state has made him capable of, I think Michael has been deliberately misleading. And I think he has more yet to reveal."

Gage's pale eyes had gone hard, and I had to look away. I was forced to admit I held the same worries about Michael, and it was more than a little unsettling to find that a man I thought I could trust was turning out to be so unreliable. But it had happened before, and in far more difficult circumstances.

Gage unlocked the door and guided me through.

"I wanted to ask him," I told him, hearing the click of the lock being thrown back in place. "I wanted to ask Will if he knew anything about Miss Wallace or this girl in the asylum and end all of this ridiculous speculation." I wrapped my arms tighter around my middle, trying to soothe the worry tying my stomach in knots. I shook my head. "But I couldn't. Not seeing him like that, so tired and worn down. He could barely lift his head off the back of the chair in the end. It just didn't seem fair to question him like that. Besides, what genuine proof do we have to involve him in these matters?"

Gage reached out to clasp my shoulders, forcing me to look up at him. "You were right to wait." His eyes were kind. "There's no reason to alarm William until and unless it's absolutely necessary. As you said before, I think if he had something he believed he needed to tell us, he would do so. It can do no good to worry him over matters that may have nothing to do with him."

I nodded, grateful for his reassurance.

"In any case, Michael would not have thanked us for questioning his brother without his being present, and though I'm cross with him right now, his wishes on that matter should be respected. Now, come." He turned me toward the stairs. "I'm sure Cromarty and your sister are eager to depart and waiting for us to make an appearance."

The expression on his face was grim as we turned the corner to the central staircase.

"You know, I can continue down myself," I said, guessing at the source of his distress. "I'm sure they wouldn't be insulted if you missed their leave-taking."

He sighed. "No. I'm a gentleman. I'll not snub your sister or her husband simply because we've had a disagreement." His lips twisted, and he added under his breath, "Though I do hate it when Cromarty's right."

I had to agree, even though I didn't know exactly what they'd argued about. Except that it had to do with me.

When I had anticipated Philip and Alana's departure to be something of an emotional occasion, I had failed to account for the presence of the children. My nieces and nephew were simply not capable of making a peaceful good-bye, and for once I was grateful for it. Rather than my sister and I clinging to one another while indulging in a spate of needless worrying, our embrace was necessarily brief, as she attempted to assist the nursemaid in corralling her children.

Malcolm and Philipa were not eager to climb back inside a carriage after almost a week restricted to its confines. They were far happier chasing each other around the dooryard. Even Greer, who was still shy of sixteen months old, began to kick and fuss as her nanny carried her toward the coach door. Lady Hollingsworth did not help matters by complaining. Her declarations that *her* children had never behaved so shabbily only served to irritate my sister further, making Alana even shorter with Malcolm and Philipa.

Caroline seemed to be the sole person capable of ignoring them, wrapped up as she was in her own grief over leaving Michael, and her anxiety over the precarious position of their engagement. Philip had been able to convince Lady Hollingsworth not to break the engagement, but, as predicted, she had insisted on following her nephew and his family to Edinburgh, separating Caroline from the dangers of Dalmay House and its master. The only surprise had been Lord Damien's insistence on remaining behind. Lady Hollingsworth had objected strenuously, but Damien proved to be just as stubborn as his mother. He intended to act as his family's representative in the subsequent explorations of the soundness of Lord Dalmay's mind and he would not be persuaded otherwise.

I felt a new respect for Damien at his determination to do right by his sister, and I knew I wasn't the only one, if the gleam in Philip's eye was any indication.

Caroline began to weep as Michael bent over her hand to kiss it, the pained look in his eyes telling us he was fighting a strong emotion of his own. My heart went out to the couple. If only Michael hadn't determined that he must lie. I understood his caution in revealing where his brother had been kept over the last decade, but couldn't he have called in Philip to ensure Caroline's family would keep William's secret when he asked for her hand? So much grief could have been avoided.

Lady Hollingsworth did not allow Caroline's hand to remain in Michael's grasp for long. She pulled her daughter away from her fiancé and dragged her out the door to the line of carriages, leaving only Philip to say his good-byes.

He watched his aunt's hasty retreat, and then sighed and shook his head. I felt some pity for him as he turned to me with a tight smile. It would certainly not be enjoyable to spend the day dealing with an ill wife, a shrewish aunt, a weeping cousin, and three rambunctious children, even if they were his own.

"Are you certain you don't want to join us?" he asked with such forced hopefulness that I couldn't help but smile.

"Not for all the gold in the world," I replied.

"Ah, well." He shrugged. "I had to try." He took hold of my hand and I pressed my other hand to his shoulder, holding him back before he could say good-bye.

"I have a favor to ask of you."

He stared down at me expectantly.

"Could you ask around in Edinburgh about this Dr. Sloane? Perhaps Alana's physician or one of the surgeons at the Royal College could tell you something about him. I . . ." I dropped my gaze, hesitant to say what I must next, but knowing it might prove necessary. Time was of the essence, and credible intelligence on Sloane invaluable, regardless of my feelings on the matter. Swallowing my trepidation, I stared at where my hand still rested against the shoulder of Philip's deep blue coat and forced myself to speak, though my words emerged haltingly. "I believe Sir Anthony's former assistant is an instructor there—a Dr. Renshaw. If you mention my name, I feel relatively certain he will speak with you."

I could sense the tension in his frame and lifted my gaze to meet his again. His soft brown eyes shone with curiosity, but he did not voice the questions that I knew must be piling up on his tongue.

"Of course," he replied. "I'll write to you when we reach Edinburgh, and as soon as I have any information for you."

"Thank you."

He nodded while his eyes searched mine, for any sign of wavering in my decision, no doubt. Then he leaned forward to press a kiss to my left cheek. "Take care, Kiera," he murmured. "And if you must trust someone in my absence, let it be Gage." He pulled back just far enough so that he could look down at me. "I know it may not always seem it, but he *can* be trusted."

Before I could reply, he pressed my hand and walked away, leaving me to stare after him.

I drifted through the doors after the others to wave as the carriages one by one rounded the drive, their wheels crunching on the gravel, and sped away from us down the lane like a trail of lumbering ants carrying food back to their colony. I could feel the warmth of Gage's body where he stood beside me. His attention was on the departing carriages, and he gave no indication that he had heard Philip's remarks, but there was a slight puckering on his brow that made me suspect he'd heard at least a portion of his comments.

In any case, I wasn't about to mention it, and I doubted he would either, so I turned away, determined to ignore the feelings of frustration Philip's well-intentioned words had dredged up inside me.

Luncheon was a stilted affair, even without the antagonizing presence of Lady Hollingsworth. Most of us were too wrapped up in our own worries to appreciate Laura's attempts at conversation, and eventually she gave up trying.

Only after the fruits and nuts at the end of the meal had been taken away did Michael mention he had received a reply from Mr. Wallace, the missing girl's father, inviting us to call at our earliest convenience. "I thought we could ride over this afternoon."

"I just need twenty minutes to change into my riding habit," I told him and Gage as I placed my napkin on the table and prepared to rise.

"May I join you?" Miss Remmington surprised us all by asking.

"Elise, I'm not sure . . ." her brother protested while Michael fumbled for a response.

"Please," she interrupted. Her eyes shone with sincerity. "I knew Miss Wallace, and I want to express my condolences and offer my help."

"You knew Miss Wallace?" Michael seemed as taken aback by her admission as I was.

Miss Remmington flushed, perhaps in response to our astonishment. "Yes. We met a few times while out walking." Her gaze darted between Michael, Gage, and me. "I liked her," she added as if that were particularly important.

Michael looked to Gage and me. "I have no objections."

Lord Damien, who had been observing this exchange with a scowl, spoke up for the first time. "If Miss Remmington is accompanying you, then I should like to as well."

Miss Remmington turned to frown at him.

"Now, see here, this isn't a social call," Michael replied in irritation. "We are going to offer our condolences, but we are also going to question Mr. Wallace and the authorities to see what can be done to assist them in their search for Miss Wallace. We don't need either of you causing trouble."

"I will merely be there to observe," Damien assured him. "And to offer my assistance if called upon."

"Elise, perhaps you should remain behind," Lord Keswick told her, not unkindly.

"No. I have more reason to visit Mr. Wallace than any of them. At least I knew his daughter. Besides," she added when it looked like her brother would argue further, "Aunt Edna always said it was our Christian duty to comfort the sorrowful and aid the despairing."

"Aunt Edna also quoted, 'For Satan finds some mischief still for idle hands to do,'" Keswick added dryly, "but you certainly didn't agree with her then."

Miss Remmington scowled at him.

"Nicolas," Laura protested gently, reaching out to press her hand to her husband's forearm. "Let her go."

He frowned at her interference, but relented with a stiff nod.

Michael, who had observed their exchange with growing agitation, rose from his chair with one stiff movement. "It matters not to me who joins us, but we leave in half an hour, whether you are ready or not."

CHAPTER FOURTEEN

When I reached the stables twenty minutes later, as I had promised, Michael had already had a dappled mare saddled for me. Her soft gray coat was speckled with creamy white dots, as if someone had flicked a paintbrush across her flank.

"Aren't you a beauty?" I crooned as I ran my hand down her long neck, allowing her to get to know me. I laughed as she tossed her mane playfully, agreeing with my sentiment.

"Well, isn't she a vain one," Gage remarked in good humor, as he rounded the corner of the building leading a chestnut gelding.

"Hush," I told him. "She has reason to be. Don't you?" I murmured to the mare, who was watching me closely. She lowered her head to snuffle the skirt of my crimson riding ensemble and I chuckled. "Ah, now, be calm, ye wee beastie," I scolded the horse, imitating Philip's Highland stable master. "Yes, I have something for you."

"Bribing the horses."

I turned to see Gage shake his head in mock condemnation while I offered the mare the carrot.

I smiled and turned back to check the horse's bridle. I could feel Gage's eyes linger on me, and I flushed with pleasure, knowing I looked my best.

Clothing rarely mattered to me, but for some reason I

always felt rather fetching in my riding habits. This particular ensemble featured the stylish new sleeves puffed from the shoulders to the elbows, where it narrowed through the wrists. Matching crimson buttons marched up and down the sides of the bodice in a military style while the fabric tapered to a sharp vee in the front. A small ruffle at the bottom of the jacket in the middle of my back added a bit of flair to the view from behind. I even enjoyed wearing the top hat with its trailing ivory sash that completed the ensemble.

The promising weather of the morning had blossomed into a beautiful autumn day. In the shelter of the stable yard, the sun's rays were almost too hot inside my woolen dress, but I knew once we mounted and rode out into the open, the blustery wind would cool me.

It appeared Gage was just as warm inside his deep evergreen riding coat, for he shifted closer to the bit of shade on my left cast by the stables' upper story. He turned away from me to run his hands over his horse's flank, checking the equipage, and commented in a deceptively indifferent voice, "Do you really think Dr. Renshaw will be able to tell us anything useful about Dr. Sloane's methods?"

I frowned at his back, knowing it had been too much to hope that he had not been listening in on my conversation with Philip earlier. "Maybe," I replied vaguely, hoping the man would drop the matter, but already knowing he would not.

Gage swiveled his head to look at me, though I refused to meet his eyes. "But why would you specifically suggest that your late husband's former assistant may be acquainted with Dr. Sloane? And why do you think he would be more willing to talk by mentioning your name?"

"You do know that was a private conversation?" I bit out in clipped tones. I ran a soothing hand down the mare's neck as her ears flicked, hearing the tension and displeasure in my voice.

"Well, when the parties involved make little effort not to be overheard, it's difficult not to hear what one shouldn't."

I turned to glare at him.

His deliberately antagonizing smile slipped and he took a step closer to me. "Come now. Why would this Renshaw be able or willing to help us?"

"To help *me*," I pointed out.

"Yes, help *you*," Gage relented, reaching up to run a hand down the other side of my horse's neck.

I pressed my lips together and considered refusing to answer, especially in light of all the times he had refused to answer my questions. But in the end, I knew that doing so would only make a bigger deal than necessary out of such a small matter. So what if Gage knew about Renshaw? He was no great secret.

"Dr. Renshaw was particularly interested in the brain, and understanding why we do the things we do. He wanted to study how changes to the brain, from head injuries and illnesses and the like, affect our behavior. My guess is that Dr. Sloane's interests are similar, and with the Larkspur Retreat so close to Edinburgh, I imagine Dr. Renshaw may have heard something of the man and his methods."

Gage considered my words and then pressed. "Yes, but why . . ."

"Because I always suspected he was displeased with Sir Anthony's treatment of me," I snapped, aggravated that he was being so bloody persistent. I sighed and stepped back from the mare before I spooked her. Crossing my arms over my chest, I lowered my voice, lest the stable hands hear me. "Dr. Renshaw was already my husband's assistant when we married. He was not present during the first few times Sir Anthony forced me to sketch and document his dissections, but soon after he was allowed to attend. My husband always did like having an audience he could lecture to," I remarked bitterly. "At first, I was mortified. But soon after, I realized that Dr. Renshaw was just as discomfited. He seemed horrified by my husband's actions, a speculation that was confirmed when Sir Anthony left us alone to complete the dissection of a man's head one afternoon."

A cloud passed over the sun, temporarily dampening the bright sunlight shining down on the stable yard. "After our discussion that day, I had hopes that I had found a champion. And, indeed, I'm quite certain he did at least protest my treatment to my husband." I shook my head with a sigh. "But it was to no avail. I never saw Dr. Renshaw again. Sir Anthony dismissed him." Albeit with what must have been a glowing reference, as Renshaw had found himself a position at the Royal College in Edinburgh soon after. "And he declined to take on any future assistants."

"Didn't this Renshaw complain to anyone about your husband's conduct?" Gage's brow was furrowed in displeasure.

I shrugged, having long ago accepted the futility of expecting Renshaw's aid. "Who would he have told? It was his word against Sir Anthony's, one of the most influential and distinguished anatomists of the realm and surgeon to the royal family. Dr. Renshaw's career would have ended, without even an investigation being opened into the matter. His complaint would have been less than useless."

Gage's expression did not lighten. "That may have been so. But he took the coward's way out by leaving you behind to suffer."

I did not argue, feeling much the same way. "Well, regardless, I feel fairly certain his guilt, if nothing else, will impel him to assist us in any way he can."

"As long as the 'nothing else' isn't Cromarty's fist wringing the life out of him."

I turned to look at Gage with widened eyes. "Oh, dear. I hadn't thought of that. Philip is likely to expect the worst of him."

"Don't fret," Gage replied, turning to face my horse so that I couldn't see the expression in his eyes, though I could hear the relish in his voice. "Cromarty won't do anything to him that he doesn't deserve."

The crunch of gravel drew my gaze toward the house. Michael was striding across the drive, a thunderous expression on his face. Miss Remmington struggled to keep up, while

Damien trailed behind, glaring daggers at her back. I turned to share a look with Gage, much less enthused with this excursion than I had been before their trio of surly faces arrived on the scene.

With our host's impatient urgings, we were all quickly mounted and riding almost due south. Michael explained that the nearest bridge across the River Almond lay several miles upstream from Cramond. A ferry often ran back and forth across the river from the village proper to the north shore, but five humans and their horses would never fit on the small barge, necessitating our taking the bridge. Fortunately the Wallaces' home, Lambden Cottage, lay south of the village and closer to the bridge, forcing us to go only a mile out of our way rather than the extra two it would have taken us to reach the village.

While we were forced to travel away from the sparkling waters of the firth, the countryside around us was not without its charms. The forests blazed with the colors of autumn and were bordered by fields waving with golden wheat and barley. Orderly rows of orchards, the sweet scent of their fruit perfuming the air, spread out to the west, followed by the winding ribbon of one of the roads leading north and west away from Edinburgh. We joined the road just before the bridge spanning the River Almond. The clop of our horses' hooves over the three arches of stone echoed off the water below us.

When we reached the east bank and turned north toward Cramond, I dropped back to ride beside Miss Remmington. She had been quiet and thoughtful since we set out, and I wondered if she was thinking of her friend.

"How long have you known Miss Wallace?" I asked her, hoping she might be able to enlighten me on the missing girl's character.

Miss Remmington glanced at me distractedly. "A few months."

"You said you met while out walking?"

She blinked and turned to face me fully. "Yes." She spoke

hesitantly at first, as if gauging my actual interest in the topic, and then with more enthusiasm as she realized I wasn't merely making polite conversation. "I've always taken long walks, and as there has been little else to do while my brother and Michael and Laura fussed and worried over Lord Dalmay, exploring the Dalmay estate became one of the only options to relieve my boredom."

My hands tightened on the reins at her almost derisive tone. "You could have visited Lord Dalmay yourself," I pointed out, trying to keep my tone even lest she realize her attitude had galled me. "After all, I've never known his lordship to be *dull*." I couldn't resist putting a bit more emphasis on that last word than was necessary.

Miss Remmington gave me a look that said I didn't know what I was talking about. "He knows nothing about fashion or poetry," she stated as if those two things told her all she needed to know about a man. "Besides, I wasn't allowed to visit with Lord Dalmay the first few weeks after our arrival. Not until my brother could be certain he wouldn't harm Laura or me."

So even Keswick had been hesitant around William at first. I had wondered. The viscount had not seemed like the sort of man to take such things lightly, even if the man in question was his wife's brother. That Will had been able to win Keswick's trust said a great deal in Will's favor, in my mind.

"I will admit that I was curious to meet his lordship. I had heard the stories. As soon as everyone in London discovered my brother was wed to one of the Dalmays, people couldn't resist telling me the tragic tale of the dashing war hero gone missing. And the stories my maid brought to me from the servants' hall were enough to send shivers down my spine, both good and bad." She straightened in her saddle, arching her neck in prideful defiance. "I even fancied that Lord Dalmay would take one look at me and be instantly cured."

I shared a glance with Gage behind Miss Remmington's

back, surprised to hear her admit to such a romantic notion. Perhaps acquired from reading all of that poetry.

"But when I met him, it was nothing like I imagined." Her mouth screwed up in distaste. "And he was old enough to be my *grandfather*."

I couldn't resist darting another look at Gage, who appeared rather displeased with this pronouncement, himself being only seven years younger than Will.

"Oh, I don't think he's quite that old," I told Miss Remmington, resisting the urge to smile at Gage's annoyance.

"Well, I *do* know he's more than *twice* my age," Miss Remmington said in a voice that said even that was ancient.

I repressed a sigh and tried to bring Miss Remmington back to the matter at hand. "So did you meet Miss Wallace after one of these visits with Lord Dalmay?"

"Oh, no. I met her weeks before that. On the path that runs along the shore. I had caught the skirt of my redingote on a briar patch and I was afraid of tearing the fabric. She happened along and helped me to get it loose."

"That was kind of her."

"Yes. Miss Wallace is very *kind*," she replied, imbuing more meaning in that simple little word than I'd ever heard. "Most people aren't, you know." She turned to look at me and I was surprised by the sincerity shining in her pale brown eyes. "They pretend they are, and they say the right things, but they're really just looking out for themselves, their reputations." She glanced away, fidgeting with the wrist of her left riding glove. "I don't blame them. I'm the same way. But Miss Wallace truly is kind, in every sense of the word."

I watched the girl as she continued to scrutinize her gloves and wondered if something had happened in London. I had assumed she was popular because of the sophisticated air she liked to put on, but anyone could feign a confidence they didn't feel. I knew firsthand just how mean and nasty debutantes could be, especially if you were in any way different from them. Was Miss Remmington, with her isolated upbringing, too dissimilar?

"What else can you tell me about Miss Wallace? Was she pretty?" I asked, realizing I was testing Miss Remmington as much as I was curious about the missing girl.

She tilted her head in thought. "Not in the traditional sense. But there was definitely something about her that was attractive."

"What?"

I could see from her intense expression that she was mulling this question over seriously. "I don't know. Perhaps it was the way she held herself. She always seemed so confident, so assured. As if she knew who she was and that she was where she was supposed to be. Do you know what I mean?" Miss Remmington turned to me to ask.

I nodded. My maternal grandmother, Lady Rutherford, for whom my sister had been named, had been like that, and even as a young child it had struck me as something unique. She had died when I was five, but I remembered her vividly: her white hair and laughing blue eyes—lapis lazuli, the same shade as my own—her musical voice. And that distinct presence that was so powerful, and yet soothing, that seemed to say that she had made peace with herself, and nothing you could do or say would change that.

I also recalled the things people whispered about her when they thought a small child wasn't paying attention. The scandal over her marriage to my grandfather. The unnatural appeal she seemed to have, had always seemed to have, to other men, before her marriage and after. Her family's lowly origins as Irish nobility. In Ireland, Grandmother Rutherford's family might have been well respected, with the blood of ancient Irish kings flowing through their veins, as well as that of the transplanted English nobility who took over their land in 1606 under the direction of King James VI and I, but in Scotland they were less than nobodies. Which made the way my grandmother had held herself all the more fascinating, in defiance of them all.

Did Miss Wallace also have something in her past she had overcome? Some hardship that tested the mettle of a person and forced her to accept herself as she was, because no one else was going to do that for her?

Realizing that Miss Remmington was still speaking, I shook aside my own thoughts.

"She also seemed so . . . knowing." She shook her head in bafflement. "I can't explain it any other way. It was as if she knew things before you ever told them to her. Nothing, and no one, seemed capable of shocking her." She reached out to run a hand down her horse's neck before murmuring, "It was comforting."

It sounded as if Miss Wallace was good at reading people. But if that was the case, if she was so astute, so aware of the people around her, then why was she now missing? Perhaps someone she didn't know had surprised her. If so, then that made our search all the more difficult and widened its range considerably.

Of course, there was another explanation. Maybe Miss Wallace had not been taken but gone into hiding of her own accord. And if that was the case, what was she hiding from? What had she discovered or read in the intention of others to make her flee?

I could feel Gage's eyes on me where he rode to the side and a pace behind Miss Remmington and me. I knew he had been listening to our conversation and I was eager to hear his thoughts on the matter.

"Did you and Miss Wallace meet often?" I asked, wondering how much credence to give Miss Remmington's observations.

"Twice a week, without fail. Until last Friday, that is. I worried when she didn't meet me at our usual place, but I know she has responsibilities in the village and at home." Her face tightened. "I thought maybe she just had other things to do."

When Miss Remmington said "other," I knew what she really meant was "better." That she feared Miss Wallace had better things to do than meet her.

At the top of a rise, we paused to stare down at the village

of Cramond spreading out before us. The main road on which
we had been traveling paralleled the river on its way toward
the sea. Most of the buildings were concentrated on this thor-
oughfare, their uniform white stone bright in the sun. The
Cramond Kirk, with its square, medieval tower and its surrounding kirkyard, stood to the right of the road about halfway down the hill. Through the trees beyond the church, the
very top of a stone tower could be seen—the derelict remains
of Cramond Tower, Michael told us. At the base of the hill,
the road met the firth, pointing straight like an arrow out to
the tiny island I had seen from the shore of the Dalmay estate,
named for the town it lay so close to.

Lambden Cottage stood on a tree-lined lane at the crest
of the hill. The home had evidently been built in two stages
and resembled nothing so much as two squat, square blocks
offset so that the back half of one connected with the front
half of the other. Simple, rectangular windows were all that
alleviated the pale gray stone of the façade and the dark
black slopes of the roofs other than the stark white door.
The Wallaces clearly favored clean lines over fussy colors
and shapes.

As we dismounted, two stable boys ran around the corner, jostling each other as young boys do, and skidded to a
halt at the sight of all of us. I laughed silently at their eagerness to take the reins of Gage's gelding and Michael's spirited brute, a stallion named Puck, of all things, clearly
named for his disposition and not his size. From the lads'
reactions, it was apparent the Wallaces didn't have the same
taste for fine, expensive horseflesh as the Dalmays.

The footman who answered the door appeared to have
been expecting us, for he bowed and led us toward the drawing room, promising to inform Mr. Wallace of our arrival.
An assurance that proved unnecessary, as the man in question emerged from another room down the passage just as we
arrived at the door to the parlor. He was frowning quite
ferociously at whatever the man beside him was saying.
When he caught sight of us, his expression transformed into

a strange mixture of relief followed swiftly by dismay, and I couldn't help but wonder why our presence should cause him such a conundrum.

The other man stopped talking and followed his gaze toward us. I suspected he might be the village constable, or whatever title he went by. Small Scottish villages rarely employed anyone specifically for the purpose of keeping law and order, often relying on their citizens to police themselves with the help of retired soldiers. Only the larger cities had anything resembling a police force, because to establish one officially required an Act of Parliament. With Edinburgh so close by, Cramond might have followed the Scottish capital's example and appointed a constable, but until the man was introduced I couldn't be certain.

He wore no exterior accoutrements proclaiming his office, but he had the bearing of a man who enjoyed being in charge, and I judged from the way his eyes narrowed as he caught sight of us that he did not take kindly to having that authority questioned.

"Sir, Mr. Dalmay and his guests," the footman announced to his employer. "I was just escorting 'em to the drawing room."

The constable appeared delighted by this news, his red mustache fairly quivering with importance. Mr. Wallace, on the other hand, looked less than pleased, and I began to suspect that this was the source of his dismay—having the constable sit in on, and attempt to overrun, our conversation. And, in fact, it was the constable who strode forward quite rudely ahead of Mr. Wallace to introduce himself. I resisted the urge to scowl at the man, who was using his current position of power to overstep the bounds of propriety.

"Mr. Dalmay, 'tis a pleasure to meet ye, sir. M' name's Paxton, Cramond's constable. I woulda visited ye mysel' if I'd kenned ye had any information for me."

Michael shook the hand the man had thrust at him. "I'm afraid, as such, we don't have information for you. We simply wished to express our condolences over Mr. Wallace's justifiable distress, and offer our assistance in any way we can." He delivered this last looking over Mr. Paxton's shoulder at our host.

"Thank ye, Mr. Dalmay," he replied. "Shall we adjourn to the drawing room? I'm sure the ladies would appreciate a seat." He smiled kindly at Miss Remmington and me, though the light did not quite reach his eyes.

"O' course, o' course," Mr. Paxton said, preening at the realization that he'd been able to manipulate his way into the drawing room. Policemen were not, as a rule, gentlemen, as from Mr. Paxton's manner and speech it was evident he was not, and as such, they entered the houses of the nobility and gentry through the servants' door and were not escorted to the best rooms of the house, such as the drawing room. If offered any kind of refreshment, it was done in the kitchens. Sir Anthony had received much the same treatment as a surgeon, as opposed to a gentleman physician, until he'd been granted his baronetcy, boosting him into the ranks of the nobility.

We filed into the drawing room, ignoring Mr. Paxton's response, and settled ourselves on the worn but well-cared-for furniture clustered near the center of the room. The chamber was warm from the rays of the sun shining through the west-facing windows. I opted for a Chippendale chair positioned near the empty hearth and Gage claimed its twin.

Mr. Wallace was an elderly man of about sixty with a head full of hair that had managed to remain mostly dark. He sported only a streak of gray at the top, much like the picture I had seen of a polecat from North America, and a dusting of silver at the temples and sideburns. His eyes were dark, though I suspected they were deepest blue rather than brown, and clouded with fear and worry. He was making a valiant attempt to hide his fatigue and anxiety, but it was evident in the slouch of his shoulders, the dark circles around his eyes, and the twitching movements of his hands as he straightened his jacket or snuck a glance at his pocket watch.

Michael began the necessary introductions. I noticed that he failed to mention Gage's famous father, or his occupation, but from the tightening of Mr. Paxton's mouth he was not to be fooled.

"Yer father is Captain Lord Gage, is he no'?"

Mr. Wallace's face drooped with weary resignation. He had clearly hoped Mr. Paxton would miss the connection.

"He is," Gage answered with aplomb, as if the association had no bearing on our current situation. I had to admire the effort, even if Mr. Paxton did not.

"I'm sure we appreciate his lordship's help, but we've got matters weel in hand," he pronounced with a determined gleam in his eye.

"My father didn't send me."

The constable appeared baffled. "He dinna?"

"I'm not here in an official capacity, Mr. Paxton." Gage smiled disarmingly. "I'm simply staying with a friend and wished to accompany him on his visit to his neighbor. I have every confidence you are conducting your investigation with the utmost diligence and skill."

Mr. Paxton seemed to be caught off guard by this compliment, for he shifted in his seat. "Why, thank ye, sir."

"Such a sad circumstance. Mr. Wallace, you must be sick with worry."

He nodded. "That I am. Mary was never one to disappear like this. I always knew where she was going and who she would visit, even if she was only going doon to the village," he replied, his Scottish brogue emerging, whether from fatigue or because he had no care to affect the English accent as other Scottish gentlemen had been taught to do.

"Well, then you've been able to trace her movements that day."

"That we have," Mr. Paxton cut in. "And I was just tellin' Mr. Wallace that we think we puzzled it oot." His pronouncement was met by a stony glare from our host, one the constable chose to ignore.

"And what is that?" Gage prompted.

"She mun have failed to begin the crossin' from Cramond

Island afore the tide came in, and it dragged her oot to sea. It's happened afore and it'll happen again."

"And I told ye, my daughter knows that crossing weel. She'd never start if she couldna make it across," Mr. Wallace argued. "She's no' daft. She understands the danger."

The constable crossed his arms over his round stomach, unmoved by his arguments. "She would if she were in a hurry."

Mr. Wallace sat forward in his seat, his face reddened with anger. "Are you presuming to tell me what my daughter would or wouldna do?"

"Wait," I interrupted. "I don't understand." I glanced around at the others, wondering if anyone else was as confused as I was. "Why would the rising tide cause a woman in a boat so much danger? And wouldn't she have asked someone to row her across? Where are they if she's missing?"

"It's a tidal island," Michael explained. "At low tide the water recedes far enough so that there's a path that connects it to the shore. But the distance is nearly a mile, and when the tide comes back in, it does so quickly. More than one person has lost their life by trying to make the crossing too late."

I allowed this information to digest for a moment before asking the obvious. "But why do you think Miss Wallace made such a crossing?"

"Because Miss Wallace paid a visit to Mrs. McCray that day," Mr. Paxton answered before the girl's father could utter a word. "The McCrays ain an ole farmstead on the island."

"And Mrs. McCray was the last person to see her?" I asked, leading the man on in hopes he'd let slip more information.

"Aye!" He nodded at me in approval, seemingly pleased that I'd caught on. "No one's seen hide nor hair o' her since she left the McCrays. If she'd made it back to the mainland someone woulda seen her."

"Except Mrs. McCray told ye my Mary left wi' plenty o'

time to cross before the tide." Mr. Wallace fisted his hands in his lap. "It makes no sense."

Mr. Paxton waved this away as inconsequential. "Mrs. McCray was in bed wi' the ague. How could she ken the time? And besides, she's always been a wee daft. What with her talk of bogles and beasties." He leaned toward Damien and lowered his voice. "Claims she saw a selkie."

Mr. Wallace's scowl was fierce. "Ye do the ole woman an injustice. Just because she's a wee superstitious disna mean she's daft. And she wouldna lie aboot my daughter leaving in time." Mr. Wallace turned away from the constable to appeal to Michael and Gage and me. "In any case, Mary woulda been mindful. If she had misjudged the time she woulda stayed the night wi' the McCrays and come home in the morn. It's happened before. 'Tis why I didna know she was missing until the next day." His last words were heavy with guilt. It was clear the man blamed himself for not realizing his daughter had gone missing sooner. What could have happened in those twelve hours or more between her last being seen and his raising the alarm?

"What of the other residents on the island?" Gage asked. "Would she have gone to any of them?"

"The only other person livin' on Cramond Island is Craggy Donald," Mr. Paxton answered with a frown, unhappy to have the conversation taken away from him. "We questioned him and searched his croft, but he wasna any use." He shook his head stubbornly. "Nay, it looks like the lass tried to make the crossing and got swept oot to sea."

I wasn't willing to concede to his conclusion, not so quickly, but it was Gage who spoke up.

"Perhaps, but what time does the tide . . ."

"Mr. Gage," Mr. Paxton interrupted, an edge of warning in his voice. "Official visit or no', I'll warn ye to stay oot o' my investigation. Cramond is my patch, and I'll handle it as I see fit."

Gage stared at the trumped-up policeman evenly, his

demeanor carefully indifferent, but I could sense the fury bubbling below the surface and tightening his jaw.

"And what if I decided to hire him in an official capacity?" Mr. Wallace challenged. It was clear he'd had enough of the constable and his posturing. "You hav'na found her, and you've had over four days to do so. Maybe it's time I gave someone else a chance. I might have better results."

Mr. Paxton's round eyes narrowed to slits. "That is your choice, o' course, Mr. Wallace. But I mun say, I'd have to view such a move as very suspicious."

Mr. Wallace stiffened.

"May be ye have somethin' to hide."

"Are you threatenin' me?"

"Nay, sir. Just offerin' ye a bit o' friendly advice."

I bit my tongue to withhold the insults I wanted to hurl at this man. It was men like him, manipulating it for their own means, who had made me so wary of the law. Mr. Paxton enjoyed the power his office gave him, and he would use any means necessary to keep it. The feelings of even Mr. Wallace, a gentleman of some fortune, mattered little. Mr. Paxton clearly cared nothing for the missing girl, and I questioned whether he had the imagination to solve any crime that wasn't straightforward. I could only hope that Mr. Wallace would complain to Mr. Paxton's superior, heedless of the man's threats.

"Noo, I'm sure we want to allow Mr. Wallace to rest after his shock," Mr. Paxton said, his gaze still locked with the man in question, and without an ounce of compassion tinting his expression or his voice. "I'll send Dr. Littleton to ye."

Mr. Wallace looked as if he might wish to argue, but kept his lips clamped in a tight line. I half wished he might, just to set a flea in the constable's ear, but I knew we would never make headway in the matter today with Mr. Paxton looking over our shoulders. Even if we got more information out of Mr. Wallace and his servants, we would never be able to question anyone in the village.

We rose to our feet, preparing to take our leave alongside

174 · Anna Lee Huber

the constable, but before the man could usher us out, I crossed the room toward Mr. Wallace determined to offer my sympathies. If the man's daughter had, indeed, been caught in the tide and swept out to sea to drown—and I couldn't even begin to imagine the grief a loved one's dying that way would cause a person—he deserved our kindness and consideration. But Miss Remmington beat me to it.

"Mr. Wallace," she murmured, her voice wavering slightly, "I don't know if your daughter mentioned me, but I considered her my friend."

"O' course, Miss Remmington." He offered her a kind smile. "She mentions you often."

Her eyes brightened, and I could tell she was choking back tears. Whether it was because she had started to speak of her friend in the past tense or because Miss Wallace had spoken of her to her father, I didn't know, but I thought perhaps it was a little of both.

"I hope they find her." Her voice was no louder than a whisper. Mr. Wallace nodded and squeezed the hand she had offered him.

I hesitated to say anything after such an emotional scene, but Mr. Wallace looked up at me and spoke first. "Lady Darby, you are the sister-in-law o' Lord Cromarty, are you no'?"

"Yes," I replied, wondering if he was acquainted with Philip.

When his eyes strayed toward where Mr. Paxton stood near the door keeping a close watch on Gage and Michael, I realized it was for an entirely different reason. Apparently the tale of my recent actions at Gairloch had preceded me; the constable just hadn't realized it.

Mr. Wallace leaned toward me and spoke in a hushed voice. "Mr. Paxton travels to Edinburgh tomorrow morn, should you and Mr. Gage like to call on me again." His gaze met mine significantly.

"Of course," I told him, doing my best to appear as if I were offering him my condolences should Mr. Paxton look our way. "Shall we say nine o'clock?"

He bowed over my hand, following my lead. "Your servant, m'lady."

I nodded and turned from him, lest we give ourselves away.

Gage did not question me as we mounted our horses and rode away from Lambden Cottage, leaving the constable behind in a cloud of much-deserved dust, but I could feel his gaze on me. As we reached the road and turned south toward the bridge, he drew his mount up next to mine.

"Nine o'clock tomorrow," was all I needed to say, as I was certain he had observed my exchange with Mr. Wallace. I saw Gage smile out of the corner of my eye.

CHAPTER FIFTEEN

Michael dropped back beside me as we turned off the main road and back onto Dalmay land, shaking his head at the trio in front of us. Seeing my look of query, he explained. "Lord Damien is trying to impress the worldly Miss Remmington with tales of his exploits." I could hear the sarcasm in his voice. "And, unfortunately, Gage is only egging him on."

"But Damien hasn't had any exploits."

"And Miss Remmington is not in the least worldly, though she likes to pretend it."

"Oh, dear," I murmured.

His eyebrows arched in agreement. "This can only end badly."

"Should we try to separate them?"

He sighed. "I doubt it would do any good."

I stared at the back of Gage's evergreen coat. It was fairly quivering with suppressed humor. "Then perhaps we should trust Gage to handle it."

Michael glanced at me, a gleam of levity entering his eyes as he comprehended my meaning. Pulling on his reins, he checked his stallion's pace.

I smiled and directed my mare to follow suit, allowing an even larger gap to open between us and the trio of riders.

The mare seemed perfectly happy to have the stallion all to herself and tossed her mane playfully.

"You are rather vain, aren't you?" I scolded her with a chuckle.

"Don't be too hard on her. All the ladies preen for Puck." Michael patted his horse's shoulder. "Don't they, boy?"

I shook my head. "That name."

"I know. Blame the stable master. I jokingly told him that this horse was going to be 'quite the buck,' but he misheard me. Quite deliberately, I might add," he said, speaking louder to be heard over my laughter. "I found out later that Laura had been reading *A Midsummer Night's Dream* and described it to one of the stable lads one day when he accompanied her on her ride. The lad told the tale to the others in the stable, *including* the stable master."

"Well, at least Puck doesn't seem to mind his name," I offered.

"Yes, happily he doesn't know what it means."

"Just please don't tell me this mare's name is Titania."

A smile quirked his lips. "No. That is Dewdrop."

I reached out to brush a hand over her dappled coat. "Quite fitting."

"I thought you would appreciate her."

We fell silent as we crossed beneath the bower of one of the forests, losing sight of the others for a moment around a curve in the road. A few birds still twittered in the gloom of late afternoon under the trees, but the predominant sound was the clopping of our horses' hooves on the smooth dirt track. The closer the calendar crept toward the end of the year, the swifter the sun set, and I knew by the time we reached Dalmay House the sun would already be approaching the horizon.

I'd been reluctant to bring up the scene in Mr. Wallace's drawing room, but I decided it was necessary if we were ever to discover the truth.

"I take it you've never met Mr. Paxton before."

Michael turned to look at me. "No. But I've heard of him."

"And today's actions only confirmed what you'd heard?"

He nodded.

"Which is another reason why you would not want the authorities involved should Will become suspected in Miss Wallace's disappearance." I could only imagine how Cramond's constable would behave in such a circumstance. He would be out of his depth, but refuse to admit it.

"Do you place any credence in his proposition that Miss Wallace was swept out to sea while crossing back to the mainland from Cramond Island?" He was careful not to appear too eager to accept such a possibility, particularly as it almost certainly meant the girl's death, but nonetheless I could hear the ring of hope in his voice.

I had been too distracted by Mr. Paxton's provoking attitude and Mr. Wallace's obvious frustration to contemplate what the constable's theory meant for Will. If it were true, then Will could be cleared of all suspicion in her disappearance. The problem was there was no way of proving it. What if she had made it back to the mainland and walked west to the trails leading onto the Dalmay estate?

Of course, that would necessitate her taking the ferry across the River Almond to reach it, and I would have supposed that Mr. Paxton had questioned the ferrymen. What were the chances that those men had forgotten they'd helped her across that afternoon? They couldn't shepherd across more than a few dozen people each day, and I was willing to wager they would remember someone as highborn as Miss Wallace. So, if she didn't take the ferry, then the odds of Will having gotten to her were infinitesimal, and that was supposing he wanted to do her harm.

Yes, the odds were looking more and more in favor of Will's innocence. But without finding Miss Wallace there would always be that small sliver of doubt, and I would prefer not to leave that to fester.

"I don't know," I told Michael. "But I would rather find Miss Wallace alive and well."

"Of course," he replied, abashed. "I didn't mean to imply that I wished Miss Wallace ill."

"I know." I offered him a reassuring smile. "You're just looking out for your brother."

Deep furrows of worry etched his forehead.

"Did Gage tell you, he and I are going back tomorrow while the constable is away."

Michael's eyes widened. "Would you like me to accompany you?"

"No. I think the fewer of us there are to draw attention the better. Besides, Mr. Paxton is liable to cause trouble when he hears of our interference, and I'd rather the man not harbor any resentment toward you."

Michael grimaced, knowing I spoke the truth. It would be best if the constable caused as little trouble at Dalmay House as possible, particularly for William.

"I'm glad you're here," he told me. "And Gage." He closed his eyes as if in prayer. "Thank goodness he sent me that letter."

"That he was finishing a case in Edinburgh?" I prompted, having wanted to know exactly how Gage ended up at Dalmay House at such a propitious time.

"Yes, and asking if he could come for a visit."

I sat up straighter.

"Told me some fiddle-faddle about how he was worn out from working so many investigations for his father. I didn't believe it for a minute, of course. Gage's work has been his life these past few years. He seems enthralled by it. But I was happy to welcome him, in any case, and badly in need of some friendly advice regarding my brother."

I *knew* there was more to Gage's presence here than mere coincidence. And when I'd asked him about it, he'd lied straight to my face, the weasel. He'd told me he'd written to Michael upon his arrival in Edinburgh, not upon the completion of his latest investigation. And then he'd implied that *Michael* had been the one to invite him to Dalmay House, not that he had effectively invited himself.

But why? Why had he lied to me, if not in a barefaced manner, at least by implication and omission? It was one thing for him to withhold the truth about his past from me. I understood that was his right, even if I didn't agree with him. But to lie about the origins of his invitation to Dalmay House, that simply didn't make any sense.

My eyes narrowed. He had to be hiding something, something he didn't want me to know, something important, or he would never have taken the risk of being so easily caught out. Gage was smarter than that. But what could it be?

"Is everything all right?" Michael asked.

I glanced up at him, realizing I'd lapsed into silence. "Of course." I offered him a quick smile. "Sorry. Just woolgathering."

"About what?" His eyes shone with curious concern. "Your expression was quite intense."

I considered sharing my doubts about Gage, but only for a moment. This was an issue between Gage and me. There was no need to bring Michael into it, especially when he already had so much on his mind.

"Just . . . wondering if Philip and Alana made it to Edinburgh without incident."

He nodded. "You're concerned for your sister's health."

"Yes," I replied honestly.

"Once Philip has her settled in Edinburgh, she'll be fine."

I turned to stare at the low-riding sun where it peeked between the trees to our west, dappling us with light. "I hope so."

When we emerged from the trees and came into sight of the manor house and stables, we could see a black gig parked in the stable yard. Michael leaned forward, narrowing his eyes to study the carriage.

"That's Dr. Winslow." He spurred his horse faster.

From his reaction, I deduced he must be Will's physician and urged my mare into a gallop. The others glanced at us in confusion as we rode past, but followed without question.

When we reached the stables, Michael threw his reins to one of the hands who had run out to meet us and slid from his horse's back. "Walk them out," he ordered. He whirled around as if looking for something, and when he caught sight of me, he pushed aside the stable lad who was assisting me and reached up to wrap his hands around my waist and lift me out of my sidesaddle. My feet had barely touched the ground before he was pulling me toward the front door.

"I wasn't expecting him today," was all he murmured, and I was struggling too much to catch my breath to ask questions.

I glanced over my shoulder as Gage's long stride caught us up, but his attention was focused on Michael, a deep furrow of concern running down the middle of his forehead.

Michael's butler met us in the entry hall.

"Is he with his lordship?" Michael asked as we passed into the space.

"Yes, sir."

But Michael was no longer listening. He halted at the base of the stairs, staring up at the gentleman descending toward us.

I pressed a hand to my abdomen, grateful my riding habit did not require a restrictive corset beneath it. I would have passed out by now, first from the gallop and then the mad dash across the front drive. I glanced up at the man we were in such a hurry to see to find his gaze already rested on me. His hair was shockingly white, particularly for a man I estimated to be no more than fifty. His frame was slight and thin, but straight as an arrow.

"Mr. Dalmay," he said, interrupting whatever Michael had been asking him, "I'm not certain what the rush was, but perhaps you should allow Lady Darby to sit down. She appears a trifle winded."

Michael glanced down at me and flushed. "Of course. Tea?"

Dr. Winslow smiled benignly as he reached the bottom of the stairs. "Mrs. MacDougall has already promised me a cup."

He nodded and laced my hand through the crook of his arm and led us toward the drawing room. Hearing their quick steps, I turned to look over my shoulder as Lord Damien and Miss Remmington entered the house. Gage paused to have a few words with them, likely discouraging them from joining us, before following us alone to the drawing room.

"Have we met?" I asked the physician as Michael handed me onto the pale blue and white damask settee before the tea table.

He tilted his head quizzically.

"How did you know my name?"

"Ah." Dr. Winslow sank into the chair opposite. "Lord Dalmay has been telling me of you. But, of course, he didn't speak of you as Lady Darby," he added, glancing at Michael. "He was as informal as always, and he seemed to have trouble remembering you by your recent title, though he was aware of your marriage."

"William has preferred first names since his release," Michael explained. "Especially for those he knew before. And he has trouble retaining new information, such as your and my sister's new title."

"Then how . . . ?" I started to ask Dr. Winslow, and then stopped when I realized he was probably aware of my reputation. I dropped my gaze to the tea and began pouring.

When I looked up to hand him his cup, his eyes were kind. "Yes, I know who you are. But you'll hear no condemnation from me." He frowned into his tea. "I've seen too much of the world to pass judgment."

I watched the man take a sip of the hot brew. "War?" I guessed.

He nodded.

I finished pouring Gage's tea and was just adding his

cream when he spoke up as if he'd been contemplating the matter.

"Isn't it rather odd for a physician to take part in battle? I thought the army and the navy employed mostly surgeons."

Dr. Winslow bobbed his head in acknowledgment as he leaned forward to set his cup down. "That they do. But I wasn't there in the capacity of a physician, though my fellow officers often came to me with their problems rather than visit the sawbones." He glanced at Michael. "In fact, I served alongside Lord Dalmay for a time."

I sat up straighter at this admission.

"At Salamanca and such. Lord Dalmay's regiment took part in some of the heaviest fighting of the war. And I could tell, long before he and his remaining men were shipped home, that he was suffering from what I call battle fatigue."

"What do you mean?" Gage asked.

Dr. Winslow tapped the fingers of his right hand against the chair arm, as if deciding how much to tell us. "It starts with exhaustion, from too much marching and too many restless nights, and then the exertion of battle, some that last days on end. But it goes far beyond that." He spoke slowly, as if choosing his words with care. "The sights and sounds and smells begin to prey on the mind. In the short term, extreme cases can lead to disconnection with one's surroundings, indecisiveness, slow reaction times, and an inability to think straight—all of which can be deadly during combat." He sighed heavily. "I saw soldiers who had charged across many a battlefield, bravely and without hesitation, suddenly stumble to a halt and glance around them in confusion, unable to accept where they were or what they should be doing."

He frowned. "But it's the long-term effects that can be so worrying, and those are the symptoms I witnessed in Lord Dalmay. Difficulty sleeping, nightmares when he did, startled responses to lights and sounds, loss of concentration or, alternatively, a sort of extreme vigilance, especially when it came to his men. But mostly I noticed he had trouble forgetting. It was like he couldn't stop reliving the horrible things that had happened to him and those around him." He nodded to indicate Michael. "From talking to Lord Dalmay himself, and his brother, I now know that's the case."

I turned to stare out the windows at the lengthening shadows, seeing William as he had been ten years before when he first took over as my drawing instructor. The perpetual dark circles under his eyes, the sometimes restless pacing. His refusal to receive me if there was even a hint of a thunderstorm threatening, as if I wasn't already aware that the thunder and lightning bothered him. The despair he dragged behind him like a ball and chain.

I never pointed out the things I observed, but he knew I saw them anyway. It was a polite illusion we played, even if both of us recognized it for the fiction it was. To speak of it now felt wrong, even if it was necessary. We'd danced around the edges the previous night, hinting and insinuating, but now thoughts and suppositions were laid bare.

"What about his time spent in the Larkspur Retreat?" Gage was asking. "Are the effects of his being locked up there similar to this battle fatigue?"

"Yes and no." Dr. Winslow settled back to consider his answer. He rubbed his thumb and index finger over his temple and forehead. "He certainly encountered some upsetting circumstances, as evidenced by his sketches, but some of his other symptoms are far more extreme than I've ever seen in conjunction with battle fatigue. He absolutely abhors the dark, and I've witnessed for myself the absolute panic it evokes when the window in his chamber is not left open at least a crack, even on the coldest of winter days. I can only speculate he was kept in some room where he was denied light and fresh air, and the thought of being without either is no longer tolerable."

I set my tea down on the table, unable to stomach any more of it. Poor William. I had contemplated such a thing briefly, but the idea of being locked in that sort of room, for possibly years on end, was too horrible to imagine.

I could feel Gage's eyes on me, his concern, but he continued to ask Dr. Winslow the questions I seemed incapable of phrasing. "And these episodes, like the one last evening? Do you know what is happening then? Or what is causing them?"

Dr. Winslow looked to Michael, as if asking permission to divulge something, and Michael nodded.

His brow lowered as he thought back. "When I first examined Lord Dalmay after his release from the asylum, I was worried there was nothing that could be done for him. Beyond his troubling physical condition, his mind seemed incapable of grappling with anything he saw or heard. And worse, he would lapse into these half-conscious states, like you witnessed last night. Frankly, I was convinced he wouldn't survive for more than a week. There was little that could be done for him except to take care of his physical needs and try to reassure him that he was now safe." He shook his head as if in amazement. "But when I returned a fortnight later, Lord Dalmay was still living, even if barely.

"We deduced that part of the problem was that he wasn't sleeping. He paced the floor of his room night after night, as if trying to outrace slumber. We tried several medications, even some home remedies, like valerian root tea and warm milk. It took some doing, but we were finally able to convince him to take a mild sedative that would help him sleep so deeply there would be no dreams, for it seemed that was what he was afraid of."

"They drugged him," Gage guessed. "At the asylum. That's why he didn't want to take the medicine you offered him."

Dr. Winslow nodded. "Unfortunately, it's quite common in those types of establishments. The patients are dosed with laudanum, or some other tincture of opium, to keep them quiet and complacent."

I frowned at the delicate white china tea set on the table. The question had to be asked. "Can't people grow to rely on those medications?"

"Yes. And I believe Lord Dalmay may have been forced to take it so often that he did so in some capacity. But he also feared it as much as he craved it, and that helped him to overcome his need for it. He still takes small doses of laudanum from time to time, particularly after having one of these episodes, but they've grown less frequent in the last few months. His last one was—what? Over five weeks ago?" He looked to Michael for confirmation.

"Yes. Almost six."

"When I received your note this morning, I was quite saddened. I thought perhaps your brother had finally beaten them." He sighed. "Ah, but I suppose we should be happy with whatever progress can be made."

"Thank you for coming so quickly," Michael told him.

He waved it aside. "I was on the way out the door to visit your neighbor Lady Gaston anyway."

"Do you know what's causing these lapses?" I asked, determined to find an answer.

Dr. Winslow offered me a grim smile of apology. "I do not, Lady Darby. But the symptoms, when they come over him, present themselves suspiciously like that of a case of extreme, short-term battle fatigue—confusion, detachment, failure to recognize his surroundings and relate to those around him. This makes me wonder if he's not responding by instinct to some stimulus."

He shifted forward in his seat, leaning toward us. "He says he feels as if he's trapped inside the asylum again, that it becomes his world. I can't get him to tell me anything else. But if that is the case, then something must be taking him back there. A sight, a sound, a smell, a circumstance— something that connects to a memory. Like when you hear a song that reminds you of your childhood. Or smell a flower that reminds you of your wife's perfume."

"Whatever it is," Gage remarked, "it must be a very powerful memory."

Dr. Winslow nodded. "I agree."

"Could they be brought on by a display of force?" Michael asked, glancing up from his contemplation of the rug. The dread tightening his features made the breath stutter in my lungs. "Early on you warned me against using force to make Michael do anything. You said that physically compelling his compliance might remind him of the asylum."

Dr. Winslow tapped his chin, considering the matter. "Yes. It's possible. You said in the beginning that something as simple as urging his lordship to remove his clothes so that he might bathe could drive him to either fight you or sink into one of his melancholic stupors." He stopped to look at Michael, who was clenching and unclenching the spindly arms of his chair. "Do you think one of your servants is using unnecessary force with your brother?"

"I don't know." He sounded agonized by the thought. "I don't . . . want to believe Mac or Donovan would do such a thing, but . . . what else can it be?"

Gage, Dr. Winslow, and I shared a look of mutual uncertainty, none of us having an easy answer for him. The idea that either of these men, who had been hired specifically to care for William, might be abusing his power over him and driving him into these episodes made me sick to my stomach.

Dr. Winslow shifted forward in his seat. "Well, I'm sure you all have much to discuss. If you have no further questions for me, I should be on my way home."

A glance at the west-facing windows told us the sun had already set, casting red light over the long streams of clouds left in its wake.

"You know how to reach me should you have need of me," he told Michael as he bent to gather up his black satchel. "The only advice I can leave you with is to try and discover what's causing these melancholic incidents, if, in fact, anything external is causing them at all. Then we can progress from there."

"But do you think that's what's halting his recovery?" I asked, stopping the doctor before he could rise to his feet. "I mean, *if* we can stop these episodes, do you think he can truly begin to heal? To lead a normal life again?"

He sank back into the cushions of his chair, and the look he fastened on me was one dreaded by every person who has ever been given grave news about a loved one. It was the look that, peering through the stair banisters as a child, I had seen the physician give my father when he explained my mother would not recover from her illness. And the look the doctor who examined Sir Anthony after his apoplexy had given me when he explained my husband was dead.

"Stopping these episodes will help, yes. But I'm afraid Lord Dalmay has been too damaged by his confinement and treatment at Larkspur Retreat. His mind was already fragile from his efforts to overcome his memories of the war, and I have long suspected they exploited that. So, no, Lady Darby, I do not think he will ever lead a 'normal' life again."

"But he's made so much progress already," I protested. "Does that not encourage you?"

"Of course it does . . ." he started to say, but I talked over him.

"He's drawing again. That's what he did after he returned home. After the battle of Waterloo, and being part of the occupation force. Not immediately," I admitted. "But once he started transposing the memories from his mind to canvas and paper he began to improve. Is that not what he's doing now? And once he gets them all out . . ." I broke off, unable to find words in face of the sympathy I now saw reflected in Dr. Winslow's eyes. I didn't want his sympathy. I wanted him to cure William.

Gage had shifted over to the settee sometime during my speech and taken hold of my hand. I allowed him to do so, needing the comfort, wherever it came from.

"He's drawing the same images over and over," the doctor told me.

I glanced at Michael in surprise.

His soft gray eyes, nearly identical to Will's, were clouded with concern. "The others are in the attic. And we've had to repaint the walls of his bedchamber twice already."

I pressed a hand to my forehead, trying to come to grips with this new information.

"We need to accept that, while Lord Dalmay may continue to recover, he will never be the man he was before his confinement," Dr. Winslow said gently. "We will all have to adjust our expectations."

I gripped Gage's hand tightly in my fist, not wanting to hear any of this. He had to be wrong. I just couldn't accept it any other way. To say that Will could never return to the way that he was—did Dr. Winslow not understand to what kind of life he was condemning him? A stunted life, one of fear and isolation, of scorn and ridicule.

"Kiera." Gage leaned toward me to whisper in my ear, but I closed my eyes and turned away, unable to face his sympathy, his pity. Remembering how he had spoken similar words to me the night before about Will never being able to make a full recovery. Those words and the doctor's each felt like a knife thrust to the chest. For if Will could never completely recover from his ordeals, would I? Could I?

I understood that Will's situation, his suffering, had been far worse than mine—and the realization of what I had narrowly escaped in not being confined to an asylum as my accusers had wished made me grow cold—but I still couldn't help wondering if I would be forever grappling with memories I couldn't forget.

Dr. Winslow said his farewells and then rose to stride across the room toward the door, satchel in hand. Realizing there was one more thing I needed to ask him pulled me from my brooding, and I called after him. He waited for me by the door.

"I wonder if I might ask you one more question."

His eyes searched mine, as if to be certain I'd recovered from my distress. "Of course."

I lifted my chin and looked him levelly in the eye, determined he take my query seriously. "What, if anything, can you tell me of Dr. Sloane?"

From the lift of his brows, I could tell he perceived my query was far from idle curiosity. "I'm afraid I know very little of the man. I've never had the misfortune of making his acquaintance." He paused to study me closer before adding, "But I do hope, having seen his handiwork, that you find what it is you're looking for, my lady."

A feeling of solidarity passed between us and I continued to meet his gaze to let him know I understood. "Thank you."

He dipped his head. "You know where to find me should you require my assistance, in any way."

CHAPTER SIXTEEN

When I returned to my seat, Gage and Michael were already discussing the potential problem with Will's two manservants.

"I can't believe it would be Mac," Michael said with a distressed shake of his head. "The man served with William during the war, and he's been a loyal retainer of the Dalmay family since before I was born. He accompanied me when I went to retrieve Will from the asylum, and I've never seen a man be more gentle, despite Will's struggling and confusion. Mac was honestly aggrieved by what had been done to my brother. I would swear on my life about that."

"Then what of Donovan? What do you know of him?" Gage asked. His pale blue eyes sought mine out as I settled back onto the settee next to him.

I offered him a tight smile and gently placed my hand on his where it lay on the cushion between us to reassure him as I turned to hear Michael's answer. I glanced back in surprise when he turned his hand over to grip mine as I began to lift it away. He squeezed my fingers in silent communication, holding on to them for a moment longer than necessary before he slowly released his grip and allowed me to pull away.

"I hired him because of his references," Michael was saying. "He worked as a surgeon's assistant at the Royal Infirmary of Edinburgh and then the Glasgow Royal Infirmary. The man is quiet, keeps mostly to himself. The other servants seem to have accepted him readily enough. There've been no problems that I've been made aware of."

Which didn't mean there hadn't been difficulties. Butlers and housekeepers often liked to handle the disciplining of their own staff before any troubles reached the ears of their employers.

"Well, speak to the head of your staff," Gage told Michael. "Find out for certain." Gage's head tilted in thought. "Incidentally, did you actually check with Donovan's references?"

He blinked in surprise. "Yes. I wrote to the addresses he supplied."

Gage frowned. "Well, write to them again. And don't use the directions Donovan gave you. Write to whoever is in charge of hiring their employees. The infirmaries should be able to direct your query to the correct person."

Michael seemed shocked. "You think his references might be forged."

"I don't know any such thing. But I would rather be certain. I've seen similar tricks pulled in London." Gage crossed his arms over his chest. "In the meantime, tell me how they alternate shifts. I take it you haven't noticed a pattern. Whether one man is always on duty when Will slips into one of his episodes."

"No. Donovan was on duty yesterday afternoon when it started, but Mac was just coming to relieve him." Michael's brow furrowed in concentration and then he shook his head. "I couldn't tell you who was with him the last time it happened."

"And their shifts?"

"Eight hours on, eight hours off. When William was first brought home they took twelve-hour shifts, but it became too much on the days when he was particularly difficult and refused to sleep. Eight hours was more manageable, and neither man wanted to switch back once Will settled." Michael frowned. "I thought the shorter shifts would help them to better keep their tempers. I spent enough time with my brother after his release to understand how trying he could be, but I never dreamed . . . that one of these men would actually harm him."

"Let's not jump to conclusions," I told Michael, even though I felt some of the same gut-burning betrayal that he must be feeling tenfold. "We don't know for certain that either of them is at fault yet. And until we do, we can't assume guilt." I needed that reminder as much as he did.

"Kiera's right," Gage said. "Let's work with just the facts."

Michael nodded stiffly.

"Does anyone else help care for William? What happens on their days off?"

He rubbed a hand across the back of his neck. "One of our footmen, Lachlan, helps out when we need him to. Or I sit with my brother."

"And this Lachlan?"

He shook his head. "He's never been around when William had one of his episodes, except once in the very beginning. I would remember that." His expression was wry. "Lachlan's somewhat more timid than Mac and Donovan, and Will . . . notices it. On his better days, he likes to harass the lad."

I was so surprised to hear that Will had the presence of mind to see even the tiniest sliver of humor in his situation, or at least enough to be teasing someone about it, that it startled a laugh out of me.

A smile curled the corner of Michael's mouth. "I felt the same way the first time I realized my brother was badgering the lad on purpose." His gaze turned distant and thoughtful. "When I confronted him about it, I think it was the first time I'd seen him smile since I'd brought him home."

My chest tightened, and my smile stiffened into something far more bittersweet.

"We'll need to interview Mac and Donovan," Gage said, reminding us of the matter at hand. "Not only about this, but also to discover whether William has confided in either of them about his confinement. There's still the issue of Dr. Sloane's accusation to deal with, and whether he lied to discredit William."

"And the missing girl," I added, and then sighed. "But I'm afraid not much can be done about that until we visit Mr. Wallace again tomorrow." And with four days—rather, five—having already passed since her disappearance, I was beginning to worry there wasn't anything we could do at all, especially with Mr. Paxton's interference. All of the urgency certainly seemed to have drained out of the situation, even for Mr. Wallace. I wondered whether that was because he secretly believed Mr. Paxton's theory or because he had other reasons to suppose his daughter was beyond our assistance.

Michael nodded. "I'll make it known to both Mac and Donovan that they're to answer your questions, if you want to speak with them now. I'm not sure I want to be present."

"It's best if you're not," Gage answered his friend. Then he turned to me, and I could tell from the look in his eyes that whatever he said next would not be pleasant. I braced for it. "And if they can't or won't provide us with the information we seek, I'm afraid we're going to have to take a look at those drawings of Will's in the attic."

I dropped my gaze, not relishing such a task, not if they were anything like the sketches currently decorating Will's walls or, perhaps worse, like the paintings he had made of the war.

Michael's voice was stretched thin. "I understand."

I tried to catch his eye, to offer him some reassurance, but he would not meet my gaze, and I had to wonder why. Were the drawings worse than we'd seen thus far? Or was he hiding something else from us? Something he didn't want us to know about. I worried it might be the latter.

M ichael accompanied us to Will's rooms, knowing we would find at least one of the men with his brother. And, in fact, we found both of them exchanging terse bits of information at the door to his parlor, in the midst of changing shifts. Michael asked us to wait a little ways down the hall while he spoke with the men.

Donovan merely nodded at his employer's instructions, but Mac proceeded to argue. Whether that was because he did not trust Gage or me, and being an older retainer he felt more comfortable disagreeing with Michael, or because he had something to hide, I didn't know. Mac had always been rather grim and surly, but I didn't recall him being so out-spoken ten years ago. Then again, a fifteen-year-old girl was not a very threatening figure. Perhaps he'd had no fear of what I might discover.

In the end, Michael had to be firm with him, but he received Mac's begrudging agreement.

"His lordship needs seeing to," he told Michael tersely in his deep brogue, while glaring down the hall at Gage and me. "They can blather at me later." And with that pro-nouncement he closed the door in our faces.

Michael frowned at the offending piece of wood. "You can speak in the parlor at the end of the hall," he told Don-ovan and us, leading us back down to the intersection of the two passages just before the locked door near the stairs.

The room was dark, but Michael grabbed a brace of can-dles from the table beside the door and lit the tapers on one of the wall sconces in the hall. Gage followed suit.

It appeared that Michael didn't want the other servants knowing we were questioning Mac and Donovan—otherwise why hide us away in this little-used room at the top of the house? In light of all the gossip I'd been hearing from Lucy, I couldn't argue with him. But I wished we could have conducted the interview in a more comfortable place. I glanced at the unlit fireplace and wrapped my arms tighter around my torso. Even my warm woolen riding habit could only hold so much cold at bay.

The room had visibly been cleaned—the hearth was swept and the furniture was free of dust—but it still held that somewhat musky stench of a room too little used and too long closed. The heavy drapes were pulled shut against even the starlight, and the corners were almost pitch-black with shadows. Gage set one brace of candles on the tea table before a heavy chair and the other on the table beside the door. With a nod to Michael, he closed the door and then gestured for Donovan to take the chair. When I took my seat in the corner of the settee Gage had indicated with his eyes, and he sat in the chair next to me, I realized how clever he had been. The candles on the tea table were directly in front of Donovan, allowing us to see his eyes and face clearly, but the candles by the door were at Gage's and my back, concealing ours.

"Now, Donovan, if you will," he began, "tell us how you found out about this position?"

His gaze was cautious, but he did not shift in his chair or attempt to evade the question. "A friend o' mine from Edinburgh heard a doc askin' roond. He kenned I were lookin' for somethin' different."

"Than your job at the Glasgow Royal Infirmary?"

"Aye."

"Why did you want to leave the infirmary?"

"For a position like this?" he replied, as if the answer was rather obvious. And it was. "Better pay. Better food. And I only have the one patient to mind, no' a whole ward o' 'em."

His answer implied that caring for Will was a far easier job than his previous assignment, which meant the rigors and demands should have been no problem for him. I wasn't sure whether he was simply answering our questions honestly or if he had anticipated the reason for our visit and was already presenting his defense. A man of Donovan's bulk should not have had to use force to convince Will to do what was needed, but that didn't mean he didn't enjoy using it. There had been a boy in the village where I grew up who liked to bully the rest of us just because he was bigger. My brother had come home with more than one bloody nose from standing up to the lad and his mean-spiritedness.

Gage tilted his head, studying the man across from him. "I imagine the men in some of those wards could become quite riled." He spoke conversationally, but I knew his comment was far from innocent.

"Aye. Injured men be like bairns. When one comes in hurtin' and carryin' on, the others join in. Canna have one screamin' and hollerin' wi'oot the others."

"How do you manage it when that happens?"

"Careful like. If ye can get the first one settled, sometimes the rest 'll follow. And if no', mayhap they need a wee more meds. For the pain."

Gage's eyes narrowed. He hadn't missed the way Donovan had tacked that last bit on at the end either. "I imagine it requires a firm hand."

Donovan's expression did not alter by one flicker of an eyelash, but I could have sworn he knew exactly what we were hinting at. "Aye. Firm, but no' too firm. They be like horses. Ride 'em too hard and they'll be more ill-tempered than ye started wi'."

I wasn't certain I liked the idea of Will and others like him being compared to babies and then horses, but I understood the point he was trying to make.

Gage tapped his finger twice on the arm of his chair, seeming to understand he was going to get nowhere with this line of questioning. Not if he didn't have something specific to accuse him of. So he switched tactics.

"Were any of your patients in the infirmary with you for a long period of time?"

I could tell from the way Donovan's eyes suddenly widened that he had not been expecting such a question. His reply was uncertain. "Sometimes."

As if scenting his prey's unease, Gage shifted forward in eagerness. Not enough to alarm Donovan, but enough that I, seated so close to his left side, noticed. "They must have grown quite comfortable with you. Spending day after day in your company. Relying on you for some of their most basic necessities. Did any of them ever start to think of you as a friend? Did they ever confide in you?"

Donovan was definitely suspicious now, his body tense,

his eyes narrowed, trying to penetrate the gloom surrounding our features. "A few."

"What about Lord Dalmay? Has he ever confided in you?"

The man's shoulders relaxed and he sat deeper in his chair. "Nay," he said, crossing his arms over his body. His eyes took on an almost satisfied gleam. "And he wouldna. He'd talk to his brother or Mac afore me."

Out of the corner of my eye, I could see Gage's mouth twitch downward. "Is he close to Mac?"

"Aye. As close as ever I've seen a laird to his servant."

I frowned. And just how many lords and their valets had Donovan witnessed? Not many, I'd wager.

Gage seemed to have the same thought. "What do you mean?"

"Weel . . ." Donovan scratched a hand over his jaw, taking his time answering. "They served together in the army, so I reckon it's only fittin', but if ye ask me, Mac is a might too possessive o' his lordship. He dinna like anyone but himsel' takin' care o' him. He caused a right stramash when Mr. Dalmay brought me in to assist 'im."

"Do you think he was objecting to having anyone else care for his lordship, or you in particular?" Gage made it a point of asking.

I questioned, too, whether this was a source of contention between the two men.

Donovan shrugged. "It could be me. But he also glares at wee Lachlan."

I stared across the flickering flame at the man, wondering what it was he wasn't telling us. He was deliberately holding something back, almost toying with us. I scowled, liking him even less than I had before.

A stray draft of cold air from somewhere suddenly blew across the back of my neck, making the hairs there stand up on end. I shivered and wrapped my arms tighter around me. And as I did so, Donovan's gaze shifted from Gage to burrow into my corner of the settee. His eyes still gleamed with smug amusement, but I could see a flicker of something else in their depths. Was it anticipation?

"Why do you view Mac's protectiveness as a bad thing? Isn't that his job? And yours, for that matter?" Gage asked, still trying to probe Donovan for answers.

"Aye. But you wouldna see me cleanin' up what I shouldn't. Or pretendin' the things that have happened haven't."

"What are you implying?" Gage demanded crossly.

Donovan leveled his gaze at him. "I willna say. You'll have to ask Mac. But when ye do, ye might wanna ask him aboot the walks he and his lordship take doon by the water."

I sat up straighter at his mention of the firth. Just what was he hinting at? We knew Will liked to walk there. Michael had told us as much. So why the intimation that there could be something troubling about those outings?

I looked at Gage fully for the first time since we'd taken our seats in the shadowy parlor. His eyes showed the same confusion, though he was doing a much better job of hiding it than I was. He studied Donovan across the table, and I could tell he didn't like the other man's smug certainty either. If Donovan knew something, he should simply tell us, not make vague insinuations and gloat over our lack of comprehension.

"Is there anythin' else?" he asked.

Gage's expression was hard. "No. Thank you for answering our questions, Mr. Donovan. You are free to go."

I bit my tongue as he rose from his seat, bowed almost mockingly, and walked around us to exit the room. When the door clicked shut, I turned on Gage. "Why didn't you press him?"

"Because he was only toying with us. I could tell from the look in his eyes that he had no intention of telling us more. Only smirking about it." He scowled at the table. "Besides, I'm not entirely certain I believe anything he says." His pale blue eyes lifted to mine, appearing soft gray in the gloom. "He's hiding something. I know you sensed it, too."

I didn't deny it. "What do you think it is?"

His mouth tightened into a thin line. "I don't know. But he definitely didn't like us prying into his past. Did you see how wary he became when I asked him about his previous patients?"

"Then why didn't you push him harder?" I demanded.

His eyes flashed. "Because I didn't know what to ask. Poking around an old wound is worse than useless if you don't know what you're looking for. Subjects will only withdraw, and they'll be more reluctant than before to let you meddle where they don't want you."

I frowned, but had to concede his point.

"Perhaps Michael's queries into Donovan's references will lead us somewhere. But in the meantime, I think our next course of action must be to question Mac to see if there is any truth in Donovan's words. Depending on how Mac reacts, we may have our answer."

"You want to question him now?" It had only been about a quarter of an hour since the irascible man had slammed the door in our faces.

Gage rose to lean over the table and blow out the brace of candles. "What better time than when his temper is less than even? It may lead him to say more than he usually would."

The smoking wicks made my nose wrinkle. "That or he'll refuse to cooperate."

As it turned out, I wasn't far off.

The muscle in Mac's cheek had jumped when he answered the door to our knock, and again when Gage had insisted on speaking to him, but he had bowed to the order. He had directed us to sit in the parlor and asked, or rather, more accurately, threatened us, to speak in low voices so as not to wake Will, who was sleeping in the next room. From the way Will had looked when we visited him that morning, the exhaustion that had dragged at him, I wasn't surprised to hear he was resting. But I *was* surprised by the almost tender expression I glimpsed on Mac's face as he peered through the bedchamber door to check on him. However, by the time he turned back to us, his features had returned to looking stony and unyielding.

That jaw muscle jumped again the moment Gage started peppering him with questions and small talk, and now even his neck was rigid. His answers all measured three words or less, and he bit them out in the most belligerent tones, until Gage questioned aloud whether he was truly qualified to be caring for a man in Will's condition. That set a fire blazing in his dark eyes.

"I been lookin' after Cap'n Dalmay since he was fifteen. I followed him to school, and then into the cavalry. Looked after him, patched him up, and made sure he came home again. I stayed wi' him at Swinton Lodge 'til he was taken, and I'll be wi' him 'til I die. *No* one cares for him better."

"What did you do before you became his valet?" Gage asked. It was a legitimate question, for I certainly couldn't see him as a footman, the normal route to such a position.

He glared at Gage. "Worked in the stables."

"That's a strange leap of position."

"Aye."

"How did that happen?"

"Cap'n Dalmay chose me."

Apparently we were back to short answers.

Gage tilted his head. "Where did you work during the nine years of Lord Dalmay's confinement?"

"The stables."

"Did you know where Lord Dalmay was being held?"

"Nay," Mac answered forcefully. "I wasna there the day he was taken. The housekeeper told me he went wi' his father, so I hurried here. But the ole Lord Dalmay . . ." he seemed barely able to speak the former baron's name ". . . said he wrote a letter sayin' he were goin' away."

"And you believed him?"

He shook his head. "Cap'n Dalmay wasna goin' anywhere, and if he were, he'd ha' taken me wi' him." He narrowed his eyes. "No, I kenned something was wrong. Searched for him, even found oot aboot a carriage that was at Swinton. Trailed it to Edinburgh, and lost its track." His voice lowered in defeat at the last, and I could tell from the shame in his eyes that he felt guilty he'd not tried harder.

But remorse could be a double-edged sword, making us lash out at those who made us feel such regret. How was it for Mac?

Gage laced his fingers together in his lap, a motion I knew meant he was on to something. "So you feel a responsibility to Lord Dalmay?"

"Aye," Mac answered more calmly.

"A need to protect him?"

He nodded his head once.

"Would do almost anything to see him kept safe from further harm?"

"Aye."

"Would you lie for him?"

I held my breath as Gage dropped the question into the silent room.

Mac's wrinkled face folded into deeper lines and his scraggly gray eyebrows lowered over his eyes. Gage didn't re-pose the question, but stared at the older man, ordering him to answer. For a moment, I felt convinced Mac wouldn't speak, but then he raised his chin in challenge.

"You're askin' the wrong question."

Gage arched his eyebrows.

"Aye, I just might lie for him. But have I?" He paused, making us wait. "Nay."

I blew out my breath in a rush of air, not knowing if I believed him.

"Are we done?" he snapped. "I've his lordship's dinner to see to."

"One more question," Gage replied calmly. "I've been told that Lord Dalmay likes to take walks down by the firth."

Mac's face stiffened. "Aye. He needs the light and fresh air."

"I can understand that. The view is quite spectacular."

I studied Gage out of the corner of my eye, wondering where these questions were leading.

"Miss Remmington admitted she likes to stroll there as well. Have you and Lord Dalmay ever encountered her there?"

Mac's expression was stony again, but this time it was fueled far less by anger than by some other emotion. "Aye," he bit out.

"I believe she meets her friend Miss Wallace down there." Gage paused, letting that knowledge sink in. My stomach clenched, suddenly seeing what he was hinting at. I had to resist the urge to reach out and smack him. I knew we were supposed to be proving either Will's innocence or his culpability in the girl's disappearance, but I had been hoping it was the former. If Gage was able to establish that Will had known her . . . That certainly would not prove his guilt, but it would put a large dent in his defense.

"Did you by chance have the pleasure of making her acquaintance?" Gage finished asking Mac.

"Nay. I'm afraid no'."

He answered with a convincing amount of indifference, but rather than sounding truthful it had the opposite effect. My heart sank.

"She's the missing girl, no?" he surprised me by asking.

"Yes." Gage's eyes narrowed in suspicion. "How did you know about her?"

Mac glowered at him. "Servants do talk. Everyone kens aboot her."

He rose to his feet, signaling it was time for us to leave. I was reluctant to depart without seeing Will, especially in light of this most recent worrying discovery.

"Could I just look in on him?" I asked.

Mac scowled down at me.

"I promise not to wake him. I just . . . want to see for myself he's well."

Something in my voice or my expression must have won him over, for he reluctantly nodded, leading me to the door. He eased it open and I peered through the gap.

William lay on his back in the middle of the bed. His face was turned to the firelight, which limned the eyelashes resting against his cheeks in gold. One leg was bent beneath the covers and his left hand lay draped over his middle. My heart warmed at the sight of him like this—so peaceful, his face unlined by trouble. A soft smile curled my lips as I silently wished him sweet dreams.

I glanced up to thank Mac, only to discover he had been watching me the entire time. A strange expression marred his brow and, unable to decipher it, I was about to simply turn away when he spoke.

"I remember you," he murmured softly. "You're the lass he tutored, who lived o'er the Tweed."

I nodded.

His face cleared of the remaining hostility that had been stamped there since our return to Will's chamber, and he bobbed his head in respect—his version of a tug to his fore-lock, I suspected.

I dipped my chin in acknowledgment, glad to know the gruff man now understood I truly was a friend to Will, and then turned to go.

Gage was waiting for me by the outer door, his back turned to me. I preceded him through the door, feeling my ire rise with each step down the corridor, but I waited until we were almost to the end of the hall before I turned on him.

"What was that?" I demanded.

I was surprised by the answering anger that flashed in his eyes. "Just following a hunch," he responded in clipped tones. His long stride swiftly outdistanced me, and I had to struggle to keep up.

Suddenly unwilling to do so, I halted in midstride. If we were going to have an argument, I would rather it be here in this deserted corridor than in one of the more public parts of the house. "When did you realize what Donovan had been hinting at?"

Gage whirled around. He stared at me for a moment, his gaze difficult to read in the flickering light of the wall sconces, before marching back to me. "As we were speaking with Mac."

"And you couldn't have waited to ask him?" My voice rose with my anger.

He frowned and stepped toward me, crowding me closer to the wall. "Why? Why should I have waited, Kiera?"

"S-so that we could have discussed it first," I stammered out. I lifted my chin, determined to show him I was not intimidated.

"The truth is the truth, is it not? And that is *why* we took up this investigation, isn't it? To discover the truth about this missing girl, and whether Lord Dalmay was involved in her disappearance?"

"Yes, but . . ."

"But, nothing," he replied sharply. "You cannot arrange an inquiry to suit your purposes. You must be open-minded and impartial, taking into account *all* evidence, whether you *like* it or not; otherwise, the result is flawed." He leaned in even closer, his pale gaze boring into mine. "And we both know what happens when the results are flawed."

"Oh, is *that* why you dismissed my doubts so readily during our investigation at Gairloch?" I sneered, pressing my hands back against the wall so that I could rise up on the balls of my feet to meet his gaze more evenly. I didn't want to admit that his words had struck a chord, that I was scared Will might be guilty.

"Your doubts were based on intuition, not evidence. And I have already apologized for that twice now. I will not do so again."

"But you will not tell me why. Why, Gage? Why did you turn your back on me?" I heard the hurt creeping into my voice and shook it aside. "After all, the truth is the truth, is it not?" I snapped, throwing his words back in his face.

I gasped as he pushed forward and flattened me against the wall, his hands splayed on either side of my head. He glared down at me and I glared back, pouring all of my rage, frustration, and pain into my gaze.

Why couldn't he be honest with me? Why was that so difficult? I wasn't a demanding person. And I certainly didn't expect much from him. I knew he couldn't give me what I had only begun to suspect I secretly wanted in the deepest recesses of my heart. All I needed was his honesty, and perhaps a little of his trust. Was that so much to ask?

Whether Gage could read my expression or not I didn't know, but his own became more conflicted. His pupils dilated, swallowing the flecks of silver that sparkled when he was angry or amused. His body, which had been rigid with fury, softened, and the next thing I knew, his hands cradled my head and he kissed me.

Whether this went on for seconds or minutes, I don't know, but by the time he lifted his mouth from mine, I was tingling from head to toe. I leaned against the wall, afraid my knees wouldn't hold me up if I tried to step away from it. Gage continued to cradle the back of my neck in his hand as he gazed down at me, our breath sawing in and out of our lungs in unison. I was too dazed to form words and it pleased me that Gage seemed similarly affected.

I'm not certain what either of us would have said next had the sound of a lock turning not interrupted us. He stepped back just before a footman entered through the hall door carrying a tray of food. The footman jumped at the sight of us, almost spilling the contents of Will's dinner all over the floor. Fortunately his reflexes were quick, and Gage was sufficiently recovered to mumble some sort of pleasantry while ushering me through the door.

We were silent on the stairs, both of us absorbed in our own thoughts. Mine mostly ran the gamut of what one was supposed to say after being kissed breathless in a hallway— it was a novel experience for me. I was afraid that Gage, on the other hand, being far more experienced, was trying to come up with an apology or a reason why he could never do so again. I didn't want to hear either.

And in the end, I didn't have to, for Lord Keswick was standing at the base of the stairs, already dressed for dinner. He asked Gage a question, and I excused myself to go change, hurrying down the hall away from the men before Gage could catch up with me.

CHAPTER SEVENTEEN

After dinner, a rather uncomfortable affair for me, being seated next to Gage as I was, we gathered in the drawing room, where the butler entered a few moments later with a pair of notes delivered late from Edinburgh. The first was for me, and I took it up eagerly, having been expecting word from Philip and Alana of their safe arrival. The second was handed to Gage, who accepted it with a frown.

I opened my letter and gave it a cursory glance to see that it was indeed from my brother-in-law, saying they had reached their town house in Charlotte Square. I told the others as much and then excused myself to sit at the dainty writing desk in the corner to finish reading the missive.

Philip assured me that Alana and the children were now settled, and they were already feeling better for arriving home at their journey's end. I breathed a sigh of relief, knowing that my sister was probably tucked up in bed with a hot water bottle at her feet and a warm cup of tea on the nightstand beside her. Philip would take care of her. And I trusted he would write me should any of her new physician's instructions prove questionable, as he promised in his letter. I smiled. Alana must have told him about my terse directives.

However, the last paragraph of Philip's missive proved the most interesting. He had already uncovered a small bit of information about Dr. Sloane, and from an unexpected source—his servants. Apparently several of the housemaids had heard gossip about him from the servants in the neighboring town houses.

It appears Dr. Sloane has developed something of a fearful reputation for being interested in unusual subjects. Rumor has it that a young maid in a household on Princes Street was examined and taken up by Dr. Sloane because of her marked stammer and extreme shyness. Where this maid was said to have gone, and from which establishment she was to have come from, the maids could not say. I do not know if there is any way of verifying this information, but, regardless, this Dr. Sloane seems to be viewed by the servants as a figure to be feared.

I frowned, turning to stare at the tapestry that hung on the wall to my left as I considered Philip's words, but the sight of Gage seated at the larger writing table in the opposite corner of the room made my thoughts pause. His arms were crossed over his chest and his face was tight with displeasure as he glared down at the letter on the desk in front of him where he had dropped it. He eyed it like an offensive piece of rubbish that he knew he must take care of but wished he could simply turn his back on and ignore. I couldn't help but wonder whom it was from, and what it said that so aggravated him.

Determined to ignore him for the time being, I turned back to my own letter and took up a piece of parchment to pen a response. I expressed my relief to hear of their safe arrival and thanked him for the information about Dr. Sloane. Then I asked if Philip could also make a few inquiries about Donovan, particularly at the Royal Infirmary of Edinburgh. The man's insolence and sly manner had raised my hackles, even more so than Mac's surly attitude and belligerent replies, and I wanted to be sure he was who he said he was.

I slipped the letter and its reply into the pocket sewn into the side of my pale green dinner dress trimmed with white lace and crossed the room to rejoin the others. Gage still sat at the desk in the corner struggling over a response to his own letter.

Michael had been explaining to his sister and her husband about our trip to Mr. Wallace that afternoon and Mr. Paxton's theories about Mary Wallace's disappearance.

"Oh, how awful," Laura exclaimed, pressing her hand over her heart. "I can't imagine how Mr. Wallace must be feeling. Does he think the constable's theory might be correct?"

Michael's gaze strayed to mine. "I received the impression he wasn't ready to believe such a thing. Not yet, in any case. Not without proof."

"Well, of course. I should think if it were my child I would want to be certain every possibility had been exhausted before I even considered such a thing. Who wants to believe their child is dead, especially by such horrible means?" She glanced at her husband. "I would rather think they were missing, no matter how anxious I was for their safety."

We fell silent, considering her words.

Laura sighed. "So sad." She tilted her head to the side in thought. "It reminds me of the Duke of Montlake's daughter. Do you remember when she went missing . . . oh, it must be several years ago now?"

Michael nodded, but I shook my head, having been in London.

"It was big news, splashed all over the newspapers in Edinburgh, her being a duke's daughter and all. Apparently she was taken from her home near St. Andrews in the middle of the night. Vanished without a trace. The duke searched far and wide for her, even offered a handsome reward for information regarding her whereabouts, but no credible source came forward. The old duke died last year, still without having found her. They say he died of a broken heart."

"Could she have run off?" I asked. "Perhaps with a suitor her father had not approved of?"

Laura smiled grimly. "It's not likely. Lady Margaret was the apple of her father's eye. He doted on her so. I don't think he would have denied her anything. And, in any case, she suffered from the falling sickness."

I lifted my eyebrows in surprise.

"She rarely left her father's estate, except to travel to Edinburgh once a year to replenish her wardrobe, and she confided in a mutual friend of ours once that she hated even to do that because the travel was certain to bring on the fits."

"What do they think happened to her?" I asked, curious what could have befallen such a girl. If she had been kidnapped, certainly the culprits would have sent a ransom note.

"The authorities suggested she might have fallen into a hole or crawled into a cave while having a fit," Lord Keswick replied.

And they had not been able to find her? I screwed up my mouth in response to that bit of ridiculousness.

"Or . . ." he glanced cautiously at his wife ". . . that she had been injured after being taken, either by her captors or because of a fit, and so the villains had never contacted the duke asking for her ransom."

"Quite an honest group of kidnappers," I commented wryly. In my experience, though it was limited, if a man would stoop to abduction, he would have no qualm in lying to get the ransom without returning the captive.

Lord Keswick's mouth quirked upward in a semblance of a smile. "Yes."

In any case, sad as Lady Margaret's story was, by now she was likely dead, and if not, she would never be found. I could only hope she was happy wherever she was.

Gage dropped into the chair between Lord Damien and Michael, a frown still marring his otherwise handsome features.

"Trouble?" Michael asked.

He pressed his lips together tightly before responding. "Just my father being my father."

Which was a rather curious statement. Michael opened

his mouth, but hesitated to speak, as if uncertain whether to ask him to elaborate.

Gage glanced up at me before turning to his friend. "Nothing to worry about."

I could tell he was lying, but I wasn't going to push the matter. Not here anyway. Not only would it be impolite, but I knew he wouldn't answer anyway. If he wouldn't talk to me about the events at Gairloch, his time in Greece, or the real reason for his being here, he wasn't likely to discuss his father with me.

"Your father fought in the war against France, didn't he?" Miss Remmington surprised us all by asking.

She had been quiet this evening, even more so than this afternoon. Seated in the far corner of the room, she held a book open in her lap, but I had yet to see her flip a page. Her puckered brow made me suspect she was worried about her friend. I could understand that. I was worried for Miss Wallace myself, and I had never met the young woman. What I did find curious was the sideways glances she had been sending Michael's way all evening. Being seated across the table from her at dinner, I'd had plenty of opportunities to observe these apprehensive looks, but I was no closer to understanding what was behind them.

"Yes," Gage replied guardedly. "He served in the Royal Navy for almost forty years."

Which was about as brief an answer as a man could give about the service of Captain Lord Gage. He was not only a war hero but also a great friend to the king and many other highborn citizens, who frequently called upon him to help them out of troublesome situations. His son often assisted him in these matters, which was why Philip had asked him to conduct the investigation into Lady Godwin's murder at his estate two months before, and how I had come to be acquainted with him.

"Do you recall . . ." Miss Remmington began hesitantly. "Did he come home with nightmares?"

I glanced at her in curiosity, wondering why she was asking such a thing.

Gage fastened her with a sharp look. "I don't know, Miss Remmington. I don't believe so." She dipped her chin as if he had confirmed something for her. However, before she could speak, he added, with a twist of his lips, "But I really wouldn't know."

I glanced at Gage, curious whether he realized how revealing that statement was about his relationship with his father.

"And, in any case, you must remember he served on a ship. Although he fought at Trafalgar and such, he spent much of the latter part of the war on the blockade and running troops and supplies back and forth from England."

Her mouth tightened at that, and her eyes dropped to the unread pages in her lap.

"What's troubling you, dear?" Laura's voice was soft with concern.

Miss Remmington glanced at Michael first and I followed her gaze. Why did she keep looking at him that way? I caught Gage's eye, and from the watchful expression I saw there I could tell he understood far more than I did.

Miss Remmington lifted her chin, as if prepared for a confrontation, and addressed her sister-in-law. "I just don't understand why Lord Dalmay had so much trouble forgetting the war. Especially when other soldiers did not."

I frowned at the girl's petulant tone.

"Elise!" her brother snapped, but Laura reached over to lay a restraining hand on him.

"No," she said calmly. "Don't scold her. She has a right to ask." Then she turned back to Miss Remmington with a grim smile. "We don't know exactly why. But that's not really a fair assessment, now, is it?" She tilted her head, urging the girl to consider the matter. "How can we know how many returning soldiers struggled with the same problems as William?"

"But surely we would have heard about it if they had."

"That's not likely." Gage stared down at the swirled pattern of the rug before him. "Battle-hardened soldiers are far more likely to endure in silence. It's all they know. And if they were to admit to having difficulties, who would they tell?" he asked Miss Remmington. "Our society doesn't exactly welcome such confessions."

I bowed my head. One only had to look at the old Lord Dalmay's reaction to his son, and his decision to place him in a lunatic asylum, to understand that. Our nation was eager to welcome home conquering heroes, not broken men.

But Miss Remmington was not placated by such answers. "But, truly, how bad could it be? Men have always gone off to war and come home again. The history books don't talk about them coming home with nightmares." Her hands fisted in her lap and she scowled. "It seems to me Lord Dalmay must have done something particularly awful if it troubled him so much."

A bolt of pure fury shot through me, stiffening my spine. "And who are you to judge? You who've never been asked to take up a sword or a rifle and kill someone in the defense of your king and country. War is a nasty, horrific experience, not handsome men in uniform marching side by side with flashing sabers. It's slogging through muck, and scrounging for food when the supplies do not come through. It's witnessing the devastation trampling armies have wrought on the countryside and the livelihoods of innocent people. It's watching your friend die in a muddy field full of corpses."

"Kiera!"

"Or watching a crow pick out the eyes of a soldier long dead by the side of the road."

"Kiera!"

I broke off at Gage's second shout, throwing him a mutinous look.

"That's not necessary."

I turned to see the others staring at me with horrified expressions. Miss Remmington's face had bleached of all color, and her eyes were wide with shock. I dropped my gaze. I knew I'd gone too far, but, *really*, the girl deserved it. How dare she! What gave her the right to condemn William, especially when she understood *nothing* about what he'd been through? She could show a little compassion at the very least.

Damien rose from his seat to pour a cup of water and crossed the room toward Miss Remmington. "War is not like that," he protested, glowering at me over his shoulder. "You're just trying to scare Miss Remmington, and I think it quite ill-mannered of you."

"And what do you know of it, *Lord* Damien?" I snapped, angry that the pampered marquess's son should criticize me. "Have you ever seen a battlefield? Are you saying that soldiers aren't forced to shoot and stab and slash, trying to kill as many of their enemy as they can before the enemy kills them? Do you think that bullets and blows do not strike home? That blood does not flow? Well, you're deluding yourself, for I can assure you that battlefields are not a pretty sight. They are not populated by tin soldiers to be tipped over and stood up again at will."

Damien, who had kneeled beside Miss Remmington to help her with her glass of water, glared daggers at me. His face reddened at my insult to his intelligence. "And how do you know?" he spluttered. "You've never been to a battlefield, so you don't know what you're talking about either."

I turned away, staring sightlessly at one of the Goya tapestries hanging from the wall. My hands gripped the arms of my spindle-backed chair so hard that I thought the wood might just crack in my bare hands. In my mind's eye I could see one of the worst of William's paintings—the chaos, the carnage of battle—an ocean of broken and bleeding bodies in blue and scarlet and green surging up against a crumbling wall. It looked like one of the nine circles of hell.

I closed my eyes, trying to erase the image. "I've seen pictures," I murmured. Opening them, I looked into Michael's soft gray ones, seeing the same tortured recognition. I pushed to my feet and mumbled some excuse before fleeing the room.

I'd only made it to the first landing on the central staircase before Gage caught up with me. I'd heard him calling my name, but I hadn't wanted to stop. Not here, not now—where anyone could see. My thoughts were too disordered to fight, my emotions too unguarded. His hand wrapped around my arm, pulling me to a stop and forcing me to face him.

"Gage, not . . ."

"Shhh . . ." he soothed, and he wrapped me in his arms and pressed my head against his chest, where it fit just below his chin.

I let him. I didn't fight. Mainly because I had not expected it, and so I had no defense against such tenderness. I had anticipated a scolding, an argument, not this gentle assault.

I closed my eyes and drew a sharp breath, inhaling Gage's scent and his spicy cologne, and allowed myself to relax into his hold. I had forgotten what it was like to be held like this by a man. The strength of his arms, the sense of being protected, cherished, sheltered. My father had never been particularly demonstrative with his affection, not since I was a little girl and he would cradle me in his arms or hold me on his lap, and my brother had followed suit. Sir Anthony certainly hadn't been the affectionate type, nor had I wanted him near me after the first fortnight of our marriage and the revelation of his deception. So it came as something of a shock when I realized how much I'd missed this undemanding affection. It warmed something deep inside me I hadn't even known was cold and consoled me in a way I had not thought possible.

When finally he released his tight hold on me and allowed me to look up into his face, I hardly knew what to say, but I felt much more capable of speaking without falling apart.

"What happened in there?" he asked softly.

"Bad memories, I guess." I sighed, knowing I had more to admit. "And I lost my temper."

He nodded. "Miss Remmington's criticism was startling and uncalled-for, but I never expected you to react so furiously." His pale blue eyes searched mine.

I dropped my gaze, knowing an explanation was necessary. "He's not here to defend himself. And I couldn't just let her comments stand. But you're right. I shouldn't have responded so angrily." I pressed a hand to my forehead. "Or vividly." I grimaced. "Did I really say something about a crow pecking out someone's eyes?"

His eyebrows raised in gentle chastisement. "Yes."

I groaned, allowing my head to fall back. I would need to apologize to both Miss Remmington and Damien for my harsh comments, though the idea left a sour taste in my mouth when I thought about the remarks they'd made that had sparked my responses in the first place.

"I'll make an apology," I muttered. "But I don't understand how Miss Remmington could suggest such an awful thing about William."

"I'm more interested in why."

I furrowed my brow. "What do you mean?"

Gage glanced over his shoulder at the base of the stairs and down the corridor toward the drawing room. Then, taking hold of my arm, he escorted me up the staircase. "Miss Remmington is certainly something of a hoyden, but she does not strike me as the type of person who would make such nasty accusations for no reason other than to cause trouble. She's upset about something. And if I'm not mistaken, it has to do with Michael."

"So you noticed the suspicious glances she's been sending him all evening, too?"

His mouth twisted into a wry smile. "How could I miss them? She may have thought she was being subtle, but she failed to recognize she had two nosy busybodies seated across from her at dinner."

I arched my eyebrows, humored by his absurd description of us.

"Speaking of which . . ." He stopped and turned to me. "You were very quiet at dinner."

I felt a blush slowly begin to burn its way up my neck and into my cheeks.

He cleared his throat. "I hope something didn't put you off your appetite."

"No," I replied, not wanting him to think I'd disliked his . . . attentions earlier, or for him to think I was some sort of green girl, bashful and unworldly. "I just . . . I don't . . ." I then stammered, proving exactly how inexperienced I was.

There was a gleam in his eye, telling me he had returned to his normal conceited self. "Yes, sometimes I have that effect on people."

I scowled at him and replied tartly, "And here I thought I was the only one having difficulty coming up with words simple enough for you to understand."

Gage chuckled and drew me away from the stairs where we could hear others below stirring. "In all seriousness," he said, still sporting a grin, "what do you know of Miss Remmington? Is there any reason to suspect something between her and Michael or William?"

"Not according to her, or anything I've observed."

"Agreed. Then it must be something she knows. Perhaps something we don't."

I considered the possibility.

"In which case, one of us will need to get her to confide in us . . ." He trailed off expectantly.

I frowned. "Me?"

He nodded.

I sighed. "Which means I really will have to apologize to her."

He smiled tightly.

"Fine," I griped, wrinkling the pale green silk of my skirt between my fingers. I heard the crinkle of paper. "But it can wait until tomorrow."

He did not push the matter further and I began to feel guilty for being so snappish. I really needed to get some rest. The previous night's sleeplessness and the long day had taken its toll on my temper and my self-control.

"I'll wish you a good night, then," he said, stepping closer.

"Wait," I gasped, my heart beating faster. "Are you returning to the drawing room?"

He tilted his head. "Yes."

"Would you mind setting this on the tray in the hall?" I pulled the missive I'd penned to Philip and Alana from my pocket. "I meant to leave it there on my way up the stairs."

"Not a problem. I have my own to mail." He patted the inside pocket of his coat.

"Is your father well?" I asked cautiously, not wanting to be handed another evasive response, but unable to forget the look on his face after he had read his letter.

"Yes," he replied, sliding my letter into his pocket with his own.

I nodded, having expected that was all he would say.

But he surprised me by adding, "He . . . doesn't like his orders to be disobeyed." There was a cynical twist to his lips. "Still thinks he's on the quarterdeck of a ship, in that regard. And, let's just say, visiting an old friend does not rank high on his list of priorities for me at this moment in time."

I offered him a grim smile of commiseration, wondering just what exactly those priorities were. Did Lord Gage have a case he wanted his son's assistance with in London? Or was there some other pressing matter that demanded his son's attention? There was no way of knowing, of course, unless Gage decided to share, which I did not anticipate happening. However, his willingness to confide what he had buoyed my hope that he was beginning to trust me.

"Well," he murmured, that gleam returning to his eyes as he slid closer to me.

My heart sped faster as I realized what was coming.

"I'll wish you a good night then."

"Yes. Good night," I replied breathlessly.

He reached forward with a single finger and tipped my chin upward, sealing my lips with the kiss I had been anticipating. I felt him smile against my mouth as he pulled away, a satisfied smirk that was both appealing and infuriating.

That smile never left his lips. Even when he turned away to retreat down the stairs, I could still feel the power of it.

Pressing a hand to my still-tingling lips, I backed into the shadows of the corridor, lest he catch me staring after him like some lovesick fool.

I knew I shouldn't be allowing Gage's kisses to distract me—that I probably shouldn't be allowing them at all—but I couldn't help but feel happy. I had never been pursued like this, not when it wasn't some lecher trying to win a bet with his friends as part of yet another mean-spirited wager made at my expense in the betting books at one of London's gentlemen's clubs. It was exciting and flattering, and a whole host of other emotions I wasn't certain I'd ever felt, at least, not quite in this way.

I knew I should be demanding explanations. And I would. But for the moment, it was simply nice to feel that for once a man was interested in *me*, and not how my talents could benefit him, or how bedding me would enhance his reputation for daring to seduce an unnatural woman like me.

I understood that whatever this relationship was between Gage and me, it could only go so far. It would be imprudent to think otherwise. But for the moment, I didn't want to contemplate the future. I just wanted to be.

I returned to my bedchamber, surprised to find Lucy once again waiting for me. I studied her closely, hoping she was in a more cooperative mood. And she was, insomuch as she didn't handle me roughly as she unlaced my clothing or gore me with my hairpins as she removed them. But she also didn't speak.

Now, Lucy was not as garrulous as some maids, but she always had something to say, and more often than not, more than one something. Not tonight. Her lips were sealed into a tight line and her brow gently puckered in an expression that some might mistake for concentration, but I knew better. I repressed a sigh.

"Are you still angry with me?" I asked her as she pulled the last pin from my hair.

I could see her pause in the reflection of the mirror before setting the pin in the enamel box where they were stored.

"Don't lie," I told her.

She looked up to meet my gaze, still not saying anything.

This time I could not hold back a sigh of exasperation. I was as irritated with myself as I was with her. Most of the ladies of my acquaintance couldn't care two figs for the happiness of their servants. They were there to do a job, and that was that. I should have been the same way, but I could not quite manage to ignore their feelings, particularly when they unsettled my own.

"Do we need to discuss it?" I asked as she ran a brush through my hair.

She shook her head.

Fine. If she didn't want to talk about it, I wasn't about to argue. Instead, I would try a different tack. "Were you able to learn anything about Donovan?"

She hesitated again, halting the hairbrush in midstroke, before continuing on as if nothing had happened. "Just that he worked at an infirmary in Edinburgh before comin' here."

"Yes, and at one in Glasgow. I discovered that, too."

She glanced up at my reflection and then set the brush aside to braid my hair. The concentration she was exerting to do a task she'd done perhaps five hundred times before was excessive, and it made me suspicious.

"There's nothing more?"

She lifted her chin. "Nay, m'lady."

I couldn't be sure, but I was almost certain she was lying. It wouldn't do to push the matter. I knew just how stubborn Lucy could be. However, my sense of responsibility for her drove me to caution her again.

"I know I warned you once, but given the fact that your family is not here to look after you, I feel I should remind you again to be careful there."

Lucy tied the ribbon at the end of my hair with a sharp tug. "I dinna need lookin' after. And asides, I told ye, he's no' likely to pay me mind. Is that all, m'lady?"

I opened my mouth to argue, but then thought better of it. The girl was in no frame of mind to listen. "Yes."

She bobbed a perfunctory curtsy and was gone.

CHAPTER EIGHTEEN

I was surprised to find Miss Remmington already in the breakfast room early the next morning. We had the chamber to ourselves, save for the footman stationed by the door to assist us, so I decided it was as good a time as any to make my apology. She accepted it with a dip of her head, her eyes scarcely meeting mine. I couldn't decide whether she was embarrassed, or intent on being angry and churlish, but either way, she expressed no regret over her own words spoken in the drawing room the previous night.

Following her lead, I focused on my breakfast and mostly ignored her presence, difficult as it was with her seated across from me. The longer we sat in silence, the more awkward it became, until I was relieved to see her rise from the table to take her leave. I hated to dash Gage's hopes, but if the cautious glance Miss Remmington gave me before exiting the room was any indication, she was not going to be confiding in me anytime soon.

Moments later, Lord Keswick entered, looking back through the door at his retreating sister, no doubt. His steps faltered when he caught sight of me, but only for a moment, and I knew I would be making another apology.

After he'd filled his plate and settled in the chair Miss Remmington had so recently vacated, I swallowed my frustration at his sister's silence and expressed my regret over the previous night's actions. Unlike Miss Remmington, Lord Keswick listened with easy acceptance, making the words less bitter on my tongue the second time around.

"I understand you were trying to defend Lord Dalmay," he told me. "You simply let your words get away from you, and who of us can say we have not done the same at one time or another." His mouth curled into a gentle smile. "I'm sure my wife and sister would tell you I have."

I released a deep breath. "Thank you for being so gracious."

He looked to the door again. "I hope my sister made her apology in return."

I did not know how to respond to such a query. I had no wish to be a tattler, or to get Miss Remmington into trouble with her brother, even if I had found her failure to reciprocate rude. Nevertheless, it seemed my silence was answer enough.

Lord Keswick sighed. "Then you must allow me to make her apology for her."

"That's not necessary."

"But it is," he insisted. "And I'm certain my sister knows how inappropriate and offensive her suppositions about Lord Dalmay were. But she . . ." His gaze dropped to his plate, where his fork hovered over a bite of kippers ready to be lifted into his mouth. "Well, she doesn't take criticism well. I'm afraid that is my parents' fault as much as my aunt's and uncle's."

It seemed to me the fault was her own, but I let him continue his explanation without argument.

"You see, my parents doted on her. In their eyes, she could do no wrong, and they let her run rather wild, for a young lady—gallivanting across the countryside. When they died . . ." I could hear the sadness in his voice ". . . I was still attending Oxford, and had yet to reach my majority. I had no idea how to care for a twelve-year-old girl, or what grooming or lessons she would require. So she went to live with our aunt and uncle."

His expression was pained. "If my parents were indulgent, my aunt and uncle were the exact opposite. They immediately set about reforming Elise. I discovered later, to my regret, that their methods were not the kindest. They constantly harangued and berated my sister, quoting Bible verses and calling her wicked. Elise, being who she is, rebelled, which only made matters worse. By the time I came of age and finally realized what was happening, she had been in their care for over three years. Now she views any attempt to correct her as an attack." He shook his head. "I've done my best, but I'm afraid she resists all instruction."

I wondered if he understood how haughty he sounded when he publicly chastised her, and if that might be part of the problem. But it was not my place to intervene in the care of his sister. I could only listen to his story and decide whether it excused Miss Remmington's appalling behavior. I rather thought it didn't, but I was more sympathetic to the girl now that I knew her life had not all been a pampered bed of roses.

I finished my breakfast and crossed the yard to the stables, where Gage was waiting for me with Dewdrop and his chestnut gelding. It was another fine day, with high clouds in a robin's egg–blue sky. The morning air was crisp, but I could tell the temperature would warm considerably by the afternoon, so even though I was shivering in my royal blue and gold riding habit now, I knew I would be comfortable later.

Mr. Wallace received us in his study rather than the drawing room when we arrived at Lambden Cottage. "Come in, come in," he exclaimed as he rose from his seat behind his desk and moved toward a more intimate arrangement of furniture before the hearth. "I apologize if this seems a bit informal, but I find my study preferable to that stuffy parlor."

I smiled at his easy manner and offered my hand in greeting. He bowed over it and then looked up into my face, giving me a chance to view the lines of worry and fatigue radiating from the corners of his eyes and mouth and carving grooves into his forehead. He turned to shake Gage's hand and I used the opportunity to survey the room.

It was a cozy little chamber, though by no means was it truly small. Bookshelves lined two of the walls, packed cheek by jowl with books, mostly leather tomes. Mr. Wallace's massive oaken desk sat before one of these bays, its surface littered with papers and open texts. The heavy burgundy curtains were pulled open to reveal a view of the back garden. Autumn flowers bloomed drowsily in the sunshine, where an errant bumblebee flitted from petal to petal. The furniture arranged before the oaken fireplace was upholstered in matching burgundy damask, with shots of pale gold and cream brocade. I admired the rich fabric for a moment before allowing my eyes to stray to the true centerpiece of the room—the two portraits hanging above the mantel.

It was clear they had been arranged so that Mr. Wallace might look at them while he worked at his desk. I quickly deduced that the woman on the right must be his late wife. She was a lovely woman, with caramel-brown hair and dark eyes, but I found my attention focused on the second subject—our missing girl. Miss Wallace sported the same coloring as her mother, but her eyes were more almond shaped, more catlike, and her chin was pointed and dainty like the fae, like her father's.

Mr. Wallace caught me looking up at them and confirmed my suspicions. "My wife and daughter. I like to have my Janet wi' me. And it only seemed right to hang Mary next to her." He sighed. "Noo it's all I have o' 'em both."

"Have you come to agree with Mr. Paxton's theory, then?" Gage asked as we settled into our seats. There was one for each of us. Or one for what had been father, mother, and child.

"Nay," he told us firmly. "I dinna believe Mary did something so foolish as to cross the land bridge wi' the tide coming in. No' unless she was forced to. And I canna think of any reason she would be. The McCrays have a boat. If there were some sorta urgency, she coulda had Connor McCray row her across. Nay. It makes no sense."

"Then why is Paxton so set on this idea? He strikes me

as something of a tyrant, but he doesn't seem wholly incompetent."

Mr. Wallace's expression was sour. "He's no' incompetent. He's just too quick to latch on to the simplest answer, be it proven or no'."

"It seems a bit shortsighted for him to declare that is what happened when he has several people telling him she would never do such a thing, no witnesses to say she entered the land bridge while the tide was coming in, and no . . . evidence to say otherwise." By "evidence" I knew Gage meant the girl's body. "It's pure speculation. For all we know she could still be somewhere on that island."

"We've searched it from top to bottom." Mr. Wallace sounded despondent. "It's only nineteen acres. And we found nothin'."

Which made it highly unlikely that we, two strangers, would find something the locals had missed.

"Did your daughter have any enemies?"

Mr. Wallace looked up at me in surprise.

"Perhaps 'enemies' is too strong a word," I corrected, before the man could take offense. "I've heard of her kindness and that she was generally well liked, but even the best of us have people who dislike us for one reason or another. Did Miss Wallace have any detractors? People who didn't get along with her, who might wish her harm?"

The furrows in Mr. Wallace's brow deepened, and he turned to the fireplace, where a low fire still crackled. "There is one thing."

I shared a look with Gage, curious as to what it was the man seemed so hesitant to share.

"I didna want to tell ye because it clouds some people's view o' Mary. But in light o' this . . ." His gaze lifted to meet mine. "Lady Darby, your mother was Scottish, wasna she? And a Rutherford o' Clintmains, at that." He spoke under his breath as he continued to study me. "And come to think o' it, I believe your grandmum was also Irish." He nodded, almost to himself. "You might understand, then. I s'pose I'll have to chance it."

Gage was watching me closely now, too, but I had no idea what Mr. Wallace was hinting at by quoting part of my lineage.

He squared his shoulders. "My daughter is gifted wi' the second sight."

I couldn't stop my eyes from widening, not having expected this.

"Ye ken what that is?" he demanded of me. I nodded, and he turned to Gage. "Mr. Gage?"

"She can see the future before it happens?" Gage replied, seeming careful to keep his voice and expression neutral.

"*Some* o' the future," he emphasized. "Major events and what God chooses to show her. My wife had it, too."

His eyes darted back and forth between us, gauging our reactions. I had no idea what to say, and I knew better than to look at Gage, lest I see disdain.

I honestly didn't know what I thought about second sight. Certainly the belief was a time-honored tradition in Scotland, one that many accepted as truth. As a child I'd heard people whisper that my grandmother had it, the same Irish one Mr. Wallace had referred to. I'd never thought much of it, though I suppose if I'd been forced to give an answer, I would have said that people simply exaggerated. That whatever "ability" my grandmother had had was the product of a quick mind and strong intuition.

I didn't necessarily disbelieve in things like second sight, however. After all, I had heard enough myths and legends from my mother and our Scottish nanny growing up that I liked to allow for the possibility of unexplainable occurrences. But I was also logical, methodical, and I had yet to meet someone who could prove they were capable of foretelling anything that keen observation could not. That didn't mean such people didn't exist, just that I had never met them, nor was I likely to.

"And she has enemies because of it?" I said, speaking to

the effect her claimed ability had on the investigation, not whether I believed it to be true or not. "People who don't believe her dislike her for it, or even envy her?"

"Most accept it readily enough, and are even grateful for it. Like Mrs. Ross. Mary saw she was going to have trouble delivering her bairns, and so she convinced Dr. Littleton to visit her in the midst o' a terrible storm. Made it just in time, or those bairns and Mrs. Ross woulda died." He sighed and bobbed his head in resignation. "But there are others who aren't so pleased aboot it. Be it disbelief, dislike, or envy, I dinna ken, but there are some who watch her wi' mistrustful eyes."

"Like Mr. Paxton?" Gage guessed.

"Aye. He be one o' them. Mr. Munro is another." He scowled. "Though it's his own fault for no' heeding her warning. Mary told him no' to fix his roof that day, but he didn't listen. And when he fell and broke his leg, he blamed her for calling a curse doon on him."

"Would he do something to your daughter to get back at her? Maybe not murder her, but harm her in some way?"

Mr. Wallace considered the matter, rubbing his fingers over his pointed chin. "Nay. Munro is a loud complainer, but he's no' violent. And if ye considered him, you'd also have to consider Mrs. Ogston, and she was just overcome wi' grief. She didn't mean her threats."

Gage glanced at me. "What threats?"

Mr. Wallace pressed his lips together, and I wondered if he wished he hadn't said anything about the woman. "Sometimes Mary has visions that are no' so happy."

I frowned. None of her visions thus far had seemed particularly pleasant, unless she hadn't liked Mr. Munro. Then the prospect of his breaking his leg might have given her some kind of enjoyment. But I refrained from making this remark.

"She saw that Mrs. Ogston was going to lose her bairn before its time. All she could do was warn her to be careful, but it happened anyway. And Mrs. Ogston blamed her for it. Called her a witch and accused her of telling the devil to take her bairn."

"And threatened to what?" Gage persisted.

Mr. Wallace faced us grimly. "Send her to hell."

I blinked. That was quite extreme.

"But as I said, she was overcome by grief. I dinna think she meant it, though I ken she doesn't wish my daughter weel."

"How long ago was this?"

"A few months. Less than half a year."

Gage looked to me with a skeptical gleam in his eyes, and I knew he would want to question this Mrs. Ogston. I was of the same opinion as Mr. Wallace—grief could make people say terrible things—but I decided it couldn't hurt to find out what her attitude toward Miss Wallace was now.

"Is there anything else we should know about your daughter?" Gage asked. "Anyone you think we should talk to while Mr. Paxton is away? We may not get another chance."

Mr. Wallace settled back in his chair with a sigh. "I s'pose you intend to visit the island."

"Yes. And speak to a few people in the village, as well as the ferrymen."

"I canna think of anyone else in particular, except maybe Calum MacMath and his ole cronies. They sit ootside the inn on fair days, gossiping like a bunch o' magpies while they watch the ships come in."

I cracked a smile at this affable description. Every village in the British Isles must have had at least a trio of these older men who congregated in the public inn or tavern to while away their hours. They were often the best source of gossip in any village, even more so than their wives.

"We'll speak to them, then," Gage said, hiding his own grin of amusement. "Now, before we go, if we could see Miss Wallace's room and speak to her maid, one of them might provide a clue that Mr. Paxton has missed."

Mr. Wallace sat up in surprise. "But why would there be anything in her room? She couldn't have kenned she was going to go missing."

"No, but she might have come into contact with someone suspicious and made a note of it or kept a record of her visits and we can deduce a pattern from them. I don't ask to alarm you." Gage's voice lowered to a soothing tone. "There may be nothing there at all. But I do have some experience with this sort of thing, and I would rather have a look now than discover later that there was a clue waiting for us there all along."

Mr. Wallace nodded tentatively at first and then with more certainty. "Aye. I dinna think she kept an appointment book, but you'd best look. And I spoke to her maid the moment I kenned she was missing, but I reckon ye should speak with her, too."

"Thank you."

M iss Wallace's maid was a stalwart Scottish lass, and I was relieved to be facing a composed woman and not a timid, sobbing mass of petticoats, though I could tell from the red rims and puffiness around her eyes that she had wept at some point, and recently. She perched on the edge of a ladder-back chair while Gage and I searched Miss Wallace's bedchamber.

"Nay, Miss Mary doesna keep a 'pointment book. She keeps it all up here." Kady tapped her head with her forefinger. "Has a mind like a trap, that'n."

"What about a journal or a diary?" I asked as I glanced back and forth between the maid and the bookshelf I was perusing.

The maid shook her head.

"Something to write her visions in?"

She hesitated to respond, drawing all of my attention to her. Kady didn't seem to know how to answer, and I suddenly realized her dilemma.

"Mr. Wallace told us about her second sight."

She searched my eyes and, apparently finding me trustworthy, replied, "She doesna write them doon. No' those horrible things." Her brow lowered into a fierce frown. "They're a curse, I tell ye. And she's told me more than once she wishes she could make 'em stop."

I abandoned the bookshelf and moved forward to perch on the edge of the bed closer to the maid, leaving the search to Gage. Somehow I could sense that this conversation was far more important than whatever we would find in this room.

"I understand that most of her visions are quite unpleasant."

"Aye. Many o' 'em come as nightmares. When she was but a wee lass, she would wake up screamin' like a banshee, puir dear. I took to sleepin' at the foot o' the bed jus' so I could be here when she woke."

"Are they always like that?" I asked in some concern. What kind of existence was that, to fall asleep afraid to dream? Unbidden, an image of Will pacing his floors in an effort to outrun sleep flashed through my mind.

The kindhearted older woman reached forward to pat my hand where it lay on my knee. "Nay. The older she grew, and the better she got at understandin' 'em, the less they troubled her. The real bad ones still upset her somethin' awful, but she's learned to live wi' the rest." Her face clouded with worry and her gaze turned distant. "That is, 'til recently."

I glanced at Gage, who had looked up from his search of Miss Wallace's desk drawer at the change in the maid's tone of voice.

"Why recently? What happened?"

Kady looked up at me, her face lined with worry. "I dinna ken for sure. Maybe it's because she seemed so happy the few weeks afore it happened. Happier than I've ever seen her. But then the nightmares began again."

My heart clenched in dread.

"Worse than ever afore." Kady clasped her hands together in her lap, the knuckles turning white as she relived her memories. "She'd wake up thrashin' and screamin', beggin' for whatever it was to stop. Woke her da' a time or two in his room doon the hall. I asked her what it was . . ." She sounded like she was pleading with her charge again. "But she wouldna' tell me. A time or two when she'd just waked I heard her babblin' aboot the cold and the darkness, but that's all I ken. And all I could think to ask her was if they were aboot her da'. She told me nay. That's when I realized . . ." She broke off, unable to speak the words.

So I spoke them for her. "That it might be her."

She nodded. "I didna want to ask her. Didna want to even think it." Her face crumpled, and she came close to losing her composure. But she took a deep breath and swallowed her grief and guilt. "But it might've been."

I pressed a hand to my chest, where my heart pounded furiously, having trouble coming to terms with the information the maid had just given us. If Miss Wallace had foreseen her own death, and if it had been as unpleasant as her reaction to her nightmares suggested it was . . . heavens! How could she live with that knowledge? How could she go about living her life, day after day, knowing it was only a matter of time before her nightmares came true? The very thought made me dizzy with fright.

I jumped at the feel of Gage's hand on my shoulder. He squeezed gently, reassuring me, and I inhaled sharply.

Kady offered me a tight smile in commiseration. "Aye. The *an da shealladh* is a dark thing," she told me, using what must be the Gaelic term for "second sight."

"Did Miss Wallace mention anyone she might have quarreled with?" Gage asked, turning the subject. "Someone who might wish her ill or hold a grudge?"

Kady lifted her eyes in contemplation and then shook her head. "Nay. Though she doesna talk to me much aboot people. She mostly keeps her opinions to hersel'." She squinted one eye. "But I can read her reactions fairly weel. Like when that fool Munro yelled oot his window at us after he fell off his roof 'cause he didna listen to her warnin'. Tried to blame her, the sod. I could tell she didna feel the least bit sorry for the man, though to all else she looked fair concerned."

I felt a measure of my equanimity return during her story, especially considering the fact that I had had a similar thought about Mr. Munro and what Miss Wallace's reaction should be to him. I even felt a certain amount of calm. Until Kady spoke her next words.

"And then there was that doctor. Miss Mary didna like him," she added, shaking her head.

The hairs stood up on my arm. "What doctor?" I demanded.

"I dinna ken his name." Her eyes had widened at my sharp reaction. "He approached her in the village and she refused to talk to 'im."

"When was this?" Gage asked. I could hear the same heightened level of interest in his voice as mine but his had taken on an angry edge, which I wasn't sure he was even aware of.

"A few weeks ago, I guess it was noo," Kady said, stumbling over her reply.

Gage nodded to her and then turned to me. "I think we need to speak with Mr. Wallace again."

I rose to follow him to the door, but before going I paused to ask the bewildered maid one more question. "Just out of curiosity, did Miss Wallace encounter the doctor before or after her nightmares began again?"

"Why, I think it was afore," she replied in surprise.

I thanked her and turned back to Gage, who was watching me with an expression that said we would be having a conversation about this later.

"His name was Callart," Mr. Wallace told us in reply to Gage's query.

We had found him in his study where we had left him, deep in unhappy thought, if the frown on his face was any indication.

He rose to cross the room to his desk. "He came to call one afternoon, offering his services to help my daughter. Said he was some *brain* specialist and he'd heard of my daughter's 'affliction.'" He lifted his gaze, a martial gleam in his eyes. "I told him to sod off."

I had to smile at that, despite my uneasy suspicions.

"Did he try to pressure you?" Gage asked.

Mr. Wallace bent forward to rummage through the papers in a drawer. "Aye. Had to threaten to throw him off my property to get him to leave."

"Did you know he accosted your daughter in the village?" I inquired.

He straightened and moved back toward us. "Nay. Who told you this? Kady?"

. I nodded.

"Impertinent leech," he growled. He handed the card he'd taken from his desk to Gage. "Dr. Thomas Callart. Noo I'm glad I kept his card. Do ye think he's behind my daughter's disappearance?"

"We don't know," Gage replied cautiously after making a cursory inspection of the business card and tucking it into the inside pocket of his coat. "Can you tell us what he looked like?"

"Short, round, rather like a partridge. No' particularly attractive."

"Well, then, let us know if you think of anything else," Gage told him. "We'll send word as soon as we have any news."

CHAPTER NINETEEN

"Do you think Dr. Sloane used an alias?" I asked, having to hurry to keep up with Gage's long stride down the hall. "Do you think this Dr. Callart could be him?"

"No."

I was so taken aback by the certainty in his voice that it took me a moment to respond. "What do you mean?"

I had to wait for his answer, as the Wallaces' butler appeared and handed us our hats and gloves. It took me but a moment to affix my hat atop my head and pin it at its jaunty angle, but Gage was already outside, taking the reins of our horses from the waiting stable boys.

"How can you be so certain?" I persisted.

I allowed Gage to boost me up into my saddle, looking down at him expectantly while he fiddled with my stirrup, the length of which had been perfectly fine on our ride over to Lambden Cottage.

"Because Dr. Sloane is tall and thin," he finally replied. "There is no way he could be this short, round man who calls himself Dr. Callart."

Gage mounted his gelding while I digested this bit of information. "You know what Dr. Sloane looks like?"

He cut a look of annoyance in my direction as he directed his horse to walk on. "It isn't difficult to ask. After all, Michael has seen the man."

"Yes, but . . ." Everything he was saying was true, but it didn't explain his restless movements or why he was avoiding looking into my eyes. So I decided to be direct. "Have *you* ever seen him?"

It took a moment for him to respond—the silence that fell between us broken only by the clopping of the horses' hooves and the jangling of their harnesses—and when he did it was barely louder than a murmur. "Yes."

A bolt of alarm ran down my spine and I sat straighter. But before I could voice my next question, he spoke again.

"We can't discuss it right now." He turned to look at me, his eyes earnest but also commanding. "I promise you, I *will* tell you. But not here." He gestured with his head to the old tower of the kirk and the pale stone buildings that lined the street at the base of the hill just coming into view out of the trees that shaded the road.

I bit back the words forming on my tongue, for I knew he was right. Whatever argument was brewing between us, whatever revelation Gage was about to make, would have to wait until we'd interviewed the villagers about Miss Wallace. We had to present a united front in our inquiries. And though it tied a knot inside me not to know, I did not try to force the words from him. However, I could not stop my mind from conjuring up all manner of possibilities.

We left our horses at the livery stables behind the Cramond Inn and walked through the village on foot. We stepped into the shops and stopped people on the street. The general consensus seemed to be that Miss Wallace was a kind, well-liked lass with a good head on her shoulders. Several people had seen her cross the land bridge to Cramond Island at low tide on Thursday last, but none of them had seen her return, not even Calum MacMath and his cronies. They swore they had been seated in front of the inn from midday through sunset, and that if anyone had seen her return, it would have been them. MacMath also made it a point, as several others did, to tell us that Mary Wallace was no fool to be risking her life crossing when the tide was already coming in, but that Mr. Paxton might just possibly be.

If nothing else, the local constable seemed a bit unpopular, but that was not an uncommon reaction to policemen in small towns, whose people liked to handle such matters in their own ways. I couldn't see Mr. Paxton exercising compromise or compassion. He enjoyed his power too much.

No one seemed to flinch at the mention of Miss Wallace's second sight, and the majority, even the reverend at Cramond Kirk, seemed to look on it with favor rather than disapproval. There were a few that frowned and shook their heads or rolled their eyes, but no one voiced a harsh opinion of her or her supposed ability. Even Mr. Munro and Mrs. Ogston seemed contrite over their earlier condemnation of her, though it may have been our positions as investigators into Miss Wallace's disappearance that kept their tongues civil.

Whatever the truth, Mr. Munro's leg was mended and Mrs. Ogston was round with child again, and I suspected these developments had done more than anything to heal any lingering animosity.

We ate luncheon at the inn, waiting for the tide to finish going out, and then traversed the mile-long trail, slick with seaweed and shingles washed smooth by thousands of years of ocean currents, to the island. I felt a little bit like Moses and the Israelites crossing the Red Sea, though there were no walls of water surrounding us, only a wide stretch of wet sand on either side and the gently undulating ocean lapping at the edges. I was grateful for my kid leather riding boots and the extra layer of woolen socks I had donned that morning as our feet sank into the sand and shale of the ocean bottom.

The island itself was green and gold with brush and lush grass and gently sloped toward a small wood roughly at its center. As we drew closer, I could see white fluffy sheep dotting the fields, nibbling at tufts of grass. The briny air whipped at my little hat until I feared I would have to remove it or else watch it blown out to sea.

When we reached the island, we followed the little path that wound up toward the wood, where we had been told the McCray farmstead rested. Nestled among the trees, the stone buildings were crude, but snugly built.

When we entered the yard, Mrs. McCray was already at her door, hands on her hips. "Are ye here aboot Mistress Mary, then?"

"Yes," Gage replied, removing his hat. "We're investigating on Mr. Wallace's behalf." He introduced us while the farmwife looked us up and down as if we were bits of useless frippery.

"Ye'll already ken I'm Mrs. McCray. Ye'd best come in."

We followed her through the door, ducking our heads so as not to smack them on the low lintel. She offered us a seat at the scarred, wooden table at the center of her kitchen and then turned to the great stone fireplace to swing a kettle over the fire. The room was worn, but cozy and clean. I cringed at the sight of our muddy footprints on her otherwise spotless flagstone floor.

She reached up high inside a cabinet and pulled out a lovely china teapot and three cups. I could tell from her handling of them that they were cherished possessions, quite possibly the nicest things she owned, and only brought out for special company. She set the tea things on the table and began spooning some of the precious leaves inside the pot. When the kettle whistled, she was ready for it.

"Noo, then," she declared, taking a seat across from us as the tea steeped. "Ye'll have heard from Mr. Wallace how I had the ague and Mistress Mary were kind enough to come visit me."

"Does Miss Wallace visit you often?" I inquired.

"Oh, every few weeks, and when me or me boy is ill." She paused and then added, "Mr. McCray dinna get sick." The way she said this made me suspect her husband was a stubborn man.

"How ill were you?" Gage ventured to ask. "Mr. Paxton made it sound like you were too sick to even stand."

Mrs. McCray scowled. "That ole fool. What'd he say? That I couldna tell the time." She blew through her lips, dismissing the man. "I had a bit o' a cough, no' consumption. And I tell ye, Mistress Mary left wi' plenty o' time to cross afore the tide. That's a fact. So it's a daft notion that the lass got swept away into the sea."

She poured milk into our cups and then carefully added tea and sugar.

Gage sipped his tea. "What of this Craggy Donald? Would she have visited him?"

"Maybe. But it's no' likely. He dinna like visitors much."

"Who is he?"

"Just an ole hermit. Keeps to himsel'. He dinna bother us so we leave 'im be," She shook her head. "Paxton and his cronies tore his place apart, intent on findin' somethin' to arrest him for."

"But you think he's innocent."

"Aye." She nodded her head decisively. "People who dinna understand him think him strange, but he's harmless. It's far more likely they'd harm him than the other way aroond."

We thanked her for the tea and set off in the direction of Craggy Donald's hut. She'd pointed us to a grown-over trail leading down toward the beach on the northeast side of the island, facing out to the North Sea. As we rounded a curve in the path, we could see a puff of smoke rising away from the hillside farther down where the shanty must stand. The clouds were moving faster across the sky now and the sea here seemed a sterner gray. I could imagine what it looked like in a storm, with roiling clouds and thrashing waves. If I were Donald, I should be afraid my little hovel was going to be dashed into the ocean. But perhaps that was how he liked it.

As we drew closer, we were able to see that the hut itself was built into the hillside, so that only two walls of wood were visible. Even most of the roof was earth. Gage approached to knock on the slatted wood door, its boards crudely lashed together, leaving gaps at the top and the bottom. It was warped and nearly falling off its hinges. There was no answer.

"Maybe he's down at the beach," I suggested. "If he rarely goes into town, he must do a lot of fishing."

And sure enough a man carrying a fishing rod and a rope strung with fresh fish emerged over a rise in the path leading down to the water. He halted at the sight of us, staring at us with blank eyes.

"Craggy Donald?" Gage guessed, taking a single step toward him before he stopped, mindful not to scare the man away. "We just want to ask you a few questions. We're here on behalf of Mr. Wallace." When the man still did not move, he added, "I'm not one of Paxton's men."

He studied us, not betraying by the twitch of a muscle what he was thinking. As to be expected, his clothes were old and worn, but kept in good repair. I could see three carefully stitched patches on the front of his trousers alone. His grizzled gray hair was kept tied back neatly in a queue and his matching beard was carefully trimmed so that it would not get in the way of eating. But it was his face that was the most remarkable thing about him, and evidently the source of his nickname. Worn and beaten until it was as thick and rugged as leather, with deep furrows grooving his forehead and the corners of his mouth and eyes. It was obvious that he had been a career sailor, be it on a merchant ship or in the Royal Navy. Given his neatness, I suspected it was the latter.

I glanced at Gage to see if he had realized the same thing. Surely, with his captain father, he would know a seaman when he saw one.

Deciding we must be trustworthy, or at least that we weren't going to toss his abode into disarray, Craggy Donald climbed the path toward us. He stepped around us to hang his catch of fish from a hook protruding from the wall.

"Where did you serve?" Gage asked.

He paused in leaning his rod against the wall by the door, as if surprised by the question. But then he replied in a low, scratchy voice. "HMS *Warrior.*"

"Whom did you serve under?"

Craggy Donald turned to look at Gage. "Cap'n Phipps."

He nodded. "I never had the pleasure of meeting him. I'm Sebastian Gage. My father is Captain Lord Gage."

He eyed him closely. "Golden like an angel, but with the devil in his eyes. Aye, I s'pose ye could be his get."

Gage smiled tightly.

"Why're ye here?"

"Visiting a friend who happens to be concerned about Miss Wallace." He faced the man squarely, speaking to him like an equal, and not some lowly cur to bully, as evidently Mr. Paxton had behaved, from the condition of Craggy Donald's kicked-in door. "I know you've already been asked before, but I need to ask again. Did Miss Wallace come to visit you on Thursday last?"

He answered with calm assurance. "Nay."

"Did you see her on the island—or anywhere, for that matter—on that day, or any day after?"

"Nay."

Gage sighed in disappointment and turned his head to look out to sea. I felt the same exasperation, but, then, we'd known it was unlikely that anyone could tell us anything we didn't already know.

"What about anything suspicious?" He sounded like he was clutching at straws now. "Did anything out of the ordinary happen on that day or the days around it?"

I fully expected Craggy Donald to say no, but something flickered in his eyes, arresting Gage's attention and mine.

"Well, there was one thing. A boat. A coble, from the looks o' its size. I didna see it leavin' the island, but it seemed it mun ha' came from here."

"This was on Thursday?" Gage clarified.

"Aye."

"Where were they headed?"

He pointed. "Oot to sea."

That meant that if Miss Wallace had been on that boat she could be anywhere by now.

"Why didn't you report this to Mr. Paxton?" I asked in some frustration.

His eyes turned hard. "He didna ask."

Just set about destroying his property.

I could hear the words left unsaid. I sighed, unable to blame the man despite my agitation. It was doubtful Mr. Paxton would have even listened to him if he'd tried to tell him about the boat.

"Is there anything else you can tell us? Could you see anyone aboard the coble?" Gage shifted on his feet and I knew he was ready to be off.

Craggy Donald shook his head. "'Twas too far off."

Gage thanked him and we started back up the path at a speed too quick for me.

"Slow down," I gasped.

He complied, but without so much as an apology for making me winded. He was too deep in thought.

"How much would you wager that Mary was on that boat?"

"I'm not wagering anything," I told him, though I did feel a surge of hope that we might be able to clear William after all. But our chances of finding Mary Wallace were looking slimmer and slimmer. "In any case, we need to talk to the ferrymen."

Gage turned to me with a bright smile. "No bet, then. But if those ferrymen don't confirm that Miss Wallace never crossed the river that day, keeping her far away from Dalmay House, I'll . . ." his eyes lifted skyward, as if searching for inspiration ". . . eat a haggis for dinner."

I felt a swirling in my stomach. One that I knew was due to Gage's rising confidence in Will's innocence rather than any nausea at the idea of eating haggis.

And as expected, Gage did not have to choke down the traditional Scottish dish. None of the ferrymen had seen Miss Wallace on Thursday, and they knew her well. It appeared she had something of a routine, and rarely crossed the river on Thursdays. So they promised they would remember the oddity of such a departure from the usual. There was absolutely no reason to doubt their truthfulness. So it was with a lighter heart that I began our ride back to Dalmay House, though my thoughts were still troubled over the whereabouts of Miss Wallace.

The trail wound in and out of the forest that bordered the firth, giving us glimpses of the water and then taking it away. But all the while we could hear the soft roaring of the waves as they approached the shore. Sycamores and elderberry trees lined the path with pale white asters sprinkling the ground between their trunks. Here and there stood patches of bramble bushes, reminding me that this was where Miss Remmington and Miss Wallace first met, and where they often strolled together. It was a lovely little wood, allowing just enough sunshine through the canopy above so that it did not feel isolated or confining.

I glanced at Gage, who seemed to be puzzling through something—his brow furrowed, his body loose and swaying to the gait of his horse. He had not spoken since asking his questions of the ferrymen. I knew there were things we needed to discuss, questions I needed to ask, but I was almost reluctant to voice them. I had not slept well again, my mind too full of worries and fears I dared not speak aloud. This was the most serene I had felt since arriving at Dalmay House—no, since leaving Gairloch Castle, when my sister promptly fell ill a mile into the journey—and I was reluctant to end it. Whether it was the peaceful setting or the mounting evidence that Will could not have had anything to do with Miss Wallace's disappearance, whatever had exerted its calming influence on me, I knew it would end the moment I addressed the secrets between us.

I wanted to pretend they weren't there. I was so tired of fighting with Gage. I tried to tell myself that whatever he was keeping from me couldn't be that bad; that I didn't need to know. But I did. I knew I did. And it would nag at me, affecting everything I did until I had the truth.

I gazed across the short distance between us at Gage's

profile, watching the light and shade shift across it. I was weary of all the secrets. He needed to either tell me or leave me be.

"I know," Gage surprised me by saying.

I worried for a moment I might have spoken aloud.

He turned his head to look at me. "I know we need to talk. But first . . . there's something I want to ask you." He paused, his eyes heavy with some strong emotion, and I realized he was waiting for my response.

I frowned, uncertain what he needed to ask me. "All right."

His eyes turned forward again. I wasn't sure whether he didn't know how to phrase his question or if he was working up the courage to ask it.

When he spoke, it was slow and hesitant. "Are there really no romantic feelings on your part for Will?"

I scowled at him in irritation. Why did he continue to persist in this?

"I know it's impertinent," he told me. "I just . . . need to know."

I studied him, trying to understand why my answer seemed so important to him. Was this because he'd kissed me? Was he worried he was trifling with another man's woman? Particularly since Will was Michael's brother, and hardly in a state to defend my honor, if necessary.

"Gage," I spoke softly, leaning forward to try to catch his gaze, "I care for Will, I do. But there is nothing romantic between us," I assured him.

When I finished speaking those words, he finally looked up at me.

I shook my head. "I am never going to marry William Dalmay, even if he asked me." It was my turn to look away, to gaze out at the strip of sea emerging through a gap in the trees. "I don't suspect I ever will marry again," I murmured. I'm not sure what made me add the last, but if we were going to be honest with each other, I suppose I decided to lay it all before him.

I turned back and, seeing his expression—which I read as somewhat pitying, though perhaps it was meant to be sympathetic—I smiled tightly. "Now," I declared, jumping straight into the fire to hide my embarrassment, "where have you seen Dr. Sloane? Did you meet him somewhere?"

Gage adjusted his seat on his saddle, making his horse snuffle. He reached down to pat the gelding's shoulder, and when he looked up again, it was as if he was on his way to face the gallows. His expression did not reassure me.

"When I was finishing up my last investigation in Edinburgh," he began, "I received a letter from a man needing my assistance with a tricky matter. I agreed to meet with him, though I was none too pleased with the information he had to give me or the matter he asked me to investigate."

I felt a gnawing sense of dread, making it difficult to breathe.

"He said he was concerned for the safety of one of his former patients and the people around him. The patient had turned violent while in his care and murdered a girl, but the family would hear nothing of his concerns when they demanded his release into their custody. I hesitated to take on the inquiry," he said, glancing at me warily. "It seemed wrong, disloyal. But then I realized that if I didn't agree to investigate, he would find someone else to do it. Someone who was far less discreet, or less disposed to see the accused in a favorable light." He began pleading with me then. "You see, I *had* to take the inquiry. I couldn't leave it for someone else, someone less understanding, who could care less for the Dalmays or what harm they suffered because of it."

"This man . . ." I began, unable to complete the sentence.

Gage nodded slowly. "Was Dr. Sloane."

I stared down at my horse's mane, too overcome by hurt and anger to speak. I felt as if I were choking on it. To think I'd begun to believe the bulk of Gage's deceits were behind us. But this . . . *this* was even worse than his refusal to share his reasons for dismissing my doubts during the murder investigation at Gairloch.

"Say something," Gage urged. "I know you must be upset . . ."

"Upset!" I gasped in disbelief. "Upset? I'm bloody furious! How could you? Michael trusted you. *I* trusted you. And all the while you've been investigating for—for *that man*." My horse whinnied and danced to the side.

"Kiera, please. I had no choice. How do you think another investigator would have treated them?"

"I don't know," I spat back, leaning over my mare and trying to soothe her. I knew she was reacting to my agitation, but I couldn't control that. "And right now, I don't care. Why didn't you tell us?" I shook my head. "I *knew* there was another reason you were here. I knew you were *lying* to me. Do you ever tell the truth?"

"Of course," he replied, actually having the audacity to sound hurt.

"When?" I demanded. "Because all I seem to ever get from you are evasions and half-truths. I can't trust you." The admission hurt like a knife stabbing into my very heart.

"Kiera, that's not true." He frowned. "You're overreacting."

"Oh, am I? Tell me one time, just *one*, when you have been totally honest with me."

He opened his mouth to reply but I spoke over him.

"Even the way you present yourself is a lie."

His mouth snapped shut and he scowled.

"You're not a rake." He looked like he was about to argue, but I cut him off again. "Just because you slept with a few widows doesn't make you a rake. It makes you a man. I understand how the world works. But you flirt and pretend you're one."

His voice was hard. "It's an image I have to cultivate."

"For your investigations?" I replied derisively.

"Yes. It's no different from the things you let others assume about you because of how awkward and aloof you seem in public."

"But I don't deliberately set out to deceive them. If they got to know me, they would see it's not the truth."

"It's the same with me. If they got to know me . . ."

"But you *don't* let anyone get to know you!"

He fumbled over his reply. "Well, you don't let anyone get to know you either."

"I let you."

Gage fell silent, and that look I couldn't decipher was back in his eyes. Was it sympathy? I turned away, feeling sick.

"Kiera," he murmured.

"No! Just . . . don't." My horse shied underneath me again and I struggled to bring her around. I wanted to let her break free to take me away from there. "I can't listen to you right now." I loosened my hold on the reins and tightened my knees against Dewdrop's flanks. "Don't follow."

CHAPTER TWENTY

The horse shot off like something had stung her on the flank. I leaned low over her neck, letting the wind whip at my clothing. I felt my jaunty little hat rip free of its pins and go sailing into the firth, but I didn't stop to worry about it. My hair began a cascade, and soon all of it was billowing down over my shoulders and behind me.

We had emerged from the trees and the trail was running directly alongside the shore now. I let Dewdrop veer toward the firth to gallop in the surf. The water she kicked up was cold against my ankles, and I knew the hem of my gown would be soaked, but I didn't care. The wind tasted sweet and salty on my tongue, washing away the bitterness Gage's revelations had left behind, and it dried my tears almost before they had a chance to fall. I couldn't even be sure whether my eyes were watering because of the wind or because of Gage's betrayal, although from the continued ache in my chest I suspected it was the latter.

Banbogle Castle loomed up ahead, its craggy walls dominating the landscape, and I set it as my destination. I had not heard Gage follow, and I was glad he'd listened for once. Thankfully he understood that I did not play coy. I truly couldn't be around him right now. I was too angry, too . . . hurt.

How could he do such a thing? Take on an investigation for Dr. Sloane? Perhaps he hadn't known about the man's ill treatment of William at first, but surely it was obvious that if a doctor was making such claims, his institution was shoddy at best. In any case, what kind of man tries to get back a patient who has been removed from his care? Gage must have seen there was more to Dr. Sloane's eagerness to see William returned to the Larkspur Retreat than a simple concern for the safety of the public. There had to be something he was afraid would become known, something he was worried that Will had already revealed or might reveal in time. And Gage had agreed to help silence him.

How could he look Michael in the eye knowing he was being so disloyal? I was half tempted to tell him about Gage's perfidy, but I knew it would only hurt him. To think we had believed he was our ally when all the time he had been working for the enemy.

I had heard his claim that he'd done it for the Dalmays, fearful of what another investigator might do, but I could not accept it. Couldn't he have simply warned them of Dr. Sloane's intent? Why all the subterfuge?

Unless he thought Dr. Sloane's claims might be true—that Will *had* killed a woman? It would explain his extreme aversion to my spending any amount of time with Will from the very beginning. If that was the case, what did today's revelations mean? That he no longer suspected Will of foul play, be it to Miss Wallace or this woman at Larkspur Retreat?

I could hardly turn back and ask him the answers to those questions now, not after riding away from him in such a fury. I would just have to save them for later.

For a moment I had an irrational fear that I would return to the manor to find him gone, disappeared from Dalmay House like he had from Gairloch, without giving me any answers. But then I realized he couldn't leave. Not with this investigation still hanging over his head and the fate of Miss Wallace unknown. He was trapped there by his duty, and by whatever sense of obligation he felt in his friendship with Michael. He couldn't escape me so easily this time.

I checked my horse's gait as we neared the crumbling castle and was surprised when I passed a bit of overgrown scrub grass to see Mac standing there watching my approach. William was perched on a rock from a tumbled section of the wall not far away. Now that they had seen me, I couldn't ignore them and ride off. And, I realized, I didn't want to.

I turned Dewdrop toward the pair, pushing a hunk of fallen hair out of my eyes. I'm sure it looked a ratty mess, but I knew they wouldn't care. William was grinning, and so I couldn't help but offer him a smile in return.

"Good afternoon," I said as Mac took hold of my reins. "Enjoying the fine weather?"

"It's not quite the same from my bedchamber window," Will replied.

"No, it isn't," I agreed.

Mac guided Dewdrop over to a flat stone to be used as a makeshift mounting block, and I unhooked my left leg from the pommel of the sidesaddle and slid off the horse's back. On the beach, not far away, there were the charred remains of a fire. I wondered if Mac had built a blaze here on a recent excursion to keep Will warm. Will scooted over, offering me part of his rock. I sighed as I settled on the hard surface, and then breathed deeply of the fresh air. It was a lovely prospect. If only Will's ancestors had kept the castle in good repair it might have been their family home still.

"You're distressed," he said, and I was taken aback by his perceptiveness.

"I was," I admitted. "But I'm calmer now."

"What happened?"

I considered lying to him, but then I realized that would make me no better than Gage. I could try evading the question, but that seemed just as bad. He was looking at me with such steady patience that I decided it couldn't hurt to confide in him. He'd always been a good listener. There was no reason to think he wasn't now just because of where he'd spent the last decade.

"Mr. Gage and I had a fight."

He searched my face. "About me?"

"Partly." My answer was deliberately unclear. I didn't want to have to lie to him, but I also didn't want to tell him about Gage having been hired by Dr. Sloane. There was no telling how he would react.

In any case, Will did not seem to mind my hazy response. He turned back toward the sea, seeming to take pleasure in the way the waves rolled up onto the sand and pebbles, leaving foam in their wake. It was such a soothing sound, the wax and wane of the ocean. Only the kittiwakes crying overhead disturbed the tranquillity.

And Will's next words.

"Kiera, I'm well aware of the risk I pose to you and everyone else. You cannot blame Mr. Gage for wanting to protect you."

I frowned, unhappy to discover what Will believed I meant by my vague reply, and displeased to hear him admit so readily that he was a danger to others. "This wasn't about protecting me."

"Are you certain of that?"

The candor in his voice made me look up.

"To a man, the protection of those he cares for is of the utmost importance. It's ingrained in us at birth, and our training as gentlemen only amplifies it. To see someone we think of as ours suffer, be it physical or emotional pain, because we failed to protect them from something we should have, well . . . it diminishes us. It . . . tears at who we are."

His gaze had turned inward, his words pensive, and it made me think that he was talking about himself as much as Gage. Who had Will failed to protect? The soldiers under his command? Or had it been someone in the asylum? I thought of the girl Dr. Sloane had accused him of killing. Did he feel guilt because he had been unable to protect her from whatever had happened to her? The idea that he might be carrying around such a burden wrenched my heart.

His soft gray eyes were clear again when he arched his eyebrows at me in gentle chiding. "It's plain to see that the man cares for you. And therefore your safety and security are very much on his mind." The corners of his mouth tipped up in the semblance of a smile and a teasing light entered his eyes. "I know you dislike being cosseted, but give the poor chap a chance."

Was that it? Was Gage really just trying to protect me? From what? The pain his lies had caused me? Well, he'd certainly failed in that regard.

I scowled at the sea, still smarting from the sting of his most recent betrayal. How was I supposed to continue working with Gage when I couldn't be certain he was being honest with me? How was I supposed to look him in the eye knowing I'd let him kiss me, even *wanted* him to, all the while ignoring the indications that I shouldn't trust him?

Yes, there had been contradictory information. Philip and Alana both believed in him and had urged me to do so. But as highly as I regarded their opinion, I also recognized they didn't have all the facts, nor did they risk so much by taking the man into their confidence. Though, as far as I knew, Gage had not betrayed the information I had shared with him about my past, nor Will's, for that matter. And he'd proven quite ably that he would risk his life to protect mine. Even now, angry as I was with him, I couldn't seem to quiet the instincts that told me I would be safe with him.

The man was beyond infuriating! Why couldn't he just have been honest and forthright with me from the very beginning?

I turned to find Will again contemplating the sea. I was surprised he could derive so much enjoyment out of it even knowing Inchkeith Island was out there. Did it comfort him to stare across the cold, choppy, sometimes violent waves of the Firth of Forth and know they stood between him and the asylum? Or was he drawn here, unable to turn his back on the place that had caused him so much pain, either out of lingering fear, morbid compulsion, or disbelief?

"You like to come here, don't you?"

He shrugged. "I grew up here. Michael doesn't remember it much, and Laura was born at Swinton Lodge, but I spent the first decade of my life in this drafty, old castle."

I glanced over my shoulder at the crumbling tower. I hadn't thought of that. Sometimes I forgot that he was fifteen years my senior, even with the gray hair at his temples. He had lived his entire childhood before I had even been a speck in my parents' eyes. My gaze snagged on the crenellated battlements, reminding me of something his brother had told us.

"Michael talked about your ancestor Sir Roger Dalmay and his dog. How the hound howled at his death."

"And how he howls at each subsequent laird's death?"

I turned to him, surprised by the unconcerned tone of his voice. "Doesn't that bother you? That a dog will supposedly foretell your demise one day?"

"No." Seeing my anxious expression, he offered me a tight smile. "I've been waiting for death a long time now, Kiera. It no longer has the power to frighten me."

I wasn't certain I liked hearing that, yet, under the circumstances, I thought I understood. But I desired to change the subject anyway.

"What was it like living here?"

He looked a question and I hastened to explain.

"I've spent a good deal of time with my sister at Gairloch, but it's been so modernized that sometimes it doesn't feel much like a castle. Banbogle has hardly seen any renovations."

He sighed. "Cold, drafty, damp, smelly. Chunks of the ceiling used to fall sometimes, and once the north stairwell caved under the weight of a footman."

I gasped, but he merely smiled.

"But it was home. And great fun when we'd play King Arthur or Rob Roy."

I looked behind me again at the castle. Moss and lichen had nearly overtaken the walls on this side of it, and a great gaping hole opened into the ground floor, one a person could walk straight into, if she wasn't afraid of the rest of it coming down on her head.

"It's too bad it's no longer safe to explore," I remarked, twisting further around to see what the object was that had caught my eye.

"Oh, I can still move around in there."

I snapped my head back to look at him in wide-eyed shock.

He chuckled. "Don't worry. I'm careful. And I don't do it often." He nodded to where Mac stood, one leg propped up on a rock as he stared out to sea. My horse stood nearby, her head bent to nibble at the grass growing along the verge of the path. "Mac doesn't like my clambering about the ruins. Worse than an old nursemaid, he is."

As if he sensed we were talking about him, Mac turned to look at us. He watched us for a moment, a contemplative look on his old, grizzled face. And then it was gone and he was striding toward us. "Time to return?" he asked Will.

"Aye," Will replied, imitating his thick brogue.

Mac nodded, not reacting to his employer's jest, and turned back to gather the reins of my horse.

Rather than taking the time to bustle the train of my riding habit, I draped it over my arm and rose to walk with Will down the path back toward Dalmay House. Mac trailed behind us, leading Dewdrop.

The afternoon was so fair, with its bright blue sky and the blazing autumn foliage, that it suddenly seemed absurd to believe Will was capable of anything nefarious. I was aware that Michael and Gage might not be happy with me for doing so, but it felt like the height of ridiculousness that we hadn't simply come out and asked Will about Mary Wallace. What was the worst we could uncover?

So I did just that, starting by asking if he knew who she was. I heard Dewdrop snuffle behind me, as if Mac might have pulled on her reins too hard, but I ignored the old man.

Will smiled warmly. "Oh, yes. We've met a time or two. Lovely girl. Do you know her?"

I felt a sudden chill, not having expected him to answer in the affirmative. And then I scolded myself for it. So he knew her. That meant nothing.

"Uh, no. But I spoke with her father recently," I answered with care, uncertain how much he knew about Miss Wallace's disappearance, if in fact he knew anything at all. "He seems like a very nice man."

"I haven't had the pleasure. But Mary speaks of him with great affection."

I was surprised to hear him speak of her in such a familiar manner, but then I remembered that Dr. Winslow had said he was often overly familiar with people's names—a side effect from his time spent at the Larkspur Retreat.

From the tone of his voice, it seemed obvious that Will did not know anything about Mary Wallace being missing. He was not concerned, nor did he seem frightened for her. So if he'd had anything to do with her disappearance himself, then either she was safe or he didn't remember. The latter did nothing to cheer me; nor the former, for that matter. But could Will really have harmed a person and not remember it? It seemed so unbelievable. And yet Dr. Sloane's accusation hung over it all like a pall.

"I was told she likes to stroll along the water. Is that where you two met?"

He nodded. "Miss Remmington introduced us."

It was my turn to be shocked again. "When?"

Hearing the unease in my voice, he hesitated.

"I'm just surprised she never mentioned it, is all. She was telling me how much she liked Miss Wallace."

He nodded. "I suppose I can understand that. I got the impression when she was forced to introduce us, oh, a few weeks ago now, that she was not happy about it. I thought it might be because of my time spent in the asylum, but then I realized it was also because she didn't wish to share her new friend. After that I tried my best to avoid meeting up with them so that Miss Remmington would not feel I was intruding."

As Will gave this speech, I realized that the sunshine and fair weather must have been having the same effect on him as it was me. He spoke more freely, more easily. And he smiled, albeit softly and slowly—something that had been rare even a decade ago during our drawing lessons—especially as he talked about Miss Wallace. I watched his expression closer.

"But you met her at other times?"

"Yes. We stumbled upon each other during our walks." And when he said 'stumbled' I knew he meant that it had not been entirely by chance. "I know you would like her. She is kind and quiet, and she listens." He tilted his head, contemplating me. "She's a bit like you actually. You both have something that makes you hold back and observe rather than taking part. In you, I think people suspect it's boredom or disinterest, and in Mary, they think it's shyness, but they're wrong on both counts. You simply don't know how to participate without revealing the differences you so try to hide."

I didn't quite know how to respond to this speech. That Will had so much insight into who I was surprised me enough, but the fact that he had compared me to Miss Wallace, a woman who claimed to have the second sight and was now missing, bothered me more. Perhaps it shouldn't have. A hundred years ago we might have been burned at the stake together. She because of her ability to see future events and me because of my ability to see into the heart of a person and render it in paint and ink. My unnatural stillness and "witch bright" eyes, as they'd been called by others in London, also did not help.

But Will wasn't privileged to these thoughts, so he did

not know how unsettled his comments had made me. "Kiera, you're the same as you ever were," he added with a crooked smile. "Just maybe a bit . . . sadder, lonelier. I'm sure your marriage to Sir Anthony Darby did not help."

I sighed. "No. It didn't."

"Why did you marry him?"

I gave a huff of humorless laughter. "I didn't want the bother of picking a husband, so I asked Father to find a match for me. My only stipulation was that I be allowed to continue painting." I glanced up at Will, a wry curl to my lip. "Sir Anthony failed to tell any of us just why he was so elated with my artistic talents, or that there would be a condition to my being allowed to continue to paint portraits."

"Your father was a good man, but he wasn't, perhaps, always the most astute judge of character."

I glanced at him in puzzlement.

"He hired me to be your drawing master that last summer, didn't he?"

"Now, that's nonsense," I protested. "You were an excellent tutor. Quite possibly the best I ever had. Did you know that?"

"I doubt it," he replied. "But, anyway, it doesn't matter. You've become a fine artist. A brilliant one, at that. If you were a man, the royalty of Europe would be clambering for you to paint them. But I suggest you trust your own judgment in choosing your next husband."

I opened my mouth to tell him there wouldn't be a second husband, but his next words cut me off at the quick.

"I know my opinion hardly matters, but I like this Mr. Gage of yours."

I couldn't manage to say anything for a moment and then I spluttered, "Gage is not *mine*."

Will gave me a chiding look that made my heart begin to beat faster.

"The man barely tolerates me," I protested.

He shook his head. "Oh, Kiera, for a woman who is normally so astute, how can you be so blind?"

I frowned. "You're wrong. If Gage were seriously interested in me in that way, I'd know."

"Kiera, a man does not have to kiss you for you to know he's attracted to you."

I felt a blush burn its way up into my cheeks. I snuck a look at Will out of the corner of my eye, and, seeing him narrow his eyes like an outraged older brother, I decided it was time to change the subject before I was forced to admit to something I didn't intend to.

"How often do you go for walks?"

He still eyed me suspiciously, but answered my question. "Whenever I can. Every other day or so if the weather is fine."

"Does Mac always go with you?"

"Or Donovan."

I studied his innocent expression. "Or you go by yourself?" I asked leadingly.

His jaw hardened in stubbornness. "If I can manage it."

"Is that safe?"

"I don't know. But I can't be caged." He looked at me, determined to make me understand. "Do you know what that's like?"

My chest tightened at the evidence of his distress.

He shook his head. "I spent nearly ten years locked up like an animal, and I can't live that way. I have to know that if I wanted to I could get free. I need that assurance."

I nodded, thinking I understood. However, his admission did nothing to comfort me.

And neither did the realization of what I'd seen earlier in the shadows inside that crumbled section of Banbogle Castle.

Will and I were passing by a shed not far from the main block of the stables, and its door stood open, allowing us a peek inside. The hull of a rowboat, about the size of a small coble, tipped on its side caught my eye and held it. There had been a boat inside the castle, and not an old, dilapidated one, to judge from the glimpse of the wood I had seen.

I glanced at Will again, remembering how he'd said he liked to scramble around inside the ruins of Banbogle. If so, he must know about the boat. Had he put it there? And, if so, why?

I tried to shake aside the uneasy feeling settling in my gut, but Craggy Donald's words to us about a boat leaving Cramond Island on the day Miss Wallace disappeared would not let me.

CHAPTER TWENTY-ONE

I separated from William and Mac at the top of the main staircase and turned toward my chambers to change out of my soiled riding habit. I knew Lucy was going to sulk when she saw the state of it and my windblown hair, even though I was the one who would suffer through the detangling. If I was lucky, she would be in a better frame of mind this afternoon. Maybe she would even have my bath prepared for me.

I picked up my pace and had just turned the corner when I heard giggling at the end of the corridor—familiar giggling. I backed up a step to peer around the corner. The door to the servants' stair stood open, held that way by a brawny arm, and Lucy leaned against the door frame laughing at whatever the person behind her was saying. Before the maid stepped to the side I already knew who was with her.

I scowled at Donovan, not caring when he looked up and saw me. He stared right back and mumbled something low to Lucy that I could not hear. She glanced over her shoulder guiltily at me, but her anxiousness at being caught quickly faded to something more belligerent.

"Lucy, I need to change," I told the maid in a sharper voice than I intended.

I watched in dismay as her chin lifted, but did not stay to see if she followed. I couldn't bear to stand there faced with Donovan's self-satisfied smirk when I knew the man was only toying with the girl. In any case, Lucy wouldn't dare disobey. Or so I hoped.

Even so, it took her several moments longer to appear than I expected, and that had given me several moments longer to grow angrier. "He's not likely to fancy you, eh?" I mocked the girl, throwing her own words back in her face.

She scowled and marched across the room toward the adjoining bathing chamber. "Would m'lady like to bathe?"

"Lucy, I am not going to overlook what I just saw."

She ignored me and disappeared into the bathing chamber to begin drawing the water. I stood in the middle of my bedchamber fuming. Stripping off my gloves, I threw them down onto the vanity with a satisfying thwack and then began picking out the hairpins still snarled in my hair. They each landed on the wooden table with a ping.

I heard Lucy return to the chamber but did not bother to turn around and face her. "After this evening, I will no longer require your services," I told her.

The girl gasped.

"You can return to Gairloch on the mail coach. I'm sure the earl would be happy to welcome you back into his staff as an upstairs maid."

"Oh, m'lady, please. I dinna want to return to Gairloch."

"Well, I cannot keep you on as you have been."

"But I've done my job," she argued. "Ye canna say I hav'na."

I turned to face her, close to screaming at her for her defiance. Instead I spoke in as calm a voice as I could manage. "You have been surly, and borderline disobedient, for days now. You were unhappy the moment we left Gairloch, and you have been insolent since we arrived at Dalmay House. Why on earth should I keep you on?"

"Please, m'lady," she begged, tears now threatening in her eyes. "If ye send me back, the others'll ken I botched it."

I sighed, unable to remain so harsh in the face of her tears. "You can tell them you got homesick."

She shook her head fiercely. "Nay. They'll ken I'm lyin'. And I dinna want to go home. No' when I just left it."

"But you've been so unhappy. Do not lie and tell me you haven't," I ordered her when she opened her mouth to do just that.

"It's just all so new," she murmured in bewilderment. "And I'm no' a fast learner. It took me months to learn to use the curlin' rods wi'oot burnin' me hands."

"Things are always going to be like that when we travel. And in Edinburgh or London or wherever we end up, until you become used to your new surroundings. New places present new challenges."

"I can manage it. I just needed to get my bearin's is all."

"Speaking of which," I said, hearing the trickle of water. "The . . ."

"Och! The bath!" Lucy dashed into the bathing chamber. "It's all right," she called out to me a moment later. "I caught it afore it spilled o'er the edge."

I crossed the bedroom and peered inside the tiled room at my maid, who was balancing against the edge of the tub while she carefully reached in to extract the plug to drain out some of the water. It was filled so close to the brim that I thought for sure just the insertion of her hand would send it cascading over onto the floor, but it didn't.

There was a pop and a gurgle and she let out a relieved breath. When she extracted her hand, I could see it was red up to her elbow.

"How hot did you make that water?" I asked her.

She glanced at me sheepishly. "I had a bit o' trouble gettin' the temperature right. It'll be cool enough by the time we get ye undressed."

I frowned at the water level. "Well, don't let it drain too much. Otherwise we'll be wasting more of the water from the cistern."

I turned away and marched back into the bedchamber. I removed the amethyst pendant my mother had given me and stared down at it, watching the deep purple stone flash in the late sunlight shining through the windows. Lucy stepped up behind me and immediately began unfastening the buttons that ran up the back of my riding habit. I could hear her worried thoughts as loudly as if she'd spoken them.

"Are ye really goin' to send me back?" she finally found the courage to ask.

I set the pendant on the vanity. "I don't know what else to do, Lucy. I'm worried about you."

"Ye dinna have to be worrit aboot me, m'lady. I'm a good girl. I ken what men are after and no' to give it to 'em. My mother and my brothers taught me well."

"That may be so," I told her as she helped me peel the fitted garment down over my wrists. "But there are more things at stake here than just your virtue."

I could see her puzzled look in the reflection of the mirror and endeavored to explain. "The job of a personal maid is far more than pressing clothes and styling hair. In a way, it's also being a sort of confidante, knowing the secrets you do about your employer. And I'm not just talking about the size of her waist or how much face powder she puts on every morning. Lady's maids, and valets for that matter, know who their employers are keeping company with, in and out of bed, and often when they are sick or expecting a child before they even do. They are privy to some of their most unguarded thoughts and fears." I turned to look down at her, seeing the guilt of disloyalty already stamped across her features. "Lucy, I need someone I can trust, and you are proving not to be that person."

Her gaze dropped to her feet. "I'm sorry, m'lady," she said tearfully. "I didna mean to tell Donovan anythin' aboot ye. But he was so kind. And he was the only one who would tell me the truth aboot Lord Dalmay." She blinked up at me accusingly through her tear-flecked lashes.

"And what was that?"

She hesitated, but just for a moment. "That he spent nine years in a lunatic asylum, and he's kept under lock and key for everyone's protection."

"That's true."

She gasped in outrage.

"But did Mr. Donovan tell you that the reason he was kept in that asylum was not because he was mad, but because of his father's own treachery?"

Lucy's eyes widened.

"I thought not. He led you to believe exactly what he wanted you to so that you would feel grateful to him for his honesty and angry with me for lying."

The reality of the man's deceit slowly began to dawn on her. "But he's kept locked up . . ."

"More for his own good than for anyone else's protection. He gets confused sometimes. We all would if we'd been confined to a dark, dank cell for a decade. I've visited with him three times since our arrival at Dalmay House, and he's never come close to anything resembling violent or aggressive. You have nothing to worry about. And I don't know why Mr. Donovan has decided to make you think so. Unless it's to get something from you."

Her gaze was filled with a world of hurt. I sat down on the bench in front of my vanity and bent to begin unfastening one of my boots. A moment later, Lucy kneeled to unlace the other one.

"I feel like such a fool," she muttered, but I was relieved to hear more anger in her voice than pain. "I kenned a man like Donovan would no' fancy someone like me. Dinna I say so?"

I scowled. "Lucy, the issue of your attractiveness, which I think you underestimate, is not the matter at hand."

"I ken that. But his interest shoulda been a red flag anyway. I never shoulda trusted 'im." She fell silent as she worked the boot off my foot and set it beside the other one to be cleaned later. She helped me step out of the skirt of my riding habit and unlaced my corset, but before she removed my chemise, she paused to look me straight in the face. "I'm more sorry than I can say, m'lady. Is there no way ye could give me a second chance? I'll prove to ye I deserve your trust. I willna let ye doon again."

Her voice was so pleading, her face so earnest, I felt myself beginning to yield. I liked Lucy—I always had—and until this journey we had always gotten along well. Was our working relationship worth salvaging?

I crossed my arms over my chest. "If you tell me what Donovan was so intent to learn about me, it'll be a start."

She nodded and proceeded to explain how curious he'd been about my background, particularly the time I'd spent married to Sir Anthony, which, fortunately, Lucy knew very little about. However, what she did know was enough to damage a reputation. But a large portion of Great Britain, or at least the majority of the upper class and their servants, must already be aware of my scandalous past. Gossip traveled swiftly among the elite. So what use could Donovan have for it? Blackmail? He would fail in that regard. I had little money of my own, except that which I earned from the sales of my artwork, and even less inclination to keep secrets that were already known to a large portion of the country. No, he must wish to use it for leverage of some kind. I just didn't know what. And that thought made me uneasy.

For the most part, I ignored Gage at dinner that evening, uncertain yet how to interact with him, especially in front of an audience. I was still angered by his revelation about working for Sloane, but the hours since our argument had given me time to think, and I thought I better understood his reasons for doing so, even if I wasn't quite ready to forgive him. There was much we still needed to discuss, but dinner was not the time or place. And in the meantime, we had an investigation to continue.

I had taken the opportunity after dressing for dinner to jot off a quick note to Philip asking for information on Dr. Thomas Callart. Perhaps he couldn't be Dr. Sloane, but that didn't mean he wasn't working for him. It seemed somewhat unlikely—after all, there must be dozens of physicians and surgeons in Scotland alone who claimed to specialize in afflictions of the brain—but I had learned not to doubt my intuition, and it was telling me there was some connection. How, I didn't yet know, but I had hopes I soon would. Or else I would have to take seriously my concerns over Will's professed ability to escape whenever he wished and the boat I had seen stashed in the ruins of Banbogle Castle.

Rather than following the others into the drawing room after dinner, Michael made our excuses and led Gage and me toward the central staircase. I glanced at Gage in confusion, but upon seeing the watchful look in his eyes I realized where we were headed. My stomach knotted in dread.

I'd known we would have to view Will's sketches and paintings sooner or later, since Donovan and Mac had been unable or unwilling to shed light onto Will's melancholic episodes or the events that had occurred in the asylum—the ones we believed Dr. Sloane was so eager to keep hidden—but I had not been looking forward to the endeavor. Ten years ago Will's artwork had given me nightmares, and though time and experience had hardened me, I still did not think I was prepared to see those images again. However, I didn't dare voice my trepidations. I could imagine Gage would be only too happy to leave me out of this task, and I was determined not to shy away from it, particularly knowing what I knew about his involvement with Dr. Sloane.

At the top of the stairs, rather than turning right toward the staircase we had always taken to the next floor and Will's rooms, Michael turned left and led us to the door at the end of the hall. My thoughts had been troubled by this door ever since late that afternoon, when I had seen Lucy and Donovan hovering there. It clearly led into the servants' staircase, which descended two stories below to the kitchen, and now I could see it also led two flights up to the attic as well.

"Michael," I murmured as we approached the door leading into the corridor beyond the first locked door on Will's floor, "you told us you keep all the doors locked so that Will cannot get out, but what about this one?" I recalled the footman who had brought Will's dinner the previous night, who had almost stumbled upon me and Gage kissing. He had come through the door off the main staircase, not the servants' stairs.

"It's locked, too. Only Donovan, Mac, and I have keys." He pushed against the door in illustration and nearly fell on his face when the knob turned and the door unexpectedly swung inward. "Bloody hell," he exclaimed, righting himself. "This isn't supposed to be open."

"Could this be how William is escaping?" Gage asked, voicing the same question I was thinking.

"I don't know. But if it is, Mac and Donovan have a lot of explaining to do." He reached into his pocket to extract a set of keys. They clinked as he shuffled them between his fingers, and upon finding the right one, he locked the door with a satisfying snick.

We resumed our journey to the next floor, Michael leading and Gage at my back. There were no wall sconces lit in the stairwell leading up to the attic, so both men grabbed a brace of candles from their recesses in the wall. Their flickering light in the draft of our movement danced over the walls around us, gleaming off the woodwork.

The attic was pitch-black and freezing. I shivered in my thin, vermilion satin evening gown and tightened my ivory shawl around my shoulders. I had expected there to be at least some living presence up here in the form of the servants' quarters, but apparently in this house they had been built belowstairs rather than above.

Michael led us to the second door on the left and unlocked it. The door swung open easily and silently, despite the fact that I had been expecting an ominous groan. I peered around Michael's shoulder at the contents inside. Crates and boxes were stacked next to old canvases resting on their sides and draped in heavy cloths. Everything was covered over with a fine layer of dust, except the box sitting on the top of the stack closest to us.

Following my gaze, he explained, "That's where I've been

storing his most recent sketches. Like the ones you saw the other night."

I stepped forward hesitantly. "May I?"

Michael was silent a moment and then choked out his response. "Yes."

I lifted my arm to open the lid on the box and then stopped with my hand poised in the air. My heart pounded in my chest. I suddenly felt as if I was about to dive over a precipice—one that I wasn't sure I wanted to traverse—and wondered whether there would be something there to catch me when I landed.

The floorboards shifted behind me and I felt the warm press of Gage's hand on my lower back. "Go ahead," he urged me.

I swallowed and lifted the lid from the box. Immediately the ashy smell of charcoal assailed my nostrils, its normally comforting scent now distorted by my concern over what I might find rendered by it inside. I reached in and lifted out the top stack of sketches, those that had been scattered across the floor of Will's room two nights past.

Flipping through the rough paper slowly, I saw the same crude renderings and scribbles I remembered. And the stacks below them were not much different. Some were more detailed and horrifying than others, but they all depicted the same scenes of helplessness and despair. The tortured images on his walls, of people drugged or strapped to beds or with their heads forced underwater, repeated themselves. There were also several more where people milled around a central courtyard, some fighting, some crying, and some laughing while the rest wandered around aimlessly. But predominately the drawings were scribbles of nothingness, of darkness. One depicted a pair of round, frightened eyes surrounded by nothing but black swirls of charcoal.

I set them down and turned away a minute, trying to regain control over my emotions. Tears were threatening at the backs of my eyes and I could feel the corresponding lump at the back of my throat. I swallowed hard, forcing it down.

"Is this all?" I asked Michael. "I take it he has not been painting." That would require a much more concerted effort, and when Will went into these . . . trances he was drawing by instinct, ignoring artistic skill.

"No."

Gage moved across the room, resting his hand on one of the blanketed canvases. "Are these from before he was confined to the asylum?"

Michael's gaze was filled with apprehension. "Yes."

Gage continued to stare down at them for a moment and then glanced back up at Michael, asking his permission.

He nodded.

Gage set his brace of candles on a stack of boxes to his left and slowly peeled back the heavy cloth. A fine cloud of dust rose from the fabric, forcing Gage to turn his head away. I wrinkled my nose against the musty stench. Part of me wanted to turn away before I saw something I didn't wish to, but another part of me held my eyes captive to the painting, wondering if I had imagined the horrible depictions Will had rendered after the war.

Fortunately, the first one Gage revealed was not one of the worst. A young woman was painted in the center, her clothes being torn asunder as she struggled with the soldier who was assaulting her. An arm hid the girl's face while the soldier smiled lasciviously down at her. However, an old woman stood behind them—her expression tortured by what she must do—with a knife raised above her head ready to strike the soldier.

Having seen enough, I turned away, facing Michael where he still stood in the doorway. His eyes were fastened on the painting and his mouth had thinned into a straight line. I watched as weary resignation spread across his features. When his gaze lifted, meeting mine, I braced myself, knowing today's revelations were not over.

"There's one more thing," he admitted.

Gage and I shared a look of mutual misgiving, wondering what Michael had hid from us now. I suspected we both had been waiting for something like this. I couldn't even summon up the anger I had felt on first learning of Michael's dishonesty. Now I only felt deep disappointment.

He crossed the room to the farthest corner and carefully extracted a rolled piece of parchment from behind several crates. Whatever it was, he had certainly hoped no one would ever find it. That realization sent a quiver of alarm down my spine.

"William drew it during one of his episodes several months ago." Michael offered no explanation for his omitting to tell us about it, just handed it to Gage and moved away from us toward the other sketches. He shuffled them together and stuffed them back in the box, keeping his back to us.

I stared at the innocuous-looking piece of paper in Gage's hand warily, wishing we did not have to open it. I held my breath as he slowly unrolled the parchment, tilting it toward the light cast by his candles. The drawing made my blood run cold.

It was a crude sketch done in charcoal, like the others, but there was one main difference, and it was instantly apparent that this was what had impelled Michael to hide it. All of Will's other drawings, even those sketched after the war, had been drawn as an outsider looking in. However, this sketch had been drawn from the artist's perspective, staring down at a woman draped across his lap, her head cushioned by his thigh. The positioning of her body and the way she looked up at him would have seemed romantic, but for the hand the artist pressed over her nose and mouth. The woman didn't appear to fight him, but actually seemed to be holding his hand where he had positioned it over her face.

I gasped and turned away, unable to keep looking at it. If Will was the artist, and he had drawn this from his point of view, that meant it was his hand over the woman's nose and mouth. Until I saw this sketch, I would never have believed Will was capable of such a thing. To smother a woman with his bare hands! My mind rebelled at the idea. There must be some other explanation. Maybe the image in the picture was not what it seemed. Maybe it was harmless. But then why had it so haunted Will that he'd drawn it along with all of the other disturbing images he'd depicted?

Had he been forced to kill her? I just couldn't accept he'd done it willingly. The William Dalmay I knew would never have harmed a woman. But if the suspicions raised by this drawing were true, if he had . . .

"Heavens! What did they do to him?" I whispered. I knew neither of these men had an answer for me, but I looked to them anyway.

"I don't know," Gage replied without emotion. "But we aren't finding our answers in these drawings, only more questions."

I followed his gaze to Michael, who still stood with his back to us. "We need to speak with William," I told him, realizing that Gage had been waiting for me to make this statement instead of him. Whether he thought Michael would listen better to me or he wanted me to come to this same conclusion on my own, I didn't know. "He's the only one who might be able to answer our questions. To explain this." I gestured to the parchment now rolled again in Gage's hands. When Michael did not respond, I had to implore him. "Michael, it's time."

He spoke so low it was difficult to hear him, even in the silence of the attic. "All right. Just . . . not tonight. He does better in the daylight."

I had witnessed the very same thing earlier that day, so I agreed.

Gage stepped forward, clasping a hand on his friend's shoulder. "We need to find out the truth, whatever it may be. Will you promise me you'll stop hindering that? That you'll let us do what you asked us to? We can't clear your brother's name or, if necessary, get him the help he needs, otherwise."

Michael nodded and finally turned to face us. "I haven't intentionally kept anything else from you. At least, not that I'm aware of."

He had aged before my eyes just in the two and a half short days since my arrival at Dalmay House. The man who had laughed and joked with us in the entry hall had been eaten alive by his worries. How had he managed to hide it for so long? His anxieties must have been consuming him for months. Why hadn't he done something about them sooner? I understood that he did not wish to upset his brother with accusations, but surely Will could understand his brother's concern over his drawings, especially this one with the girl. Maybe it was not so straightforward, but if tomorrow Will was able to explain everything to us, Michael was going to feel pretty foolish.

But I should have known it would never be that simple.

CHAPTER TWENTY-TWO

"Ugh!" I cringed a short time later when I returned to my room. I lifted an arm to cover my nose. "*What* is that *awful* smell?"

"'Tis valerian root tea, m'lady." Lucy stepped forward with the cup of the foul brew, holding it away from her face. "I noticed ye were havin' trouble sleepin', and Cook swore it would put ye right oot, like a bairn."

"Truly?" I asked doubtfully, taking the cup from her.

"Aye."

I stared down into the pale brown liquid and leaned forward to smell it more closely. "Ugh!" I turned my nose away. "It smells like stale sweat and . . . and dirty feet."

Lucy bit her lip and then offered helpfully, "Ye could try pinchin' your nose. That's what me mam used to do whenever we didna want to take our medicine."

I hesitated, but seeing the eager look in the maid's eyes, I decided to at least try. It was clear she was trying to make up for her earlier lack of judgment, and though I would have wished for a better token of apology, I couldn't disappoint her without at least making an effort. So I followed her instructions and lifted the cup to my mouth, but before it even touched my lips I gagged and had to turn my head aside. I shook my head and handed the cup back to her. "I'm sorry. I'm grateful for your effort. Truly. But I simply cannot drink that."

"I understand, m'lady." Lucy wrinkled her nose at the concoction. "It do reek. I dinna think I could drink it either."

I instructed Lucy not to worry about me—I could slip out of this dress alone—but just to get rid of that fetid-smelling tea before it made me ill, and then get herself to bed. I saw her out the door, balancing the tray of tea as she would a basket filled with snakes, and then crossed the room to stand before the hearth, knowing the stench would be less near the fire. Once the scent had cleared from my nose, I settled down to wait.

The foul odor of the cook's valerian root tea was not the only reason I had urged Lucy to leave without helping me to change. I expected a visitor, and I had no intention of again being put at the disadvantage of wearing my night-clothes. I wanted to be ready this time, for I suspected I had just as much to say to him as he had to say to me.

I realized that perhaps I'd been a bit precipitous in condemning Gage for beginning an inquiry on Dr. Sloane's behalf. His motives for doing so had not been completely unjustified. He was right. Another inquiry agent would not have been so concerned with protecting the Dalmays, and their reputation, at the very least, would likely have been damaged irreparably in the process. At least I could take comfort in knowing that Gage had their best interests at heart. I could see now that he had been placed in an impossibly difficult situation and he was proceeding the only way he knew how. It still irritated me he hadn't confided in me sooner, but I better understood why he hadn't.

I also realized that maybe I expected too much from Gage, that perhaps I needed to be a little less demanding when it came to the information he chose to share with me. If he wasn't comfortable sharing the details of his past, then I needed to accept that. Just because I wanted the truth didn't mean he owed it to me. I had secrets of my own, and I didn't share those freely, whether a person deserved an explanation or not. The fact that I had chosen to share some of those secrets with Gage did not mean that he had to reciprocate. Maybe if I were his wife, or fiancée, or even being seriously courted, I could expect more, but as we stood now, in spite of those kisses, I was nothing more than a temporary partner and perhaps a friend.

In any case, we had to put this dispute aside, because if this evening had proved nothing else, it was that I needed Gage's help if I was to finish this investigation. Things had become too dark, too difficult, and I wasn't certain I could do it alone. Not facing the prospect of the truth we might uncover about William. I was too close to this one, my emotions too involved. I needed Gage's impartiality. And perhaps his shoulder to cry on if things did not end as I wished.

I twisted around in my chair, checking the clock ticking steadily away on the mantel. Enough time had passed that I began to worry I'd misjudged him yet again, but then a peremptory rap sounded on the door.

Gage strode through it without having been given permission to enter. He glanced around the room, clearly looking for me, and it took him a moment to find me in the shadows cast by the rounded sides of my wingback chair.

I arched my eyebrows at him. "I suppose I should be happy you at least knocked."

He ignored my comment, crossing the room toward me. "You were waiting for me."

I tilted my head, watching the firelight flicker over his features. "You're becoming predictable."

He did not scowl as I expected him to, but instead trailed his eyes over my figure where I lounged in the chair. "Maybe."

I felt a lick of heat everywhere his gaze touched and had to fight the urge to lift my hand and cover my décolletage. Perhaps I had miscalculated. I now suspected I might actually feel more secure in my high-necked night rail and wrapper than the thin silk and rounded neckline of this gown, despite all the layers of undergarments.

I frowned, irritated that he had managed to make me

question my composure while he didn't even show a flicker of remorse for barging into my private chambers. "Did you stop to consider that you could have simply asked me to meet you? Perhaps somewhere a little less scandalous?"

He replied by asking me a question instead, one of his more annoying habits. "Would you have come?"

I answered without hesitation. "Yes."

My reply seemed to catch him off guard. His body stiffened and his pale eyes widened. I watched him study me, trying to tell if this was some kind of trick. I thought he would have realized by now that I didn't play such games. At least, not like other society ladies.

He moved forward and sat on the edge of the other wingback chair positioned beside mine before the fireplace. Leaning forward over his knees, he pressed his hands together and started to explain, "I'm sorry I didn't tell you and Michael about my working for Dr. Sloane from the start. I should have trusted you to understand." His eyes when they lifted to meet mine were heavy with regret.

"It's all right," I replied softly. As much as I'd wanted to hear his apology, I couldn't allow him to bear the full weight of responsibility. "I know why you didn't. And . . . I can't really say you were entirely wrong."

"You . . ." He halted in midsentence, as if he had trouble digesting my words. "You do?"

I nodded and turned to stare at the flames licking along a log of wood. "If you had been completely up-front about it with Michael, with William, with any of us, from the start, you would never have gotten to the truth. Michael has already been hiding evidence from us since the very beginning, and possibly only making things worse for his brother. And had I known about you and Dr. Sloane . . ." I sighed. "I can't in all honesty say that I wouldn't have kept things from you, too."

I could feel Gage's eyes quietly assessing me, but I didn't have the courage to meet them.

"I can."

I turned to him in surprise.

"If I've learned anything about you, Kiera, it's that you're not only extremely loyal, but also unfailingly honest."

My conscience smarted at the thought of the lies of omission I'd made to Will earlier, as well as Lucy. "Not unfailingly."

A small smile curled his lips. "All right. But I still know that, had I told you about my investigation for Dr. Sloane, you would have found a way to tell me all while still remaining loyal to Will."

I did not argue, knowing that assertion was about to be tested.

He sat farther back in his chair, getting more comfortable. "Incidentally, what made you change your mind? About what I did?" he clarified. "Earlier you seemed angry enough to have me drawn and quartered. I came here expecting to grovel."

"I suppose I spoke too soon, then. I would have liked to see that."

He tilted his head, a teasing light entering his eyes. "I'm quite certain someday you'll get another chance."

Something inside me squeezed and then released at his flirtatious comment. "I realized I responded more heatedly than perhaps I should have," I admitted, running a hand over the chocolate-brown twill of the chair arm. "That you were given little choice in the matter and you were only doing what you felt you had to." I glanced up at him through my lashes. From his grim expression I could tell that the matter still did not sit well with him. Whatever else might be bothering Gage, it was clear he did not enjoy lying or spying on his friends. "One or two things did occur to me later, though."

"Such as?"

"Did Dr. Sloane tell you the name of this girl Will allegedly killed?" An image of the woman in that sketch, lying in Will's lap, her hair trailing out behind her, flashed through my mind, but I pushed it aside.

Gage's brow furrowed. "No. And I did ask. It bothered me at the time, but he told me that it was a very important person's daughter. Supposedly this 'very important person' didn't want word spreading about where his daughter had been."

I frowned. Dr. Sloane was keeping his cards very close to his chest, and I viewed that as even more of a reason not to trust his word, regardless of that sketch.

"What else did you want to ask me?" Gage shifted in his chair, trying to look calm and at ease, but I could see the tension in his frame—the tautness in his shoulders and jaw, and the gleam in his eye that told me he was paying close attention. It was the same gleam he got when he was interviewing a suspect or a witness. In this case, however, I knew he was not trying to interrogate me. He was simply nervous about what I had to say, and since I was anxious, too, that made me feel more on equal footing with him.

"This evening's discoveries may have altered your answer somewhat, but I was wondering what you thought about Will's innocence. I suppose I assumed you wouldn't have revealed your relationship with Dr. Sloane had you not believed Will blameless in Miss Wallace's disappearance."

"You're correct," he replied, staring down at his black evening trousers. "I did not, and *still* do not, think he had a hand in Miss Wallace's kidnapping."

I leaned toward him. "So you think it *was* a kidnapping?"

"Little else makes sense. Though what has become of her, I cannot say." His eyes narrowed in thought. "But it just seems too coincidental for them not to be linked in some way. Lord Dalmay *must* have known her."

"He did."

He looked up at me in surprise.

"After I galloped away from you this afternoon, I happened to stumble upon William and Mac." I held up my hand to forestall any argument. "Don't scold me. I didn't know they would be there, and I wasn't about to be so rude as to ignore them."

Gage did not react, though I saw the strain it caused him not to do so in the muscles of his neck.

"I walked back to Dalmay House with them, and Will was in such a relaxed and talkative mood, I chanced asking him about Mary Wallace."

"And?"

"Miss Remmington introduced them."

"Really?" Gage asked in genuine interest.

I nodded. "Will spoke very highly of Miss Wallace. And, if I'm not mistaken, he might be a little taken with her." My next words were sobering. "He didn't seem to know that she was missing, and I didn't think it my place to enlighten him."

"No. It was probably best you didn't."

I wasn't certain what that was supposed to mean, especially spoken in the quiet voice he used, but I chose to ignore it.

Besides, I had weightier worries on my mind. I eyed Gage surreptitiously, wishing he hadn't paid me such a compliment on my honesty, not when I was already struggling with my decision over just how much to reveal about my interaction with Will that afternoon. Part of me wished to divulge all, while another felt that would not be in Will's best interests. After all, what if those suspicions that were nagging at me proved to be nothing?

But that sketch of Will and the girl shed a different light on all of this, one that was far darker and more ominous. What if Will was responsible for the death of that girl in the asylum and Miss Wallace's disappearance? I had not wanted to even contemplate it, but I could not ignore that drawing or Will's own words to me. If I said nothing and Will harmed someone else, I wasn't certain I could ever forgive myself.

I inhaled deeply. "There are two other things you should know about my conversation with Will this afternoon," I murmured solemnly.

He listened quietly, maintaining a neutral expression as I told him about the boat stored in Banbogle's ruins and how Will had told me he could escape from his chambers anytime he wished. When I finished, he laced his hands together over his stomach and considered the matter. "How is he making his escapes? Did he say?"

I shook my head. "But my guess, at least after this evening, is that it's through that door to the servants' stairs."

"And no one saw him or thought to stop him?"

I couldn't answer that. In such a large manor house there was likely another servants' staircase on the other side of the building; perhaps that was the set most often used.

"Who is leaving that door unlocked and why? I'm sure you realize it must be Mac or Donovan. Or Michael," he added as an afterthought. "Though, his anger this evening at finding it unlocked seemed genuine enough."

"What of the boat?" I asked, reluctant to hear his opinion, but unable to stop myself from asking.

"You're thinking of the boat Craggy Donald saw leaving Cramond Island, are you not?"

I nodded.

He tilted his head. "If it was Lord Dalmay, why was he headed out to sea instead of back toward the Dalmay estate?"

"I wondered the same thing," I admitted, though I didn't add the only explanation I could think of—that he'd deserted her body farther out to sea, in hopes it would never wash ashore. Even so, I could see from the look in Gage's eyes he had already thought of that.

I turned away to stare unseeing at the fire, letting the bright flames sear my retinas. As if that would burn away the image of William pushing Mary Wallace's lifeless body out of a boat and into the steely blue waves of the North Sea.

No! I just couldn't believe it. It made no sense. I had seen the tender look in his eyes when he spoke of her. If he had harmed her, murdered her, how could he have talked about her in such an affectionate manner? I just couldn't believe Will could be evil enough to do such a thing. And I couldn't believe he'd rowed over to Cramond Island, abducted and killed Miss Wallace, and then returned to Dalmay House, all without realizing what he'd done. We had to be wrong.

"Just more questions to add to our list for tomorrow," Gage said, sounding somewhat daunted by what was to come. "I only hope he has some answers for us."

I did, too. Because if he didn't . . . well, it didn't bear thinking about.

"Have you given any thought to the identity of this girl Will supposedly killed? Or her important father?" I asked, intrigued despite myself. Was the girl's identity the secret Dr. Sloane was so desperate to keep? Or had Sloane been hiding nothing at all, other than his barbaric treatment of his prisoners. Though, from what I understood, many lunatic asylums handled their patients similarly.

"A little," Gage replied.

"Could he be a royal?"

He considered my suggestion and then shook his head with a heavy sigh. "I don't know. I can't think of anyone from the British royal family who is unaccounted for. But the girl could be illegitimate. Or come from any of a dozen countries in Europe."

I hadn't thought of that, but it widened our field of potential candidates considerably. I could barely keep track of my own sovereign's acknowledged kin, let alone those born out of wedlock or belonging to another country.

"Kiera."

The solemn tone of Gage's voice made me pause.

"I also have something I need to tell you."

I sat up straighter, alarmed by the look of dread that had washed the color from his face.

He swallowed, making the Adam's apple bob in his throat. "You wanted to know why I doubted your intuition and refused to listen to you at Gairloch . . ."

I leaned forward and snatched hold of his left hand, stopping his words. "Gage, no." I shook my head. "You do not need to tell me this. It was selfish of me to keep pressing you."

He swallowed again and a new determination settled over his features. "I *want* to tell you. Please. Will you listen?"

I studied his face and, seeing the certainty there, nodded.

He offered me a faint smile and turned his hand over to squeeze mine before releasing it.

He turned to stare at the fire, and a muscle worked in his jaw, telling me how difficult this was for him. I had wondered at the truth for so long, but, seeing the distress it caused him, I wasn't sure I wanted to hear it anymore. For whatever it was had affected Gage very deeply, and if he was ready to share it with me of his own free will . . .

I thought of the words Alana had said to me before her departure. About how when Gage was ready he would tell me, and I would know then just how much he esteemed me.

Watching him now while he wrestled with some strong emotion, I couldn't help but feel a corresponding ache in my chest.

When finally he turned to me, he appeared composed, but the pain in his eyes was raw and aching. "My mother was murdered," he stated flatly.

I drew in a sharp breath and pressed my clasped hands against my stomach.

"She was poisoned."

I wanted to touch him, to hold his hand or wrap my arms around him, but I could tell that was not something Gage would welcome at the moment. It was written in the stiffness of his posture, the hard line of his jaw. So I squeezed my hands together more tightly, making the knuckles turn white, and waited for him to find the words to continue. Somehow I knew he had not shared this story with many people, and it would be a difficult one for him to tell.

He rose from his chair and crossed the chamber toward the windows. He lifted aside the curtain to stare out at the darkness beyond. I wondered if he found it easier to speak that way. "I was in my second year at Cambridge," he began to explain slowly. "Upon my admission to the school a year earlier, I had received special permission to live in a cottage with my mother not far from campus." He flicked a glance at me. "My mother was sickly, you see. She always was. She would get these terrible racking coughs that seemed to last for hours, sometimes days, on end. They drained her, sucked the life out of her." He grimaced with remembered pain. "They would send her to bed for weeks. I remember as a little boy being so frightened because she couldn't seem to catch her breath." His entire being seemed to tighten with emotion. "Her face would sometimes turn blue."

My heart ached for that little boy, terrified for his mother. "Was your father there?" I asked, standing to move closer to him.

He shook his head, almost absently. "He was in the navy, and in those years he was sailing with Nelson, and then manning the blockade against France. At age eleven, I was supposed to join him, but my mother begged him to let me stay with her, and my father relented." His smile was wry. "I didn't want to go anyway. So, in a way, she saved me from a grueling life on the seas." His voice turned pensive, making me wonder if he thought about this often. "How different my life would have been had I joined the Royal Navy and fought against Napoleon."

He might have died. My heart twisted at the thought. So many young men had lost their lives in that war, and when he went off to fight he would have been merely a boy. I could sympathize with his mother.

"When I came of age to attend Cambridge my mother insisted I go. All of the men in her family had attended, and she and my grandfather did not want me to be any different. But I refused to leave my mother alone in Plymouth, not with her so ill. So we reached a compromise, and my grandfather helped me find a suitable cottage close to the university." He shifted his gaze and I knew he was no longer seeing the world outside my window, but a house at the edge of Cambridge. "She seemed happy in our new home, and for a while she even seemed to improve. I started to believe it was the sea air that so incapacitated her, and inland she would begin to make a full recovery."

Hope still rang in his voice, even after all these years. But

I already knew the outcome would not be a happy one. I hugged myself tightly as a cloud crossed over his features.

"Then in the autumn of 1815, she began to worsen. She couldn't keep any food down; her strength began to fail. And then the cough returned. The physicians couldn't do anything for her." He swallowed, and his voice, which had steadily risen with remembered anxiety, was suddenly hoarse and flat. "She slipped away just before Christmas."

I couldn't help it then. I stepped forward and reached out to take his hand in mine. I knew he had more to tell me, but I had to touch him in some small way, to offer some comfort. He squeezed my fingers, clinging to them, but he did not look at me.

"There was an inquiry. My father insisted upon it. Napoleon was exiled to Saint Helena; the war was over and he was home on leave. You could say it was my father's first taste of the profession he would take up when he retired." His smile was humorless. "I resisted the investigation, insisting Mother had simply succumbed to her illness. I believed Father was trying to make up for being absent so often. During the war, if we saw him four weeks out of the year, Mother and I counted ourselves lucky." He did not sound bitter about such a truth, but resigned. Life in the Royal Navy was difficult in the best of times, and wartime made it almost unbearable.

"Father and the local magistrate swiftly found evidence of foul play, and it pointed to my mother's maid, Annie. Apparently, just before my mother fell ill that last autumn, some of the other servants had overheard her scolding Annie for her insolence and her shoddy work, and threatening to let her go. However when mother's sickness returned, Annie was suddenly needed again to nurse her, for no one seemed able to comfort my mother so well. Father suspected Annie first poisoned her so that she could keep her position, and then continued to do so so that her services would always be required. Whether she had dosed my mother with too much of the poison that last time, or the cumulative effects of the poison combined with mother's illness had simply became too much for her weakened body, Father didn't know, but he felt certain the maid had some part to play in it."

Gage's eyes were heavy with grief when he finally turned to look at me. "I didn't want to believe it. I told them they were wrong, that Annie could not have done it. She was like a second mother to me. And she loved my mother. Or, at least, I thought she did." A lump formed in my throat at the desolation in his voice. "I defended her, sheltered her, protested her innocence . . . up until the night my father caught her trying to dose us with the same poison to silence us."

I gasped.

"She claimed she'd had no idea, insisted that someone had tampered with the pantry." He shook his head. "She swore to the very last that she was innocent. And I almost believed her." His gaze bore into mine, wretched and dejected. "I almost helped her get away with murdering my mother."

I slid my arms around his torso and rested my head on his chest, trying to comfort him in the same manner he had consoled me on the staircase landing after Miss Remmington made her nasty implications about Will's service during the war. He embraced me back, holding me so tightly that I knew I had done the right thing.

"I'm sorry you had to experience such a thing," I rasped into the white folds of his cravat. "I'm so sorry your mother was murdered."

I felt the muscles in Gage's throat work as he laid his head against my hair. "Do you understand now why I didn't want to hear your doubts over our suspect's guilt during our last investigation?" he murmured softly. "And why I didn't want to tell you?"

I nodded. It had reminded him too much of his defense of Annie after his mother's death. And it had been too private, too painful to relive, unless absolutely necessary.

"Regardless, I'm sorry I didn't listen to you. Your concerns were not unfounded. As was proven," he added wryly.

I squeezed him tighter, telling him all was forgiven.

He squeezed me back. "I understand that not every case is like my mother's. And as an inquiry agent I certainly can't be effective if I allow such a plank in my eye." He brushed a hand over my hair, smoothing it back from my face. "That's why I became so cross with you for defending Lord Dalmay's innocence so blindly, and for trying to block my finding out from Mac if he had met Mary Wallace."

"I know. I'm afraid I've been so concerned with making certain everyone treats William fairly, that they not jump to conclusions about him because of the time he spent in the asylum, that I failed to realize I had leaned so far in the other direction that *I* wasn't treating him fairly either." I sighed. "Perhaps we should have insisted Michael let us question him about Dr. Sloane's accusations and Miss Wallace's disappearance from the very beginning. We've been so intent on protecting him from the pain of further accusations, coddling him like a baby, that we haven't treated him like a man." I looked up at Gage. "I think he's stronger than we realize."

He lifted his hand to trail his thumb over my cheekbone. "I would agree. He survived the horrors of the Peninsular War and then a decade confined to a lunatic asylum, after all. The war alone could have ruined a man."

There was something in his voice, in the pale winter blue of his eyes, that told me he was speaking from experience.

"Were you involved in the revolution in Greece?" I asked, not wanting to press him for answers, especially after tonight had already seen so many difficult revelations.

His gaze met mine, and I could see the sting of those memories, whatever they were, shimmering below the surface. I had expected him to hide them from me, but because he was vulnerable or he'd decided to trust me, he didn't. "For a time," he replied. "But I would rather not discuss it. At least, not now."

I nodded, accepting his answer. Just the fact that he had decided to confide in me that little bit was enough.

His expression loosened in relief and he bent his head to kiss my brow, and then my lips.

When he pulled away several agreeable moments later, he tucked me in close to his side and turned to stare out the window. I pressed my cheek to the soft fabric of his coat, where I could smell the musk of his skin mixed with the starch of his clothes and the spicy scent of his cologne, and followed his gaze to the windowpane. But rather than trying to peer through the darkness to the forest beyond, I focused instead on our reflection. In the softly rippling surface, our images almost merged into one, but the shadowy outline was so faint that I swore if I blinked it would vanish. I clasped Gage tighter and kept my eyes open.

CHAPTER TWENTY-THREE

The next morning, I was shaken awake by my maid.

"M'lady, Mr. Gage is askin' for ye. He says it's urgent."

I pushed myself upright, rubbing the sleep from my eyes while Lucy bustled over to the window to throw back the curtains. I shied away from the light, soft as it still was so early in the morning.

"What is it?" I asked. "Did he say?"

"Nay. But he'll be waitin' for ye oot front with the horses."

Ten minutes later I hurried through the front door to find Gage already mounted.

"What is it?" I asked while a stable hand helped boost me up onto Dewdrop. Two quick adjustments to my saddle and I was following him down the drive.

"We've found Miss Wallace," he told me grimly when my horse drew abreast with his.

I didn't like the tone of his voice.

"Where?"

He directed his horse east toward the firth. He glanced over his shoulder at me, a solemn, angry look in his eyes. "On the beach."

Neither of us said much on the ride over. We didn't need to. Both of us understood what the discovery of Miss

Wallace's body on Dalmay property meant. The likelihood of William Dalmay being involved had just increased from possible to plausible. I tried not to jump to conclusions, not before I'd had a chance to see the body, but I couldn't ignore the simple fact that this was the stretch of land where Miss Wallace and Will had met.

Gage had set a guard over Miss Wallace's body, and we found him standing several feet away from the corpse, trying not to look at it. The servant, a man who worked in the Dalmay stables, if I was not mistaken, looked up at us in relief as we rode out of the forest at a trot. We drew our horses to a halt and handed the man the reins.

"He was visiting his family in Cramond," Gage told me as we approached the beach. "Found her on his return to Dalmay House this morning."

I was listening to him, but all of my attention was focused on the figure lying in the sand at the edge of the water.

"Kiera." He stopped and turned to face me, blocking the sight of the woman. "I had to send a footman to Cramond to fetch the constable, so we haven't much time." I looked up into his face, understanding now the extreme urgency. "The lad was instructed to dawdle a bit, but there's only so much dallying a man can do."

I nodded, and moved to step around him, but his hand came up to stop me. I looked up in surprise.

"You do not have to do this," he told me. I could see the war raging behind his eyes, between his need for answers and his desire to shield me, shield any woman, from this. "I just . . . I need another's opinion. And I don't trust Mr. Paxton's. And with your knowledge . . ." He hesitated, reluctant to speak of the years of unwilling instruction in anatomy I had received from my husband.

"It's all right," I assured him.

He searched my gaze, as if to be certain I wasn't lying.

"Now, let's not waste any more time."

He dropped his hand from my arm and followed me

across the path and onto the rough sand beach where the girl's crumpled form lay.

"We're certain this is Miss Wallace?"

"Yes. It looks like her portrait. And the man who found her . . ." he nodded back toward the stable hand minding our horses ". . . recognized her."

I braced myself, trying to prepare for whatever I was about to see. This wasn't the first corpse I'd seen, I reminded myself. Nor even the first murder victim. It couldn't be any worse than the last, whose throat had been cut from ear to ear. Fortunately the morning air was crisp, and the brine of the sea had masked most of the stench of decomposition. I took even, shallow breaths and leaned forward to look into the girl's face. It was flecked with sand and grit, like the rest of her.

"Did you turn her?"

"Yes."

I allowed my gaze to travel carefully over her body, taking in the state of her hair and clothes, and the gray-white cast to her skin. Her caramel-brown hair was a tangle of snarls, and her clothes were dirty and unkempt. As to be expected, they showed signs of dampness, but she had been lying on the beach for enough hours that the wind had begun to dry them.

"Gage," I murmured in distress, "this is all wrong." I shook my head. "If Miss Wallace had been swept out to sea by the current and drowned like Mr. Paxton suggested, she would not have washed up onto the beach here."

"So she was placed here, either on purpose or because she was killed nearby."

"And look at her clothes. They're old and shapeless, and made from very poor quality wool. Miss Wallace would never have worn this."

"Or the coat," Gage pointed out. "It's a man's."

I stared at her face, at the rigidity of her expression. "Look at this bruising," I said, kneeling next to the body. The cool, damp sand shifted under my weight. A large purple contusion had formed on her forehead, and another bruise had blossomed on her left cheekbone. "These were made before death."

I lifted her hand, finding that the fingers moved far easier than I expected, while her arm was still stiff. "Her nails are broken, chipped, and dirty, her knuckles scraped."

"So she must have struggled." I could hear the supposition in his voice as he tried to piece together the facts, but my attention was already on my next discovery.

Pushing up the sleeve of the coat, I sucked in a harsh breath. The skin on her wrist was raw and tattered. Gage crossed to the other side of the body and lifted the other sleeve to reveal the same result.

"She was bound," he said, stating the obvious. "What about her feet?"

They, too, were damaged from some kind of restraints, though not as severely. I became sickened further by the bruise I found on her calf as I slowly inched her skirt up, and the scrape on her knee, and by the huge purple welts on the insides of her thighs. Unwilling and deeming it unnecessary to see more, I lowered her dress and looked away, taking a moment to compose myself.

I closed my eyes and took several deep breaths of the cool sea air, trying to block out the horrible knowledge filling my head. The briny scent of the sea helped me to swallow some of the acid on my tongue. I forced myself to listen to the cries of the seabirds and the waves lapping at the shore. But when I heard Gage shift impatiently behind me I turned back, aware that our time was running out.

Grateful for the leather covering of my riding gloves, I reached out to unfasten the top half of the buttons on Miss Wallace's dress and her chemise. Peeling back the edges, I found another bruise and the greenish discoloration on the skin of her abdomen I had been looking for.

"I can tell you she's been dead for longer than twenty-four hours."

"You're certain?"

I nodded, buttoning her back up. "Sir Anthony used to

say that he knew he'd gotten a fresh body when the skin of the abdomen had yet to turn green. Although then he often had to contend with the rigor of the corpse." I lifted the hand, showing him how the fingers bent. "This body has gone past rigor and is returning to pliancy."

I had hated the "fresh" bodies he made me sketch while he dissected them even more than the others, particularly when I began to realize that many of them weren't criminals come straight from the gallows. I had felt an uneasy suspicion that my husband, or rather the grave robbers I knew he must have employed, had gotten them by even more nefarious means than their normal scheme of digging up newly buried corpses. When it came to the procurement of the cadavers my late husband used, I had not wanted to know the details. I would not have been able to bear knowing, not without a shadow of a doubt, not when there was almost nothing I could have done about it. My supposed active participation in that process had been one of the most macabre and vicious rumors about me. I was said to have lured young men into being the victims on Sir Anthony's dissection table.

Gage knew all this, for I had admitted it to him during our investigation at Gairloch, so he didn't ask now, and I was grateful.

I pushed up the sleeve of the ratty brown coat to look for more bruising and also found the distinctive marks of the spring-loaded lancet used in bloodletting at the inside of her elbow. "She's been bled. And recently."

Gage examined her other arm. "From this arm, too."

One of the images drawn on William's wall suddenly flashed before my eyes. The one of the man with rivulets of what looked to be water running down his arms. I now felt more certain than ever that they were supposed to be blood.

I re-covered her arm and laid it gently beside her body, considering all of the evidence. "I don't think she drowned. An autopsy could tell us more. If there's water in her lungs. But I don't think we'll find any."

He rounded the body and offered me his hand to help me stand. "How did she die, then?"

"I don't know. She was clearly mishandled and abused, restrained, and almost certainly bled." I stared down at the girl's pale face. "Surely the wounds made from a bloodletting done before she went missing would have healed before she died around a day, a day and a half ago."

"All of those things could still have happened to her, and she still could have drowned," he pointed out, but I could tell he agreed with my original conclusion.

"Yes, but that still means her body was moved here. The only way she could have drowned and washed ashore here is if the killer chased her into the firth along this stretch of beach and either knocked her unconscious or held her head underwater." I found my gaze straying toward Banbogle Castle and a chill crept down my spine. "But I rode along this stretch of shore just yesterday afternoon," I reminded myself as much as Gage. "I would have seen her."

"Maybe, maybe not, depending on how fast you rode by here and how much attention you were paying to your surroundings."

I had been so hurt and angry. All I remembered were my riotous emotions and the wind in my face as I urged Dewdrop onward. The thought that I might have ridden past Miss Wallace's body in the shallows near the shore without noticing made me sick to my stomach. If only I hadn't let my temper get the best of me maybe I would have been more observant, and better able to say for certain whether or not the body had been in the water just offshore.

"But if it's any consolation," Gage told me, correctly reading my horrified expression, "I think you're correct. Whoever killed her brought her here deliberately to make it look like a drowning. Or, possibly, something worse."

I was about to ask him if he meant what I thought he did when the sound of approaching horses made me turn back toward the trail. Two horses had emerged from the forest and I was surprised to see Miss Remmington on one of them. She ordered the stable hand to help her down and began striding across the distance between us.

"Is that her?" she yelled.

I looked at Gage in alarm and we moved forward to intercept her.

"Is that her?" she demanded, her voice rising almost hysterically. Her hair was streaming down her back and her eyes were wild.

"Please, Miss Remmington, let's not . . ."

"No!" she shrieked, jerking away from Gage. "Is that her? Is that Mary?"

I stepped in front of her, wrapping my hands around her upper arms to keep her from moving any closer to the corpse. Her expression was agonized and I could do nothing but tell her the truth. "Yes."

Her head reared back and then she began to shake it in denial. "No." She pushed against me, trying to move past, and I pressed back, forcing her to look me in the face.

"Yes," I repeated gently.

Her bottom lip began to tremble and her eyes filled with tears.

"Oh, dearest," I crooned, not knowing what else to say.

She crumpled before my eyes and Gage was there to help me gather her into my arms, letting her sob wildly on my shoulder. He met my gaze over her head, telling me it was time for me to be on my way.

"Come away from here," I told Miss Remmington and urged her back toward the horses.

"But . . . but I want to see her," she choked out.

"No, you don't," I assured her, and that only made her cry harder.

Lord Damien stood in the middle of the path gazing helplessly at the girl in my arms.

"Gather the horses' reins," I told him. "All except Mr. Gage's."

He obeyed and followed us down the path through the forest back toward Dalmay House. I knew Miss Remmington was too upset to sit a horse, and I wanted the opportunity to think. I had underestimated Miss Remmington's affection for Miss Wallace. Mary Wallace must have been quite a friend to make such a lasting impression on so short an acquaintance, for Miss Remmington did not strike me as overly sentimental.

I hoped Constable Paxton would see reason when Gage spoke with him, but I had a sinking feeling he would not. That Gage had been the first to examine the body would irritate him, and I could see him sticking to his theory that Miss Wallace had been carried away by the tide while trying to cross from Cramond Island just to spite him. Perhaps Mr. Wallace was the man we would have to reason with, though I hated to bother him when he had been dealt such a horrible blow. But surely he would want to know the truth about what had happened to his daughter.

In any case, sanctioned or not, I was not going to stop investigating, and I doubted Gage would be so easily deterred either. The location of Miss Wallace's corpse suggested one of two things. Either Will had been responsible for her disappearance and death or someone was trying to make it look like he was. And I was not going anywhere until I had the truth, whatever that might be, and no matter how painful. If he was innocent, I owed it to Will. But even if he wasn't, I now owed it to Miss Wallace and all of the people who had loved her to bring her killer to justice.

About halfway back to Dalmay House, Miss Remmington's sobs lessened and she began to take herself more in hand. She still sniffled into her handkerchief, but she no longer openly wept. "I introduced her to Lord Dalmay," she gasped between hiccups.

"I know."

Her eyes widened. "You knew?"

I nodded, but decided not to reveal my source. "Why didn't you tell me before?"

She frowned, considering her answer. "Because Michael Dalmay seemed so eager to protect his brother. I thought that was what he wished me to do."

"Because you were worried we would think Lord Dalmay's acquaintance with her would make him a suspect in her disappearance," I clarified.

Her face crumpled. "And now he's killed her, and it's my fault."

"Now see here," I told her sternly, not needing her to presume anything, "we don't know anything for certain. Mr. Gage and I are investigating the matter, and we plan to get to the bottom of it."

"But she was found on this beach."

"And she could have been deposited there by any number of means."

Miss Remmington's expression was dubious.

"There are a lot of factors to this investigation you are not privy to. We need to be certain we have the right culprit before any accusations are made." Her gaze was flat and unreadable, and that made me uneasy, which forced me to press her. "Will you give us a chance to conclude our investigation before you decide who murdered your friend? Can you do that?"

"But you do believe she was murdered?" she asked anxiously.

I hesitated, wondering if I should have left room for doubt. "Yes," I replied, unable to lie to her.

She sighed. "I suppose that's better than that *stupid* constable who believed she was swept out to sea." She glanced back at me and nodded. "All right. But do it quickly." Her hands tightened into fists. "I want the man to pay."

I resisted the urge to nudge the autocratic girl into the patch of bramble bushes on the right side of the path, but only just barely.

I was seated in the drawing room reading a letter when Gage returned from the firth shore and stormed into the chamber in a towering fury. I watched as he paced up and down the floor and cursed Constable Paxton for a bloody fool, the many capes of his greatcoat snapping out behind him as he pivoted.

"I take it he refused your assistance."

"The *idiot* actually threatened to have me brought up on charges for interfering with his investigation."

I grimaced. "I guess he heard about our visit to Cramond yesterday."

"Oh, yes. Some helpful biddy passed along that choice bit of information." He whirled around on the heel of his boot and charged back across the room. "He refused to listen to any of our findings today or yesterday, even about the boat Craggy Donald saw moving away from the island. He said the man wasn't to be trusted and we should just ignore whatever he told us."

I scowled. "Did you ask him about the damage he did to Donald's hut?"

"To be sure, but of course he denied it."

"Of course." I crossed my arms over my chest. "So he's going to rule Miss Wallace's death a drowning by misadventure?"

"Yes." He paced the length of the room one more time before planting his hands on the back of a golden wingback chair and leaning over it toward me. It creaked beneath the force of his weight. "Can you believe that man actually accused me of being a ghoul when I suggested he have the local surgeon or someone from the Royal College perform an autopsy to discover if there was water in her lungs?"

I sighed. "I was afraid of that. People do have a fear of dissection. Many still believe it's an unholy practice, that the soul can't be resurrected if the body is desecrated."

"Yes, well, while they worry about that, Miss Wallace's murderer may very well go free." He scraped a hand back through his golden hair and with a huff rounded the chair and dropped down onto its cushions. "So that avenue is closed to us, unless you want to go harass her father. I'm sure Mr. Paxton will have gotten there ahead of us, painting our suggestion in the worst possible light, but we could try. Though I loathe asking a grieving father to do such a thing."

"No. Not when all we wish to discover is if there is water in his daughter's lungs. We're already relatively certain she didn't drown."

He nodded and leaned forward with his elbows braced on his knees, staring down at his feet. His hands were spread wide and he kept bouncing the fingertips of one hand off the other in nervous agitation. When he noticed me watching him he nodded to the paper in my lap. "You were reading when I came in."

I lifted the letter. "It's from Philip."

Gage sat straighter in interest.

I opened the sheet of foolscap to look down at the handwriting. "He spoke to Dr. Renshaw, Sir Anthony's former assistant," I reminded him.

"What did he say?" From the look in his eyes I knew that wasn't all he wanted to ask, but he stuck to what was most important. I would have disappointed him on the other anyway, because Philip had said nothing of the man—or whether he had been rough with him—other than to relay his words about Dr. Sloane.

"Apparently he's familiar with Dr. Sloane's work." I arched my eyebrows.

"That doesn't sound good."

"It's not. He says that Dr. Sloane likes to collect oddities—people with interesting mental afflictions." I glanced back at the letter, reading from Philip's notes. "He was dismissed from his position at the Royal Infirmary of Edinburgh, and he received disciplinary sanctions from the Royal College of Surgeons because of a series of unorthodox experiments he performed on several of his patients." I lifted my gaze to meet Gage's. "Including his daughter."

He stiffened in surprise. "His daughter?"

I nodded, having felt the same shock upon reading the words. "Apparently she suffered from uncontrollable manias

300 · *Anna Lee Huber*

and melancholia, and his experiments began as a way to find a treatment for her."

"Where is she now?"

I hesitated, feeling a pulse of horror at the whole situation. "She killed herself."

Gage sank back in his chair and ran a hand through his hair, looking as stunned as I felt.

"That's what prompted the investigation into his experiments in the first place."

"His own daughter?" he muttered, staring unseeing at the muted morning sunlight shining through the windows to his right. "What was he doing to her?"

I shook my head, wondering the same thing.

"Did Cromarty confirm these statements?"

"Yes. Though he had to exert his position and authority to do so." It made sense that the Royal College would not want word of one of its members' radical actions made public to taint their reputation more than it already was by Dr. Knox's part in the infamous Burke and Hare case. Dr. Knox had purchased the bodies of the victims Burke and Hare had murdered, believing they were robbed from graves like most of the bodies he procured for dissection. Or so he said. Public opinion had recently turned against the anatomist and lecturer at the Royal College, blaming him for providing incentive for the killings, at the very least.

Of course, Dr. Sloane's sanctions must have occurred years ago, prior to the Burke and Hare scandal, otherwise Dr. Sloane wouldn't have been conducting his experiments in a lunatic asylum on remote Inchkeith Island instead of in Edinburgh. Unless he had been doing both.

I shivered at the thought.

In any case, while I could understand the Royal College's desire to keep his actions quiet, I heartily disagreed with them. The man's perfidy should have been made known to the public to protect families from unwittingly consigning their loved ones to Dr. Sloane's care. Families like the Dalmays. Although I still could not comprehend the old Lord

Dalmay's decision to confine his son to an institution like the Larkspur Retreat, I wanted to believe he would never have given him over to Dr. Sloane's care if he'd known about the man's unorthodox experiments and the reprimand he'd received from the Royal College.

"Does he mention what these experiments were?" Gage asked.

"No. But I think we can only assume that some of Will's drawings depict them." And the idea that he might have done these same things to his daughter, his own flesh and blood, made me sick to my stomach. I could tell Gage's thoughts had followed the same path, for his brow furrowed in concern.

"Perhaps it is these experiments, and not the identity of the girl he claims Dalmay murdered, that Dr. Sloane is so eager to keep secret. After all, the man was already sanctioned once for his actions. And quite possibly lost his daughter because of them, though I suppose there's no proof. He could easily have blamed her death on her melancholia. But, either way, it would explain the tight security at Larkspur, and why Michael was never allowed past Dr. Sloane's office."

I nodded, worrying my lip. "Both possibilities give him reason enough to want to see William silenced and returned to his care." I studied Gage, who was rubbing his hand over his brow in deep thought. "Do you think it's possible that's what is happening here? That Dr. Sloane is somehow manipulating events in order to discredit William and see him brought back to his asylum, whether by frightening Michael into recommitting him or dragging the authorities into it?" The idea seemed ludicrous, but without blaming William the list of other suspects was quite short.

"Perhaps," he replied, sounding unconvinced.

I could tell he was trying to consider other options for my sake, and I appreciated it. But by the very fact that he needed to try, I knew the circle of blame was tightening around Will. There were just too many facts that pointed to him. Too many things we would be forced to overlook if we were to attempt to shift the blame elsewhere. If William were not who he was, if neither of us cared for him, I knew we would already be interrogating him and demanding an explanation.

"It's time to talk to Will," I declared, knowing I needed to be the one to say it.

Gage nodded slowly.

"No more handling him with kid gloves. We need answers. Mr. Wallace deserves to know what happened to his daughter so she can rest in peace."

I turned away, unable to bear the compassion in Gage's eyes. I might have been determined to get answers, but I was not looking forward to hearing them.

CHAPTER TWENTY-FOUR

Once we had explained the morning's discoveries to Michael and our renewed intentions to question his brother, he insisted on joining us, first and foremost to inform him of Miss Wallace's death. He asserted that if his brother had not harmed her—as he said he believed, though his eyes belied him—then Will would need his support. We could not force him to leave the matter to us—Will was *his* brother, after all—and I thought his refusal to abandon him somewhat admirable, under the circumstances.

However, Michael's confident words did not translate to his behavior. He was so jumpy and anxious I was afraid his emotions would be conveyed to William. In an effort both to better control the situation and to relieve him of the weight of such an onerous duty, Gage offered to do the talking. After all, he was far more accustomed to such charged situations than Michael or I, and quite skilled at putting people at ease in order to question them. But Michael insisted he would do it. That Will was his brother, and he needed to be the one to speak to him.

So when we entered Will's bedchamber, finding him seated by the same window Gage and I had found him gazing out before, it was Michael and I who took the seats next to him while Gage and Mac stood by the door. His bright smile at our arrival quickly faded at the look on his brother's face and he waited in quiet anticipation for whatever Michael had come to say.

"I'm afraid we have something sad to share." Michael swallowed, but his voice still wavered on his next sentence. "I'm sorry to have to tell you this, but . . ."

Unable to resist doing so, and despite my doubts about him, I reached forward to take Will's hand. He grasped mine back, but he never removed his eyes from his brother's.

Michael swallowed again before rasping, "Mary Wallace is dead."

Will's entire body stiffened and he gripped my hand tighter, but other than that there was no discernible reaction. He just stared at his brother as if he hadn't spoken, as if he couldn't hear him.

When a moment of tense silence had passed without anyone moving, or hardly daring to breathe, Michael shifted in his seat. "Will, did you hear me? Do you understand?"

His gaze flickered, allowing just a glimpse of the raw pain he had locked behind his eyes. I wasn't sure if anyone but me had seen it—Gage and Mac being too far away and Michael being too wrapped up in his own worries—but it tightened something, a vise, around my chest and squeezed the air from my lungs.

"How?" he said, his voice void of emotion.

Michael glanced at me in uncertainty. "Well, we don't know yet. The constable thinks she drowned."

Will's eyes swung to mine, and I struggled to keep my emotions in check under his penetrating gaze. "But you don't."

It was a statement, not a question, and I found I didn't want to lie to him. "No."

"How?" he repeated in the same emotionless voice, but with a shade more force.

"I . . . I'm not certain. But there were too many other . . . markings. And the drowning just doesn't make sense."

Something in his face changed—a tightening of his brow, a flattening of his lips. "You've seen her, then?"

I realized what I'd said and nodded.

Michael cleared his throat uneasily. "Will, there are some questions I need to ask you." His words were halting. "You obviously knew Miss Wallace. Did you . . ."

"What markings?" Will asked me, ignoring his brother.

Michael's words stumbled to a stop and his brow furrowed in concern. I could see Gage shift, out of the corner of my eye, and I knew he was hesitant to reveal such details to the man who was our chief suspect. But Will just waited patiently, watching me with those pained eyes. I could see more hurt in them with each passing second.

"She'd been bound," I replied, my voice hoarse with suppressed emotion. "And there were . . . bruises, many bruises." I couldn't reveal those details. It was too much to put into words.

Will seemed to understand them anyway, for his grip tightened so hard on my hand that I worried he might break it. His breathing became labored and his eyes unfocused. I shifted forward in my seat, trying to soothe him.

"Will. Will, look at me," I told him, pressing my other hand to his shoulder and then reaching up to cup his cheek. He closed his eyes and shook his head, almost violently. I pulled my hand back and Michael leaned forward.

"William. It's all right," he urged, but his voice was anything but comforting.

Will's hold on my hand was now becoming too much and I tried to pull it away from him, but he wouldn't release it. I wasn't sure if he was even aware he was holding it.

I sucked in a sharp breath at the pain. "Will, you have to let go of my hand." My voice shook. "Will, you're hurting me."

Gage and Mac entered the scene then, Mac holding Will back in his chair, while Gage tried to pry Will's fingers loose from mine. There was a tussle and Will shouted. He jolted forward in his chair when Gage managed to remove his hand from mine, but his other hand shot out to wrap around my arm.

"Did they bleed her?" he demanded, his face inches from

mine. His eyes were wide, ordering me to tell him what he wanted to know. The others struggled with him to remove his hold on me and the muscles in his neck stood out from the strain it took to maintain his grip. "Tell me! Did they bleed her?"

I blinked wide eyes at him and gasped. "Yes."

His face slackened in pain, and he released me so abruptly that I fell backward into my chair. Gage lifted me from it and pulled me toward the door before I could say a word, even though Will had gone ominously still and silent. All I could see moving was the rise and fall of his chest as he fought for breath.

Gage urged me into the parlor, blocking my sight of Will, and turned me into the shelter of his arms. I could feel that I was trembling, but I thought it was more from shock than fear. I had never expected to see Will behave in such a manner. I had known it was possible—Michael and Philip and Gage had all warned me of it—but being told something could happen and actually experiencing it were two different things. I inhaled, trying to pull in as much of Gage's comforting scent as I could, and held it before releasing it on a shuddering breath.

When the worst of my trembling had stopped, Gage loosened his embrace to look down into my face. "Are you all right?"

I nodded absently, rubbing the spot on my arm where Will had grabbed hold of me.

"Are you hurt?" He lifted my hand, running his fingers gently over the bones. The calluses on his fingers rasped over my skin.

"Just bruised, I think."

I watched his fingers, flinching when he hit a tender spot near my little finger.

"Maybe we should ask Dr. Winslow to take a look at it, just to be sure."

I began to argue, but then realized it was my right hand

we were talking about, my painting hand, and nodded in acceptance. Surely Will hadn't done any permanent injury to it—my stomach clenched at the thought.

Gage must have read the worry in my eyes, for he pulled me close again.

"Kiera, I'm so sorry," Michael exclaimed as he emerged from Will's bedchamber. His expression was agonized. "Had I known he would react that way, I never would have told him about Miss Wallace with you so close to him."

"I thought you said he hadn't attacked anyone in months," Gage snapped before I could respond.

"He . . . he hasn't," Michael stammered.

"Damn it, man! He nearly broke her hand."

"Please!" I interjected, having never seen Gage so upset or Michael so distressed. "I'm unharmed. I . . . I don't think there's any lasting damage." I pressed the other hand to Michael's arm. "How's Will?"

Gage scowled at me. I didn't know whether that was because I'd halted his tirade or because he couldn't understand why I was asking about the man who'd just injured me. Perhaps both.

Michael seemed just as taken aback. "He's . . . he's quiet. He's not responding to our questions."

"Is he about to have another one of his episodes?"

He thought about it and then shook his head. "No. This is different. I think he's aware we're there, he's just unable . . ." he hesitated ". . . or unwilling to respond."

I crossed my arms over my stomach, thinking back on Will's reaction to Mary Wallace's death. I had seen so much pain in his eyes, so much anguish. And, yet, he had *hurt* me. I wanted to shake that aside and focus on his emotion, but I couldn't. Not while my hand still ached and my insides quavered.

"Well, which do you think it is?" Gage demanded of Michael, his voice rising again with his temper. "Is he unable or unwilling?"

"I don't know . . ."

"Because if he's unable, that's one thing, but unwilling . . ." He stepped forward to crowd Michael, towering over him by a good six inches. "You do realize he's the main suspect in Miss Wallace's murder, and with that, the murder of that girl in the asylum is looking more likely. And if he's refusing to answer questions and hindering our investigation, that makes him even more suspicious."

"He might just be incapable of answering now," Michael argued, trying to stand up to Gage, but his voice continued to waver. "He clearly cared for Miss Wallace."

"And he doesn't care for Kiera?" Gage shouted. "His affection is not a mitigating factor. He crushed her hand."

"He didna ken what he was doin'," Mac argued.

We all glanced up in surprise to see him standing outside Will's bedchamber door.

"He wouldn't ever hurt her ladyship." He shook his head. "No' on purpose."

"How can you say that? He just did," Gage snapped.

"Wait," I interrupted, pressing a restraining hand to his arm. "Mac, what do you mean he didn't know what he was doing?"

The older man frowned, his scraggly brows lowered over troubled eyes. "'Twas the injuries ye were describin'. The bruises and bindings. It's like at the asylum. They treated 'em like bloody animals. Ye've seen his drawings."

"And they bled her," I murmured, thinking of the image of the man with blood running down his arms still inscribed on Will's bedchamber wall. I had connected Mary's wounds to it the first time I saw them, but had overlooked the implication.

I glanced up at Mac and he nodded in confirmation. "Aye."

"So you don't think he realized he was hurting me?" I asked, moving a step closer to the cantankerous manservant.

Mac shook his head.

I heard Gage open his mouth to argue, but held up my hand to forestall him. "But he did."

Something in Mac's gaze shifted at these words and I moved a step closer to look up into his face.

"He did hurt me." I let the full pain and shock of that realization show in my face. "I never wanted to believe that he could, but . . ." I gestured weakly with my bruised hand.

Mac's eyes dropped from mine, and I knew he understood what I was trying to say.

"I want to help him," I told him. "I want William to be better. But if he harmed Miss Wallace, if he killed her, whether or not it was an accident, we are not helping him by leaving him free to potentially hurt other people."

His anger sparked again. "But that Dr. Sloane . . ."

"Not Dr. Sloane," I said, shaking my head. "Not Larkspur Retreat. But there are more humane asylums. Places where you can visit the patients to be certain they are being well cared for. And if that is where Will needs to go, we're not helping him by lying to keep him with us."

I waited a moment to allow my words to sink in. "Mac, we need the truth."

I had not thought it possible for Mac's perpetually grim face to fall even more, but it did. And its bleakness touched me.

"Aye. I'll tell ye."

I glanced at Gage, whose temper had cooled considerably in the face of the man's willing cooperation. "How is it that Lord Dalmay is able to escape his chambers whenever he wishes?" His voice had an edge to it, telling me he was keeping himself tightly restrained. "Is it through the servants' stairs?"

Mac's gaze darted to Michael, who looked unhappy. "Aye. When he first came back to us, I noticed that Cap'n Dalmay didna like feelin' trapped, as he had been at the asylum. It made him upset. So I thought it would do no harm to let him think he could escape. And I always followed him when he did." He scowled. "But then there were a couple o' times when he got by me wi'oot me bein' aware. Oh, we found 'im right quick, but it bothered me that he'd gotten to be so cunning. So I started lockin' the door again when I wasna on duty. I was worrit he'd do himsel' harm."

"We found it unlocked last night." Michael's voice snapped like a whip. "Was that you?"

He had the grace to look abashed, which gave the manservant a rather hangdog look. "Aye."

"What of the boat?" Gage asked.

"What boat?"

"The one stored in the ruins at Banbogle Castle." He nodded toward me. "Lady Darby saw it there yesterday afternoon."

Mac's grizzled brow ruffled in confusion. "I've ne'er seen a boat there."

"You didn't notice the boat inside the crumbled section of the wall?" I asked.

"Nay. Are ye sure it was a boat?"

I considered the matter, wondering if I'd been seeing things. It had been tucked in the shadows and I hadn't gone any closer to be sure. "Yes. There was a boat," I stated, not willing to be swayed on this.

"I'm sorry," he said, sounding genuinely regretful. "I didna see it."

I nodded, deciding to believe him. In any case, it wouldn't do any good to press the matter. "Do you recall who was on duty with William Thursday last, particularly in the afternoon?"

"I was," he replied with a great deal of confidence. "And then Lachlan."

"Lachlan? Where was Donovan?"

"He had the day off."

I cast a fleeting look at Gage, wondering if he found that piece of information as interesting as I did. "Did he tell you how he planned to spend it?"

Mac scoffed at the idea. Obviously the two men were not good friends. "Nay. Just that he left the estate."

"And William. Can you tell me with any certainty whether you or Lachlan was with him at all times during that day?"

"Aye. He ne'er left my sight. And wee Lachlan woulda told me had he escaped his. That lad is scairt o' his ain shadow, as well as me."

We'd heard from Mac's own lips just how stealthy Will had become. He just might have escaped without them knowing it.

But for the several hours it would have taken him to row to Cramond Island and back? Could he really have gone missing for that long without it being noticed? And where had he kept Miss Wallace? She had not died until the night before last, five days after being taken.

The only place I could think of was Banbogle Castle. Which would mean that her body could have been lying inside, long since gone cold, while I chatted with Will just yesterday. The idea sent a chill down my spine. The castle would have to be searched. I only prayed we didn't find evidence I was right.

CHAPTER TWENTY-FIVE

Since William was still unresponsive, Gage and I decided our next course of action should be to speak to Donovan and find out just where he'd gone on the day Miss Wallace disappeared. I followed Gage down the hall away from Will's rooms, nearly colliding with his back when he hesitated at the junction of the corridor. The door leading to the main staircase was to the left, but he glanced to the right, toward the servants' stairs. With a wry glance over his shoulder at me, he strode down the hall to this second set of stairs. As suspected, the door was unlocked.

"Well, Mac is on duty." I sighed.

Gage arched an eyebrow, but gestured me through the doorway. It would be quicker to take this flight of stairs straight down to Donovan's room in the servants' quarters. We descended a flight and a half only to stumble to a halt at the sight of the person coming up.

Miss Remmington glanced up at us guiltily, her eyes still rimmed in red from crying.

Taking in the sight of her clad in cloak and bonnet, her cheeks pink from windburn, I gasped. "Oh, no! Tell me you didn't!"

She wrapped her arms around herself and bit her lip.

"Good heavens, you did!" My voice echoed in the enclosed

space. "You promised me you would let us finish our investigation."

She lifted her trembling chin in defiance, her eyes shining with tears. "Someone had to alert the authorities. Lord Dalmay has to be punished."

I rushed down the remaining stairs to stand over her. "But what if he didn't kill her, you foolish girl! And now you've brought that power-hungry oaf of a constable down on our heads. Do you think he cares about being sure he's found the real culprit? About getting justice for Miss Wallace?"

"But I thought . . ." Miss Remmington murmured, her rebelliousness crumbling before our eyes. "He *has* to have done it," she said, sounding less certain. "Who else could it be?"

"There are a few other possibilities." Gage descended the stairs to join us, some of the tension and anger he had restrained coming unleashed. "But now that you've alerted the constable we'll be wasting our time dealing with him instead of interrogating them."

Miss Remmington began to cry in earnest. "I didn't know."

"Because you didn't listen. Next time you're so bent on vengeance, be sure you have all the facts."

She buried her head in her hands, but he was having none of it.

"Pull yourself together," he snapped. "You're going to help us. Now, what exactly did you tell Mr. Paxton?" He took hold of her upper arm and shook her. "What did you tell him?"

"J-j-just that I had intr-troduced Lord Dalmay to Miss Wallace." She hiccuped. "And that he had spent time in a lunatic asylum."

"That's it?"

She nodded.

"Good. Now, you are going to tell Michael Dalmay what you've done."

314 · Anna Lee Huber

She gasped in dismay.

"*You* were the one who accused his brother of murder before a foolhardy constable, so you can be the one to tell him so. And you need to do so now. Mr. Paxton will have gathered his associates and be making his way here. We need to be ready for him when he arrives."

She blinked up at him with weepy feminine delicateness, but it did nothing but anger him further.

"Do you want to help fix what you've done or not?" he snarled.

She startled. "Yes."

"All right, then. Michael is in his brother's room. Go straight up. The door at the top of the stairs is unlocked. Go!"

She scrambled past us up the stairs, her feet rapping against the wood, in as much of a hurry to get away from Gage's fury as she was to help, I thought.

"What are we going to do?" I asked, panicked now that some of my anger had faded.

"Defy him," Gage replied with a stubborn tilt to his chin. "I'm not about to hand William Dalmay into Constable Paxton's custody, whether he's guilty of murder or not."

I was relieved to hear it, but uncertain just how he was going to manage that. But I knew better than to question him when he had that determined look in his eye.

Rather than continuing down the next flight of steps to the kitchens and servants' quarters, he hauled open the door to the ground floor. The sound of another door closing below made me turn back as Gage hurried into the entrance hall corridor, but I could hear no footsteps approaching from below. I considered investigating the noise, but Gage was already so far ahead of me down the passage that I chose to ignore it.

When Constable Paxton and his two associates rode up to Dalmay House less than an hour later, he was greeted by a phalanx of angry men. Gage and Michael, wearing their most forbidding expressions, stood side by side on the drive before the front door, blocking his entrance, while Lord Keswick and Lord Damien took up positions behind them, looking none too welcoming themselves.

I had been surprised by Damien's willingness to step into the fray, considering the doubts we all still held about William's innocence. I could only assume that his loyalty to his family had weighed heavily in the decision. After all, he couldn't wish for his sister's fiancé's brother to be taken up in shackles. Imagine the resulting scandal. And Lady Hollingsworth's shrieking fit when she found out. She was already going to be angry that word of William's stay in an asylum had gotten out, but if he were arrested, Caroline would never be allowed to marry Michael.

A pair of the Dalmays' burliest footmen flanked the entrance and bolstered the number of men Mr. Paxton would have to fight his way through to six. Laura and I stood in the doorway and refused to be shooed away by either Keswick or Gage—or the sanctimonious butler glaring disapprovingly at our backs. Miss Remmington had long ago retreated upstairs, but I suspected she found a window to peer through in order to observe the scene below. Had I been in her shoes, I wouldn't have been able to resist, no matter how guilty I felt for causing the confrontation.

We could see the dust kicked up by their horses' hooves long before we actually caught a glimpse of them. It was like watching a thundercloud approach from the distance, growing louder and fiercer as it neared. The analogy was not inapt, as the sky today was far less friendly than it had been over the past week. The misty banks of clouds we were so familiar with in Scotland had overtaken the sun, preventing its warm rays from breaking through. I suspected rain would move in before nightfall, and I wouldn't be surprised if the wind followed, blowing some of the bright autumn leaves that had been clinging so stubbornly to their branches to the ground.

I doubted Mr. Paxton had anticipated receiving such a

reception, but the time we'd had to watch his approach down the long, straight drive, he'd also had to prepare for our unfriendly greeting. He might have been a prideful buffoon, but he was no idiot. He knew we weren't all standing out there to welcome him.

And his response to this was antagonism. Not the smartest course of action when faced with six men, two of whom by this point were towers of fury. He drew his horse to a stop at the last possible moment before he would have crashed into Michael and Gage, making me flinch, though they didn't seem to react at all, except their postures became stiffer and angrier.

Mr. Paxton glared down at them like they were insects. "I'm no' here to argue wi' ye, Dalmay. I'm here for your brother. Where is he?"

"Not going with you."

Mr. Paxton's eyes narrowed. "Dinna make me arrest ye, too. The man's committed murder. He needs to be locked up."

"And how do you know that?" Gage asked. "Just this morning you declared Miss Wallace's death an accidental drowning."

Mr. Paxton's face reddened. "I'll no' be talkin' to you, Mr. Gage. You've been interferin' wi' my investigation, and by all rights I should have ye taken up for it." He stabbed his finger toward Gage. "You should've been the one to tell me aboot William Dalmay's affliction and no' Miss Remmington. She's the only one wi' a lick o' sense."

"That's *Lord* Dalmay, to you," Michael corrected him in a hard voice.

"He's no' really a lord," Mr. Paxton protested.

"Yes, he is," he enunciated carefully. "And has been since our father died."

"What, are ye daft, man? He spent time in a madhouse."

"That changes nothing. They cannot strip a man of his title simply because he's declared insane, *which* my brother is not."

The constable huffed and opened his mouth to argue, but Michael cut him off.

"He's *not*. He never received a proper hearing before the Court of Chancery regarding his mental state. He has never been proved to be anything but sane."

"Then how'd he end up in the madhouse?" He sneered.

Michael's shoulders were taut, his hands clenched into fists by his sides. "He was confined to that asylum against his will. He's the victim here, not the perpetrator. And I'll thank you to remember that."

Mr. Paxton's horse shifted, but he paid it no heed, merely tightened his grip on the reins. "Regardless o' how *you* say he got there, the fact remains that Will . . ." Michael glared at him and Mr. Paxton puckered his lips in distaste, but corrected himself. "*Lord* Dalmay spent time in a *lunatic* asylum. He canna be in his right mind. And Miss Remmington believes he killed her friend."

"She's overwrought." Gage spoke up again. "She misspoke."

"Ye can force her to take back her words, but I heard the ring o' truth in her statement, and ye won't convince me to believe otherwise."

I couldn't see his face, but I could tell from the tone of his voice that Gage was losing his patience. "What you heard was a woman grieving and desperate to avenge her friend's death, and she picked the closest and easiest target. You can't arrest a man on such flimsy evidence."

The shade of Mr. Paxton's skin now rivaled the deep red of his hair and mustache. "I can. And I will. Now step aside."

"You have no authority here."

"I do. And I'll arrest all o' ye if ye stand in my way a moment longer."

"You can try." I tensed as Gage stalked closer to Mr. Paxton, worried the constable or his horse might lash out at him. But Gage seemed not to share this fear, and he reached out to grab hold of the horse's bridle. "But as I said, you have no authority here. Lord Dalmay is a baron, and as such, a member of the peerage, which gives him the privilege of being exempt from civil arrest."

I stifled a gasp and shared a glance with Laura, who seemed not to have forgotten this fact, to judge from the smile of enjoyment that curled her lips at seeing the constable's reaction.

The man's chest puffed out like an angry robin and his eyes bulged so large I worried they might pop out of his head. "The man is no' a peer."

"Oh, but he is," Gage replied silkily. "So unless you have a warrant—which I know you do not, because no magistrate would ever dare to issue one on such flimsy evidence, especially for a peer—then you haven't the right to even threaten to arrest him."

He turned to the two men Mr. Paxton had brought with him, who seemed content to merely observe the proceedings. I suspected they were simple villagers, maybe retired soldiers, who were only doing as the constable had asked of them.

"I suggest if you don't wish to be brought up on charges of unlawfully detaining a peer along with Mr. Paxton here that you return home."

The men looked at each other and one shrugged, as if to say this wasn't his matter. Then they slowly began to turn away.

Seeing that his reinforcements were abandoning him, the constable snarled. "This isna over. I'll be reportin' you all to my superior."

"You do that," Gage replied without concern. Then in one smooth motion he released Mr. Paxton's horse and stepped far back from the man and the horse's reach.

With one last furious glare at all of us, he pulled his horse around, its hooves scrabbling for purchase in the loose gravel, and rode down the drive after his men.

Gage and the others watched to make sure the constable didn't return or veer off the lane and attempt to approach the house from another path.

"Damn the man!" Michael exclaimed.

Gage reached over to clasp him on the shoulder, guiding him toward the door. "I'm afraid your efforts to keep hidden your brother's whereabouts for the last decade have all been for naught. Paxton is going to tell every man he knows and then some."

Michael nodded dejectedly and turned to Lord Keswick, who was trying to apologize for his sister's actions.

"Why didn't you remind me about the rules of privilege?" I demanded of Gage, linking my arm through his as he passed by me into the warmth of the entry hall. "Had I remembered, it would have made this confrontation much less anxiety ridden. I couldn't figure out how you were going to thwart Mr. Paxton."

He offered me an enigmatic smile. "What? And ruin the excitement?"

I arched a single eyebrow in chastisement. "So if we discover that Will is guilty of murdering Miss Wallace, he will be tried before the House of Lords, not the criminal courts?" I asked in clarification.

"That is correct. But in his instance, it's far more likely he would receive a hearing before the Court of Chancery first to decide if he's insane. If he was found to be, then he and his property would be placed in the custody of the king, and he would be detained in an asylum of the Lord Chancellor's choosing."

"Does the Lord Chancellor allow the family members any say?"

Sensing my concern, Gage pressed his hand over mine where it rested on his arm. "He might. But even if he doesn't, there's no cause for alarm. The Lord Chancellor would never choose a place like the Larkspur Retreat."

"So, effectively, if Dr. Sloane were still trying to get William back, he's now lost all ability to do so."

Gage stopped to look at me as if I'd just said something important.

"William's stay in a lunatic asylum is no longer a secret,

so should he prove to be innocent but still require more care than Michael can give him, Michael can search wherever he likes for another place to take his brother," I elaborated. I doubted Michael would ever do such a thing, but should he have to, there were no more concerns over secrecy.

Gage pressed a hand to his head. "Bloody hell! Why didn't I see this before?"

I widened my eyes in alarm. "See what?"

He paced away from me a few steps and back again. "Dr. Sloane. He's been truly manipulating us all."

"What?"

He stood staring down at his feet for a moment, almost in awe.

"What do you mean he's been manipulating us?" I demanded.

Gage's eyes turned hard and he shook his head. "The bloody bastard."

"Gage," I exclaimed, growing agitated.

He glanced up at me. "I'll explain. But first . . . Michael," he called across the room to where Michael was deep in conversation with Keswick. Michael looked up in question. "Do you want to help prove your brother is innocent?"

He straightened. "Of course."

"And you, Keswick?"

He murmured his assent.

"Keswick, take a pair of footmen with you to Banbogle Castle. Check to see if there's a boat stored there, and if there is, send word back, but don't let it out of your sight."

"What is this all about?" Michael asked as Keswick departed. He looked as bewildered and exasperated as I felt.

"I'll explain. But I need you to make sure Donovan is not in your brother's chambers."

"Donovan?"

"Yes. And if he is, bring him down to his room in the servants' quarters. Either way, we'll be waiting for you there."

Gage hurried away before he could answer, toward the

flight of servants' stairs we'd used earlier. I had to practically run to keep up.

"Gage. Gage!" I grabbed hold of his arm just as he was opening the door and pulled him around to face me. "Would you mind telling me what's going on?"

He wrapped his hand around my upper arm and pulled me into the dim stairwell. He cast a fleeting look up and down the stairs to be certain we were alone and then began speaking in a hushed voice. "All along we've suspected that Dr. Sloane was eager to have William Dalmay back at his Larkspur Retreat. You yourself suggested he might know something Sloane doesn't want revealed. So he decided to control the situation. He put one of his men in position to keep an eye on Dalmay and report back to him."

My eyes widened as I realized what he was saying. "Donovan?"

"That's my guess. Did you notice that Dr. Sloane once worked in the same infirmary Donovan gave as a reference—the Royal Infirmary of Edinburgh?"

I gasped, wondering how I'd missed that connection.

"I don't think that's just a coincidence."

I scowled. "Did I tell you he's been cozying up to my maid?" From his frown I could tell I hadn't. "He wanted information from her—about me, about my past."

He stiffened and his eyes turned watchful. "I hope you reprimanded the girl."

"I did," I replied, still trying to read his expression in the low light. "And I hope she's had the sense to stay away from him since. I'm still considering sending her back to Gairloch."

He turned away abruptly and guided me down the steps with a warm hand to my back.

"I still don't understand," I said. "Has he been manipulating us through Donovan?"

"Partly. But you remember Dr. Sloane sought me out and specifically asked me to investigate. I'm beginning to wonder if he knew all along that Michael and I were old friends, and so I would be more inclined to see his brother confined to an asylum than face a public trial. And . . ." he paused in his descent of the stairs to look at me ". . . most importantly, that I would be more eager to keep Dalmay's crimes hidden from the authorities."

I began to comprehend. "Dr. Sloane was relying on the fact that all of us would want to keep Will's past and his current mental state secret. So if he could convince us through a series of incidents that William was a danger to himself and others, and that Michael was incapable of caring for him, he hoped we would then urge Michael to realize that his brother was better off at Larkspur Retreat rather than risk revealing his condition to the rest of the world."

"Exactly."

The entire scenario sickened me to the point that I felt physically ill. "That's . . . that's . . ." I stumbled over my words, unable to think of a description horrible enough. "That's *evil*." I clasped my amethyst pendant, running my fingers over the smooth, cold stone. My mother had given it to me as an amulet of protection, and I needed the comfort of it, and her, now. "Do you think that's what's really happening here?"

"That's my theory."

I leaned against the wall at my back, feeling a little weak-kneed. "And so Mary Wallace . . . He killed Mary Wallace just to make us doubt Will?"

Gage's answer to this was slower in coming. "Possibly."

"But why drag her into this?"

"She befriended Dalmay, didn't she?"

"Yes, but if Dr. Sloane was so keen to keep the matter contained then why didn't he nab Miss Remmington or Laura or me instead?"

"Perhaps it was simply a matter of opportunity. He could make Miss Wallace's death look like an accidental drowning, keeping the authorities from investigating too closely, while still making all of us doubt."

I shook my head, having trouble accepting all of this.

Gage stepped forward to cup my elbow. "I know it all seems unbelievable, but from the beginning I've had a hunch that nothing was as it seemed. And without declaring Will insane, and blaming all of this on him outright, I can think of no other explanation." His gaze was so intent I couldn't look away. "I'm trying to keep an open mind."

For me. He was keeping an open mind for me. That was what he left unsaid. He was testing every avenue, even those that seemed somewhat ludicrous, so that I wouldn't have to accept that Will might be beyond my means to help. Gage himself was not convinced this was anything but an outrageous theory, but he was willing to consider it, for me.

That realization warmed me from the inside out, blunting the icy fear Dr. Sloane's potential involvement had caused me. "Do you think you can make Donovan talk?"

"I don't know." His features hardened. "But I'm determined to try."

CHAPTER TWENTY-SIX

He pulled open the door to the servants' quarters, frightening a maid, who stood on the other side clutching a stack of clean linens. He reached out a hand to help her steady the toppling pile and murmured an apology before asking for directions to the men's lodgings. Making only one wrong turn through the dimly lit corridors, we eventually located Donovan's room among the bedchambers for the male staff.

There was no answer at the door when Gage knocked. I could tell from his lowered brow and the way he had compressed his mouth into a tight line that he wasn't happy about this. Without waiting for Michael's permission, he pushed the door open and strode in. I smiled awkwardly at the footman who was watching us with some curiosity from his room across the hall and followed Gage inside.

The room was small, as most servants' quarters were, with bare walls and a single window high up near the ceiling. The window was too small for even a petite adult to squeeze through, and it let in so little sunlight that Gage was forced to light the candle we saw sitting on the dresser. The only other piece of furniture was a bed, neatly made, but so short and narrow that I had difficulty imagining brawny Donovan fitting in it.

I stood near the door and observed while Gage rifled

through Donovan's belongings. "Aren't you worried he'll be upset if he discovers you searching his things?"

"I don't particularly care," Gage replied, kneeling to dig through the bottom drawers of a dresser.

I watched him another moment before venturing to inquire, "You do realize Miss Remmington has spoiled his plan by alerting Constable Paxton?"

He slammed the drawer shut. "Yes." Then his voice was muffled as he bent over to search under the bed. "And I'm worried Donovan will now flee, taking whatever evidence there is with him. Now," he murmured, reaching his hand up under the frame, "what have we here?"

He sat back holding a tin of some kind and I leaned closer to see what it was. But before he could open it, the shuffle of footsteps distracted us.

Michael paused just inside the door, glancing around in confusion. "He's not here?"

"No," Gage said. "And I take it he wasn't in your brother's chambers either?"

He shook his head.

"Dash it!" His expression turned grim. "Well, let's hope Keswick finds that boat." The implication being that otherwise Donovan might have already fled.

I frowned, wondering if he had been listening in the stairwell when Gage and I confronted Miss Remmington. If so, he'd had a good hour and a half to make his escape without our knowing it. I cursed myself, wishing I'd taken the time to check on the noise I'd heard. If Donovan got away, we might lose our only chance to find the answers we sought and to clear Will of suspicion for good.

I admitted I still had doubts. Could Dr. Sloane really have manipulated events so skillfully? It seemed improbable, if not impossible. But after what he'd done to Will in that asylum, I knew it wasn't inconceivable.

However, if he *had* been influencing us, I could say with certainty that no matter what Dr. Sloane had made us believe about Will, we would never have recommended that

Michael return his brother to that cesspit called Larkspur Retreat. But maybe Dr. Sloane had already known that was unlikely. Maybe his real intention had been to discredit Will and cast doubt on his sanity. After all, if no one believed what Will said, then Dr. Sloane's secrets were safe.

That thought made me uneasy, for I certainly had my doubts now about Will and just what he was or was not capable of. It troubled me to think that at least some of my misgivings might be at the behest of a devious man.

I moved closer to peer over Gage's shoulder as he lifted the lid on the tin he'd found under Donovan's bed. It scraped against the base and the odor that wafted up from it immediately made me take a step back.

"Ugh!" I pressed a hand over my nose and mouth to block the stench.

He scrunched up his nose and reached inside to sift the sawdust-looking material through his fingers. "It's dried valerian root."

"I thought I recognized it. Lucy brought me a cup of valerian root tea last night," I told them, speaking through my hand. "Vile brew. She said your cook had told her it would help me sleep."

"Yes," Michael replied. "It's one of her better remedies. We tried to give some to Will when he first came home from the asylum, but he reacted so strongly to it we never tried again."

The back of my neck began to tingle. "What do you mean?"

"Well, he kicked up a right fuss and then threw the cup against the wall. Shattered it. The stain never did come out of the wallpaper. It was there until we removed it to get rid of the first round of his drawings."

I thought back to that first night at Dalmay House, when we had entered Will's room and I had seen him hunched in the corner scrabbling at the wall with his charcoal.

"It's the valerian root," I gasped.

Gage and Michael turned to look at me.

"That's what's triggering Will's melancholic episodes."

Gage glanced back at the tin, his jaw hardening.

"But we haven't tried to give him valerian root tea since that first time," Michael protested.

I shook my head. "It's not the tea. It's the smell. It reminds him of the asylum."

He frowned. "Because they served it to him?"

"No." Gage rose to his feet to explain. "She means the scent must be similar to what the asylum smelled like. I admit, it is quite rancid."

Michael still looked confused. "It smells like an herb."

I stared at him in amazement. "What are you talking about? It *reeks*! Like stale body odor and . . . and smelly feet."

A grin tugged at the corners of Gage's mouth. "I'd heard there were people who didn't actually mind the smell of valerian root, but I've never actually met any. Until today. I guess you and your cook simply enjoy the smell of rancid feet."

Michael scowled.

"I smelled this in Will's bedchamber on the night we arrived," I said, gesturing to the tin in Gage's hands. "I caught a whiff of it as I was approaching Will. I remember thinking it was body odor, but as I moved closer it dissipated. Donovan must have put this in something or wiped it on an object. He must have introduced it to the room on purpose, knowing it would upset Will." I pressed my hand to my nose again. "Close that," I told Gage.

The lid clanged against the container as he pressed it down. "Donovan must have noted Dalmay's reaction to the valerian root tea when you tried to give it to him. Then he began introducing it to Will's environment when he thought no one would notice or when he wanted him to have an episode. Clearly he was up to mischief when he provoked a fit the other night. Sabotaging your engagement, I'd wager, when he heard you'd told your fiancée and her family about Will."

Michael rubbed a hand across the back of his neck and stared at the tin as if it were a snake about to bite him. "Could it be he had trouble sleeping and he simply used it to make himself a cup of tea?"

Gage's expression was dubious. "If it were something so innocent, why did he feel the need to hide it in a place few people would think to look?"

He had no answer for that.

I felt sorry for Michael—he appeared horrified by the realization that the man he'd hired to take care of his brother had, in fact, been doing him injury—and, yet, at the same time, I was furious with him. He was so protective of Will, even willing to go so far as to lie for him, but he hadn't noticed that one of his staff was hurting him. If he truly couldn't sense how awful the valerian root smelled, perhaps I could forgive him for missing it. However, I couldn't help thinking that if Donovan had been so capable of harming Will in this way, how many other little things had he done to impair him? Had Michael missed those, too?

I crossed the room to lean against the door frame, staring out into the corridor. Perhaps I was being too hard on him. But I couldn't offer Michael any words of comfort just then. And I knew if I couldn't dredge up enough sympathy to do that, I might say something I regretted.

"I need to speak to Lucy," I told the men, without looking back or waiting for a reply.

I could hear the clang of pots and the thwack of a knife up ahead and followed it into the kitchen. The scent of bacon lingered in the air from breakfast, mixing with the sharp aroma of the onions one of the maids standing at the butcher-block table was chopping. The girls looked up at me in surprise.

"I'm sorry to bother you," I told them with a reassuring smile. "I'm looking for my maid. Could you point me in the direction of the women's quarters?"

As they stood gawking at me, I began to realize how

absurd the situation was—ladies did not go belowstairs to seek out their servants—and felt a blush sting my cheeks.

"Well, dinna just stand there gawpin' like fish," a little, round woman in a long apron scolded, entering the room behind me. "Answer 'er ladyship."

The maids continued to stare, neither of them seeming to be able to find their tongues.

The woman sighed and shook her head. "They dinna have a lick of sense betweenst the both of 'em." Then she turned to look at me, as if she conversed with ladies in this manner every day. "Yer maid's quarters'll be doon that hall. But I think ye might find 'er quicker in the servants' hall across the way. Heard the maids in there twitterin' away like magpies just a moment ago."

"Thank you," I said and followed the direction of her pointing finger.

As I drew closer, I could hear the maids as well, giggling about something. Hesitant to give them as much of a scare as I'd given the kitchen maids, I reached up and rapped on the open door. The laughter straggled to a stop as I peered around the corner into the chamber. The maids stiffened in surprise as they realized who I was.

"M'lady," Lucy gasped and rushed forward, smelling like starch. "Were ye callin' me? I dinna hear ye ring."

"I didn't."

"Oh, was I s'posed to be waitin' for ye in your rooms?"

"No, Lucy." I grabbed hold of the frazzled girl's shoulders. "You haven't done anything wrong."

Her face was still crinkled in worry. "Then why are ye doon here lookin' for me?"

I shook my head impatiently. "I'll explain later. I need to know everything you learned from Donovan. Was there anything he told you about himself?"

Her eyebrows lifted toward her hairline.

"Lucy, it's important," I added when she didn't speak right away. "He must have told you *something*."

"Well," she finally murmured. I didn't know if her dithering was due to a misguided loyalty she still felt for Donovan or because of my frantic demeanor. "He told me where he worked afore, but ye already ken that. And that he grew up in a small village near Kirkcudbright."

"Twynholm," the maid across the room stitching the hem of a gown muttered, making us all glance over at her. Her cheeks reddened as if she hadn't meant for us to hear her. "Me mam came from the area," she explained. From her broad Cumbrian accent, I pegged her as either Laura or Miss Remmington's maid, likely Miss Remmington's.

I turned back to Lucy, who was studying the other maid in unhappy suspicion, and released her shoulders.

"What about the people here? The Dalmays or the other servants. Did he talk about them?"

"Sometimes," she answered guardedly, flicking another glance at the other maids.

"Did he talk about Lord Dalmay?"

"Nay." Then she ventured to ask a question of her own. "Did that constable really come and try to arrest his lordship?"

I could see the other maids were interested in this answer as well, for they leaned forward. "He tried," I replied, unwilling to gossip about William. "What about Miss Wallace or anyone from Cramond? Did he mention any of them?"

Her eyes widened. "Nay."

I swallowed a sigh of frustration. What on earth had she and Donovan talked about? Surely they hadn't discussed me the entire time. "Did you notice anything suspicious? Was there any topic he seemed to avoid?"

"Why are ye askin' me this?" Her gaze searched mine for what I wasn't saying. "Has he done somethin' wrong?"

I hesitated to disclose such a detail, but I decided it would be best to destroy any romantic notions she still held about the man while I still had a chance of extracting useful information from her. "We found proof that he's been harming Lord Dalmay."

Lucy pressed her hands over her mouth.

"And we suspect he might be involved in Miss Wallace's death."

"How?" she stammered.

"I'm not going to reveal that to you. But I need to know about his suspicious behavior."

Her eyes grew bright and she shook her head. "I'm sorry. I dinna see anythin' suspicious."

"I did," the same maid who had spoken up earlier announced. A slightly older maid seated in a chair nearby, polishing a brooch, hissed her name, but she lifted her chin and ignored her. "I saw somethin' suspicious."

"And you are?"

She quickly bobbed a curtsy. "Irene, m'lady. I'm Miss Remmington's maid," she told me, confirming what I had guessed.

"What did you see?"

"I saw Donovan sneak oot o' the house one evenin' and take the trail doon to'ard the ole castle, and I followed 'im." She flushed, as if realizing what such an admission might say about her, and lifted her nose farther in the air to add, "I caught him flirtin' wi' Nelly, one o' the kitchen maids, early in the day, an' I thought it'd be jus' loike her to meet 'im in a place loike that. But when I got to the castle, he weren't wi' Nelly, but talkin' to some bloke."

My heart began to beat faster. "What did the man he was speaking to look like?"

"Tall, brawny. I didn't get a good look at 'im."

"Did you ever ask him about it?"

"Didn't have to. He caught me watchin' and threatened to tell Lord Keswick and have me sacked."

"Which is why you didn't tell anyone this until now?"

She gave a sharp nod of her head. It would also explain why she'd been so eager to share it with me. I didn't for one second believe Irene had followed Donovan down to Banbogle just to get Nelly in trouble. She'd likely been involved with Donovan herself and perhaps was afraid he was dawdling with the other maid. That was what Donovan had threatened to reveal to her employer—loose behavior was a far more serious offense than leaving the manor at night. And from the pain and disillusionment on Lucy's face, I knew she had also realized it.

In any case, the reasoning didn't matter. I still believed Irene was telling the truth.

Her story told me that Donovan had been using the grounds of Banbogle, if not the castle itself, for his own purposes. So it wasn't too far of a leap to think he might store a boat there. I also recalled the remnants of a recent fire I had seen on the beach in front of Banbogle. At the time, I'd thought the ashes were left from a fire lit by Mac to keep Will warm, but now I wasn't so sure. Donovan could have used the fire as a signaling device to someone out in the firth. It would be easy to see from the water, but hidden from Dalmay House by the large stone block of Banbogle.

The fact that he had threatened Irene to keep her from telling anyone about his meeting with that man said volumes about how desperate he was to keep his clandestine appointment secret. What I wanted to know was just how many of these meetings he'd had over the course of the last nine months of his employment, and just who this man was he was conferring with.

"Thank you," I told Irene and then turned to retrace my steps back to Donovan's room, eager to share my discovery with Gage.

"M'lady," Lucy called. Her feet pattered against the hard floor after me. "I forgot. I put this in my pocket to give to ye. Thought ye'd want to see it straightaway."

I glanced down at the letter she handed me, seeing Philip's familiar scrawl. I felt another surge of excitement, hoping he had information for me. But first I thanked Lucy and hurried to find Gage.

He was still in Donovan's room with Michael, but Lord Keswick was also with them and, judging from the looks on their faces, he had not brought good news.

"The boat?" I gasped.

"Gone," Gage replied. Angry frustration shone in his eyes.

I pressed my hand to the door frame, feeling like someone had punched me in the gut. I couldn't believe it. He'd gotten away. To where, I didn't know. And it didn't really matter. The fact was, our chances of catching up with him now were slim. And even if he'd gone somewhere close, like to his suspected employer on Inchkeith Island, we would never be able to flush him out of the asylum. Not without building a strong enough case against him to get the authorities involved, and I wasn't sure we could do that.

I relayed the information Miss Remmington's maid had given me, adding to the pile of evidence against Donovan, all the while knowing it wasn't the proof we needed to convince a magistrate of his guilt. Then, while the men discussed the matter, I broke the seal on Philip's missive. It was brief and to the point, but enough to make me exclaim, "I *knew* it."

Michael halted in midsentence as they all turned to look at me.

"This Dr. Thomas Callart, the man who tried to examine Mary Wallace," I reminded Gage. "It turns out he was an apprentice to one Dr. Alan Sloane, when they worked at the Royal Infirmary of Edinburgh together."

Gage's scowl turned black.

"Well, doesn't that give us proof that Dr. Sloane was part of this?" Keswick asked.

Gage shook his head. "It's all circumstantial. It might convince a magistrate to interrogate them, but that doesn't mean they would tell the truth or admit their part." He crossed his arms over his chest and widened his stance. "No, what we need is irrefutable evidence that Donovan worked for Sloane, that they had nefarious intentions toward Lord Dalmay and Mary Wallace, and that they carried through with them. Right now all we have is the testimony of Craggy Donald saying he saw a boat leave Cramond Island."

"And head out to sea," I interjected. "Which is, incidentally, in the direction of Inchkeith Island."

He arched his eyebrows. "Yes, but he never saw who was in it. We have a tin of valerian root . . ." he nodded toward where it lay on the bed ". . . and the word of a lady's maid that Donovan secretly met a man down by the beach. Our strongest evidence is that Donovan is missing, and yet we have no definitive proof of wrongdoing."

"What about the markings we found on Miss Wallace's body?" I said. "She was clearly bound and beaten and bled. Couldn't we show her wounds are consistent with the manner in which Dr. Sloane's patients are treated in the asylum?"

Gage shook his head. "The magistrate will argue that they're consistent with any violent abduction."

"But the bloodletting marks?" I pressed. "Why would a simple kidnapper do such a thing?"

His eyes narrowed in consideration. "That may just be our linchpin, for it won't be easy for them to explain away. We need to speak with a surgeon, to make certain there are no contingencies for bloodletting we have not considered that would ruin our argument." He turned to Michael. "We also need to better search Lord Dalmay's chambers and the surrounding area to make certain we're not missing something. Can you send some of your men out to search the woods and to ask around in Cramond and Dalmay village, and even as far away as Queensferry? I don't want to discover later that Donovan fooled us by making us think he escaped by boat when actually he walked away on foot."

CHAPTER TWENTY-SEVEN

I spent the remainder of the afternoon helping Gage search Will's rooms and then buried in the library. Our exploration of Will's chambers achieved nothing except to heighten my concern for Will as he lay unresponsive first on his bed, and then on the settee in his parlor while we examined his bedchamber. Whatever Donovan had used to introduce the scent of valerian root into Will's rooms had been removed, as well as any other incriminating evidence.

The library had also yielded no new information, but in this case, that wasn't such a disappointing thing. Will and Michael's father had amassed quite an amazing collection of medical treatises and textbooks, perhaps purchased in an effort to find information to help his battle-fatigued son. Regardless of how they got there, I was grateful for the selection, and after several long hours scouring their pages, I felt relatively confident we could combat almost any potential argument that Miss Wallace's being bled could be related to something other than the asylum. The only point of contention I could not entirely refute was the reasoning that it would have temporarily weakened her, but I felt we could argue the redundancy of such an action when Miss Wallace had already been bound and beaten. There were also the marks themselves to consider, for they had obviously been done with some skill, pointing toward a perpetrator who had experience with the procedure—either a surgeon or an apothecary. Dr. Sloane neatly fell into this group.

I stood to stretch my back and glanced out the tall wall of windows toward the overcast skies. The already hazy light of late afternoon had begun to fade with the approach of thicker clouds from the west. I hoped those who'd gone out to search wouldn't be caught in the rain. I began to wonder if we should have searched the ruins of Banbogle in the off chance there might be evidence there that could be washed away by a downpour, when Michael rushed into the room.

"William has escaped."

My head snapped around and Gage shot to his feet, dropping the text he'd been reading on the table in front of him with a thud.

"What?" he shouted.

"He nearly knocked Mac unconscious with a wooden tray before bolting out the door."

I pressed a hand to my mouth in shock.

Gage rounded the table toward Michael. "Are we certain he escaped—and wasn't taken by Donovan or that fool of a constable?"

"Yes. He darted past a maid on the servants' staircase, frightening her half to death."

"Is Mac all right?" I ventured to ask.

Michael's mouth flattened into a thin line. "Yes. He's got a devil of a headache, and he's beyond furious, but he'll recover. Mrs. MacDougall is stitching him up right now."

I cringed at the realization Will had hit him hard enough to draw blood. "I don't understand," I said as I joined the men near the doorway. "Why would he run off like that? Why would he attack Mac?"

Gage's expression was grim, and I could read the bleak thoughts shining in his eyes before he even voiced them.

"No." I shook my head adamantly. "Don't tell me you think him culpable of Miss Wallace's murder after everything we've discovered about Donovan and his association to Dr. Sloane." There was anger in my voice, but also desperation.

We were so close to proving Will's innocence. I simply did not want to contemplate the possibility he might not be. That he might actually have killed the girl.

"I don't know." His voice was carefully modulated, but I could hear in it the concern that raised it a pitch higher than normal. "There are too many other factors to consider. Other reasons he could have fled. The best thing we can do is find him."

I bit my lip and nodded.

"Have any of the footmen returned from their search of the woodlands and villages?" he asked Michael.

He shook his head. "And neither has Lord Damien or Keswick." They had volunteered to ride to Queensferry, some distance off.

Gage inhaled deeply and exhaled, the muscles in his shoulders flexing in an eagerness to act. "Then that leaves just the two of us. Where do you think he's gone?"

"What about me?" I protested. "I can help."

"We need you to stay here and direct the search. Should the others return before we do, you can send them back out to look for Dalmay."

"But surely Laura or Michael's butler can do that."

"But I'm asking *you* to do it."

I scowled at him in frustration. "Gage, you are already short on men . . ."

"Yes, so Michael and I need to set out, not stand here arguing with you."

I bristled, furious that he would speak to me in such a way.

"Kiera," he added, gentling his tone, "pause to consider the matter. What if Dalmay should return of his own accord? Someone he trusts needs to be here to receive him."

I was not happy with his orders, but I had to concede his point. Someone should be here to manage Will, and with Mac injured and Laura ignorant of much of what was happening, that left only me. However, from the intensity of his gaze, I suspected there was more to his determination to see

I stayed safely inside the walls of Dalmay House than simple common sense. Perhaps bad memories from our last interaction with a murderer.

"All right," I murmured. "I'll do as you wish. But you do realize this isn't like at Gairloch."

His pale blue eyes flashed with some nameless emotion, but all he said was "Thank you."

I nodded and returned to my books, leaving him and Michael to decide where they would search for William first.

Ten minutes later, I watched through the open front door as Gage's and Michael's horses galloped down the drive toward Cramond. With any luck, they would overtake Will, whom they assumed to be on foot, before he left the Dalmay property. He couldn't have gone far. I just hoped there was a reasonable explanation for his strange actions. I hadn't liked the blank stare he wore earlier when we searched his rooms, but he had seemed so dejected that he appeared harmless. Perhaps I had misread the situation.

I still couldn't believe he had clubbed Mac over the back of the head with a wooden tray. I would never have believed Will capable of such a thing. But, then again, I had never believed he would harm me. I flexed my right hand. I suspected I wouldn't be able to hold a paintbrush or writing implement comfortably for several days, but I could tell now there was no permanent damage. I didn't need Dr. Winslow to confirm that, but Michael had sent for him anyway—for me, for Will, and now for Mac.

Stepping back from the door as the two men on horseback disappeared from sight, I turned to retreat to the drawing room and gasped as I almost collided with a man's chest.

"Mac." I pressed a hand over my pounding heart and gave a breathless laugh at my jumpiness. "What are you doing here? I thought you were supposed to be lying down."

A thick white bandage was wrapped around his grizzled head, stained with blood on the right temple above his eye. There were deep lines around his eyes and mouth, telling me he was in pain, but he seemed determined to ignore it. "Where are they goin'? To search for Cap'n Dalmay?"

"Yes. To Cramond."

Mac's scowl deepened. "He's no' in Cramond."

I crossed my arms over my chest. "Oh? Then where is he?"

His gaze met mine levelly and suddenly I knew without his saying a word.

"Of course!" I exclaimed. I whirled back toward the drive, realizing it was too late to catch up with Gage and Michael. They were far out of sight, the dust already settled in their wake.

I pressed a hand to my forehead, considering what I should do. I could wait for one of the footmen, or possibly Keswick and Damien, to return and send one of them after Will. But that could be hours from now. It would be dark soon, and it was growing colder by the minute. I doubted Will had thought to dress warmly before his mad dash to escape.

I bit my lower lip and turned to look at Mac. The only alternative was for us to go after him, and if I was reading Mac's expression correctly, that was what he was determined for us to do. I knew Gage wouldn't like me leaving the safety of Dalmay House, but what other choice did I have? I couldn't stand here and pace the floor when I knew where William was. He could catch a dreadful chill, or fall victim to an accident. The ruins of Banbogle Castle were not exactly a safe place. I glanced back out the door toward the ominous clouds building in the west. And it would start raining soon.

That decided it. If he was clambering around on those crumbling, drafty ruins in the middle of a rainstorm he would probably slip and bash his head open or break a leg.

Mac must have read the resolve in my eyes, for he offered to come with me before I even told him I was going.

"Are you certain you can manage?" I protested, eyeing Mac's bloodstained bandage.

"'Tis no matter," he replied.

I didn't argue, but grabbed my cloak from its hook and

followed Mac out the side door. I made a quick detour to the stables, where I ordered the old stable master to saddle a horse and ride after Gage and Michael. The old codger began to argue with me, but one look at Mac's scowling visage silenced him. Then we rejoined the path leading into the woods between Dalmay House and Banbogle. Mac weaved a bit when he walked, as if his world was not quite steady, and the crease between his eyes had deepened, but he soldiered on, determined to accompany me.

The air was crisp, and ripe with the scent of approaching rain. Beneath the trees, the trail was already steeped in shadow, giving the tense situation an even more sinister feel. I wrapped my cloak tighter and did my best to ignore the noises of the woodland, ones that normally wouldn't have fazed me. Twice I jumped, once at the rustle of the underbrush made by some small woodland creature and again at the sound of a nut or piece of fruit striking the ground after falling from a tree branch.

I was sure Mac thought I was daft. I caught him sneaking glances at me once or twice out of the corner of his eye. We didn't talk. What was there to say? Either we would find Will at Banbogle or we wouldn't. If we did, we would bring him back.

If only it had been that simple.

We swiftly reached the edge of the forest and the castle's tall, crumbling shape loomed over us. From this angle, I could see little but weathered stone and the section of the ceiling that had caved in over the nursery. But as we rounded the castle to the side facing the firth, at the very top, seated on the edge of the battlements, I saw a familiar figure.

My stomach dropped to my knees. "What is he doing?" I gasped.

Mac and I rushed forward, dodging around or vaulting over chunks of stone. I tripped and nearly took a tumble over one large piece.

"Will!" I shrieked. "You come down here this instant." Fear made my voice wobble. "Will! Do you hear me? Will!"

He didn't look down at us, but just continued to stare off in the distance out over the firth. Could he not hear us? Or was he ignoring us?

I glanced around me frantically before turning to Mac. "One of us has to go up there," I said, at the same time I apprehended the danger we would be putting ourselves in. The floor could collapse beneath us, or a piece of the ceiling could come crashing down on our heads. But we couldn't just leave Will up there. "Has . . . has he ever done this before?"

Mac shook his head and then grimaced, pressing his hand to a rock to steady himself.

In the course of our mad dash, I had forgotten his head injury. He couldn't go up there. Not in his current state. Not without the risk of his taking a tumble or passing out on the way up the stairs. Which left only me.

My gaze traveled up the four stories of ramshackle masonry from the scrubby brush at its base to the battlements where Will's legs dangled over the edge. Swallowing the bitter taste of fear flooding my mouth, I pressed a hand to my pounding heart. "I'll go."

Mac looked to me, and I could see he was torn by the realization that he must let me be the one to face the danger.

"It's all right," I assured him. "Just . . . just keep him in your sight."

Without waiting for a response, I turned to clamber over the rocks littering the yard. The entry yawned before me, its heavy wooden door long since removed for scrap wood elsewhere. The castle was dark inside, and I wished I'd brought a candle or a torch, something to light my way. Who knew what kind of animals and insects made their home here now? The thought of walking straight into a spiderweb made me shiver in revulsion.

I shuffled across the floor, careful of fallen rocks and other debris that might lay in my path, and was guided only by the wall on my left. I tried to touch it only when necessary, wary of what I might find crawling across or growing on its surface. From the rank stench of damp and earth I suspected the space was overgrown with moss and mold. Halfway down the passage, the light passing through the crumbled section of the wall offered enough light for me to see the doorway into the staircase on my left, tucked into the stone separating the central hall block from another large chamber. The darkness inside yawned blacker than even the entrance passage, and I inhaled several shallow breaths, trying to muster the courage to enter.

Deciding it would be better to have it over and done with, I began to climb at a fairly rapid pace, praying that I would not encounter too much debris littering my path. The stone steps were worn smooth and dipped at the center from the weight of centuries of people treading up and down them. At the back of my mind, I recalled Will telling me how a staircase had crumbled beneath one of the footmen, but I blocked it from my mind, refusing to think on it. The stairs opened briefly into a room, whose broken and exposed windows afforded me a glimpse into the dusty chamber. It was empty, save for a few pieces of splintered and discarded furniture, and a piece of tattered cloth lying against the wall that I could have sworn moved.

Not eager to discover that I was correct, I turned and hurried up the next section of stairs ahead of me, which continued to spiral around the outside of the building, so that the door to the chamber above opened at a spot on the south side of the castle rather than the east. This room was very similar, save for an irregular, two-foot hole in the stone on the west-facing wall. I did not fail to note the staircase continued to climb around over this shoddy section of masonry, and prayed the surrounding stones were still strong enough to support the walls and staircase.

I passed the next floor's chamber without peeking inside and walked straight into a tightly wound spiral staircase that was better lit than the others, for it opened onto the roof. I shivered from the wind being directed down the shaft and picked up my pace, even though my legs protested and I was panting from the exertion. The stairs in older castles had certainly not been built for the convenience of ladies in long, heavy dresses. More than once, I had misjudged the height of a step and almost fallen forward onto my knees on the dust-shrouded stone.

I gasped for breath as I stepped out onto the battlements. The wind whipped furiously at my cloak and the skirts of my Prussian blue dress, swirling them around my legs, and tugged at the pins in my hair. I glanced cautiously to the left, seeing the crumbled section of the roof that had fallen in on the old nursery. My stomach pitched and I turned away, deciding it would be best to avoid even looking at that portion of the roof.

Ahead and to the right of me, Will still perched on the edge of the battlements. His back was to me and he had not even flicked a glance over his shoulder to indicate he knew that I was there. I stepped out onto the stone roof between us, saying a silent prayer that it would hold beneath my weight. It did. So I continued forward, taking each step with care so as not to alarm Will, in case he truly didn't know I was behind him or I upset the fragile masonry.

As I approached a gap in the battlements, I could not withhold a tiny gasp. The view was magnificent. Ahead of us the Firth of Forth stretched out like a deep blue blanket, rippling and undulating in the blustery weather. Whitecaps formed farther out, crashing into the shores of Cramond Island and another island to the left toward the coast of Fife. I thought I could see yet another isle far, far in the distance, possibly even the infamous Inchkeith Island, but the fading light made it hazy and indistinct. The north and south shores stretched out like the arms of a lover opening for an embrace, the bright colors of their autumn forests now shrouded by encroaching shadows.

I looked to Will to see that he was now leaning more heavily on the merlon to his right, whether from weariness or inclination. The crenel he was seated on was wide enough for two people to sit side by side, but I did not dare attempt the maneuver, particularly in heavy skirts and a cloak. I was

not certain I could have managed it in any case—the ledge
was at the height of my bosom—or that I wished to perch
myself so precariously. My nerves were already stretched
taut at the sight of Will doing so. If he shifted forward but
a few inches he would tumble to his death. I still wasn't sure
that wasn't his ultimate goal, so I bridged the few remaining feet between us with extra caution.

When finally I stood next to him, I lifted my hands to rest
them on the crenel and studied him out of the corner of my
eye. There had still been no discernible reaction to my presence, but I knew he was aware of me. It was there in the weary
manner he seemed to accept everything lately, in the way his
breathing deepened, whether in relief or resignation.

In any case, I did not speak, waiting for him to do so first,
as I had done that first night when I saw him hunched in a
corner scribbling with a nub of charcoal, revealing so much
about his inner turmoil with just that simple act. I wanted
to shout at him, to pull him from the battlements, but I was
afraid such a drastic action would only precipitate matters, so
I willed myself to wait, trusting the roof would hold and
Will would eventually respond to me.

It took a few minutes—several long, nerve-racking
minutes—but, as expected, somehow my quiet, undemanding presence loosened his tongue.

"I thought I could do it this time," he murmured in such
a soul-weary voice that I felt the breath catch in my lungs.
"I've wanted to so many times. It's just . . . it's all too much. I
just want it to end." He was begging now, the words wrung
from so deep inside him that they were raw and ravaged.

Tears burned the backs of my eyes.

"But every time, *every time* I think I can end it, or just . . .
let it end, when it comes right down to it . . . I can't." He
began to weep; bitter tears etched trails down his cheeks. "I
always change my mind. I always fight it. Despite how much
it hurts to do so." He turned to look at me. "Why? Why
don't I have the strength to end it? Is this my punishment?"

"No," I rasped, unable to listen silently to his self-recrimination a moment longer. I grabbed hold of his hand, clasping it between my own as his image swam before me and answering tears spilled down my face. "No. None of this is your fault."

"But it is," he insisted.

I shook my head.

"It is," he sobbed. "I killed her!"

My heart stuttered in my chest and grew cold. I tried to say something, but I couldn't, and meanwhile he continued to speak.

"She was good and sweet and kind, and I killed her. It doesn't matter that I didn't want to. That I *begged* her not to make me." He turned to look out at the firth, the wind playing with his hair, but his mind was far away in memory. "But she threatened to do it herself. She just couldn't take it anymore. She said hell would be better." He shook his head. "But I couldn't let her do that. She didn't deserve that fate. She was an angel. My angel." His face tightened in revulsion. "And I killed her."

Somewhere in the midst of his speech, I had become confused. Were we still talking about Mary Wallace, or . . . I suddenly realized he was talking about the girl from the drawing, the one Michael had showed Gage and me.

"By suffocating her?" I guessed.

He nodded, too lost in his memories to wonder how I had known such a thing. "Meg told me it would be just like she'd gone to sleep. That she knew she was going to die soon anyway. The seizures were getting worse from everything they'd done to her, and she wanted to die peacefully rather than in the grips of one of those fits. She promised she wouldn't fight me, and she didn't. But I could see the pain in her eyes. She'd lied about that. It wasn't peaceful, and it wasn't kind."

I didn't know what to say. His pain, his hatred of himself was so deep, I didn't think there was anything I could do, anything I could say to even come close to touching it, to soothing it. Especially when I myself felt so conflicted about what he'd told me. Yes, he'd killed this Meg, but only after she begged him to. If he hadn't acted as she wanted, she had threatened to commit suicide. Her threats must have been very real, because after listening to him, I didn't for a second believe that he would have carried out her wishes if he hadn't feared she was speaking the truth. Suicide placed her soul in jeopardy. It could be argued that the girl was insane, either before she entered the asylum or because of what had happened to her there, and thus the sin might be forgiven, but how could Will allow her to chance it? To face eternal damnation?

And if Meg's seizures were getting worse, and she was certain she would die soon anyway, wasn't Will protecting her from further pain, despite what she felt when he suffocated her? Whatever they were doing to her in there couldn't have been tolerable, not if she was that desperate to end it.

It was difficult to absolve him completely of guilt, but it was also hard to condemn him. I couldn't help but wonder what I would have done in similar circumstances. What if Will had been the one begging me to end it for him? I couldn't with any certainty say I wouldn't have done the same thing for him that he had done for Meg.

I frowned. That name kept nagging at me, as if I'd heard it recently. But where? I didn't think I had met anyone named Meg, not in Cramond or on the Dalmay estate. Perhaps someone had mentioned a . . .

I jolted, suddenly recalling. Good heavens! Could it be true? I glanced up at Will, wondering if he knew the girl's full name or if he'd only known her as Meg. I decided there was nothing to do but ask.

"Do you know, was Meg short for Margaret?"

Will replied without looking at me. "Yes."

I swallowed. "*Lady* Margaret?"

That brought his head around, suddenly curious. "Yes."

"Was she, by chance, the Duke of Montlake's daughter?"

He nodded hesitantly.

I pressed a hand to my forehead, feeling sick. "Your sister

told us about the Duke of Montlake's daughter and how she'd gone missing several years ago," I explained. "She also mentioned that she had the falling sickness."

Something flickered in his eyes. I thought it was anger. "She told me she'd been abducted from her father's estate. That Dr. Sloane had examined her a few months before, but her father had refused his suggested treatment. So Sloane had kidnapped her." His mouth tightened into a thin line. "To be honest, I was actually relieved to hear the duke had not been so heartless as to consign his daughter to such a fate."

Unlike his own father. But that knowledge was a raw wound that even Will seemed unwilling to touch. I wasn't certain any of us would ever understand the old Lord Dalmay's decision.

"I'd long ago learned to accept that Sloane was willing to do anything to further his desires, no matter how vile. He had no regard for us as people." His voice was hollow and bitter.

I turned to study the sky behind us. Dark clouds had rolled in, blocking out the last rays of the setting sun, so that the sky to the west was as dark as that in the east. The remaining light was fading fast, and I knew we had little time before the prickling dots of rain I felt sporadically hit my face began in earnest. But I had one more question to ask him before I had to insist he climb down off the battlements and come with me. A question I'd wanted to ask from the first, but never had the courage to until now.

"Will," I murmured, tucking a strand of hair behind my ear that the wind had pulled free from its pins.

He must have heard the caution in my voice, for he turned to look at me in guarded expectation.

"What exactly happened to you in there? I've seen your drawings, but . . . what . . . was he doing to you?"

Will's eyes went a little unfocused, and I removed my right hand, the same hand that he had crushed in his grasp only hours before, from holding his to touch his lower back.

I would have hugged him, but his waist was level with my shoulders, making any embrace much too awkward to attempt.

When he finally answered it was with a hard shake of his head. "No. No, I won't tell you about that."

The horror and dread in his voice made my heart clench. Part of me wanted to argue, but it was clear that it was too awful for him to relive, so I did not press him. Especially when another part of me wasn't sure I wanted to know. Just because I had the courage to ask did not mean I had the courage to listen.

"But you should know, if you don't already," Will added, making me peer up at him through the gloom in curiosity. His next words were choked. "That Mary Wallace was taken up by Sloane as well."

My heart beat faster in my chest. "How do you know for sure?"

He stared down at me in rebuke. "The same way you do. The bindings, the bruises, the marks left from bloodletting. It all begins the same."

"Why the bloodletting?"

"To weaken us," he replied, confirming my suspicions. "Then the routine varies."

"Depending on what sort of brain abnormality he thinks you have?" I guessed.

He nodded, and then his face crumpled in pain. "I befriended her. She was so sweet and kind. And she understood me, like no one had before. And I brought her to his attention." He shook his head. "I may as well have killed her, like I killed Meg."

"You couldn't have known."

"I should have. It was my mistake to think I was free of him. He's always watching. He always will be." He looked down at me, his eyes bright with fear. "I shouldn't even be talking to you. Especially not here."

I blinked up at him. The idea that Dr. Sloane might come for me next sent a cold shiver down my spine. "He wouldn't be interested in me," I protested, trying to convince myself as much as him. "You had battle fatigue, and Lady Margaret had the falling sickness, and Miss Wallace second sight. He's only concerned with oddities. And I'm not . . ."

I broke off. I had been stared at and whispered about since I was old enough to pay attention to such things, probably before. Our nursery maid, a woman whom I knew had loved me without question, had even called me her "odd little duck" with quiet affection. I just never seemed to respond the way I was supposed to, especially in social situations. I had different interests from other women, and I had the somewhat disturbing ability to lose myself in my art, to the extent that no one and nothing else existed. I had also learned, from painful experience, to blunt my emotions when needed, something my late husband had alternately praised and ridiculed me for, but that was more a skill of survival than a desire to be stoic. I still felt the pain and fear and despair; I'd simply learned not to react.

Perhaps I didn't have a distinct affliction, like Will or Lady Margaret or Mary Wallace, but my mind certainly didn't work like everyone else's. I saw things differently, questioned them more. Would Dr. Sloane see enough peculiarity in me to make him want to add me to his collection of subjects?

I frowned. Was that why Donovan had been asking my maid questions about me? Had he been probing for information for his employer? I remembered how Gage had stiffened up when I mentioned it to him. Had he suspected something similar?

I pulled the flapping ends of my cloak tighter around me and glanced up at Will to find him watching me with a mixture of sympathy and affection.

"I see your point," I told him. "And though I don't concede that Sloane will be coming after me next, perhaps it would be a good idea to return to Dalmay House. I'm sure Mac is wondering . . ." my gaze swept the ground at the base of the castle ". . . what's taking . . ." I leaned farther out to see closer to the foundation ". . . so long. Where's Mac?"

Will leaned forward to join me in my search for Mac's familiar stooped form, but he was nowhere to be found.

My heart began to beat faster and I had to tell myself there was no reason to panic. "Do you think he decided to join us?" I would have thought his head injury would prevent him from doing such a thing, but Mac was nothing if not stubborn.

"I doubt it," Will replied and then flushed, obviously recalling the blow he had given him to the head.

I raised my eyebrows in gentle chastisement.

"I know. I'll apologize." He swiveled to the side and lifted his legs up onto the battlements. I backed up so that he had more room to maneuver, but kept my hands out should he begin to lose his balance. "I just wanted to stun him long enough to get away. I couldn't let him catch me until I reached here, where I could end it."

I breathed easier having his two feet planted safely on the roof with me. Well . . . I glanced over my shoulder at the caved-in portion of the roof, perhaps *safely* was not the right word, but regardless, I was relieved he was no longer dangling from the battlements.

"And speaking of apologies . . ." He stepped closer to me, his face pained. "I'm sorry, Kiera. I don't know what came over me."

I lowered my gaze, feeling a lump form in my throat.

"Did . . . did I hurt you seriously?"

I shook my head. "No." I lifted my right hand and let Will take hold of it. "It's just a little sore."

He cradled it almost reverently, his chill, rough fingers skimming over my skin. "Maybe they're right. Maybe I'm not fit for company," he murmured under his breath.

I squeezed his hand gently and offered him a tight smile. There wasn't time to discuss it, not with the rain beginning and Mac still nowhere to be found. I peeked over the edge of the battlements again, disturbed by the fact that Mac was no longer standing below. "Where do you think he's gone?" I asked as a fat raindrop fell on my forehead and rolled down my face. I pulled my cloak hood over my hair, wishing I'd taken the time to grab a coat for Will. His thin shirt and waistcoat could be doing nothing to protect him from the cold wind, and they certainly wouldn't keep him dry.

His face tightened with growing worry. "I don't know. It wouldn't be like Mac to abandon us." He leaned farther out, peering to the left and to the right of the castle, down the shoreline. He narrowed his eyes, trying to see better in the encroaching darkness.

I tugged on his arm. "Let's get out of the rain." And out of this derelict, old castle, I added, unspoken. "Maybe he's waiting for us under the trees on the other side of the castle, where we can't see him."

Will nodded, but there was a new watchfulness to his movements that set me on edge. I tried to follow where his gaze had gone, wondering if he'd seen something I hadn't, but he took hold of my hand and pulled me toward the stairs, taking the lead.

"Stay at my back," he told me and, upon seeing my look of apprehension, added, "I know the way better than you. I can guide you down."

I couldn't argue with that, though I knew there was something he wasn't telling me. I could feel it in the taut muscles of his shoulders and back as I rested my hands against them and began to follow him downward.

CHAPTER TWENTY-EIGHT

If I had thought the castle was dark before, it was black as pitch now. It felt like we were descending into an abyss, into a chasm of nothingness, and soon the stairs and walls and everything solid around us would drop away, tumbling us into the void. My hand fisted in the silken material of Will's waistcoat, anxious that at least he remain with me.

The rain drummed against the stone with soft thuds, picking up speed as we slowly inched our way downward. The damp intensified the stench of mold and mildew until it was almost cloying in its intensity, as if the walls themselves were nothing but slime and moss. I avoided touching them as before, grateful for Will's solid back at my front. The gust of the wind across my shoulders blown down the stairwell from above made me shiver and squirm, worried some large insect had crawled across me.

A step or two before the first landing, where the opening to the fourth-floor chamber yawned to our left, providing us with a little light, a faint howl rent the night air and made all the hairs on the back of my neck stand on end. I wasn't certain the sound had been real, and not some trick of my mind, except that Will had also stumbled to a stop, his spine bristling in much the same manner. It sounded like a dog, perhaps some kind of hound, but before I could contemplate it further, the shuffle of feet in the darkness of the staircase beyond the landing alerted us to the presence of someone else. Apparently that person had been surprised by the noise as well. And given us just enough warning to stop Will from stepping onto the landing and into the dim light cast by the chamber window.

I gripped Will's waistcoat even tighter and he reached back to wrap a hand around my hip, urging me to move toward the curving inner wall of the spiral staircase. I followed his guidance, careful not to make a sound as I did. Although my heart pounded so loudly in my ears I began to worry the intruder would hear it.

I had three guesses as to who stood in the darkness below us—Donovan, Dr. Sloane, or Constable Paxton. Of the three, Mr. Paxton would be preferable. But I had a sinking suspicion it was not the blustering lawman, and neither of the other two meant anything good for Will and me. I wondered again where Mac had gone and then closed my eyes in dread. If someone was standing seven feet away, waiting to ambush us, then it was likely he had already taken care of Mac.

I gritted my teeth, furious at myself for getting into another situation like this and not having a weapon of some kind tucked away on my person. When I had been threatened at Gairloch, I had sworn if I survived I would get a pistol to carry with me. Philip had promised to help me choose the right-sized gun and teach me to fire it when we reached Edinburgh. Unfortunately I had yet to make it there. And so here I found myself, again empty-handed, facing an assailant who I was certain had not come so ill prepared.

Will's gaunt body was pressed up against mine. I didn't think he was carrying a weapon either. So that left us with only our brains, and hopefully some element of surprise.

Time stretched, each of us waiting for the other to move. I had no idea if the person beyond knew we were there, or still believed us to be above on the roof. I suspected it was the latter; otherwise there would have been no reason for his continued silence. Clearly if he'd heard us pause here, he knew we were aware of his presence.

I shivered, growing colder and colder by the second, from the drop in temperature and the perpetual draft from above and the fear crowding out my other senses. Will's back was stiff against my hand and I could feel him tremble slightly. Our assailant was going to have to do something soon, or I worried Will was going to collapse.

Finally the man shifted again. The crackle of dirt on the stair below him seemed to echo throughout the space after all the tense silence. He shuffled his feet one more time and then seemed to come to a decision. He took one cautious step up onto the landing and then another, steadily crossing the distance toward us.

I felt Will's muscles tense, knowing he was going to spring at the man, and I prayed to God the assailant was not expecting it and did not have a weapon drawn.

The attacker was large. I could see that in the faint light, but not much else. It must be Donovan, I decided, and I cringed at the memory of the man's bulging biceps. Will didn't have a chance of defeating him.

But there was no choice now. He was almost upon us. And in the next breath, Will leaped forward into him, knocking him to the ground.

I didn't stop to see what happened next, but darted into the chamber, knowing I had to find some way to help Will. Diving into the fray would do no good. I needed a weapon, something to hit Donovan with.

Several steps into the room I found it as I bashed my shin against something, tripped, and went sprawling with a muffled yowl of pain. I sucked in a harsh breath and rolled to the side, reaching down to cradle my leg. I could feel a knot forming, but I didn't think it was broken. And, in any case, I didn't have time to worry about it. I could hear a series of punches and smacks coming from the doorway, along with grunts and groans.

I patted around the gritty floor near my feet and found the chunk of stone that had toppled me. It was half the size of my head and just small enough that I could lift it without wrenching my shoulder. I pushed to my feet and hefted the stone. Stumbling just once from the pain in my leg, I crossed the room toward the men.

I could see very little, but I could tell that Donovan's bulkier form was straddling Will's. He landed one punch to the face and then another. I raised the stone above my shoulders and brought it crashing down on Donovan's head. It connected with a satisfying thunk, the impact ricocheting into my hands.

Donovan toppled like a felled tree. I lowered the stone to the floor and knelt to help push his body off Will, panting from the effort. Whether Donovan was dead or simply unconscious, I didn't know, and I didn't care to check. All that mattered to me at the moment was getting Will and myself out of there.

Will's breath wheezed in and out of him, and I reached up to cradle his head, feeling a wetness that must be his blood smear my hands.

"Will," I gasped. "Are you all right?"

"I'm alive," he mumbled in a funny voice, and I realized Donovan must have broken his nose.

"Can you move?" I asked him, trying unsuccessfully to keep my distress from showing. It made my voice shake.

He groaned. "Help me up."

I looped my arm under his and around his back and hoisted him to his feet. Once standing, he pressed his hand to the wall to steady himself and took several deep breaths. "All right," he murmured, removing my arm from around him. "Let's go."

We resumed our descent, with Will once again in front and me at his back. Though, this time, I kept both hands securely fastened around the sides of his torso, to stop him should he begin to topple forward. I couldn't gauge how severe his injuries were in the darkness, so I had no idea what he was dealing with in the way of pain and disorientation, but it didn't appear to be too debilitating, for his pace picked up the farther we descended.

I supposed the element of surprise was gone should there be anyone else farther down waiting to jump us. They would have undoubtedly heard Will and Donovan's scuffle. I could only hope that Donovan had been acting alone.

But I discovered how wrong I was only moments later when on the third-floor landing a man stepped out of the darkness and into the dim light, pointing a pistol at us. He was tall and slim, and from the way Will reacted, becoming rigid as a board, I knew this must be Dr. Sloane. The light was too faint. I couldn't see his face. But I had no trouble imagining the nasty smile curling it.

"William," he proclaimed in an oily, cultured voice. "So good to see you. It's been some time."

Will didn't respond, just continued to stare at the man. I could feel his heart pounding against my fingertips where they were pressed to his chest.

"I see you've overcome Donovan. I must say, I'm reluctantly impressed. But, then again, you always were a fighter." The malicious tone of his voice made it clear that this wasn't a compliment. It made my skin prickle with disgust.

I wished I had something to hurl at him. Like the rock I'd dropped on Donovan's head. If only I'd thought to bring it with me. But, of course, it was far too large for me to throw.

I couldn't see his eyes, but even so, I knew they had shifted, gazing at me where I peered around Will's shoulder. It felt like the slimy skin of an eel slithering over me.

"And this must be the illustrious Lady Darby. I've been anxious to meet you."

Those words coaxed the first reaction from Will since Sloane had stepped into our path. He reached back and fisted his hands in my cloak to pull me tighter against his back, shielding me with his body when I would have stepped to his side to face Sloane directly. I didn't resist him, at the same time grateful to him for placing himself between me and Sloane and concerned about what that meant.

"I can't say I feel the same," I retorted, knowing the best way to keep Sloane from firing his gun was to keep him talking.

Sloane chuckled, a gravelly sound that grated on my nerves. "No, I suppose not. But not to worry, we'll have plenty of time to change your mind."

Will and I stiffened as one.

"She's not going anywhere," Will told him.

Sloane almost seemed surprised he'd spoken. "Of course she is." In the hazy light I could see him tilt his head. "Oh, were you hoping I'd come to take *you* back?" he crooned in mock sympathy.

Will reared back, bumping my forehead with the back of his head.

"I'm sorry, William. But I'm afraid you've worn out your usefulness. Especially since the authorities suspect you in Mary Wallace's death." He tsked. "I simply cannot have that kind of notoriety associated with my asylum, you understand."

"What did you do to her?" Will asked. "I know you kidnapped her. Just like Meg."

Sloane's voice became harder, less sardonically polite. "Yes. Meg. Did you tell Lady Darby how you killed her?"

Will didn't answer, and I couldn't bear for the man to derive any pleasure out of thinking he'd broken the news for him. "I know."

"Really?" he declared in curiosity, drawing out the word. "Well, Lady Darby, you *are* proving to be interesting."

"What did you do to Mary?" Will demanded with more force this time.

"Temper, temper, William," Sloane snapped. He raised the pistol in his hand higher, pointing it straight at Will's chest. "She proved to be too weak. Couldn't handle the days locked away."

"In the pit?"

My heart stuttered just at the phrase.

Sloane shrugged. "Her heart must have given out. Some people aren't able to bear the absence of light."

Will's voice rose in anger. "And sound and heat and food and fresh air."

"Ah, yes. I forgot you're intimately familiar with it."

I remembered then what Miss Wallace's maid had told us about the nightmares she began having shortly before she disappeared. How she'd babbled about the cold and the dark. And how Kady had worried Mary had foreseen her death. I had found the idea horrifying before, but now—knowing she'd been locked in "the pit"—I couldn't fathom it.

Dr. Sloane was a fiend and I told him so. "You're not conducting medical research. You're torturing these people! You're nothing but a monster."

"And your husband truly needed to dissect all of those bodies to write his anatomy textbook?" he calmly retorted.

I recoiled, pulling away from Will, but he gripped me tighter.

"Sometimes advances in medicine require a measure of suffering. Particularly if the brain, the body is ever to be fully understood."

"My husband may have been no saint, but at least his test subjects were dead before he tortured them. Their souls were gone, their bodies merely husks. They couldn't feel any more pain. You have no excuse. You drove your own daughter to suicide."

Dr. Sloane reared back, and I felt the full force of his anger for the first time emanating across the distance between us. His voice snapped like an icy whip. "My daughter was mad, and completely bent on destruction. I tried to find a cure for her, I tried to bring her to heel, but she resisted all my methods. And when I relented, out of *pity*, she killed her mother while in the grips of a manic rage, and then killed herself."

I stiffened in shock at his words, and he seemed to sense it.

"Oh, yes. Didn't know that, did you? She killed more than just herself. But if I'd continued my tests, if I'd kept her far from her mother, at least my wife would still be alive today."

The click of the pistol cocking jolted down my spine and I gripped Will tighter.

"I'm not going to allow sympathy to get in the way of my

research again," Sloane continued in a more even tone, though his voice was still as sharp as a knife. "The families who refuse to hand over their loved ones with afflictions of the brain are fools who must be saved from their own folly, before their unfortunate relatives harm themselves or others. And I'm afraid *you're* one of those unfortunates, Lady Darby."

An icy band of fear wrapped around my chest, holding me immobile.

"Now," he continued in the same silky tone he'd used when he first stepped out of the shadows, "I'm done wasting my time. We have a little boat trip to make across the firth this evening, though I fear the rain will hinder our journey somewhat."

"She's not going with you," Will told him, hugging me even closer to his back. I didn't struggle against him—I was too terrified—but I did worry. With his hands behind him and his body shielding mine, he was defenseless.

"Of course she is," Sloane said, his tone brisk. "With any luck, my oarsmen already have the boat pulled to shore below. We'll be gone before the blood even stops pumping from your body."

I tensed and shoved against Will, trying to get him to move, just as Dr. Sloane's pistol fired, a percussive burst of light in the darkness. Will jerked backward into me, slamming me into the wall at my back. I felt a spray of liquid splatter my cheek. My knees gave out beneath me and I dropped to the floor with Will on top of me.

The acrid stench of gunpowder lingered in the air. Dazed, I pushed Will to the side and tried to feel where the bullet had struck him. But Sloane grabbed my arm and dragged me out from underneath him. He tried to force me to my feet, but I fought against him, screaming for Will. In the darkness, it was hard to tell, but I thought he moved. Was he alive?

Sloane struck me across the temple with the gun, knocking me to my knees. Pain exploded in my head, sharp and blinding. I couldn't fight it.

I felt myself being lifted by an arm around my waist and shuffled forward a few steps. Then, from behind me, I heard Will's voice.

"I said . . . she's not going with you."

Sloane turned and dropped me to the floor just as Will seized hold of him and flung him away from me.

"Run," he ordered me before kicking Sloane where he lay crumpled on the floor just inside the third-floor chamber.

I lurched to my feet and steadied myself against the cold wall, trying to shake away the cobwebs from my mind. "Run!" I heard Will shout again, but I couldn't leave him. He was bloodied and bruised from his fight with Donovan, and now he'd been shot. If I didn't help him, he would surely die.

He groaned in pain as Sloane struck back, and I staggered toward the doorway. That was when an arm grabbed me from behind.

How I'd missed the sound of feet running up the stairs, I didn't know, but I struggled against the man's grip.

"Kiera, it's me," Gage's familiar voice shouted in my ear. I nearly collapsed in relief.

"Come. Let's get you out of here."

"No," I protested, pushing away from his chest. I could still hear the thwacks and thumps of men fighting in the chamber beyond. "We have to help Will. He's been shot."

"*I'll* help Will. You need to get out of here," he protested and tried to turn me toward the stairs.

I staggered unwillingly down a step, but turned back as soon as Gage had released me to rush into the chamber. He glanced back over his shoulder and shouted, "Go!" But I still didn't listen.

I stepped forward to watch as Gage drew a pistol from the waistband of his trousers and pulled back the hammer with a click. Sloane and Will were locked together in combat and it was almost impossible to tell them apart in the gloom. Gage waited for the men to separate long enough for a clear shot, exhibiting far more patience than I had. Will was battered and bleeding from a gunshot wound, for heaven's sake. I was about to open my mouth and scream at him when Sloane landed a blow to Will's torso that sent him crumpling to the floor. His target clear, Gage fired his weapon. The flash of the miniature explosion momentarily blinded me. We heard a thud and a grunt, and Dr. Sloane stumbled back against the wall. But rather than fleeing the scene as Gage yelled to him to do, Will pushed to his feet and lunged at Sloane.

That was when I heard the ominous crack, too loud to be bone on bone or even a pistol report. The two men paid it no heed, continuing to slam each other into the outer wall, the one with the two-foot hole in it. As I watched, the stone began to fissure, breaking apart.

"Will!" I shrieked and leaped forward, trying to warn him.

Gage had moved forward a few steps to help Will, but stumbled to a stop as the wall began to collapse. He wrapped his arms around me as I tried to move past him.

"Will!" I shrieked again, fighting to break free of Gage's hold.

With a deafening roar, the wall and part of the floor and ceiling crumbled before our eyes in a cascade of rocks and debris, swallowing Will and Sloane.

I screamed and crumpled to my knees. Then I started to cough and choke as the collapsing rubble sent up a plume of dust, enveloping Gage and me. He sheltered me as best he could, gathering me in his arms and covering me with his body. I wheezed and sobbed against his chest, clinging to him.

The castle shifted and rumbled, threatening to send more of its stones crashing down and bring us with them. But I didn't care. All I knew was darkness and heartache and Gage's strong arms.

CHAPTER TWENTY-NINE

Will's funeral was held three days later, a gray and gloomy day fitting to the occasion. The fine autumn weather we had enjoyed earlier in the week was broken, and winter fastened its grip on the world and on our hearts. Most of the leaves had fallen during the rainstorms that followed the night of Will's death, and I fancied the trees and the sky were crying for Will, too.

There were few guests. Few that were welcomed, anyway. Gawkers and newspapermen lined the perimeter of the cemetery, eager to see the ornate coffin of the war hero gone mad, the fallen laird of Banbogle, whose death had been foretold by a howling dog, like so many of his Dalmay ancestors before him.

After the service, we retired to Dalmay House for tea and a selection of savories none of us seemed to have much of an appetite for. We gathered in the drawing room, where I curled up in a wingback chair by the windows, watching the rain trail down the glass in tearful streaks. I knew the others were concerned for me—I could see it in their faces, hear it in their voices—but I could find no words to reassure them. So they hovered about me, as if they thought their presence might comfort me when all it did was remind me of their worry and make me want to burrow deeper inside myself.

Philip and Alana, who had arrived late the evening

before, sat on a settee a few feet from my chair, listening to Gage and Michael explain some of the details they had yet to hear. Alana asked specifically about the hound, and Michael explained the legend. His voice was hoarse with grief and fatigue.

"We'd originally ridden for Cramond, you see, thinking Will might have tried to visit Mr. Wallace. But we met up with a pair of my footmen we had sent to the village earlier in the day to search for Donovan. They admitted to having dawdled at a pub adjacent to the bridge over the river and swore that my brother could not have gotten past them and into the village without their taking notice." His chair shifted with a creak. "We were just about to set off again when our old stable master rode up to deliver Kiera's message. We immediately rode for Banbogle, following the firth's coastline. That's when we heard the dog howl."

That mournful bay that had frightened Will and me to a standstill and alerted us to Donovan's presence on the stairs beyond.

"And you feared it was the legend?" Alana gasped.

"Yes," he choked out.

I wrapped my arms around my stomach and sank deeper into my chair, knowing my posture was far from proper, but not caring. I still wasn't certain how I felt about the howling dog being the supposed portent of Will's death, but I couldn't deny it had happened. Not when Gage and Michael, and some of the other residents of Dalmay House, had heard it, too.

While Michael struggled with his emotions, Gage took up the tale. "We arrived in time to find two men dragging a little skiff ashore, and after overpowering them we tied them up and went to search the ruins. We found Mac near the base of the tower knocked unconscious. He was barely breathing and bleeding profusely from another wound to his head. Michael tried to rouse him, but when the wall came crashing down . . ."

It had claimed Mac for its victim as well. Michael barely had enough time to get out of the way of the falling debris.

In honor of his service and sacrifice, Mac had also been laid to rest that morning, in a grave near the Dalmay mausoleum. That way, even in death, he would never be far away from the man he had served so faithfully in life.

"And while Michael tended Mac, Gage, you went in the castle after Lord Dalmay and Kiera," Philip deduced.

I could feel his gaze on me, even through the fabric of the chair.

"What I don't understand . . ." he continued, his voice tight with disapproval ". . . is what they were doing there in the first place."

My spine stiffened, and I fully expected Gage to inform him that I'd disobeyed his order to stay at Dalmay House, but he didn't.

"Mac realized where Lord Dalmay had gone after Michael and I had already ridden toward Cramond. And fearing he would do himself harm, Mac and Kiera went to Banbogle to try to stop him. They couldn't have known Dr. Sloane and his lackeys would show up to cause trouble."

"Oh, my. Were they planning to take William back to that asylum?" Alana asked.

I shifted in my seat, not wanting Philip or my sister to know the truth about Dr. Sloane's intentions for me. They felt so much guilt after what had happened to me at Gairloch two months prior, and though I knew they would feel some remorse that I had been put in danger again, I wanted them to be spared the added horror of knowing Dr. Sloane's plans.

"He wanted to silence him. And Kiera. So they couldn't share what they'd uncovered."

I sank back in my chair and closed my eyes, grateful for Gage's discretion.

"What will become of Banbogle now?" Philip asked Michael, ever concerned with estate business. "I imagine you're not going to leave it standing."

"No," he replied, his grief now better under control, though never far from the surface. "I've already hired a contractor from Edinburgh to tear it down. I simply can't bear to look at it anymore. My father should have demolished it years ago."

I reached up to finger my amethyst pendant, thinking that if he had, Will might still be with us.

I heard Lady Caroline's gentle voice as she leaned in to murmur something to Michael. I knew he was grateful for her presence, and I was as well, at least for his sake. But I couldn't stomach the sight of Lady Hollingsworth. I imagined there would be no impediment to Michael and Caroline's marriage now that he was the Baron Dalmay. I swore that if I saw even the tiniest flicker of satisfaction in her eyes, I would not stop to think before I slapped her. But she behaved with perfect decorum, and we departed Dalmay House without a row.

I returned to Edinburgh with Philip and Alana that afternoon after the funeral. Lucy did not join us. I found I could not ignore her betrayal, and she accepted my decision without a fuss, admitting she wanted to return to Gairloch and her family. So she took the next mail coach north to resume her old position as an upstairs maid, hopefully a little wiser in the ways of men and the world than before.

Gage followed us to Edinburgh to turn over the information we had gathered about Dr. Sloane to the Royal College of Surgeons, while Michael took the same evidence to a local magistrate he respected, trusting the matter of Larkspur Retreat would be taken care of quickly and effectively. And it was. For weeks afterward the newspapers in Edinburgh ran stories about the notorious doctor and his asylum.

All told, almost two dozen patients were liberated from Larkspur Retreat, and Sloane's records and the island's tiny graveyard revealed dozens more who had not survived his brutal treatments. Patients like Lady Margaret, whose brother, the current Duke of Montlake, now knew what had become of her, and Miss Wallace, whose father could at least feel some relief that his daughter's killer could never harm anyone ever again. I hoped that would enable all of them to rest in peace.

I derived some satisfaction in knowing that it was William who, in the end, had triumphed over Sloane and effected the release of so many of his patients. That he had, in effect, conquered his demons. But it was a cold comfort.

I tried to settle in Edinburgh, to find my place again in Alana and Philip's household, but I no longer belonged there. It was like trying to fit into a garment I'd already outgrown.

Philip suggested I keep busy, that I take on a few portrait commissions. But after I honored a request made by Michael, and immersed myself in the task of painting Will's baronial portrait, spending night and day in my studio for an entire week, I couldn't bring myself to pick up a brush. It was as if whatever artistic ambition I'd possessed died with the final touches I made to Will's posthumous portrayal.

Instead I wandered the house listlessly, avoiding everyone, particularly my sister. Some days I spent hours strolling the streets of Edinburgh, from the wide avenues of the New Town to the dank, twisting lanes of the Old Town, until the cold or rain or dragging steps of the footman accompanying me drove me indoors. Once or twice I tried to pick up a book, but the words could not hold my attention, nor could the pianoforte or my viola. The children made me cross, and the sampler I tried to stitch, never my favorite activity in the first place, almost drove me to violence.

The only emotion capable of pulling me from my cotton-wrapped world was anger, but I hated the rages that seemed suddenly to come over me. They were so unlike me, and I knew they concerned Philip and Alana without their having to say a word. I could see it in their eyes, in the way they whispered together, in the way they cautiously broached a topic. Such as that of Sebastian Gage, who had effectively abandoned us since our arrival in the Scottish capital.

After the wall collapsed at Banbogle, and the castle had settled, Gage had carried me from the ruins and through the woods to Dalmay House. I remembered little of that evening except the crushing grief. He had left me in the care of Lucy and Mrs. MacDougall to be bathed and have my cuts and bruises seen to. However, I could not be comforted. So when Gage returned to check on me later, he gathered me in his arms and held me close until I wore myself out from weeping and fell asleep sometime in the early hours of the morning.

But when I awoke, he was gone. And he had been careful to keep his distance ever since. He didn't ignore me or go out of his way to avoid me, but he never sought me out, and there was a hesitation, a reserve that had not been there since the first day of our meeting at Gairloch. I wasn't sure what I had done to make him pull away from me, but with each passing day the aloofness between us had grown, until now our brief encounters on the street or at social events were so stiff and formal we might have been strangers.

I was angry and frustrated by it, and yet I couldn't bring myself to remedy it. After all, Gage had distanced himself from me once before. It wasn't my place to chase him. I hadn't the energy for it anyway. But I felt the sting all the same. Particularly since I could have used a friend. Someone other than my sister, who was smothering me to death.

So when my brother Trevor wrote to me and asked me to come stay with him at Blakelaw House, our childhood home in the Borders region, I accepted.

Alana fussed and fretted over my decision to leave, but Philip seemed to understand my need to get away for a time. My sister had recovered her appetite and some of her energy since arriving in Edinburgh, so she was no longer in danger, and I needn't feel guilty for leaving her. But, in any case, I promised I would be back before it was time for the baby to be born.

Philip talked to me of familiar comforts and country air, but I thought of nothing but escape—the confinement of the city, of my sister's household, of the pain and fury that seemed to be consuming me from the inside out. I knew I couldn't remain this way, wallowing in grief and anger. Despising the things I had always loved. Something inside me was broken, and I had to find a way to fix it, to move forward, or else all my struggles to overcome the shadows of

my past had been for naught. Gage's diving into the water at
Gairloch to save me had been for naught. Will's sacrifice had
been for naught. And I couldn't allow that to be true.

The day I was to travel to Blakelaw House was brisk and
windy, so by necessity our final good-byes were done in the
vestibule before I hurried down the steps of the town house
and into the awaiting carriage. The door was slammed shut
by the footman as I turned in my seat, and I only had a
moment to be surprised before the man seated across from
me thumped the roof with his cane and the horses set off.

Gage studied me warily, as if I might bite him. He
needn't have worried. I was too stunned even to react when
he reached across to help spread the lap blanket over me I
had lifted from the seat.

I eyed him guardedly in return, wondering what his presence here meant, and whether I would like it. It had been
over a week since I'd seen him last, at a dinner party. We'd
exchanged greetings and polite small talk, but nothing
more. I sat in my usual place at the edge of the drawing room
while he charmed the assemblage. If I'd needed another
reminder of all the reasons why we didn't suit, that had done
so quite effectively.

I rested my feet on the hot brick wrapped in cloth that had
been laid on the floor of the carriage to keep me warm and
waited for him to speak. He couldn't keep me waiting much
longer or otherwise the coach would reach the outskirts of
Edinburgh before he finished speaking, and he would have a
long walk home to his lodging rooms on Princes Street.

Unless he planned to accompany me. That thought made
my heart leap in my chest. But then I shook it away as nonsense. He would return to London soon, recalled by his
father or his own inclination.

Gage, who had long since settled back against the squabs
to observe me, finally spoke what was on his mind, keeping
his tone carefully neutral. "So you truly did intend to leave
without telling me good-bye." It was a statement, not a
question.

His words pricked my temper and I scowled. "How could I, when I've barely seen you? After all, I can't exactly call on you. I might be a bit unconventional, but I would never be so forward as that."

"You could have written."

I stared at him, trying to tell if he was hurt or simply making a point. "And you would have come?"

"Of course." His reply was spoken with quiet certainty, as if he wasn't surprised I'd asked, but he wanted to be sure I understood that I never need do so again. He leaned forward, his pale blue eyes gazing solemnly into mine. "Kiera, if you ever need me, I will come. You have only to ask."

I didn't point out that I hadn't precisely *needed* him to come to me so that I could say good-bye. But then I realized: perhaps I had. Just to know he hadn't completely abandoned me. That he still cared enough to stow away in my carriage and look at me in that way that had always made my insides melt. To show me that I hadn't lost him, like I'd lost Will.

I didn't understand why he'd distanced himself from me, but maybe he wasn't the only one who'd been aloof and reserved. I couldn't control the emotions churning inside of me, so I'd stifled them, all of them but my anger. Just like I'd done when I was married to Sir Anthony and I couldn't bear the fear and hurt and disgust he'd caused me.

I felt tears burn the backs of my eyes and furiously blinked them away refusing to let them fall. I didn't want to feel this hurt, this sadness. So I pushed it away, burying it down deep.

I took a deep breath and then nodded, telling Gage I understood.

He watched me a moment longer and then reached up to tap the head of his cane on the ceiling again. The coach immediately slowed.

"Take care of yourself, Kiera," he murmured.

I nodded, feeling like I'd swallowed a bubble. "You, too."

He reached out to open the door and rose to exit the carriage, but at the last moment changed his mind. Slamming the door shut again, he sat down on the seat next to me, and before I'd even realized his intent, he reached out to cradle my face in his hands and kissed me. For how long, I never seemed to be able to tell, but it was with sincerity and purpose, and when he pulled away, there was something in his eyes I'd never seen before. Something that made my heart stutter in my chest.

He was gone before I could put a name to it.

The carriage pulled forward again, gently rocking back and forth over the cobblestones while I sat there dazed and not unpleasantly befuddled.

Unlike our last good-bye, I knew I would see Gage again. Why he had distanced himself from me since the night of Will's death I still didn't understand, but I knew our paths would cross once more. That it would be so soon, and under such mysterious circumstances, I could never have guessed. Particularly when it involved a grave on the hallowed grounds of an ancient abbey. But if my experiences with Gage had taught me anything, it was to expect the unexpected, and this time I certainly learned my lesson.

HISTORICAL NOTE

For the setting of this second novel in the Lady Darby Mysteries I used several interesting locations that actually exist in Scotland. For Dalmay House I utilized many elements of the Dalmeny House and Estate, located along the Firth of Forth, northwest of Edinburgh, much the way I described it. Details have been altered to suit the story's purposes, but several items of interest, such as the Goya tapestries Kiera admired and the magnificent entrance hall, are very true to life.

The former ancestral residence, Barnbougle Castle, also stands nearby on the estate and was the basis for my Banbogle Castle. The castle became somewhat dilapidated after the family moved to the newly built Dalmeny House in 1817, and suffered damage when some of the explosives stored there accidentally detonated, but it was restored in 1881 by the fifth Earl of Rosebery, who became prime minister in 1894. There is indeed a legend about Sir Roger Mowbray (although I changed his name to Dalmay) and his faithful hound, whose howls supposedly presaged his death and each subsequent laird's as well. There are several versions of this tale, and even a ballad written about it, but they all center on Sir Roger's dog and either his howls or his ghostly appearance being a harbinger of death.

The village of Cramond and Cramond Island exist much as I have described them. As does Inchkeith Island, though no lunatic asylum was ever located there. It was utilized for military purposes, and historically it was used at least once for quarantine, as well as for James IV's bizarre linguistic experiment to discover the original language in 1493.

The artist Francisco Goya figured prominently in the creation of this book. I borrowed several of his pieces of artwork and attributed them to William Dalmay. First and foremost are his series of prints called *The Disasters of War*. These disturbing images were crafted from Goya's experiences during the Peninsular War in Spain. They seemed to be exactly the type of scenes that a soldier like Will would have witnessed and have difficulty forgetting. I also utilized some of the themes from Goya's paintings *Yard with Lunatics* and *The Madhouse* to help create the images Will brought back with him from Larkspur Retreat.

Like any war, the Peninsular War was riddled with atrocities perpetuated by friend and foe alike. It was bloody and horrific, sparing no one, even women and children. It's no wonder that soldiers returned home with battle fatigue, or what today we would more commonly call PTSD, posttraumatic stress disorder. However, this troubling and sometimes debilitating disorder was not acknowledged as the medical condition it was, and soldiers were made to suffer in silence or risk being branded a coward or a lunatic.

After his stay in the lunatic asylum, William Dalmay also suffered from sensory deprivation syndrome, due to the primitive conditions of his cell and his time spent in "the pit." Being deprived of our normal senses, particularly light, can be severely disorienting and often causes sufferers to experience unpleasant hallucinations to make up for the absence of stimuli. In 1830 this was also an unknown medical condition, as most mental disorders were at that time. Even the falling sickness Lady Margaret suffered from, the more common name used in that time period for epilepsy, was looked on with superstition, though at least strides were being made in the understanding of that disorder.

Lunatic asylums in the early nineteenth century were

much as I described them. Fortunately, men like William and Samuel Tuke, Jean-Baptiste Pussin, and Philippe Pinel had begun a movement years before toward instituting more moral treatment methods. However, changes in the general public's thinking took time to take effect, and so many lunatic asylums remained as primitive as ever.

In Scotland, the gift of second sight was, and in some areas still is, widely believed to exist. The expression comes from the Gaelic term for the ability, *an da shealladh*, which means "two sights."

Several of the details about Sir Anthony Darby's life were borrowed from the real life of English surgeon and anatomist Sir Astley Paston Cooper. In 1820 Sir Astley performed surgery on King George IV, removing an infected sebaceous cyst from his head. He received a baronetcy for his efforts and was appointed sergeant surgeon to the king.

Though confusing to some, in the past, particularly in the UK, there was a strong distinction between physicians and surgeons. Physicians were usually considered gentlemen, and therefore treated with the courtesy of one, being allowed to enter through the nobility's front doors and such. It was believed that surgeons, on the other hand, were of a lower class because they performed manual labor, something a gentleman did not do. So while a physician could examine you and prescribe medicines, a surgeon had to be called in to do bloodletting or set a broken bone or perform any type of surgery. Surgeons were consequently treated like the lower classes, entering through the servants' door and being denied entry to the formal receiving rooms of the house. Which is why Sir Anthony would never have been permitted even to court Kiera had he not received his baronetcy.

Also perplexing to many Americans is the fact that most surgeons in the UK go by the title *Mr.* even to this day. This tradition originated in the sixteenth century when surgeons were barber-surgeons and did not have a medical degree like physicians who attended university. When the College of Surgeons received its royal charter, the Royal College of Physicians forced the law to stipulate that surgeon candidates receive a medical degree first. So an aspiring surgeon was made to study medicine first, achieving the title Doctor. Then when he obtained his diploma to become a Fellow of the Royal College of Surgeons, he reverted to Mister as a sort of snubbing to the Royal College of Physicians. To avoid confusion, I opted not to title the characters who are Fellows of the Royal College of Surgeons as *Mr.*, but left them with the distinction *Dr.*

Through the course of history, there was indeed a set of special privileges reserved for the British peerage, namely the right to a trial by their peers in the House of Lords, access to the sovereign, and freedom from arrest. In the case of the latter, peers were supposed to be free from arrest in civil cases only, not criminal, but the law enforcement officials of the time, particularly before formal police forces were established, would have found it difficult to arrest a peer at any time without getting other peers or magistrates involved. Without definitive proof, Constable Paxton would have had trouble convincing a magistrate to arrest Lord Dalmay, because of his title. And even if he had been arrested and charged, Lord Dalmay would still have been tried in the House of Lords, if, under the circumstances, it ever came to that.